THE SPIRAL STAIRCASE & OTHER NOVELLAS

CLIVE RADFORD

CONTENTS

THE SPIRAL STAIRCASE

THE SPIRAL STAIRCASE

Computer games creator Francis Blake sat in his study contemplating, his Yale blue eyes narrowing as his mind failed to congeal ruminations into tangible ideas. Unremittingly disappointed by the lack of useable content he had jotted onto paper or coded into his computer scratchpad page, in an act of dismay he breathed out rapidly, then shifted his flop of fair hair back off his forehead in a frustrated motion. Originality still evading him, his despair increased as supplementary notions were consigned to the redundancy bin without a second thought. Wondering how to break the impasse, he stretched his tall, slim frame and yawned, his facial skin raddled taut against an angular chin and gaunt cheekbones.

Blake's preceding business assignment had been arduous. Spending many late nights and early mornings at the computer, impelled by contractually agreed code delivery deadlines, the task had near-to exhausted him. Now the latest revenue-bearing project confronted him. The challenge seemed even more demanding, a lack of a coherence constricting serviceable output to a trickle. For days, his tried and trusted methodical technique yielded diminutive fruit, clarity of address eluding him. Left flailing like a nascent programmer fresh out of code cutting school and bereft of a single scheme, his irritation boiled over, the pencil he held snapping between tense fingers.

Out of the corner of his eye, he spied his wife Jane crossing the garden, carrying a basket of freshly cut flowers before the computer screen lured his observance again, but he drew another blank. Opening the French doors, she entered his den, her summer dress catching on the *chez lounge* before she delicately removed the offending threads with her usual poise and elegance.

"My god, it's warm out there," she informed, "but it's doing wonders for the new bed I planted back in the spring. The camellias are still flowering." She thrust her cache forward. "Take a gander at this lot."

With his cerebral patterns still entrapped in solution mode, Francis hardly heard a word, let alone become seduced by the alluring array of pinkish-white and crimson hues. Whilst subconsciously flicking the mouse, he gawked at the uncooperative icons dancing about the screen. Suddenly, the kernel of an inkling popped into his mind, as if summoned by divine intervention.

Jerking his head up, the hunch morphed into the tremor of a dawning light shining through his foggy haze. "What are your estimations about the concept of a computer game centred on a Dickens adventure trail?"

Whilst arranging her flowers in a cut-glass vase, Jane furrowed her brow at the out-of-the-blue question. "Incontestably it's been done before." She glanced at him, her face ripe with criticism. "There must be other assets the world associates with Rochester apart from Charles Dickens."

"Yes…you're right," he permitted, frowning and drumming his desk with a thumb in dissatisfaction. "I'm being lazy."

Glistening affectionately at his erudite wife, he felt guilty about his lack of vicissitude. Usually, the creative process came easy to him. His ability to pull disparate filaments together to form electrifying computer games had won him abundant industry prizes, but of late, he had entered a barren patch. Gaping out into the garden, he reengaged his comprehension, hoping a flurry of constituent elements might coalesce into a bold contrivance, culminating in an innovative product.

Quick-witted to her husband's consternation, Jane came over

to him, laying a sympathetic hand on his shoulder. "I'm sorry to pour cold water on your grand design, but Dickens has been done to death." Tellingly culpable of adding to his woes, she displayed contrition before furnishing, "off the top of my head, how about Turner? He had a loose association with Rochester, didn't he?"

"Turner," Francis repeated, his tone imbued with brio. Rotating a new pencil between his palms, he pondered. "Joseph Mallord William Turner."

"The very same," Jane confirmed.

Grinning, his disaffected mood cascaded into a sunny register. "You might have hit on a mainstay. And I do like his paintings."

Pleased his anxiety had evaporated, she smiled back. "Duncan could help you out. He's the art buff."

Francis Blake had honed his computer programming skills whilst employed at Hewlett Packard. Bitten by the burgeoning gaming bug, just before the millennium, he decided to leave HP and launch his own business. Promptly flourishing into a raging success, the enterprise gained premier-class status, his concoctions adopted by sundry well-known gaming vendors, the licensing deals he bartered with them providing the means for a very comfortable and opulent *modus vivendi*. Gorging in the London fleshpots, buying Beeches, a huge house on Rochester's Esplanade opposite the River Medway and a brand-new Morgan Plus 8, all illustrated his success. Further extending his reach, he holidayed in the south of France and Tuscany, spent long weekends with his mates sightseeing in out-of-the-way destinations, joined the Savile Club mixing with fellow scientific and engineering inventors, as well as aesthetic types, and in general, indulged in rampant materialism.

Despite the revelry, a huge gap remained in his private life. Hunting for a spouse he could spend the rest of his life with surged into a burdensome and finicky chore. Many candidates came and went without the necessary connection being made, signalling a lifelong relationship. Then, like a beacon of ravishing enchantment, Jane Selby surfaced on the horizon.

Jane, Gorgeous-Jane to her confidants, not just because of her loveliness, but also for her tantalising people skills, had majored in drama at the Mountview Academy of Theatre Arts. After just six months of concentrated effort in the press to be a starlet, she accepted acting not to be her congenital constituency. However, she excelled in stage direction, finding the role a bountiful medium for artistic expression, and more importantly, a fertile vocation. Capping in a career with a national broadcasting conglomerate, she then joined independent filmmaker Spellbound Studios, headquartered at Penenden Heath, as head of production, whilst still retaining director functions of her choosing.

Francis and Jane originally met at a wine and cheese party held by their collective friends, Duncan and Natasha Bayliss. With his elegant demeanour, sharp wit, and Ted Hughes-like facsimile, Jane increasingly fell for Francis as the event went on into the early hours of the ensuing day. Contrarily, he reckoned Jane to be out of his league, her well-groomed presentation, stunning beauty and dynamic flair beyond his ken. Authentically, a woman every man craved, but few could charm. But the chance meeting proved his assumption wrong. In no way superficial, Jane became swayed more by his personality than his physical potency. Speedily fusing, they fell in love, and married less than six months later, fellow Savilian Bayliss providing best man duties.

Francis cogitated at length on Jane's Turner suggestion, formulating the uniqueness of the theme to be worthy of in-depth investigation. Thereafter, he called Bayliss, told him about the Turner-centric computer game proposal, and polled if he had any ideas *vis-à-vis* the artist's association with Rochester. Stimulated by the proposition, Bayliss arranged to come over to discuss it in more detail.

Arriving in the early evening, after Jane had gone off to Penenden Heath for a screenplay assessment meeting, Rochester High Street gallery owner and art retailer Bayliss already had a plethora of valuations about Turner's Rochester associations.

"Well," he began, "the revered man explicitly visited Rochester and many outlying villages, rummaging for landscapes and seascapes to background his tableaus." Charged up, his review segued into specifics. "You might recall he captured Upnor Castle under his meticulous brushstrokes, and assuredly used the view of the Thames from the Isle of Grain for *The Fighting Temeraire*."

"Hhmm," Blake enthusiastically responded. "Maybe we could take a peek at some of Turner's sites neighbouring Rochester. It could contribute stimuli for the computer game."

"We could, but—" Bayliss issued his oppo a cautionary visage. "If you want my involvement, Francis, I'm not available until next weekend. Natasha and I will be in Bruges this weekend, participating in a Magritte symposium. His surrealism period is very much back in vogue, and we are meeting a Belgium compiler, with a view to him awarding me a commission to trace some of Magritte's renderings going missing when the Germans occupied Belgium in World War Two."

"How is the wonderful Natasha?"

"Radiant. I swear by everything holy, she gets a little lovelier every day."

Whereas Jane held the gorgeous accolade, Natasha Bayliss moved like a ballet dancer and had become a fashion model in her youth, her attributes different to those of bosom pal Jane's, but equally attractive. Possessing a plumbless appreciation of the romantic, often Duncan eulogised about his wife *ad infinitum*, not letting the listener escape until persuaded they had an accurate vision of Natasha. Even though Francis had known Natasha long before Jane entered his life, Duncan often cornered him, conferring every detail of a new characteristic he had come to observe about his wife, the games creator unable to flee until the rich extent of the revelation had been conscientiously described.

"Oh, you do surprise me," Blake gibed. "And there's me rationalising she had kissed goodbye to her golden phase."

"*What*! Never," Bayliss retorted, brushing off the light sarcasm. Changing his deportment from defensive to focused, he declared, "By the way, returning to the main topic, there is a tenuous connection between Turner and Dickens."

"Oh no," Blake gabbled. "At Jane's insistence, I'm trying to dodge Dickens."

"Ah, it's nothing too esoteric," Bayliss guaranteed. "I'll tell you more when we meet."

* * *

Leaving Jane with Natasha, Blake picked up Bayliss from his house on St Mary's Island a week Sunday afternoon, and they struck out in the Morgan for what endured at Chatham Naval Dockyard.

"I want you to get a feel for Turner," Bayliss exhorted. "Tread the same footfalls he trod when he inspected HMS Temeraire at Chatham Dockyard."

"What's the correlation? I mean, I didn't realise the Temeraire moored at Chatham."

"Not many people do. They prefer to glamorise the Temeraire, saying she sailed homebound in honour after the Battle of Trafalgar, but it's all fallacy." Disgruntled by the delusion, he scowled, making Blake smirk at his companion's intolerance of inaccuracy. "Categorically, Temeraire took part in Trafalgar, but after, use as a prison ship awaited her and she anchored at Chatham before her ultimate indignation, the breakers yard at Rotherhithe in 1838."

"So, do you mean Turner could have primarily seen her at Chatham Dockyard?"

"Yes, to make some preliminary sketches prior to the setting we recognise in the formal painting."

Tramping the quaysides, the two men took in the revamped dockyard. No longer a naval base, though many historical elements survived, it had been rebuilt into a mixed economy of shops and offices. Walking longitudinally in the ropery, ship construction sheds and galleries, they absorbed the ambience of a bygone age. Whereas once a hive of naval activity, some of the stripped-down building carcasses now loomed more like futuristic space-frame art fabrications. Identifying influential features, Bayliss inferred their candidacy for the proposed computer game, Blake photographing the artefacts, posing more questions, and making copious notes.

Satisfied the old dockyard's possibilities had been exhausted, they moved on to the Hoo Peninsula. Gazing out on the Thames estuary vista, Blake and Bayliss pictured Turner studying the same view.

"There is the possibility," Bayliss commented, "we could be in the exact same spot where Turner erected his easel and painted the schema for *The Fighting Temeraire*."

"Yes, I must say, I am getting a feel for this," Blake frothed, his instinct for intake beginning to stream. "But—" Still to be exhaustively doubtless, he bared his teeth. "I need a touchstone to set it apart from other computer games."

"How do you mean?"

"I know you are not a computer lover, let alone a gaming enthusiast, Duncan, so let me try to position the business determinants necessary to make a successful new game." Pausing, he gathered his esteems whilst perusing the panorama. "The kind of game I put together is aimed at the intellectual, the type of guy seduced by computers, and liking to play games testing mental agility. It doesn't embody a large ingredient of the games buff genre, and its buyers are tagged by short attention span and easy boredom. If there is nothing compelling to make them revisit the game time after time, unerringly they move on to other offerings. To get repeat business with my games, I must give them a discriminating seducer. In turn, it becomes an incentive to buy the subsequent game, and so on."

Not wholly convinced, Bayliss wrinkled his nose. "I thought you did mass market games as well."

"I do, but just let's say, the up-market, top-of-the-range game feeds my alter ego, and enhances my reputation in the industry. It gets me commissions for specialist sectors, meaning as well as earning a royalty fee for every copy of a game sold, I'm also paid for the game creation." Twinkling at his buddy, he appended, "It's the challenge ahead of me now."

"I see," Bayliss acknowledged. Moving away to attain a better appraisal of the Essex side of the Thames, he scanned Coryton oil refinery and Canvey Island for articles to satisfy Blake's need but augured nothing. "Seems like we're going to draw a blank here."

"I think you're right." Blake eyed the estuary again, its ruggedness and sparsity not instrumental enough to rouse lateral conviction. Partially low-spirited by the expedition, he pushed out his lower lip and stared at Bayliss imploringly. "I've got some good material for the games infrastructure, Duncan, but I need a speciality in the plot to *really* put the hook in."

With the sun low in its autumnal arc, darkness began to creep across the flint grey-cadet blue sky, its cloud formations billowing in response to a north-easterly.

"Okay, let's go back to Rochester," Bayliss advocated. "There's something at Eastgate House that might confer what you're seeking."

"*Eastgate House*!" Blake echoed. "It's Dickens country, isn't it?"

"Trust me, you won't be disappointed."

By the time they reached Eastgate House Rochester, dusk had swamped daylight, night not far behind on her tails. Driven at an acute slant by the north-easterly, rain pita-patted on the pavement. With its austere facade and gothic chimney stacks silhouetted against the incipient stars and the moon, the Elizabethan house arose as daunting to Blake. Its right-angle frontage placement to buildings on the High Street, gave the impression a giant had come along, surveyed the main drag, and finalised the best place to plonk down the assembly to engender an architectural dichotomy.

"You'll have to be quick, sir," urged the curator, a well-built man with a military carriage, his voice resembling the pitch of Richard Attenborough's twang as the headliner Regimental Sergeant Major Lauderdale protagonist in *Guns at Batasi*. "We shut for the night in half an hour."

"Very well," Bayliss affirmed. "We'll be done before then."

Gliding onward into the inner sanctum of the fabled house, the intrepid visitors discerned its age-old character; wall panelling and fabrics dulled by ten-thousand bright dawns, and a musky, near-to-pungent smell, the stuff behind shockers and delirium.

"So, what's the connection between Dickens and Turner, Duncan?"

"It's rumoured Dickens met Turner in 1847. With *Dombey and Son* about to be published as a monthly serial, Dickens backpaddled from Switzerland to publicise the series, and begin research for *The Haunted Man and the Ghost's Bargain.* Dickens had always applauded Turner's paintings, and when they met, it evolved into an epiphany moment for the writer."

"Why?"

"Many of Turner's paintings have an eerie, ghostly feel about them. You know, shrouded in spirits, such as *Morning* or *Venetian Festival,* even *The Fighting Temeraire.*" Validating the assertion, he lifted his eyebrows.

"Yes, of course."

"Dickens talked to Turner about these paintings as a source of inspiration for *The Haunted Man and the Ghost's Bargain.*"

"So, if I perceive you correctly, you're saying I could build the ghostly aspects of Turner's oeuvre into my computer game."

"Ahh, hah." He gasped. "You've jumped a couple of stages ahead of me, Francis, but yes, such an essence could give your game an edge, and thereby a novel selling point."

"You still haven't told me what we're doing at Eastgate House."

Bayliss ignited a reticent kisser. "It's a bit tenuous, but many years ago, someone told me there were unused canvasses in the Eastgate House basement, possibly stored there by Turner in 1838, when he painted numerous seascapes off the North Kent coast, notably, *The Fighting Temeraire.*"

"And so?"

"Well—" Grimacing, he braved Blake, as if embarrassed about his succeeding recommendation. "We could take a gander at them. See if there is anything to incite your creative juices."

Bemused by the contention, Blake took a step back, beaming teasingly at Bayliss. "So—" He wavered, unsure of his interpretation. "You foresee scoping some old, unused canvasses will be heaven sent, do you?"

Blushing, Bayliss beseeched, "Only a notion, Francis. If you deem—"

Cutting him off, Blake elevated a kindly hand at his mucker. "Duncan, I'm kidding. If the combination of old house atmosphere and a few unused canvasses furnishes impulse, who am I to argue?" Gleaming at an entrance door leading into the archive, he entreated, "Come on, let's find these elusive nuggets."

Negotiating the sepulchre entrance, they made their way down a metal, spiral staircase to the large, multi-compartmentalised depository, its space only lit by the fading daylight emanating through grimy windows, their panes ringing as droplets of the autumn rain fell against them.

Since its origination by Sir Peter Buck in the 1590s, the house had been used for many functions, *inter alia* acting as a storage facility, but the likelihood of a vestige from Victorian times revealing itself rested as remote to Blake. Disclosing more dust than pearls, and the occasional bruised knee as they stumbled into semi-concealed brickwork, Bayliss began to have severe reservations about his fancy, Blake contemplating despite good intentions, nothing could result from the probe.

At the epicentre of the cavernous vault, Bayliss stopped and studied the setting. "Why don't you try further afield, while I concentrate here? With the light waning and time against us, we need to cover as much terrain as possible."

"Yes, a logical foray," Blake okayed, energised more by courtesy than certitude.

Guardedly making his way into the maze, the games creator audited ahead as he proceeded, eventually coming to rest in a secluded cranny at the far end of the cellar. In the dimness he made out a rectangular shape ahead of him, a dust cover cloaking it. Moving on, Blake mockingly mused to himself, *could this be one of Duncan's unused Turner canvasses?* Contracting his eyes, he stood in front of the object, flabbergasted to have unearthed anything at all. Gently withdrawing the cover, remarkably, a large three-by-four-feet-sized canvass shook his eyesight. Dumbstruck, he bent to delve into the cache, cracking his eyes wide, stalking for signs of the master's still evident faded touch. Then he sensed someone behind him.

Quivering his brow in disbelief, he promulgated almost triumphantly, "I might have chanced upon what we're questing for, Duncan. What do you think of this?"

Twisting around, he expected to see Bayliss, but no one came into his view. Puzzled, he glimpsed right and left, then stood to his full height, sure Bayliss must be in the next cranny. Baffled but unflustered, Blake turned back to the canvass. Again, he comprehended someone behind him. Swiftly swinging about, he saw nothing, then recoiled slightly, doubting his lucidity. Smirking to himself, he computed in the creepy environment his imagination had got the better of him. Resurrecting canvass scrutiny, he kicked into fascination, intrigued as to how a purportedly prized Turner artefact had been left to gather dust in a dank, dark catacomb. Momentarily, he peeped at the outer wall, the north-easterly still steering raindrops against the windowpanes, but though he saw them collide, he could not hear their tintinnabulation. Instead, he registered an alto-pitched ringing noise.

Again, he fathomed a presence behind him, the attendant unwelcome resonance rising in timbre and approaching crescendo.

Turning briskly, he blurted, "Duncan…is that you…Duncan."

No answer.

Blake moved away from the canvass, his perception of otherworldliness shrinking, the reverberation correspondingly in decline. *Where has Bayliss got to?* he pondered. *He couldn't be playing some kind of macabre trick, could he?* With the light reduced so much, making it impossible to see more than a few yards to his front, he tested for a sturdy datum locus. Holding his arms forward as if he had temporarily gone blind, Blake tested for solidity to affix his station. His sensitivity failing to moor him, the distance from his fingertips to whatever he aspired they might make contact with topped the infinite.

"*Duncan!*" he chimed, his voice soaring into urgency.

Still no response from his fellow comrade in search of Turner. Feeling atypically disturbed, his mouth went dry. Gulping, he licked his lips. "*Duncan,*" he bellowed.

"Hello…did you call?"

Blake strode towards the voice, his vexation mounting. "Duncan, where *are* you?"

"Keep on coming to the peal of my voice. I'm trying to find the light switch."

Moving edgily, Blake felt for the wall brickwork to aid his navigation, then he heard a click, the crib instantly flooded in fluorescent light. Raising a forearm, he shielded his dilated eyes from the sudden glare.

"Ah, there you are, Francis. I thought I'd lost you." Staring at Blake with a stumped countenance he solicited, "something wrong? You seem to be dreadfully dazed."

"Duncan, I...I'm positive you were behind me. I assumed I talked to you." Reconnoitering about, he took in the cellar dimensions behind Bayliss. "You were

standing—" Stopping abruptly, disconcertion poured from his physiognomy.

"Yes, Francis?"

He made to rejoin, his mouth dropping, then latching without a word spoken. Blinking, wonderment took hold. "Erm, er, nothing." Laughing nervously, he supplemented, "Anyway, come and see this."

When Blake peeked back to where he had come from, the canvass and dust cover had vanished. Moreover disquieted, he shifted sideways, then gawped back at Bayliss.

"What is it? What have you exhumed?"

Momentarily lost for words, Blake shuddered as Bayliss eyeballed him. Nodding, he indicated at the cranny where he reckoned he had removed a dust cover concealing a canvass beneath.

"Yes, what is it?" Bayliss pressed, befuddled by his companion's behaviour.

Aiming a jagged digit at the core of the cranny, Bayliss sighted in Blake's direction.

Making to speak, a bedevilled, ashen port dispersed on Blake's puss. "I...I saw a canvass."

"Good, lead on," Bayliss gushed. "This I've got to see."

"No, Duncan! You—" As if skeptical about his wits, he hesitated. "You don't understand."

"What? What is it? What don't I understand?"

Shaking his head, Blake reacted almost pitifully, "It's gone."

"Gone!" Bayliss imitated, glowering. "What do you mean, gone? What's gone?"

"I, er...I saw a rectangular periphery in the gloom, laid against the cranny wall over there." Signifying the precise location, Blake advised, "I removed a dust sheet exposing a blank canvass underneath."

Walking into the cranny, Bayliss perused from left to right before glimmering at Blake. "Nothing here. Are you definite this is the right one? There are many other crannies in this cavern."

Exasperated, Blake rapidly moved to the space where he calculated he had seen the treasure.

"I'm telling you, it manifested itself here," he forcefully contradicted. Rubbernecking at the spot, he confirmed, "This *is* the place."

"Mmmm," Bayliss uttered, melding an uneasy comportment. "Just wait there a moment."

Examining the nearby crannies, Bayliss dug up nothing. Reversing, he recorded his compatriot scratching his head, patently bamboozled, and talking to himself.

"Why Francis, you've gone awfully white. Are you okay?"

Evidently riveted by developments, Blake hardly noted the words. Then under his breath, he muttered, "I know I saw it. I pulled its dust cover away." Gawking at Bayliss, he blathered, "It *must* be here."

Eighteen months beforehand, Blake had suffered a nervous breakdown, sequent to strain caused by overload. He knew he had low stress tolerance, but regardless of Jane's protestations to take it easy, professionalism and fear of failure drove him on. She had nursed him over the ordeal passage, and on a variety of occasions Bayliss had intervened to tackle some tricky situation for his chum. Blake recovered, but occasionally disintegration affects crowded into his consciousness. The specialist he had consulted certifying such secondary instances of neurasthenia were commonplace, and with time they'd dissolve altogether.

Recalling the episode, Bayliss earnestly counselled, "Calm yourself, Francis."

"I know what you're deliberating." Drilling Bayliss accusingly, his eyes bloomed.

"Francis—" He furrowed his brow in a conciliatory mode. "Your derangement arose a long time ago." Moving closer, he applied a comforting grip on Blake's upper arm. Smiling, he coaxed, "You've been striving very hard recently, and we've been talking about people from the past all afternoon." Lightly tapping adjacent brickwork, he warranted, "It's just a bit of self-hypnosis aroused by these surroundings, nothing more. Now come on, Jane and Natasha are awaiting us for dinner."

* * *

"Blake and Bayliss, sounds like a detective agency, doesn't it, Natasha," quipped Jane.

"Yes, maybe they should have gone into sleuthing years ago," she airily corroborated.

Following the bizarre Turner quest, Francis and Duncan were having after-dinner coffee and Benedictine with their wives at the Blake's Rochester residence. They had told them about the sortie in fits and starts, Duncan sensitive to Francis's peculiar phantasm, and not wishing to distress Jane about her husband's possible relapse into crisis.

Noticing Francis cruised as strangely detached for most of the evening, Jane refrained from tabling the obvious question, so as not to spoil the four-way social occasion. Notwithstanding, in the middle of coffee, she could not hold her curiosity any longer.

"Duncan."

"Yes, Jane."

"What else did you two get up to this afternoon?" She issued him a curious clock. "Demonstrably, I have totally lost my husband to his new computer game design."

Shooting a glint at Francis, Duncan observed he still dwelt overtaken by events borne in the Eastgate House cellar, his pallor blanched, his expression stretched tight and fixed like it had become set in plaster of Paris. "Well," the genial art dealer began before clearing his throat, "we ended up back in Rochester at Eastgate House."

"Eastgate House," a blindsided Jane duplicated. "I understood Turner acted as the centrepiece of this new computer game."

Explaining the context of the visit, its significance falling into place for the wives, as if paralysed, Francis abided unvaryingly inert throughout Duncan's edifying vindication.

When Jane asked Francis to comment on the visit, he made some staccato responses, but still exhibited adjacency to the subject, his sojourn plainly troubling him. Knowing her husband's foibles earlier, she had picked up on constraint in his persona, hence her delicate inquiry to Duncan apropos completing the afternoon's log. Aware she'd sustain her inquisition until satisfied everything had been revealed, reluctantly he came to the shake at which Francis had undergone an illusion.

"It wasn't an illusion, Duncan," Francis remonstrated, coming out of his semi-transfixed sphere. "It was real." Gaping sincerely at Jane, he beseeched, "I pulled off the dust cover and a canvass lay underneath. Afterwards, I could still smell dust on my clothing." Addressing Duncan in a rising voice, he reproached, "I tell you, it nestled as real."

Perturbed by her husband's bravado, Jane peered at Duncan with vacant gills. Wobbling his head in affirmation, a subtle syntax for, 'yes, his collapse symptoms have reignited', she unreservedly decoded the message. Effortlessly changing the subject to her gardening enterprises, the Bayliss's played ball, Francis nestling in his own parochial world, copiously transparent to the new conversation.

When Jane escorted the Bayliss's to the front door, leaving Francis in a meditative domain in the dining room, she took the opportunity to interrogate Duncan at length about her husband's apparent fantasy.

"What happened in the Eastgate House cellar?"

Retiringly, he gyrated his head, his lineaments awash with ambiguity. "I don't know, Jane. Whatever Francis submitted to had finished by the time I found him. As to whether real, or a figment of his daydreaming, I can only guess."

Her head fell, Natasha promptly advancing and hugging her in an act of support. "It's very much like the circumstances conducive to his mental crash," Jane wearily conceded. "Overburden propelling worry and stress, and the enlargement of a hyperactive imagination."

"It could be nothing," Duncan reassured. "Just an odd circumstance. Make him take a few days of absolute rest, then see if it has passed, and he is back to normal."

"Yes, you're right. But—" She pursed her lips and gloomed, her mind travelling back to past events. "I'm still concerned about the dispossessed embodiment distilled into his countenance. It's just like when he entered his disintegration."

"Yes, I spotted his somewhat cloistered condition as well," Natasha approved. "He bristled with detachment when Duncan summed up their visit to Eastgate House, like he balked at the account, frozen in denial."

Looking daggers at his wife, Duncan apprised, "Well, I'd not go as far as that, but he hardly said a word coming back from Eastgate House, and even less at dinner. He's trying to resolve what he might have seen, or fantasised he saw." Turning to Jane, he annexed, "Anyway, as I say, make him rest for a few days."

Obliged to fulfil her professional obligations, after an early breakfast the ensuing morning, Jane went off to Penenden Heath under a doleful cloud and recurrently concerned for her husband's wellbeing.

In defiance of her goading to take a respite and desist from all code cutting, within an hour of her departure, Francis sat in the study goggling blankly into the computer monitor. He had fired up the Turner game application intent on keying in new code, but nothing came. All he saw amounted to a dust sheet covering a canvass deep in the recesses of the display.

Continuing to gaze into the screen, he began to feel cut off and stranded, reflecting he had experienced the same prodigy at the outset of his disorder. Though he knew it to be self-induced, the limpid image on the screen gawked back at him, as if challenging his perspicacity. Finding himself mesmerised by the silo's convulsion icon, he plunged into its web-like influence, unable to turn away, let alone concentrate on anything else. Falling fatally into the consuming void, the mouse residing stationary, the keyboard silent, he knew no new code could be cut until he sussed out what had happened at Eastgate House. Trying logic to rate events, it failed to impart concrete explanations.

Introspectively, he argued the hallucination, if indeed it turned out to be such trickery, had been evoked by tiredness and fatigue, then counter-argued before the event, he'd been fine, in good spirits, and far from relapse into breakdown.

So, what the hell did I confront? he mused. *What did I see and touch?* Worse, he speculated, what did the manifestation he felt behind him seek? Undoubtedly, it could not have been Bayliss. He had been too far away to transmit the imprint of being nearby. Exhausting the rational, Blake grasped at straws, appraising the most obtuse and oblique possibilities. Whatever form it subsisted in, he had to find out, or the spectre would trouble him enduringly.

* * *

A further hour of supposition went by before Blake hurried away from Beeches. Inevitably sucked to Eastgate House, he descended the spiral staircase into the gem room, the bright autumn sun illuminating the underground space much better than on his first visit. Hesitantly, he moved to the spot where the materialisation had occurred. Negotiating an obtuse-angled corner to engage the cranny, staggered by what he saw, he halted in his tracks. His mouth unlatched as a flush of alarm purged his sensibilities, his right arm involuntarily gesturing with an accusing digit. There before him, reposed the rectangular object just as he had seen previously, its dust cover jauntily disposed over to one side, but uniformly concealing what lay beneath.

Glancing to and fro, he confirmed his isolation. His mouth drying, he licked his lips, then moved on, stooped and outreached a hand to the edge of the dust cover. As he made contact, he distinguished a spook behind him, as he had done before when he anticipated it to be Bayliss. This time, he knew it could not be his co-investigator. Hastily twisting about, nothing came into view, though the creepy caress of the shadow persisted, the sensation like holding a high voltage cable, its internally conducted power engendering vibration.

Revolving, he leered at the enigma, his fingers trembling

against the dust sheet. Gently pulling away the cover to progressively expose the canvass, to his everlasting astonishment, it befell no longer blank. What Blake saw amazed him. Whereas beforehand the surface had been greying-white with mould in some areas pitting the cloth, it had now become transformed into a dazzling Turner masterpiece.

Infatuated and unable to quash the will to stop, Blake clutched the dust sheet, dragging it away. His eyes roamed over the painting, his mind noting and analysing each section, then storing its image. Similar to the seascape as witnessed from St Mary Hoo with the Essex coastline and Canvey Island on the opposite shore, as Blake envisioned it could have been in the mid-nineteenth century, its vibrant montage of bold colours and foggy symbols transported him into an otherworldly domain. Better still, the background blazed with Turner's trademark god-like, radiant, yellowy-red, with flecks of blue sky, whilst the foreground raged in a white and marine-grey tempestuous sea. As the games creator roved the painting, he detected the haunt's potency increase behind him. Near-to smelling the aroma of another being, its breath congealing on his sensitive neck skin, its intrinsic coldness chilled the air, causing vapour to condense on his forehead. Nonetheless, Blake had to taste it. He swirled around, but in doing so, the presense lessened, its magnetic pull decreasing appreciably as he backtracked a few feet towards the spiral staircase. Spinning, he ambled forward again, lurching to his knees, intent upon an in-depth inspection of the marvel.

As Blake studied the painting, the ghoul's muscle resumed a penetrating effect, the stamp of an incorporeal demon perched on his shoulder like a taunting devil much stronger. Ignoring the stalking, he explored the depiction more thoroughly, concentrating on the sky, often a sanctuary hiding phantoms and mysterious figures in Turner's work. Judging he began to see an outline of some semi-concealed being, he cocked his head from side-to-side trying to crystallise the shape into an orderly pattern. Light blond hair, an oval frontage with lofty, large cornflower-blue eyes, a fine nose and generous lips coalesced into solidity. Slowly, he got up, stood back, and bore hither and yon into the entrancement. *Is it an image of the young Turner*, he pensively contemplated?

Bolting his eyelids, he hoped to solve what he had undergone, the realm of conjecture maintained until he heard, "excuse me sir, will you be much longer, only I have to shut the house for lunch."

Startled, Blake whirled about sharply, gulping air. Recognising the Eastgate House curator, his nervousness vented, and he hurriedly breathed out. "Do you see it?" he begged, his voice on the brink of control.

Casually checking right and left, the curator embodied a mystified dial. "See it," he echoed, persevering his officious mien. "See what, sir?"

"The painting, man, the Turner, look—"

Blake gaped back into the cranny again, emptiness now filling the niche, no dust sheet, and undeniably no Turner *tour de force* to be seen. Dumbfounded, he beheld the curator, his jaw dropping, incredulity in his eyes.

Doing his darndest to retain tact, the curator requested, "If you'd care to return to the lobby, sir."

"But it *was* there," Blake protested, signalling to the vacant space. "Didn't you see it as you walked away from the spiral staircase to the corner of this cranny?"

Perplexed by the outburst, the curator replied, "I'm sorry, sir, I don't know what you're talking about."

"The painting, the painting," he prattled, his features torn with anguish. "The damned Turner."

"*Turner*, sir?" the nonplussed curator queried, jolting his head back to its neck foundation extremity. He had not been listening to Blake. Used to rounding up stray sightseers over many decades, he had acquired the art of filtering out their pleas to let them stay from his consciousness. Reconsidering Blake's words, he enquired, "Do you mean, J.M.W Turner, sir?"

"Yes, yes," the code cutter barked back.

His bafflement unfluctuating, the curator declared, "I don't think so, sir." Glimpsing about again to verify his standpoint, he then held his hands behind his back and rocked on his heels to emphasise his authority. "If there were any Turners in Eastgate

House, they'd have been unearthed long ago." Issuing the restless visitor a reprimanding expression, he proclaimed, "With respect, you've let your inventiveness get the better of you. It's easily done in historical habitats like this. Now do come along, sir."

Dejected, Blake took a last lingering peek at the cranny, then followed the curator up the spiral staircase.

* * *

Wayfaring to Beeches, Blake stopped the Morgan on the entryway, flustered to see Jane coming out of the front door. She had heard the cracking exhaust note of her husband's car whilst preparing to leave the house.

"Francis, there you are. Finding you not in, I became confounded."

"Hello, darling,"

"Having forgotten to pick up some papers needed for the afternoon's business at Penenden Heath, I had to come back." She dwelt, eyeing him suspiciously. "Where have you been?"

Not envisaging to see his wife, and thereby the need to explain his absence, in a moment of paramount truth he confessed, "I've been to Eastgate House again."

"Oh, *Francis!*" she cried, denunciation ringing in her tone. She squinted, devoured by guilt about her film commitments and thereby neglect of her disturbed husband. "I have to go, but I'll be back by six. Let's talk then."

"Yes, lets," he blandly parroted.

She gave him a loving peck on his cheek, then climbed inside her Alfa, fluttered a hand to him, and sped off along the driveway. Waving back, he momentarily forgot about the worrisome Eastgate House occurrence. Albeit soon after entering the house and making his way to his den, the Turner image dominated his mindset again.

Pacing hither and thither in weighty cogitation, occasionally he came to rest by the French doors, absorbed by the Medway's navigation channel, a few sailing vessels making their way to the mouth of the river. Distracted by their passage, the ominous beguilement receded, but as he left his station, again the spook levitated in the forefront of his mind.

Nervous about his welfare, he grilled himself as to whether he drifted inextricably into another breakdown, and the malicious imp masqueraded as the cursed factor bringing on the fallacy. Even worse, could the clash have been real, at least real as in the incarnation came from the other side. But why could only he differentiate the bogeyman and see the painting with its accessory dust cover? Irrefutably, ghosts and banshees were not selective according to the victim they hounded. Unarguably, anyone present should discern their vibes, but neither Duncan Bayliss nor the curator had made the connection. It denoted a further cave in, and the event nothing more than a counterfeit progeny fashioned in his hyperactive mind. Having already been there, experienced its decimating flipside, and spent what he perceived to be an eternity in recovery, he had no wish to be reinstalled in the foreboding refuge. Re-evaluating his maiden assent pertaining to spirits being incapable of selection to be false, he conceived maybe they only made alliances with earth-bound beings whose receptors were finely attuned to their aura. *Yes*, he concluded, incontrovertibly, it must be the answer.

Somehow, he had to exorcise Turner's ghost. Telephoning Duncan at his Rochester High Street business, he told him about the morning incident at Eastgate House, then appealed to him to accompany himself on another visit. Anxious about his compadre's palpable fragile state of mind, Bayliss agreed to the supplication, but cautioned he could not make a rendezvous until late afternoon and intended to meet Blake at Eastgate House.

· At the appointed hour, Blake sluggishly perambulated in front of the building entrance, trying to evade meddlesome stares from the curator. A north-easterly blew rain against the windowpanes again, the house made more dramaturgic in semblance under a Constable-like gunmetal grey sky, its clouds pregnant with vapour. To be certain he cruised as creditable to Bayliss, Blake recounted the morning's events in his mind again. To the wide-awake curator, he dallied fidgety like an over-wound coiled spring on the verge of breaking.

Post factum, the curator took the initiative. "Excuse me, sir, if you are coming into Eastgate House again, we will be closing—" He consulted his timepiece. "In forty-five minutes."

Continuing to pace leisurely, Blake endorsed the advice with a wave of a glove. Time began to run short. *What the hell has delayed Bayliss?* Apprehension wrought his body language. Just when he surmised he had been abandoned, Bayliss suddenly came into view, gasping for air.

"Francis, I began to picture I'd missed you," he gabbled. "I got a last-minute call from Monsieur De Vos, the Magritte collector I told you about a few weeks ago, and had to service his requirement, so apologies for my dishevelled display."

"It's quite alright, Duncan. Come on, we haven't got much time."

Undeterred, the allies went inside Eastgate House, rapidly proceeding to and opening the entrance door at the top of the spiral staircase leading to the puzzling crypt.

"Duncan, let me go first," Blake gingerly broached. "Giving sufficient time for the avatar to reappear, you trail me in a few minutes." Breaking off, he perused the hub of the archive. "I want to know what you see."

"Very well, but—" Bothered, Bayliss grew a poker face. "I do feel uneasy about this chicanery. I don't want you to—" He halted precipitously.

"Have a relapse, were you going to say?"

Accrediting fault to himself for the diffidence Blake had identified, the art connoisseur shrunk rearwards in response. "Jane would never forgive me, if anything happened to you."

"I have to do this, Duncan. Until the mystery is resolved, I will not be able to function properly." Pausing, he eyeballed Bayliss intensely, a single-minded visage filling his cast with doggedness and determination. "I have to know what it is nagging me like a menacing zombie."

Familiar with its grating squeaks and loose steps, Blake made his way down the spiral staircase. As in the morning junket, the physical conditions were the same in the nature of the cellar's damp musky atmosphere, the only change being fading native light, and the pita patter jingle of rain hitting the small windowpanes in the upper parts of the basement walls. Circumspectly walking forward, his faculties on full alert, he passed the vault epicentre and homed in on the cranny where he had hitherto seen the dust cover on the canvass.

Composing himself, Blake took a shallow breath and ventured into the aperture, a familiar sight emerging before him. Exhaling, he wheezed, reluctance to go on devouring him. Steadying himself, he held his nerve and carefully grasped the perimeter of the dust cover, pulling it away. Immediately, he distinguished the apparition reinvigorate its substantive authority enveloping him. As the cover slid away, Turner's glorious painting became revealed, its' god-scintillating-like image in a lustrous sky more brilliant than on the morning session, the icon seemed alive, moving about the canvass in a circular motion, Turner's secreted phantoms and mysterious figures mimicking its course. Remembering the initiatory encounter, Blake took a fleeting glance at the basement wall. Again, he saw raindrops hit windowpanes but did not hear their peal. Instead, the alto-pitched ringing clamour resurfaced.

Stretching a pointed digit at the engrossment, Blake divined the presense intensify its puissance. When he stroked the painting surface, it overwhelmed him, the poltergeist infiltrating his whole being. Drawn into the painting like iron filings to a powerful magnet, he trembled uncontrollably under the manifestation's crushing ferocity. Trying to withdraw only saw his finger sink into the canvass, then his hand, then his arm. Frantically, he tried to pull back, but to no avail. The compelling savagery had seized and shackled him, inalienably sucking him evermore into the seascape. He swore he touched the lapping river waves, their icy cold contact making him pant with dubiety. Then, with a greater thrust, the influence pulled him entirely into the bleak, fathomless water. Its chilliness taking effect, the chimera's towering effort, hauled him deeper into the watery void.

Kicking with desperation, Blake drove himself up to the surface, Canvey Island looming up to his front, St Mary Hoo to his rear, and above, the iridescent mug of Turner, growing larger and larger as it descended upon him. Thrashing about, he furiously struggled to stay afloat, the effort futile. His energy spent, he slithered into a bottomless chasm, breath exhaling from his mouth, forming surface-bound bubbles as he began to scream.

* * *

"*Duncan!*" Jane whooped. "What on Earth has happened?"

Bayliss stood in the porchway of the Blake's Rochester house, bolstering Francis across his shoulder, and holding his waist to stop him falling.

"Jane, have you got some brandy? He's going to need it."

She ushered them into the lounge, Bayliss depositing the spaced-out, severed from reality computer games creator on a large couch.

"I wondered where he'd gone when I returned to Beeches," Jane submitted in a wavering voice. "With no note to explain his absence, I neared calling Natasha to see if she could supply an explanation."

"We were at Eastgate House again," Bayliss told her. "He telephoned, asking me to meet him there." Knowing Jane disapproved of further visits to the Elizabethan residence, he gave her an apologetic cast. "Francis had one of his illusionary turns."

Assaying her bedraggled husband, Jane bemoaned, "Oh, he's not at all well. Like with madcap eyes, his pupils are stationary in the dilated shape with a constant blank lour, and his complexion is pallid." Reversing away as if trying to deny what she saw, she agonised, not far from breaking. "What happened, Duncan?"

Bayliss relayed on the early evening proceedings until the pinch when Francis went into the vault and petitioned him to follow a few minutes later.

"When I got to the bottom of the spiral staircase, I called out his name but got no reaction. So I switched on the fluorescent light, then went to the cranny where the foremost incidents had happened." His physiognomy cascaded into distrust. "I saw Francis writhing on his knees, as if some invisible fiend clung to his upper body he couldn't shake off."

Jerking a palm across her mouth, Jane swallowed her breath in a reactive motion of equivocation. Revelations of another breakdown permeated her immediate deliberations, fright nourishing on the heels of shock.

"I ran on, calling his name as I went, but evidently he did not hear. He didn't even register my existence. I took hold of him, but he felt like a tonne weight, as if an opposing force held him. With enormous effort, I managed to disengage him." All at once Bayliss terminated his chronicle, his kisser a mass of incredulity, his pulse racing.

"Please go on, Duncan."

Gyrating his head dismissively, he imparted, "The strangest thing is—" His doubting countenance coasted into a chilling scowl. "He had the strength of ten men resisting my assistance. When I finally got him to his feet and away from the cranny, he went limp like a washed-out rag doll, and crashed into my clasp, as if suddenly released from restraining fetters."

Not liking what she heard, Jane buckled, her puss contorted in dismay. She visualised more to the escapade existed, other than possible disintegration recurrence. "You mean, he behaved as if being held by a potency, preventing you from yanking him free?"

Feeling rather ridiculous, Bayliss judiciously avowed, "I'd not care to give credence to such a possibility, Jane. If someone had told me what I've just told you, I'd not be persuaded. It's just too fantastic to have any bedrock in reality."

Her fears about a second nervous collapse consolidated, Jane's mouth dropped open, but how could the ambiguous clash be explained? "Duncan, I just don't know what to construe in these findings. Maybe you got caught up in Francis's fantasy, unwittingly taking on its dimensions."

She glared at her stricken husband, realising he must have heard her words, but Francis prevailed immune to notions of regular authenticity, his volition lost to incapacity, his wits relegated to neutral. He had already entered a daunting, all-to-familiar zone.

* * *

Thenceforth, Francis Blake spent eight months at Oakwood Hospital, once designated the Kent County Lunatic Asylum. Near to being in a catatonic province when he entered the institution, a combination of drugs and hypnosis relaxed the symptom allowing a gradual recovery, his traumatised inhibition shifting into a more easy-going posture as his legibility began to surge into activation. Jane visited him nearly every day, and the Bayliss's most weekends, all proctoring his gradual rise into normalcy.

Soon after being admitted, Jane Blake talked to Francis's psychiatrist Mister Atterberry about his crack-up.

"What's the prognosis?" she solicited. "And what's to become of Francis?"

Singularly unsure, Atterberry conceded her husband had become psychologically disturbed. Cognizant of the investiture topple, he implied the latest episode to be on a far grander scale and caused by ingrained misconception.

"Under hypnosis," he explained, "Francis keeps on referring to the idiosyncratic peculiarities of Eastgate House, a blank canvass miraculously transmogrifying into a living painting, and the appearance of Turner drawing him into the River Thames estuary off St Mary Hoo." Lowering his head, the psychiatrist professed, "It's a timeless case of delusional paranoia, an unerring insistence the improbable is in fact a real, tangible ensemble to him. The medicines will help, but he must purge the stalking out of his system, and recognise it's not real, just a falsehood conjured up in his mind, stirred by this computer game to be founded on Turner." Discontinuing, a dubious front built on his studious comportment. "There's one phrase he keeps on coming out with under hypnosis." Thumbing through his case notes, he combed for the pertinent wording. "It's here somewhere. Ah, here we are." Gawking at Jane, he read, "*I was listening to the rain but hearing something else.*" Removing his spectacles, he subconsciously bit his bottom lip in a demonstration of bewilderment. "Does it mean anything to you, Missus Blake?"

Reflecting for a moment, Jane replied, "As a matter of fact, it does. It's a line from a song called *Marquee Moon* by Television, one of Francis's favourite bands. He listens to classical music while he cuts code, but *avant garde* rock music is his pleasure." Unglued by the line's context, she enquired, "But what has this got to do with Francis's affliction?"

Quivering his brow, Atterberry confessed, "We don't know yet. May not have any bearing whatsoever. It's just, he keeps on repeating the line under regression hypnosis, as if it has some axiomatic significance to his confusion."

Sometime later, Jane talked to Duncan Bayliss to see if he could cast any light on the *Marquee Moon* line.

"Let me ponder." Cogitating, he then snapped his fingers. "*Yes*, I remember. On both occasions I visited Eastgate House with Francis, rain fell. Even in the cellar we could hear the pita patter of rain on the panes. It must be what Francis is referring to, but the line—" His carriage zoomed into a quizzical deportment. "Say it to me again."

"*I was listening to the rain but hearing something else.*"

"Maybe Francis is saying although he saw raindrops falling on the panes, he didn't hear the chime they created. Instead, potentially, he heard an alternative chatter made by another source." Anguished by his lack of plenary coherence, Bayliss rifled about, defeated. Holding his arms out, he then slapped his upper thighs in symbolic frustration. "I'm sorry, Jane, it's about the best I can do."

"Not a problem. It's only a bi-product anyway, not the origin responsible for his collapse into neurosis. Every time I ask Atterberry about the germ behind Francis's crumble, he responds with nebulous replies, nothing exact or explicit." Exasperated, she exhaled noisily. "It's so infuriating. If I don't know the precise stimulus responsible for his mental and emotional milieu, how can I stop it happening again?"

Discomforted by her irritation, Bayliss could only bequeath soothing but ultimately ineffectual words. He too had no wish to see his marra undergo such a brutal baptism again, but the antidote or the required measure eluded him as well.

Rather than going back to the Blake's Rochester house, Jane spent many nights at the Bayliss's St Mary Island abode. Unequivocally afflicted by her husband's phobia, on some occasions they heard her sobbing into her pillow. Trying to resolve events in her own mind, in the evenings she often paced along the St Mary's Island periphery pathway running parallel to the River Medway, aiming for logic and common sense to explain what had occurred, but the maddening postscript she dissected only confirmed an ever-hardening, nondescript conclusion.

"The irony is," she began after one walk, "I proposed the Turner idea to Francis."

"Oh, Jane, don't beat yourself up," Natasha besought, shocked by her pal's tortured mind. "What has happened to Francis is not your fault."

"But it is," Jane upheld.

"Ohhh," she retorted, shaking her head. "Tell her, Duncan."

"Natasha is right, Jane," he argued in as gentle a voice as he could muster. "It's a coincidence, and pure chance Francis has suffered another attack. The trigger word could have been anything."

"But—" she restlessly began, before losing her train of thought.

Bothered by Jane's flustered irrationality, Duncan embraced her. "Please, don't do this to yourself. It won't accomplish anything and will change nothing." Tenderly squeezing her hand, he counselled, "Just be strong for Francis. It's what you must do."

Coming out of her self-imposed flagellation, Jane's enunciation lightened. "Yes, I know you are both right. It's just, I have this frenzied mindfulness of guilt hanging over me."

Natasha Bayliss's dread about Jane's own mentality ballooned. She said to her husband, Jane would join Francis at Oakwood if her sorry plight continued. Vacillating whether to jolt Jane out of her self-imposed malaise, or let the obsession percolate out of her naturally, the Bayliss's kept a wary eye on her without resorting to obtrusive disciplines. Discreetly monitoring Jane, they made judgments *vis-à-vis* her psyche, but tarried unsure as to what labours to take.

Belatedly, Jane beat them to the draw. She had to know what had happened to her husband at Eastgate House. After much debate, she persuaded Duncan to take her on the same trip, capping in Francis's unnerving hallucination in the repository. Staying at home, Natasha elected to be the anchor point for the ensuing action, should there be any further unexplained disturbances.

* * *

Duncan and Jane arrived at Chatham Dockyard on a freezing winter's day, an angry, volatile sky murmuring overhead, and a north-easterly biting to the bone. They went into the ropery and other buildings in the complex before motoring out to the Hoo Peninsula, Bayliss trying to replicate the conversations he had with Francis. He talked about Turner's meeting with Dickens, its relevance to *Dombey and Sons*, *The Haunted Man and the Ghost's Bargain*, and how the meeting had a beneficial stamp on Dickens' future writings. Back-auditing her husband's fitness, he also certified Francis sailed as both aroused and focused by the Turner-Dickens account, then quick-witted and enthused when they trekked to Eastgate House.

Sensing she could be treading in her husband's trail, Jane fluked upon some foot tracks in the marsh. Bayliss nominated the imprints were unlikely to be those of Francis, other people having tramped the marsh boundary since the visit. Nevertheless, she browsed her surroundings, imagining her husband had done the same thing.

With the weather worsening, and Jane content nothing more could be gained from the marsh setting, they journeyed on to Eastgate House, Jane approaching its entrance with trepidation as she lamped its irregular Elizabethan outline. Her seizure palpable, Bayliss gently held her, made comforting overtones, and assisted her over the threshold.

Recollecting Bayliss, the curator welcomed the visitors. He had become aware of Blake's hospitalisation when Atterberry visited Eastgate House, to see if he could cast any light on what Francis had described under hypnosis. Recalling the affair but elucidating in the negative, the curator convinced the psychiatrist such a bizarre notion to be without precedence in his appreciation. Unmoved, Atterberry took the opportunity to go into the supposed glory hole, finding nothing out of the ordinary, let alone a canvas covered by a decaying dust sheet.

Being a man of unimpeachable discretion, when Bayliss had phoned ahead, saying Blake's wife wished to make a visit, the curator had abided tight-lipped about what Atterberry told him of Blake's misfortune.

Holding Jane's hand as she nervously followed, Bayliss led the way down the spiral staircase, each step onto the creaking metal amplifying her anxieties. Bordering on an incalculable, inklike pit to Jane's unaccustomed eyes, with a few treads to go, she faltered at the prospect of advancing into the tomb, Bayliss probing reluctance in her movement.

"It's alright, Jane. I won't let anything happen to you."

Settling at the foot of the spiral staircase, Bayliss momentarily released his clasp on Jane to find the light switch. As he pressed it, she heard a click and fluorescence illuminated the cellar, the facade to her front not what she anticipated. Before the visit, she had visions of a clammy, cloistered compartment with a low ceiling, its floor festooned with decades even centuries of document-ladened trunks and packing cases crammed with third-order artefacts, deemed not important enough for public trot-out, their rotting interiors breeding a camphoraceous, sickly fragrance. Dripping water from broken drains and rats running wild completed her mental picture.

By contrast, the view frontwards came as a surprise to her, the sepulchre meticulously clean, unfettered by vermin and foul smells, its ceiling affording occupants to stand to their full height. Resembling a billet converted to accommodate snooker and pool tables, traditional pub games, and a bar where players could drink and live out their fantasies of being Jimmy White, or Fast Eddie Felson, the pool champ character from *The Hustler*, the association composed her. It also made her evaluate what Francis perceptibly saw must truly have been unreal.

Walking slowly through the depository, Bayliss showed Jane the empty cranny where Francis had his struggles, her comprehension of nothing being inauspicious, distinctly reinforced. She begged the question, had Francis simply fallen into the grip of another cave in, brought on by overexertion and stress? Holding the discernment, she schemed to discuss the insight with Duncan and Natasha, maybe even Atterberry at Oakwood. After a few more minutes of inspection, Jane had seen enough to validate her initial certitude.

Ascending the spiral staircase, she took a last lingering gander at the cavern before Bayliss extinguished the light, the basement promptly saturated in total darkness. Only meagre light from the ground floor above made for sure-footed guidance on the assent up the metal construction.

Moderating she had been unnecessarily fearful at the expectancy of visiting the hypogeum, suddenly Jane experienced a chill run up her back, its weaving passage reconnoitring every contour of its arched form.

"*Duncan!*" she wittered, her shrill grate resonating with panic.

Bayliss reengaged the fluorescent light. Immediately, the shiver evaporated. Perplexed, she gawped at him, her quandary plain.

"You okay, Jane?"

"Sorry, Duncan, I just…" She tilted her head, fixing him with dazzled eyes. "I just…"

"Yes?"

"Oh, it's nothing." She peeped into the cellar epicentre again, as if securing it stayed clear. "Can you wait until I'm back at the ground floor level before you turn off the light, please?"

He smiled up at her. "*Mon plaisir.*"

Grinning back as if feeling ridiculous, she consummated the ascent, Bayliss tracing her progress to the top before glancing back at the offending cranny, switching off the light, and joining her.

During the jaunt back to St Mary's Island, Jane lingered quiet and solitary, her inherent effervescent persona subdued, her usual sparkling properties diminished. Bayliss aced something amiss, but decided a softly, softly attitude might be best under the circumstances, and left until the evening.

Natasha met the expeditionaries at the front door of the Bayliss house.

"Come in, Jane, you must be frozen." She gave her friend a

generous, warm smile before flashing a querulous gape at her husband.

Raising a cautionary hand in response, he then pressed a finger to his lips, indicating not to make a fuss.

Speedily moving into the lounge, Jane left Natasha mooning at Duncan.

"What happened?" she fretfully entreated.

"I'm not unequivocal," he conceded, resignedly fanning out his hands. "But some unforeseen chapter happened."

"Where?"

Hesitantly, he advised, "At Eastgate House."

"Oh, my god," Natasha jabbered, her everyday calm mien devoured by shock.

After Jane had thawed out and the threesome had eaten a light dinner, Jane innately withdrawn in the course of the repast, like Francis had been after his introductory bogey spat, they retired to the lounge, Natasha asking about the Turner trail. Going into some detail recounting Chatham Dockyard, the Hoo Peninsula, and essentially Eastgate House, Duncan itemised the trek dispassionately whilst Jane curled up in a comfortable suite chair, preoccupied with her own ruminations, and outwardly oblivious to the report.

"We ended up going into the vault, so Jane could see where Francis had his moment, then—"

Before he could go on, Jane interrupted him. "Duncan." She got up, went to the window, and scoured in the direction of Rochester, less than a mile away as the crow flies, the Bayliss's watching her transit then exchanging troubled idioms. Twisting to address them, she cited, "Duncan, when I climbed the spiral staircase—" Hesitating and jittery, she began to wilt.

"Yes," he rejoindered, standing up to catch her if she began to crumple with torment.

"Did you…" Expeditiously, she ceased speaking, manifestly open-eyed about her fragile footing, but more critically, intent on not coming across as melodramatic. "…did you feel anything, when you put the light out, perhaps—" She beheld him imploringly. "Perhaps the presense Francis is so keyed up about?"

Not particularly knowing how to deal with the trenchant matter, Duncan blazed at Natasha. Nodding at him to reply, she then made a pushy mien.

"Well...no, nothing at all."

Returning to her chair, Jane licked her dry lips then scrutinised the Bayliss's with an unyielding absolute certainty. "I felt possessed."

Alarmed by the admission, Natasha instantly rose to her feet. "Oh, Jane, no, surely not."

She cast a dispirited pout at Natasha then buried her head in her hands, trying to shut out the world, tears welling up in her large oval eyes as she began to tremble. In a shallow voice she divulged, "I did feel an incongruous adversity upon me, like a slimy reptile sucking me down, but the moment Duncan turned the light on again, it dissolved."

* * *

Still disconcerted by her subsurface contention, at Jane's next Oakwood visit, she told Atterberry about her confrontation with the doppelganger.

"Self-induced autosuggestion, Missus Blake, nothing more," he proposed, smiling at her with conviction to restore confidence. "The seed became implanted by your husband's showdown. When you visited the Eastgate House crib, your imagination drove your instinct to maximum sensitivity, creating modalities for illusion. The mind took over crowning the deception."

"Maybe," she batted back. "But I'm not a person predisposed to hysteria, nor do I subscribe to a halfway house world hovering between Earth and heaven. My artistry gets enough stimulation from filmmaking."

"Yes, and the occupational aspect in itself could be the catalyst for what you visualised in the silo."

Such a possibility had not occurred to Jane. She recoiled at the innuendo, then tapering her eyes began to buy into the plausible clarification. "You mean, my mind could have been pre-loaded with premonitions because of the nature of my duties at Spellbound Studios?"

Contemplating for a trice, the psychiatrist confided, "It's possible. There have been many cases of patients so enrapt in their profession, it degrades their capacity to be sagacious. In fact, your husband fits the model. In your case, I prevail predisposed to say mesmerism is the culprit behind your candling."

"I understand your rationale, however, Francis has a history of mental hyperactivity provoked by stress and professional pressures. I have not. For me, what I detected in the cellar embodied itself as very real, not a delusion blown out of proportion owing to mind imbalance, but a corporeal spook, noted as you'd espy a human being in tight proximity behind you."

"Be assured, Missus Blake, it didn't happen," Atterberry maintained. "You said you don't believe in the afterworld of spirits and ghosts. With that in mind, the only other credible explanation is an inducement resultant from submersing yourself in the same environment responsible for Mister Blake's derangement."

Reluctantly, Jane accepted the hypothesis, though the undertaking still nagged at her cognate to the remnant of a thorn retained in soft flesh.

Caught between a vocational diagnosis and her own interpretation, Jane Blake secretly dallied skeptical. Though decidedly creative and imbued with intellectual appraisement in spadefuls, she prided herself to be a solid person, not subject to flights of fancy. She had gained a reputation as a robust thinker both at Penenden Heath and in her private life. Why should she suddenly cascade into indefiniteness stationed on flaky facts and impressions? She deduced her capricious hysteria to be of her own making, stirred by emotion and apprehension for Francis. Undoubtedly, these were the factors altering her customary predilections, the leftover elements being circumstantial. Howbeit, no matter how ludicrous the notion she conceived, she stood on quaking quicksand, her every movement no matter what its galvanising motive, drawing her intractably into the void.

Somehow, she had to find stability, or she could be of no use to her husband in his recovery period.

Fretting over Francis coupled with her own lurid wrangle at Eastgate House took its toll on Jane, her gorgeousness fading consequent from worry and suspense. Though none of her colleagues or confidants, inclusive of Duncan and Natasha Bayliss said so, it evidently occurred to them Jane suffered the paralysing burden of dread. Soldiering on, she supported her husband's revival and tried to rationalise the spiral staircase phenomena into placeable constituents in line with Atterberry's prognosis.

As Francis took upward surges in his recuperation, Jane's dismay lessened. Once again, her demeanour flowered into an optimistic and positive fettle, her gait flowed with purpose, and her unmarred-body language aerated with euphoria and joy. Lightness and elation began to shine in her lineaments, her Gorgeous-Jane moniker rekindled.

* * *

In the autumn of the sequent year, Francis Blake left Oakwood, latterly deemed well enough by Atterberry to restart family life at Beeches.

Though far from his old self, there had been a pronounced improvement in his mental health. His manner not sullen, and his body language removed from broken, he no longer wore a vacant mask. In lieu of melancholia, he signaled contentment when only a few months earlier he had sulked and scowled. Though vibrancy pulsed in his being, in part he still glided side by side with inhibition, a form Jane estimated to be the upshot from amassed foreboding.

She never mentioned her visit to Eastgate House with Duncan to him. With Francis on the mend, why re-visit the venue of the apparition? Surmising it could have an adverse downside on his permanent rehabilitation, and might cause a relapse, she preserved her secret. In preference, she went out of her way to bring extra warmth and love, confident all-embracing recovery would come out of caring domesticity. She even hired a maid to take care of

Francis's every need during the hours she tended to her duties at Spellbound Studios.

While Francis underwent extensive therapy at Oakwood, Jane had deleted the Turner game file from his computer and thrown out all the filaments and minutiae he had gathered to foster its genesis. She refereed any reminders of his ominous head-to-head with the poltergeist were the last thing he needed. She had also presumed her husband would enquire about the Turner file, but nothing eventuated. Had he made a conscious decision not to go there, she asked herself, Jane construing his lack of chastising her measure as an indication Francis did not incline to revisit the spring of his crash into the persecution complex.

After a few months of ancillary convalescence, Francis felt able to recommence code cutting. Putting out some feelers, he ascertained his reputation and kudos had not been soiled by his temporary retreat. Several companies from his computer games manufacturer client roster responded, incorporating Cyberdeception, a well-established, Warwick based games provider, who had engaged him for specialised games invention in the past. Contingent on his success, Cyberdeception contracted him to originate an interactive virtual reality game for the forthcoming 2012 London Olympic Games.

Armed with a flurry of insights, Blake set off on the task, Jane pleased to see a supplemental upward stride in her husband's recuperation. Visiting frequently, the Bayliss's were astounded by Francis's abiding recovery, and pleased Jane had wholly redeemed her splendour and buoyant personality.

Intriguingly, Francis even began to put the Turner incident into a jokey context.

"I realise now," he confessed one day when the Blakes entertained the Bayliss's, "I must have been overburdening myself. It incited stress, and the Turner hallucination transpired."

"Well," Duncan responded in a somewhat reserved intonation whilst glistening at Natasha, "we are very pleased for you. There came a time when we fancied we'd never see the old Francis again, but your restoration has been remarkable."

"Yes," Natasha endorsed. "If Mister Atterberry had said you'd be back to your accustomed self within a year of your breakdown, I'd have been very doubtful. But here you are, bright, breezy and able to put the Eastgate House event into perspective, without descending into a gibbering mess. It's nothing short of a miracle."

Beaming gratuitously, Francis took his wife's hand. "I thank Gorgeous-Jane for my fortune. Without her constant care and encouragement, I'd not be talking to you today."

Ever modest, Jane retorted, "Mister Atterberry might have also played a pivotal role."

"Unquestionably," Francis agreed, "but he lacked your charms and womanly guiles. Those were the elements pulling me out of the mire."

They all broke into laughter. Jane and the Bayliss's now unwavering Francis had come through his ordeal without retaining any legacy hang-ups.

* * *

A few weeks thereafter, with Belioz's *Symphonie Fantastique* filling the study with a vibrant melody, Blake merrily banged away at his keyboard, creating code for the Olympic Games project. Satisfied with the game's progress to date, he hummed along to the symphony, content normality had been resurrected. Perfecting a section cored on the 100m athletics event, he ran the code generating CGI. Coming to life, the program rendered athletes readying themselves for race mode. Having arranged for the program to breed a 3-D formation, as the athletes charged along the track, the configuration changed from frontal foreground to receding background with the runners dissipating towards infinity, championed by a cheering crowd spurring them on.

About to resume on the succeeding stage of coding, suddenly Blake noticed the computer screen begin to flicker. Arbitrating he had inadvertently dislodged its power plug, he bent to ensure it rested fully in place in the mains socket. When he re-examined the screen content, there were no jubilant athletes, no exultant race officials, and no drone of the artificial crowd applause he had programmed into the game.

Only a 2012 London Olympic Games banner remained in the display's top-left corner, and in place of the game icons, he saw a familiar face, Turner's face, just like he had seen in the Eastgate House cellar. Centered in the middle of the screen, the visage began to enlarge until Turner's forehead, eyes, ears, nose and chin had grown beyond the monitor screen's resolution. Then Turner's mouth opened, growing so large, it engulfed the holistic display, the Olympic Games banner disappearing down his throat.

Blake sat entranced as light-shaded anatomies arose from the depths of the throats' dark funnel. Under a murky grey sky, he began to see flecks of yellowy-red and blue twinkling like tiny lightning rods, then Canvey Island grew in the backdrop, and the Thames matured into a tempestuous sea, replete with Turner's phantoms and mysterious figures flailing in the waves. A pulsating, alto-pitched clatter accompanied the affray, its single harmonic reverberation familiar to Blake. Finally, out of the storm, a spiral staircase materialised.

* * *

Blake stood outside Eastgate House, ogling its dominating superstructure and spectral windows. In his paranoia obsessed compulsion, the latter seemed like eyes staring at him, pupils forming in the lead-lined panes and emanating their critical disdain at his arrival. At the upper scales of the edifice, guttering screeched and groaned under the push and pull of a north-easterly, the roof flexing like lungs breathing oxygen into Eastgate House. Raindrops beat against the paving stones, throwing up specks of dirt, spattering Blake's shoes and trouser bottoms. Staring earthward insouciant to the stains, his mind had become located elsewhere. He could already hear a building, alto-pitched buzz drowning out the pita patter of the rain striking the Eastgate House windowpanes.

"It's Mister Blake, isn't it?"

The incessant, shrill hum ended. So distracted with his architectural appreciation, Blake had failed to mark the nearby curator. Rotating to buttonhole him, he began to discriminate the official.

"Yes…it is."

"Are you alright now, sir? We heard you'd been unwell for some time."

"I have been, but I'm fine now," Blake confirmed, his voice almost bright with reassurance.

Losing his concentration on the curator, Blake fell out of volition, re-hypnotised by Eastgate House, superficially buckling on its foundations and shimmying its walls. Amazed by the lively, seductive motion, his eyes widened, and his jaw fell. Sniggering involuntarily at the incongruous exhibition, he then eyeballed the curator with refreshed intensity. "Tell me, is the crypt still open to the public?"

Hands clasped behind his back and emitting a vigilant comportment, the curator came over regardful. "It is, sir, but—"

Blake goggled at him earnestly. "Yes?"

Not wishing to offend, nonetheless the curator elected to counsel caution. "With respect and taking account of your previous visit's repercussions, you shouldn't go there, sir."

Mustering all his fortitude and breaking into a nimble smile, Blake slipped tranquilising digits onto the curator's shoulder. "I'm fine now," he pleaded.

A few minutes later, Blake stood at the top of the spiral staircase. Cautiously taking hold of the banister, little by little he descended, remembering each creak and ear-piercing whine the metal made against his footsteps.

Winter again, daylight had been fading since the sun's arc had patted the western horizon in the mid-afternoon. Only a gloomy streetlamp illuminated the cellar via its opaque windowpanes. Stopping halfway down the spiral staircase to seek out familiar datum coordinates, Blake strained his eyes to see into the depository recesses. Authenticating the odd fulcrum spot, he listened for indistinct clamours and refrains, but only silence reigned. Distinguishing no spectre, and no chill on the back of his neck, he resumed onward, each tread befitting a gulf, each vague echo a hollow epitaph to future's folly.

At the bottom of the staircase, he convened his bearings, reached for the light switch with fumbling fingers and fluorescent light flooded the bunker. Careful measure by careful measure, he tentatively moved into the chamber, as if finding his way up a footpath suspended in space with the abyss below. Though scared, he abided compelled to go on, the same force making him leave his den, jump into the Morgan, race to Rochester High Street, and stand outside Eastgate House, rousing the impulse.

Passing the archive epicentre, he stopped inches from the corner after which the enigmatic cranny lay, the paranormal portal to another dimension where his supernatural encounters had taken place. Closing his eyes, he edged to a locus he adjudged to be the cranny entrance, then delayed. Immediately he felt the presense encircle him, a familiar ringing vibration humming in his ear. Unlocking his eyes, Blake probed the vault windowpanes, the north-easterly propelling rain droplets against them. "*I was listening to the rain but hearing something else*," he fatalistically murmured, then focused on the source of his abstraction.

To his front, at the back of the cranny, lay a recognisable rectangular object, shrouded by a dust cover concealing the painting he knew to be beneath. Extending his fingers, he grasped a corner of the dust sheet, slowly peeling it away to uncover Turner's glorious masterpiece. As he gazed into its majesty, static emblems again took flight, their fluidic tempo exacerbating his entrancement. Changeling yellowy-red converted clouds to expanding gas plumes in a range of gold and silver flecks. Ablaze with green and purple hues, distant dark coastlines metamorphosed into vigorous chugging shapes. With waves crashing upon waves, the Thames built to a wall of Titan fury, spray sent flying up into the ozone like a volcano erupting molten lava. Making eddies in their wake, whirlpools traversed the surface, and above, the kaleidoscope sky shone with the moving air of a god-like sun. Steadily corralled into the melodrama, Blake floated above tremulous *terra firma*, unconditionally absorbed in alluring captivation.

Marvelling at the dynamism and the vivid portrayal of Turner's creation, his jugular pulsated subordinate from blood coursing through veins spurred on by adrenalin rush. Seemingly at one with the painting, with no partition between flesh and brush strokes, he lived in the waves, their rolling passage caressing his soul, quelling all anxieties. Refreshed by aqua immersion, he walked on the Canvey Island shoreline and in the St Mary Hoo marsh, his ambulation bouncy, his expression luxuriant. As the sunlight transposed into dancing shadows, green transformed into emeralds, purple into lighter violet. Flying in the clouds, he spiralled in their bathing coolness, laughing gregariously as he played tag with Turner's phantoms and mysterious figures. Liberated from all worldly volition, he darted upwards into prismatic horizons on the frontiers of space.

Wholeheartedly released, his demons extinguished, Blake's fears were neutralised. Only a welcoming light lay ahead on his travel. It beckoned him to hurry.

* * *

Jane Blake arrived back home at her usual time.

As the front door banged shut, she heard a Belioz descant coming from the study and called out, "Hello, Francis."

She took off her gloves, placing them on the hall table, hung her coat in the cloakroom, and skipped through correspondence left on the hall table.

While checking her hair in the hall mirror, she reiterated, "Francis." Raising her voice over the music, she attached, "Are you there?"

No answer. Adjudicating her husband must be eaten up by the 2012 Olympic Games computer game task, she made her way along the hallway to the study, its door slightly ajar.

"Francis, I had the most—" She desisted in mid-sentence as she entered.

Surveying his den, she foresaw seeing her husband at the computer. Instead, she saw him laid out on the *chez lounge*.

"*Francis!*" she exclaimed, almost breathing the word, before dashing to her prone husband.

Utterly still, a joyous, dogmatic smile embedded into his

lineaments, his eyes dilated, shining and wide open, his stopped metabolism had preserved his body in a relaxed, jaunty disposition.

Saddened and distressed as an emotional cry of despair leapt from her mouth, tears streamed from her eyes. Then she saw an unfamiliar item consigned to a chair by the *chez lounge*. Flicking a hand up to her mouth, she apprehensively gasped for breath as her eyes fell on the Turner, its resounding magnificence and pomp, just as her late husband described.

A few days passed before Jane read Francis's obituary in the local newspaper. Across from the text, an article on a recently exhumed Turner pronounced its finder, a Rochester man, had unearthed the treasure quite by accident in the Eastgate House cellar. It went on to say, the finder had been so overcome by the discovery, he had later expired, intense emotional shock culminating in a rapid heart-stopping seizure.

Adjacent to the print column, a photograph showed the Turner, propped up against the spiral staircase.

GROWING UP WITH THE ROLLING STONES

GROWING UP WITH THE ROLLING STONES

Fashions may come, and fashions may go, but the holy Rolling Stones go on forever. 'If you don't know who Keith Richards is, then you haven't been living on planet Earth.'

Gavin Anderson frequently said so when confronted by ill-informed goldbricks and slouches, claiming the latest rock sensation would eclipse the Stones, taking stage centre in the hearts and minds of hungry for pulse-raising music teenagers, and go on to rule the universe. Nothing met his indignation more than their sycophantic adulation of here today gone tomorrow pretenders and one-hit wonders, cashing in on the grand rock 'n' roll pantheon created by the genre's genesis pioneers. Presley, Vincent and Cochran impersonators, masquerading as the doyens of third-generation rock, when in practice they were strictly passé, especially came in for acerbic ridicule. It all smelt of big-bucks' ambitions without any credentials, and even less talent.

Worse came when the matchless second incarnation found themselves endlessly parodied by lesser beings, rock royalty members the Beatles and the Rolling Stones copied and ripped off, until their impersonators had their studio tone and live act off pat. For Gavin, only the real McCoy had genuine, gilt-edged currency, all others viewed to be fakes and flakes. Dining out on the platinum-standard bearers, he revelled in their music like it tasted of honey, read about them akin to a novice devouring the scriptures, and endlessly marvelled at their elan and verve.

If the Fabs were deemed to be Liverpool's cuddly rock 'n' rollers, when not breeding mind-blowing singles and albums, conversely, the press positioned the Stones as revolutionaries, rampaging across the hinterlands of the old Establishment, their outsider qualifications, renegade semblance, and strutting sexuality placing them firmly on the administration's bad boys hit list, whilst diametrically, securing the attention and following of young people, searching for excitement and purpose. For Gavin, Mick & Co represented high octane pleasure at its finest, an assessment made in his formative years and one maintaining credence as his life exploded into adventure and exploit, the perfect accompaniment for permanent bliss.

Needless to say, when Elvis got into his stride, Gavin remained a twinkle in his father's eye. Years later, and after much reflection, he acquired the wherewithal to pronounce on rock's great, and not so great merchants.

* * *

Greeting the entrance of Gavin Kurtis Anderson into the universe at 11:20 pm, 26th September 1960, a full harvest moon loomed large above a cloudless, magenta blue night sky. Keeping his mother Aleshia waiting a few days beyond the predicted birth date, apprehension consumed his father Garfield at the lateness of the arrival. Finally, emerging into a world dominated by the Cold War, sweeping societal change, and burgeoning monumental creation in the arts, science and industry, both mother and father beamed from ear to ear when a nurse offered the newborn to them, wrapped in blankets and gargling with vitality.

"I thought he'd never appear," Aleshia quipped as her husband kissed her on the cheek then sparkled at their new son.

Smiling at the light sarcasm, Garfield countered, "Well, it might be indicative as he grows up, he will consider all things with due diligence before acting."

"*Hah*, I didn't expect you to be so philosophical at a time like this."

"What better time to make hopes and dreams for a child."

"Yes, you're right." Gazing lovingly at Gavin, she anointed, "Let's trust he is as attentive about the bridges he will have to cross as life comes up to meet him."

Three years earlier, just before their first son Donnell's third birthday, Garfield and Aleshia Anderson bought a midsized four-bedroom detached house in Christleton, just outside the ancient city of Chester. Employed as sales manager for Knockton & Garwell, a world-famous manufacture of precision scientific instruments used in the aircraft and nuclear engineering industries, Garfield had steadily climbed the promotion ladder and aimed for further advancement. Aleshia had been ladies' department manager at premier-class departmental store Browns of Chester, but when Donnell came along, she took on the mother role full-time. Succeeding from the economic boom of the mid-to-late 1950s, by the time Gavin arrived in the family bosom, the Andersons were basking in the fruits of their occupational endeavours. Garfield's firm car had been upgraded from a Wolseley 15/60 to a Rover P4 100, and Aleshia ran around in the new car market champion from the Austin Motor Company, the Mini. Invariably, the Andersons holidayed in Devon or the Yorkshire dales, but had ambitions to venture abroad when Gavin had ceased teething, Lombardy and Poitou-Charentes their coveted destinations.

One embryonic event to touch Gavin and evermore etch itself in his memory happened when his mother left him in front of the television with Donnell and their older cousin Lucas, 17th October 1962, watching the Beatles foremost broadcast performing *Love Me Do* on Granada's magazine-type programme *People and Places*, presented by Bill Grundy.

Lucas had been into Elvis and Johnny Kidd & the Pirates, Donnell, the Shadows and the Everly Brothers, the Fabs immediately displacing these former darlings in their affections. Staring at the TV screen, then at Lucas and Donnell, Gavin wondered why they were so thrilled, before he too slid into bewitchment.

Returning from Knockton & Garwell, Garfield entered the lounge in the middle of the rendition. Calling Aleshia to join him, at the song's conclusion, they were amazed to hear Grundy say the band hailed from Liverpool, just twenty miles north-west of Christleton. Noticing additional to Donnell and Lucas, Gavin had also lost himself, riveted by the transmission, the grownups exchanged incredulous glances.

"This is the only time I've seen Gavin transfixed by anything," Aleshia told Garfield when the adults retired to the kitchen.

"Mmmm, odd. Maybe he's just reacting to Lucas and Donnell's obvious fatal addiction to this new group from Liverpool.

"Maybe. Even at a very early age, they say a child's shaping proxies point the way to their future essays."

"Yes." Frowning, he supplemented, "Just a minute. Are you saying, number two son is destined to become a pop star?"

Chuckling, she laid reassuring fingertips on her husband's arm. "Not necessarily, dear, more a case of, I'm wondering what the unveiling might mature into in the years to come *vis-à-vis* his inclinations."

"Quite. It's inevitable both our sons will slide towards the popular music of the day. Certainly, Donnell is already there. Howbeit, I don't see any downside to it, after all—" He hunched his shoulders acceptingly. "We both got caught up in the swing-thing when we were kids."

Paradoxically, just a few days afterwards, the Anderson family tuned into an altogether different and potentially life-threatening dissemination, when British telecasts screened President Kennedy's address to the American nation regarding the Cuban Missile Crisis, a stand-off between the United States and the Soviet Union, possibly leading to World War III, and the exchange of intercontinental ballistic nuclear weapons.

The juxtaposition between the two major events, the premier, a dawning moment, the second, a possible prelude to the ultimate revelation, left Garfield and Aleshia perplexed by the poles-apart news. Though the possibility of an East-West nuclear war had been apparent since the end of WWII and the advent of H-bomb tests in the early 1950s, few believed the likelihood to be real, the Superpowers posturing at each other from the safety of their own bunkers as far as it got, with the British and the French stuck on the side-lines developing their own independent nuclear weapon deterrents.

Kennedy's broadcast changed false perceptions for all grownups, kids largely abiding, oblivious to its ramifications. Responding to the emergency with propositions about constructing an underground fallout shelter, Garfield and Aleshia surveyed their back garden, later action averted when Khrushchev agreed to remove Soviet missiles from Cuba, leaving husband and wife breathing a sigh of relief.

Though the Cuban Missile Crisis lodged in the annals of history, arguably, the Beatles televisual feast spelt the Liverpool combo's inaugural leap into the nation's perpetual consciousness, and the colossal rise of the world's most significant and creative rock band.

Over the next few years, Gavin heard many more Beatles riches issuing forth from Donnell's bedroom, and on occasion, witnessed his mother singing along to *I Want to Hold Your Hand* on the BBC's Light programme and *Things We Said Today* on Radio Caroline.

Before his fourth birthday, he had his maiden acquaintance with the Rolling Stones when Lucas brought their launch album, eponymously titled *The Rolling Stones*, over to the Anderson's house. Plonking it on Donnell's Dansette record player, he set the scene alight with the band's interpretations of American rhythm & blues and blues anthems.

In subsequent years, Donnell convinced his brother, when the track *Carol* came on, Gavin tattled, 'I like this one.'

Honed on a solid diet of country and Chicago-vogue blues, Chuck Berry and Bo Diddley, the Stones assaulted the nation's sensibilities with a flurry of vivacious singles and classic covers albums, before manager Andrew Loog Oldman locked Jagger and Richards in a room, not letting them out until they had penned the band's paramount original single, *The Last Time*. After the landmark moment, it just got better and better, the band fathering a plethora of outstanding singles and albums, notably throughout the late 1960s.

By age six, Gavin had attained a genuine taste for the Rolling Stones music, often going into Donnell's bedroom and playing his copy of the band's latest single or long player, mixed in with other selections from his brother's collection. An object of wonderment to him, the Dansette could be loaded with twelve singles or eight long-players, its automatic feed operation sometimes resulting in more vinyl dropping onto the turntable from the retaining spindle stack than intended, making the unit vibrate and wobble, a backlash invariably amusing him.

Whereas other pupils at Christleton Junior School talked about toy soldiers, liquorice sherbets and TV repeats of The Lone Ranger, invariably Gavin struck up a conversation about contemporary music in general, and the Rolling Stones in particular, only a few of his classmates having the remotest idea, apropos the subject matter.

Another on-air banquet introduced him to the Jimi Hendrix Experience Christmas week 1966, when the trio played *Hey Joe* on Top of the Pops. Sitting cross-legged on the lounge floor goggling at Hendrix, his flamboyant clothing, charismatic personality and guitar gymnastics mesmerised the blossoming music aficionado.

During his fashioning years, the Stones' fascination continued, his current musical preferences also expanding to the Byrds, Cream, Fleetwood Mac, the Who, the Kinks, and habitually, the ever-inventive Beatles, filling his leisure time. Constantly dazzled by the abundance of hugely stimulating archetypal material and revelatory innovation unwrapping in the evolving derivative rock genus, he perceived involvement in a very special period of up-to-date music evolution. Often, when he assumed it had reached the boundary of excellence, a new hotshot came along to storm his faculties and blitz his mind, opening supplementary avenues of exploration into literature and the arts, and prompting investigations into the influences behind the extraordinary opus.

One day, his likings got into the outer limits when his father heard some strange brattle coming from Donnell's bedroom, only to find Gavin engrossed in the weird commotion.

"What on Earth are you listening to?"

"Oh, hello, Father. I'm listening to *I'm Waiting for the Man* by the Velvet Underground."

"Huh!" Garfield exclaimed. "I can just about get along with the usual raucous noises coming out of the boombox, but this…" He scratched his head. "…this is completely out of tune, and the recording is way too over-driven."

"That's the way it's meant to sound."

Recoiling, Garfield uttered, "Really?"

"Yes. I read in the *New Musical Express*, the Velvet Underground is experimenting with distortion and repetition in the style of La Monte Young.

"Who?"

"I went to the library and checked him out. He's an American *avant-garde* artist and minimalist music composer."

Confounded by the precise retort, Garfield scouted, "where did you learn the phrase, *avant-garde*?"

"I looked it up as well. Its French."

"Yes, I do know." Gawping at his budding, erudite son, he congratulated, "My, you are growing up quickly. I didn't learn any French until my investiture year at Wirral Grammar."

* * *

Given his play pals bawled and cried when they didn't get their way, their parents either foolishly giving into their wants or administering physical punishment, by contrast, Gavin never behaved childishly. He began to imagine he'd somehow been insulated from tantrums and histrionics, and thereby deemed himself to be abnormal, even offbeat for his age. Consulting his brother, Donnell told him, he'd been equally restrained in his germinal years and to put the apparent difference down to good parenting. Buoyed up by the explanation, Gavin concluded he'd been very lucky. Evidently, some parents didn't know what the hell they were doing. His obviously did.

Gavin had been best buddies with Colby Richmond, another Christleton minor living just around the corner from the

Andersons and coincidentally born on the same day as him, until the Richmonds moved up the River Dee coastline to Neston, just after Gavin turned seven. The only one of his contemporaries to show an interest in rock music, when Colby left, Gavin had no one his own age to talk to about the Rolling Stones, or any other diversion.

Sure enough, he kicked a ball about on Birch Heath Park with other juniors, went to birthday parties, and took part in school socials, but the opportunity to instigate conversations about modish music and other hip motifs eluded him, no one else awestruck by the Stones, any other band, or his bordering on obscure conversational topics.

Increasingly, he gravitated to Donnell and Lucas as playmates and sounding boards to bounce opinions off, not only about rock music, but the world he had begun to discover. Being in their presence inflated his familiarity with things not normally coming into the domain of a junior schoolboy. Their much more sophisticated teenager colloquial premises enlivened his absorption. Patently aware of the age gap between himself and his brother and cousin, Gavin made it his goal to function like a teenager, so as to seamlessly fit into their ranks.

Music discussions aroused him more than anything else. Attuning himself to the theme batted back and forth by Donnell and Lucas, he timed his entry into their debates, ensuring he had something electrifying, even unique to say.

"In terms of quirky, two-and-a-half minute singles, I can't see the Action and the Creation have anything more to tender than what the Who and the Kinks have come up with to date," Lucas argued in Donnell's bedroom, whilst the threesome listened to the Who's *Sell Out* album.

"All I'm saying," Donnell opposed, "is it took a while for those bands to find their feet. Both the Action and the Creation have released awfully good singles, so it bodes well for the hereafter." Shrugging his shoulders, he then conceded, "Okay, I admit neither has come up with an album yet,

but—" He grimaced.

"But what?"

"It's just, there is enough evidence from their singles to suggest when they do release an album, both bands will come up trumps."

"Pie in the sky, Cus. Both are covers bands."

"Can I add a perspective?" Gavin interjected.

"*Certainly*, junior cousin," Lucas reacted. "Enlighten us with your take."

"Well—" Slightly unsure of his ground, subconsciously he licked his lips. "The Stones started out as a covers band until they began writing their own stuff at Andrew Loog Oldham's insistence. Even the Beatles had some covers on their early albums."

"True," Lucas acknowledged. "So are you saying whoever manages the Action and the Creation, needs to do what Oldham did?"

"Yeah. Mick and Keith didn't realise they could write a song until they were made to."

Pouting at Donnell, Lucas approved, "Maybe Junior Cus has a valid argument?"

Typical of his inputs, Gavin established the more he poured over rock journals *New Musical Express* and *The Melody Maker*, plus the few books in Chester library dedicated to the rock music landscape, the more he digested the brand, enabling him to make educated comments when engaging with his seniors. Continuing in parallel with his school studies, little else deflected his energies.

* * *

Throughout the course of his junior school days, Gavin absorbed the Stones' output, his dedication not lost on Donnell and Lucas as the band bloomed from purist blues and rhythm & blues outfit into psychedelic rock, blues rock and country rock. Often, his parents viewed his predilection as both comical, and concerning, Gavin either singing the numbers whilst occupied in a household chore, or seemingly enthralled listening to the Stones music as he read *Treasure Island* or *Robinson Crusoe*.

"Do you recall saying, a child's shaping proxies point the way to their impending essays, or words to the same effect," Garfield asked Aleshia on one occasion when he heard Gavin singing along to *Down Home Girl.*

"I do. Are you reasoning it could have been prophetic?"

Blowing out, he retorted, "I figured Donnell had an overdeveloped proclivity for rock music, but it positively leaks out of Gavin. Every time I chance upon him, he is either listening to the infernal Rolling Stones or singing one of their songs."

Giggling at her husband's note, Aleshia contradicted, "It's not so bad. His school work is fine, and invariably he does his chores. Might just be a passing phase.

"Well, I calculate the passing phase has been in play for four years. Aren't children meant to be fickle, their interests rising with the dawn and waning at sunset?"

"You're right. So, what do you want to do about it?"

Pushing his bottom lip frontwards in an indeterminate manner, he ceded, "Since all is okay on the schooling and domestic fronts, nothing I suppose."

Though not totally relaxed about his brother raiding his disc hoard in his absence, Donnell allowed Gavin into the private recesses of his bedroom to access his Dansette and pile the autochanger with singles and albums. Independence came when Garfield and Aleshia bought Gavin his own Dansette for his eighth birthday, liberating him from dependence on his brother's goodwill. Now he needed more records to complement his meagre accumulation of Stones singles and albums. After a talk with Donnell, they mutually decided to buy diverse albums and singles, so as to avoid replication and maximise the Anderson boy's vinyl library, Gavin investing in all tomorrow's Stones releases, Donnell in everything else, including the Beatles, Cream and the Jimi Hendrix Experience.

Additionally, after much petitioning from Donnell, his father permitted him and Gavin to play their music on his hi-fi audio system in the lounge, comprising Technics belt-drive turntable, 50watt stereo Pioneer amplifier and twin Wharfedale Airedale loudspeakers, until then, exclusively reserved for Garfield's jazz and classical collection.

"Now," he began, eyeing his boys with a weighty aspect, the

day he granted access to his beloved stereo, "the rules for using my pride and joy are, one, no overdriving the speakers by whacking up the volume. Two, always leave the system in the pristine order in which you found it, and three, under no circumstances, not even genuine curiosity to hear what the grownups listen to, be tempted to play one of my LPs." Shimmying back, he produced an inflexible phiz. "The last one is a hanging offence."

"Got it, Dad," assured Donnell.

"Gavin," his father prodded.

"Oh, I'd agree to anything to use your stereo," he pledged, the glint in his eye making Garfield suspicious.

He need not have worried. During the period the boys used his stereo, no incidents of hanging were reported.

For the brothers Anderson, it equated to a chasm transition *ad modum* music fidelity compared to the mono dings and clanks transmitted by a Dansette, the lounge system providing superb stereo top-end frequency clarity accompanied with distinctive low-end frequency focus. Peals and reverberations remaining hidden or indistinguishable when emanating from a Dansette were made crystal clear, the listening pleasure heightened immeasurably.

* * *

Shock occurred for Gavin in June 1967, when a judge at West Sussex Quarter Sessions, respectively, sentenced Mick and Keith to three months in prison for possession of amphetamines, and one year for allowing cannabis to be smoked in Richard's West Wittering mansion. Consequently, Gavin wondered if his beloved Rolling Stones would ever enter the recording studio again?

In a show of strength for fellow psychedelic travellers, the Who released the Jagger-Richards penned masterworks *The Last Time* and *Under My Thumb* as a single in tribute to the Stones, their intention, to cut and release further Jagger-Richards tunes to keep the Stones music alive in the listening public's minds. Despite the Who's industry, much to Gavin's relief, after a few months, under appeal, the sentences against the errant duo were quashed.

Moreover, a tougher bolt to reconcile arrived for the Stones devotee when employees uncovered Brian Jones' motionless body at the bottom of his swimming pool at Cotchford Farm, 2nd July 1969. Indulging in a profusion of psychedelic drugs, unlike owners of cast iron constitutions Jagger and Richards, they markedly affected poor Brian. Often morose and shaky, his eyes glazed over, Jones' mercurial musical abilities largely deserted him. Though he had contributed to the Stones trailblazing *Beggars Banquet* album, his overtures to the follow up *Let It Bleed* recordings had been minimal. His mood swings and lack of subscription to the music concretely curtailed his continuing participation in the band, Jones fired when Mick Taylor assumed lead guitar duties for an up and coming American tour. Scheduled back in the spring, 5th July 1969 saw the Stones perform a gratis concert in Hyde Park, the band dedicating the event to Jones, Jagger reading sections from Shelley's *Adonais* as part of the tribute.

For Gavin, it represented the foremost time in his nascent life someone he admired had died. Profoundly affecting him, the watershed separated his foregoing years, filled with nothing but good times, from a dubious future. Though still formulating his take on life, he stomached death to be an integral part of the human life cycle. In Jones' case, it had come excessively early, Gavin knowing the multi-instrumentalist's dive into the shady world of California Sunshine and Mary Jane had above all been responsible for his unintended demise. A salutary recognition, it eternally stayed with him, acting as a limiter when life-threatening recreational substances were offered to him by third parties.

"Have you heard about Brian Jones?" Gavin asked Lucas when his cousin came over to the Anderson residence the evening of the announcement.

"Yeah, on the *Six O'clock News*." Fanning out his digits in a gesture of sorrow, he then sadly appended, "Might have been inescapable. Never the same again after Anita Pallenberg dumped him, it drove Brian into narcotics dependency. Albeit, it transpired fate relieved him of his pain."

"I didn't picture life could be so fragile."

Gaping at him affectionately, Lucas insisted, "You're far too adolescent to be making such serene statements. Have you cried yet?"

"No, but I'm expecting to."

"Don't bottle it up, Gavin. There's no shame in shedding a tear for someone you venerate."

"Have you cried?"

"Not yet. I'm still taking it in, but undoubtedly tears will come."

Later, when Jimi Hendrix and the Doors Jim Morrison also checked out prematurely, Gavin persisted under no delusions as to the root cause, Hendrix choking on his vomit whilst intoxicated with barbiturates, Morrison officially dying of heart failure brought on by the by-products of an astronomical intake of LSD over many years.

All three had departed aged twenty-seven, in relative terms, sixteen years from Gavin's age in his final year at Christleton Junior School. Realising twenty-seven hung not far away, he wondered if any of the demised super-luminaries could have envisaged the brevity of their lives when they were eleven? Researching the paradigm, he encountered edifying stories littered with artists, writers and musicians hooked on laudanum or some other hallucinogenic. Many barely got into their stride before the grim reaper came for them.

Revisiting the issue in his late teens, he posed, for those of an aesthetic persuasion to maximise talent, were pharmaceuticals an essential aid to achievement? If so, then lifespan could be very brief, and when not creating, the taker could be overtaken by inner demons and fears, terminating in all sorts of physical and mental ailments. Agonising over the dilemma, he identified some with an artistic bent were doomed from birth, their minds and bodies incapable of digesting stimulants without grave consequences.

Extra tragedy occurred in the rock world at the Altamont Speedway Free Festival, labelling the ending counterculture event of the decade, the headlining Rolling Stones attracting over 300,000 people, and the event billed as Woodstock West. Thirty miles due east of San Francisco, festival goers had been gathering for days before the event, the local Hell's Angels chapter hired as security by the Stones tour management to keep them away from a makeshift stage and generators.

When Jefferson Airplane played in the early afternoon, violence broke out between dazed-up-to-the-eyeballs hippies and Hell's Angels drunk on beer, scores of people badly injured and hospitalised. Dwindling in the middle of the Flying Burrito Brothers set, it simmered in the backdrop before the headliners were due to come on.

As the Stones sprang into their set under a brooding, Californian night sky, the turmoil intensified, the band's roster interrupted repeatedly by Hell's Angels pushing people off the rostrum and bashing hippie heads with baseball bats. Amidst a stirring rendition of *Sympathy for the Devil*, a fight erupted at the foot of the platform, prompting the band to pause the superlative chorale while the Angels restored order. Relative calm prevailed until the unleashing of *Under My Thumb*, when a bunch of Angels got into a protracted scuffle with one attendee. Allegedly wielding a gun, a Hell's Angel retaliated, stabbing the spectator to death. Oblivious to the crime, the Stones completed their set, only finding out about the mayhem crowning a killing after decamping from Altamont by helicopter.

When news of the cataclysm seeped across the pond, Gavin sealed overnight the goodwill and tolerance typifying the mid-sixties had been replaced by harsh tribalism and extremism, the catastrophe putting a huge dent in love generation perceptions. Rating his incipient years distinguished by concord and affinity might have been an unusual snapshot in time, he determined violence and discord were the bylaws. An unsavoury conclusion, it left him with no illusions as to the primeval nature of mankind.

Discussing the misfortune with brother Donnell, he submitted, "Life isn't all good times and having fun, is it?"

"No, I'm afraid not." Hitting Gavin with a concerned stamp, he persuaded, "Listen, I've had a bit more practice of how unforgiving the world can be, and you've got it all to come. You're going to have to get used to absorbing the rough with the smooth.

As far as I've been able to resolve, the trick is to put adversity into context, and move on confident lessons have been learnt."

"But doesn't history keep on repeating itself, and nothing is ever learnt? For example, when evaluated with impartiality, all wars are futile with minor or no net gain, but still they rage."

"Gavin—" Simpering, he plopped a comforting hand on his sibling's shoulder. "Sometimes for one so young, you're overly highbrow. I might be wrong, but because power resides with governments, not much can be done to affect global goings-on by the individual. Sometimes you have to accept the inevitability of wrong-doing and more essentially, there is no profit in agonising about it."

"You're saying, after taking in a bad event, just log it as happenstance and move on."

"Yes…or you'll propel yourself into craziness with grief."

* * *

Calamity nearly befell Gavin during a Christleton Junior School trip to Snowdonia. Led by a couple of teachers, thirty-plus ten-year olds trekked through the national park, staying at youth hostels and eating on the hoof, with the objective of valuing the beautiful mountainous region of North Wales, and overcoming personal challenges, mainly the will to go on along the often-torturous route. Game for anything, the juniors mastered walking at least eight miles a day in boots, whilst carrying backpacks, and negotiating the foothills adjacent to Betws-y-Coed and Llanberis without running out of steam.

Feeling like seasoned intrepid adventurers, when a rainy day came to ascend Mount Snowdon, shrouded in mist and billowing clouds, the prospect drew no concern. Approaching the upper reaches along the prescribed footpath, Snowdon's peak lingered wholly enveloped in swirling mist and low-lying cloud. Though cold and wet, the expedition soldiered on without complaint to the teachers. Then, out of the blue, the pathway gave way under a torrent of rainwater rushing over the mountain. Gavin and two other juniors lost their footing and slipped off the passageway for about ten feet, before stopping precariously just short of a 200ft precipice. Scrambling to the rescue, the teachers hauled the threesome up, and the party continued to the summit, welcome hot food and drinks gorged by the hikers in a cafe. Knowing the juniors were exhausted by the climb, and wary of fresh pathway slippage under the rainy conditions, the teachers decided not to take any gambles and journey down the mountain on the Snowdon Mountain Railway to Llanberis.

Being untutored in the sort of risk to life and limb, and still hovering on adrenalin rush, none of the juniors cogitated too much about the corridor being washed away. Typical of the times, the potential gravity of the incident never became recounted to parents by either pupils or the school. Only in later life did Gavin comprehend he had come close to death.

Back at the Anderson residence, Aleshia registered his energised and pumped up guise. "So, how did it go?" she casually inquired.

"*Definitely* the best thing I've ever done," Gavin replied. "Very exciting. Made me appreciate Snowdonia is a wonderful place."

"No problems then? No unforeseen incidents?"

"No," he defended in all innocence. "Nothing we couldn't deal with."

* * *

In parallel with his obsession for what history proved to be the world's greatest rock 'n' roll band, Gavin cultivated a keen penchant for cars, pestering his father to let him drive his latest firm car, a Ford Lotus Cortina Mk2 on the Anderson's driveway. Brother Donnell had already gained the privilege, but Gavin had to wait until his twelfth birthday to take the wheel of a car, his parents deeming him to be big enough to handle the controls and touch the pedals. By then the Lotus Cortina had made way for a sleek Triumph Stag, Gavin studiously parading hither and thither along the entryway in the convertible coupe whilst listening to songs from the Stones *Exile on Main Street* album on the car radio.

Manifest from a visit to Oulton Park, when the entire

Anderson family went to see a British Saloon Car Championship event, Gavin streamed into enrapture at the sights of and sounds made by Ford Escort Twin Cams, Austin Mini Cooper S's, Porsche 911s and exotic Chevrolet Camaros. Even better, the event incorporated an exhibition of vintage and veteran cars.

"Cor, take a gander at those beauties," Gavin eagerly voiced when his vision fell on a 1938 Lagonda v12 Drophead Coupe and a 1952 Jowett Jupiter.

"Yes," Garfield agreed, "cars most of us can only dream about."

"Boy," he drooled, "what I'd give for them."

"Well, ambitious son, strive for educational attainment, then labour every hour the good Lord sends, and one day a classic car might be yours."

Following the excursion, like for the Rolling Stones, Gavin devoured vintage car magazines and books in Chester library, amazed by the array of jaw-dropping chassis designs and powerful engine variants.

After Garfield had acquired the Stag, Gavin's aspirations for his subsequent car centred on an Aston Martin V8 or a Jensen Interceptor, his father telling him such top-of-the-range grand tourers were beyond both the bounds of the Knockton & Garwell car policy, and his personal bank account.

* * *

1971 brought Gavin's introductory supreme life test when he revised for the eleven-plus examination to the background cacophony of the latest Rolling Stones album *Sticky Fingers* circulating in his head. Fortunately, Keith and the boys did not deflect his concentration too much, Gavin passing the trial and the ensuing September, attending his inaugural day at the King's School Chester, brother Donnell already a member and in the upper-sixth form, Lucas graduating the prior summer with sufficient A-Level grades to take him to UMIST to read mechanical engineering.

One new face he noticed at the King's School initiation resembled a leftover from the beat generation, his longish hair, loose tie, and body language betraying his obvious aversion to authority, making him an instant icon of defiance.

Magnetised by the aura he threw off, at lunchtime Gavin made his acquaintance.

"Hi, I'm Gavin Anderson."

"Hello, Gavin Anderson." Smirking, the boy held out his hand, Gavin grasping it. "Marlon Yardley."

"Were you named after Brando?

"Kinda. My parents are involved in the film industry, and they like the rebel flicks coming out of Hollywood in the early fifties."

"How so?"

"My father began his career at Ealing Studios as a production assistant, then film editor, before being head-hunted by Granada Television to produce TV dramas and documentaries. It's where he met my mother. She's an art director."

"Wow, impressive," Gavin complimented, his eyes widening in veneration. "So er, what's your take on Kings?"

Quivering his brow, Marlon indignantly fixed, "Difficult to say after half a day. I had the choice of either Kings, or one of the grammar schools on the Wirral. I plumped for Kings because it's the nearest to where we live in Tarvin Sands. How about you?"

"My brother is in the upper sixth. He's pretty happy at Kings, so I took his word as gospel."

"What do you do outside of school?"

"Listen to rock music, mainly the Rolling Stones."

"You don't say!" Marlon blurted, surprise bursting into his inflection. "I'd pigeonholed you more for mainstream pop. So—" He grinned devilishly. "You're not a replica of the conforming sheep trying to ingratiate themselves with the masters this morning?"

"Well, my tastes tend to be left field."

"*Left field*," he babbled. "Where did you pick up such a far-out term?"

"Off my cousin Lucas. He's at UMIST. When I got into the Stones, and some other unusual pursuits for a junior schoolboy, he said I had left-field tendencies."

"I see." Studying Gavin like a compiler about to buy a rare

artefact, he drawled, "You just might be the person I'm seeking as a fellow thrill-seeker, Gavin Anderson. What are you doing this evening?"

Fortuitously, their preparatory meeting led to an in-depth, life-long friendship, Gavin soon unearthing Marlon lived up to the maverick image he portrayed, querying the masters' views on a plethora of vanilla, academic arguments, and taking delight in getting away with as much non-conformity as the Kings rule book authorised. Likening him to the Malcolm McDowell portrayed iconoclast character Michael Travis, in Lindsay Anderson's anti-establishment film *If*, Marlon grew into a colourful and hypnotic symbol of rebellion.

Gavin had seen *If* at the Chester Gaumont with Donnell and Lucas. Rigidly sticking in his memory, the film's gritty portrayal of life in a public school culminated with Travis and his coterie of disenfranchised disciples machine-gunning dignitaries, school staff and pupils alike from the school roof in the terminal inflammatory scene. A poster board hero for juveniles, akin to the Rolling Stones Travis delineated as a thorn in the side of officialdom, glorifying in mocking and destroying their cosy, insular worlds, and replacing them with facile anarchy.

In the latter phases of junior school, Gavin had also developed dissident tendencies, often at odds with approved convictions and required modus. Though conscientious about the basic three-r's; writing, reading and arithmetic, when he challenged the benefits to the pupil of religious studies, form teacher Missus Hagen severely chastised him, saying, it wasn't his place to question the school curriculum.

She also accused him of slovenly presentation, when one morning he turned up with mud splashes on his shoes consequent from walking in a sodden field on his trek to school. Slow to rub off the mud, he had been dispatched to Headmaster Mister Poynton for subsidiary reproach. Sensing diminutive contrition in his posture, Poynton sent a letter to Aleshia Anderson, stating notwithstanding her son's scholarly prowess, his general attitude to say-so had much to be desired.

Returning home from school a few days later, Aleshia

confronted him. "What's all this about your behaviour at school?" she demanded to know.

Not envisioning such a forthright inquiry, he emitted, "Pardon?"

"I've received a letter from Mister Poynton, identifying your deficiencies when it comes to behavioural criteria."

"Ohh." Rolling his eyes, he queried, "Is this because I had mud smears on my shoes?"

"It goes far deeper, Gavin." She took a quick breath, letting it out gradually whilst mentally composing her consummating address. "You're a bright boy, and your father and I are very pleased with your school reports, but you have to acknowledge your nonconformist propensity towards certain things is a negative affecting your school standing." Propping the castigation, she waggled an outstretched finger. "You're going to have to learn, to get on in this world, educational accomplishments are not enough. You'll have to bend to whatever regime you are under. Your father and I have never had to reprimand you for bad manners, so why this indiscipline at school?" Suddenly halting, another factor struck her. "I hope this rebelliousness is not coming from your addiction to the Rolling Stones."

"Mother, huh—" Shaking his head disdainfully, he then pleaded, "The Stones have influenced me, but I'm hardly in a position to copy their rebellious lifestyle, am I? I just quizzed the value of religious studies to pupils, and accidentally got my shoes muddy. They're not expulsion offences, are they?"

"No, but sometimes you are too clever for your own good. As I say, learn to bend. The time for free expression is outside of school."

"But school is meant to encourage free expression, isn't it?"

"It is, but within the confines of settled pupil bearing. You see —" Effecting an intransigent air she emphatically told him, "When you go to Kings, you'll find a lot more opportunity for individualism without incurring the wrath of the school authorities...that is, if you pass your Eleven-Plus. If you don't, then it's Rowton Secondary Mod, and you'll find even less scope for an independent propensity there, than you currently have at Christleton Junior School."

Taking note of his mother's salutary words, he decided not to make any more waves.

* * *

Buckling down to his first term studies at Kings, he found despite superhuman effort to understand Latin, it continued to be problematical, whereas mathematics came easy to him, his logical cognitive processes enabling him to master geometry, trigonometry and algebra. Much of the remainder of the curriculum absorbed his consideration, primarily the sciences, plus English and history. Others, such as art, drama, and needless to say, music were met with inquisitiveness and enthrallment.

His mother had been right regarding Kings as an institution fostering frankness and candid veracity, Gavin near to jubilant on finding sanctioned concepts and opinions could be tested without rebuke, principally in his creative English, arts and drama classes. Some of his fellow pupils, including Marlon Yardley were of the same leaning, revelling in the open-ended exchange of ideas and alternate viewpoints bubbling up from class debate on most subjects. Whereas he discerned junior school to be a necessary labour, empowering him to matriculate to a grammar, Gavin looked forward to classes every day at Kings.

Though an unlikely setting for anything deemed outrageous or disgraceful by the school's authorities, albeit no fault of his own, Gavin got involved in a lab experiment going out of control. Occurring during a chemistry class in the autumn term, it proved to be an anodyne happening, not to be duplicated.

Broken into four-pupil sized groups, they were tasked to investigate and log the endothermic and exothermic reactions between ethanoic acid and sodium carbonate. Two of the pupils within Gavin's group decided to have some fun for the exothermic experiment by oversaturating a conical flask of ethanoic acid with sodium carbonate crystals, while Gavin and the other pupil tabulated results from the endothermic experiment. Inducing an extremely volatile exothermic codicil, the solution bubbled up under conical flask confinement, *ex post facto* harvesting enough thermodynamic energy to erupt like a volcano, drenching the lab ceiling and splattering several pupils with the chemical mix. Alarmed by the prank, chemistry master Mister Argyle, a Scotsman with a shrill voice and no latitude for misbehaving pupils, or an inclination to uncover the culprit behind the mischief, dispatched all four group members to headmaster Mister Dennison for a tongue lashing and possible corporal punishment.

A man of uppermost familiarity with wayward schoolboys, Dennison knew only one or perhaps two of the four were responsible for incurring Mister Argyle's displeasure but did not intend to grill the nominees to ascertain cogent truth. Wisdom told him applying the same provisions to all the selectees, deterred the guilty from thereafter misdemeanours, and those innocents unjustly punished saw to it they did not embroil themselves in shenanigans via association again.

Admonishing them in turn, when it came to Gavin, he bayed, "Well, Anderson junior, if you are going to tread in the same illustrious footsteps as your elder brother, you will need to evade all the traps baited and set by some of your less virtuous brethren."

Dispassionately, he then proceeded to administer three whacks to the left palm of each antagonist with his trusty cane, sending them back to the chemistry lab with florid mugs, glowing ulnar nerves, and a compulsion not to reoffend.

Come the mid-afternoon break, Marlon interrogated him on his date with Dennison's corrective treatment.

"Did it hurt?"

"Surely you must know. With your surly tendency to governance, you must have had some close encounters with the cane."

Sneering at the thought, he divulged almost proudly, "Yeah, at Tarvin Junior School. I just want to know how it felt for you."

"My pride is more injured than my swollen mount of Venus."

"Oh!" Grinning at his pal's obvious indignation, he jabbered, "So you plan to dodge forthcoming disciplinary measures?"

"Absolutely. How about you, or are you predestined for, let's call it, a painful consultation with Dennison?"

"Yes, it's only a matter of time for me. I've resigned myself to incurring the wrath of at least one of the masters, once too often, and as a consequence being dispatched to the headmaster's study."

"Ouch, a bit fatalistic, isn't it?"

"More like realistic. You're right about my peevish predisposition to authority. Until it burns itself out, I anticipate meeting with the cane on a somewhat regular basis."

"You're predicting the rendezvous like it's a kind of badge of honour."

"In a way, you're right. It's the merited upshot from knowing I've challenged the mighty beyond argument, and physical correction is their only retort."

"You mean, they've failed if they have to send you to Dennison?"

"Affirmative." Swaggering into an intemperate idiom, he glorified, "Awfully masochistic on my behalf, don't you agree?"

"Yes, very profound, but you worry me, Yardley."

"How?"

Befuddled, he boiled up a vexed expression. "God knows what trouble you're going to get me into."

"Ah well, for someone like you, who likes reconnoitring the periphery of the comprehendible, unquestionably, if you can see if yourself becoming embroiled, it will be owing to my powers of fatal enticement?"

Flabbergasted by the reckless admission, he remained tight-lipped.

Tempted to fettle the actual exothermic calamity culprits, Gavin held his anger, shrewd to the incontrovertible outcome, if caught in the act, fisticuffs in the school yard led to a renewed appointment with Mister Dennison's trusty cane, and in so doing, him earning a reputation as a troublemaker. Instead, he made it flawless to the guilty parties, if they ever got him into bother again, he'd seek revenge on the rugby field, unintentionally on purpose dealing out severe tackles, rendering them cripples.

* * *

Paradise on Earth arrived for Gavin when Donnell took him and Marlon to a Rolling Stones concert at Kings' Hall, Manchester, the pair needing special dispensation from their parents because of school the next day. Agitated beyond certitude, when the band emerged to thunderous ovation and launched into *Brown Sugar*, Gavin imagined all his successive birthdays had come at once. Entranced throughout the holistic set, comprising *Gimme Shelter*, *Honky Tonk Women*, and a large selection from the band's current album *Goat's Head Soup*, he wanted the pageant to go on indefinitely, the Stones live act meeting all his wishes. Though with Donnell, he had seen Free at Chester College, Fleetwood Mac at Quaintways, and Derek & The Dominos at Manchester Free Trade Hall, all paled in comparison to the Stones astonishing display and seductive connection with concertgoers.

Whilst homeward bound in Donnell's car Gavin twisted to face Marlon, purring, "I assessed Paul Kossoff, Peter Green and Eric Clapton were all par excellence guitarists, when Donnell and I saw their bands, but the guitar interplay between Keith Richards and Mick Taylor topped their quality."

"You've seen Eric Clapton?" Marlon gushed, unmistakably dazzled.

"Yeah, when he fronted Derek & The Dominos."

"*Jesus*, Anderson, you keep on impressing me with the unforeseeable. I'm meant to be the cool hipster, but I'm damned if I can claim seeing a guitar mega-god on my meagre concert-going roster."

"Ha, ha, purely arising from having a benevolent older brother."

"Quite right, Junior," Donnell interjected. "And don't you forget it."

"I won't, but the day will come when I can reciprocate," Gavin assured.

Grinning, Donnell avowed, "I'll hold you to it."

"What's the best gig you've been to, Donnell?" Marlon enquired.

"Probably, Led Zeppelin at the University of Manchester, but the most portentous gig endures as the Beatles at the Liverpool Empire, just before Christmas 1965. Our Uncle Jeremy took Cousin Lucas and me. You see, with hindsight, the Beatles weren't musicians, they were magicians. *Sergeant Peppers* is tops, but *The White Album* is not far behind, and all of their other releases are momentous in one way or another."

"Can't disagree with you there," Marlon guaranteed. "But indisputably the Stones run an immediate second?"

"Yep, and Junior might argue since the Fabs split, Mick & Co have appropriated leadership duties."

"Too right," Gavin vociferously supported, before the threesome burst into laughter at his customary uncompromising salute to the Stones.

Years went by before Gavin appreciated not all younger siblings were permitted to join in with their older brothers and cousins' activities, teenagers seen in the company of junior schoolboys, a source of potential ridicule from their peers. If not for his grownup demeanour and the way he conducted himself, he might have been kept at bay by Donnell and Lucas.

Amassing such a foundation bestowed him with the facility to communicate with people older than himself. Twigging adaptability to be one of his strengths, he tried to put himself in their shoes, the situational alignment bonding good congress, Gavin invariably welcomed into their circles as an equal. Being tall for his age, the physical attribute helped his induction into older boys and grownup schemes during both his junior and senior schooldays. As he had done with Donnell, from a very early age, Garfield had imprinted upon him, convincing communication and interpersonal skills were the key to accomplishing fruitful relationships at all junctures in the life cycle, a smile and an outgoing and approachable constitution central to the goal. Taking notice of the advice, both his sons adjudged it to be a beneficial boon over their lifespans.

More laid back than the often-temperamental Marlon Yardley, Gavin rarely lapsed into bad temper or raised his voice, his early years spent trying to be received into the teenager fold of Donnell and Lucas imbuing him with the sagacity of calm calculation. Observing some of his contemporaries melt into trembling wrecks when accosted by an ordeal or going utterly Tonto in answer to their leg being pulled, he contented himself knowing when the same trials impinged upon him, he dealt with them in a reasoned fashion. Residing serene under trying circumstances served him well in later life.

* * *

His growing camaraderie with Marlon orchestrated some interesting and ultimately electrifying debates. Additional to discussing all kinds of music, motorbikes and cars, they also covered teenage sexual desires, often segueing into risqué territory.

Amidst their third year at Kings, their involvement with girls got underway, mainly those from Queen's Park High and Upton-by-Chester High. Capping in invitations to girl's birthday parties and other social events, behind closed doors Gavin and Marlon indulged in kissing and light body searches with the girls they fancied. Often, complementary arousing caresses from the girls got the better of them, contributing to over-excited libidos and the need to employ restraint and prolonged cold showers.

A constant companion, frustration plagued them. Both wanted the delight of broader whoopee, but neither relished the prospect of the girl denying their hungers with a brush-off, eventuating in blushes and red cheeks.

Breaking from school studies, after Marlon declared ambitions to forfeit his virgin status had come to a head, Gavin cross-examined, "So, are you saying, you'd go with a girl, just to lose your cherry."

"I guess I am. It's a barrier I have to confront, just to see what all the fuss is about." Manufacturing a skeptical puss, he warbled, "Don't tell me you haven't contemplated the same thing."

"No, I can't deny it's fallen within my rumination palette." Squinting, Gavin admitted, "But I can't see myself targeting a girl for such a design alone. We both know girls who obviously put it about, girls of easy virtue as my brother calls them, but—" He juddered his head dismissively. "I couldn't be so hard hearted about it."

"Rubbish, Anderson. If the girl is doing some unbelievable things to your pecker, and she gives you the green light, you'll do it."

"Maybe."

"*Maybe!*" he bellowed furrowing his brow to abet the rebuke. "It's doubtless. If Justine Foland wanted to sightsee your hidden parts and test out their performance, you couldn't resist."

"Well, you've selected Little Miss Perfect, the girl every boy wants on his arm. Rebuffing her charms could be a contest doomed to pleasurable failure."

Consolidating his text, Marlon pressed, "It doesn't have to be a top-of-the-range model. I'd bet if Stacey Noble did the same thing, you couldn't stop yourself from doing the business with her."

Laughing at the sentiment, Gavin then quashed the assertion. "I don't think so. She has all the peculiarities of a dweeb, a dork, better still, a munchkin straight out of Tolkien's Middle-earth, not that I've ever read his fairy-tale dribble."

"You're being inordinately fussy, Anderson," Marlon criticised before nonchalantly adding, "categorically, I'd go with any girl giving me the come-on."

Gyrating his head from side to side at the unbridled declaration, Gavin joked, "You'd fancy Destiny Angel from *Captain Scarlett & the Mysterons*, and she's just a puppet."

"Yes, but a very striking puppet," he stipulated, joining in with the gibe, "especially with her sexy French voice."

"Well, I can't argue with your comprehension." Upping the ante, Gavin catechised, "How about a girl made up to appear like Destiny Angel, and dressed in the same sprayed on, figure-hugging garb and kinky boots?"

"You mean a double, a doppelganger?"

"Yeah."

Meditating on the proposal for all of a second, he then beamed lecherously. "Sounds good."

"I'm joking, Yardley. This conversation has become

disingenuous, if that's the right word. To even consider such a proposition, I'd have to be stoned."

"*What*!" Recoiling, Marlon blasted, "You're not taking drugs, are you?"

"Of course not." Issuing his chum a speculative probe, he investigated, "Are you?"

Subconsciously jerking his napper rearwards, he prattled, "Why do you ask?"

"Last Saturday night at the Chloe Merrick bash, you were even more gregarious than you normally are, and you were very flushed."

"Oh—" His jaw dropped like he had been caught *in flagrante delicto*. "You spotted my cascade into feverish malaise?"

"What had you taken? Mary Jane?"

"No—" He sniggered. "Some low-grade amphetamine."

"Where did you get it?"

Cautiously scanning about, he inspected for school masters. "From some dude browsing the vinyl in Revolution Records on Foregate Street," he faintly proclaimed. "I just wanted know-how of the psychic voyage."

Recreational pills experimentation apart, when not at school or socialising with Gavin, Marlon hung out on the rim of Chester's teenage, wild child set, his shifty interludes into their midst disturbing Gavin. Though eminently intelligent and not a practitioner of self-delusion, Marlon's exploratory spirit drove him to try out the frontiers of acceptable society regulations and yearnings. Overarching his Kings tenure, Gavin grappled with similarly compulsive journeymen at parties and other communal events, mavens of metaphysical homage roaming in the vales of abstract concepts in the thrust for self-discovery and fulfillment, even individualism and singularity.

Fascinated by their charts and acts, howbeit quixotic and even classically poetic, Gavin refrained from joining their transcendental order. What had happened to Brian Jones, Jimi Hendrix and Jim Morrison when they tumbled headlong into the esoteric pit, still fresh in his memory. Though an amiably romantic notion, and one having its own rewards, be them somewhat transitory if tragedy occurred, he abided predisposed to retain control of his faculties in the belief superior rapture could be reached using methods and practices not dulling the mettle or frying the brain.

* * *

When Mick Taylor quit the Rolling Stones only weeks after the band's *It's Only Rock 'n Roll* album release, Marlon took bets on who'd replace the gilt-edged guitarist. It transpired multiple candidates had been tested out by the band, specifically, Mick Ronson, Bowie's foil on *Ziggy Stardust*, blues-rock virtuoso Rory Gallagher, and ex-Humble Pie joint front man alongside Steve Marriott and long-term Stones amigo, Peter Frampton. In the wake of the candidature alternates coming to light, a buzz pervaded Rolling Stones fan groups countrywide, arguing about the eventual winner.

Gavin hoped against hope that Jeff Beck prevailed, arguably, the best lead guitarist on the planet and a dead ringer for Richards. Nevertheless, the Faces Ronnie Wood hooked the vacant post, initially confounding him and making Marlon a packet on bets placed on the primary contenders. Dissecting the news and founded on Taylor's occasional glorious but undervalued showboating incurring Jagger's and Richard's disapproval, Gavin concluded another topflight player upstaging Glimmer Twins Jagger and Richards would not be repeated. A good guitarist, but explicitly not in the same rank as Gallagher and Beck, Wood represented a safe choice. With his Richard's hairstyle and happy-go-lucky sensibilities, he seamlessly fitted into the Stones without causing irritation, ending up as a permanent feature.

With longing forever enveloping their visual arts taste buds, Gavin and Marlon got to see the Stones again at New Bingley Hall Stafford, the trip needing extraordinary cajoling of their parents because the gig fell in the O-Level examinations timeframe. With no tests falling in the ensuing two days after the Monday gig date, permission was grudgingly granted. Both lads had been revising like crazy since Easter, and their January mocks had affected grade A's and B's in every studied subject. With the success in mind, they sold their parents on the basis the same grades were achievable in the formal trials.

Changing trains at Crewe travelling from Chester to Stafford, they joined some girls in a typically dirty and foul air smelling British Rail carriage compartment.

"Going to see the Stones at Stafford, are you?" asked one girl, a bubbly brunette with an infectious smile.

"Yeah," Gavin voiced. "Is it so obvious?"

"We heard you and your oppo talking about the gig on the platform."

Making introductions, it came to light that bubbly brunette with huge come to bed eyes and a tantalising shape Tina, and her similarly endowed sidekick Lorraine, were from Crewe, and also roving to New Bingley Hall. Sensing a liaison in the offing, the boys got cosy with their fellow travellers, the foursome arranging to meet up again at Stafford rail station after the gig, the comeback ride bequeathing interminable chat and protracted kissing, Gavin pairing off with Tina and Marlon with Lorraine, finalising in a summer of get-togethers in Crewe and Chester.

As the relationships germinated, Gavin and Tina got very intimate, Tina proving to be a very sexually provocative girl. One Saturday, she enticed him to her house in Crewe, her parents out for the day at Chester races. Dressed to thrill, she made it plain he could go all the way with her. Proving to be his precursory full-on sexual experience, he left Crewe with a huge smile and a feeling a separation intersection had been breached, total metamorphosis from fumbling schoolboy to burgeoning paramour realised.

* * *

In the course of Gavin's A-Level study years, when he blissed out to New Wave-pioneers Television and Talking Heads, as well as revisiting the Stones early oeuvre, Richards added to his bust infamy when arrested by Canadian Mounties in Toronto, eventually being charged with possession of cocaine and heroin with intent to traffic. Although released on bail, due to the trafficking charge, if convicted, he'd serve a seven-year jail sentence.

Conjuring up the worst, Gavin foresaw the suspension of the Rolling Stones transcription and concert profession, if not the end of the band without its Kapellmeister. Fortunately, a blind woman and diehard Stones fan privately appealed to the trial judge, saying Richards always helped her when the band toured Canada, making certain she remained safe and cared for after the shows, Richards eventually let off and sentenced to do a complimentary concert for the blind, Gavin breathing a sigh of relief when the news condensed into his consciousness. Prior to the prolonged period of vagueness, Gavin had procured Nils Lofgren's debut solo album containing the track *Keith Don't Go*, the lyric *Keith don't go, don't take my fun* becoming a plea from Gavin to Richards to stay out of jail.

"Thank god," he blustered to Marlon Yardley shortly after Richard's acquittal. "For a while I reckoned Keith had crossed one too many dangerous bridges."

"Yep, the authorities worldwide have had it in for him since the Stones hit notoriety in sixty-five. Just illustrates you can't tweak the Establishment's tail without a ton of the nasty stuff descending from above."

"Yeah, city hall can't be beat, can it?"

"Absolutely not, the dice is loaded against unorthodox bohemians, because they pose a threat to the status quo."

"*Cripes!*" He glittered. "You've just distinguished yourself in such an all-encompassing description."

"Huh, don't I know it." Wincing at the suggestion, he verbalised, "If you are going to be a thorn in the side of officialdom, the trick is to thwart their grasp by becoming so rich, you are immune from their restrictive measures."

"You have intentions to become rich?"

"It's either affluence and wealth, or I will lose my tongue from biting it so much in contempt of conforming to societal yardsticks."

Chuckling at the remark, Gavin expressed, "I guess your monochromatic perspective constitutes the difference between us.

You are an all-out dissenter, whereas, despite my free-thinking, I merely chip away at the edges of irregularity, receding back into a safe zone when the temperature gets too hot."

"Don't denigrate yourself too much, Anderson. Incontestably, I'll not be able to sustain my adopted insubordinate persona post the educational system."

"Why?"

"As I say, the ardent schismatic needs to be rich to avert societies restricting tentacles. To become rich, you need a flair paying a lot of money. Unlike Richards and co, I do not command any god-given talents. With such an inhibitor in mind, to attain even a modicum of life's judicious anticipations; good career, wife, children, I know I will need to curb and suppress my transgressor tendencies."

Staring at him with vacant gills, Gavin ascribed, "Behind your adamantine facade, you're very much the pragmatist. I suppose it's what impels me to back off when I get too near to the vaporising flame."

After the relative disappointment of the *Goat's Head Soup*, *It's Only Rock n' Roll* and *Black and Blue* albums, the Stones remastered the airwaves with *Some Girls*, Gavin cocker hoop about their resumption to searing form. Whether due to relief the band could continue after Richard's Canadian narcotics bust, or in retaliation to a new strain of zest-laden invention punkmeisters, the Clash, calling the band, 'dinosaurs', *Some Girls* echoed the wondrous format and breath-taking sonic climbs and descents on *Sticky Fingers*.

Inconsistent and questing for the right hook to hang its hat on, released two years previously, *Black and Blue* rendered a hotchpotch of jazz-tinged, funk and reggae rock, leaving Gavin deducing hiring Wood had been a mistake. However, auxiliary investigation revealed session players Harvey Mandel and Wayne Perkins, both imbued with top-notch blues pedigrees, played most of the guitar parts alongside Richards in an obligatory mambo pattern, the Glimmer Twins determining the soundscape of the album's make-up, Wood extricated from the tribunal of recriminations.

In complete contrast, honed whilst with the Faces, *Some Girls* showcased Wood's rhythm & blues and rock n' roll credentials, his dual rhythm and lead guitar sorties with Richards energising the album with purity of purpose and surety of affect. Better still, reminiscent of the band's Chuck Berry inspired undertakings on their formative albums, much of the substance rang with the same charged-up exhilaration characterising the band's ability to seize the listener's absorption from the unlocking note, Bill and Charlie on top form relentlessly driving the songs with pumping basslines and syncopated percussion, and Jagger out-snarling John Lydon on the punchiest of the tracks. His hankering satisfied, his faith restored, it all left Gavin in seventh heaven, the Stones still the genuine article, nothing punk dispensed decidedly challenging their top dog status.

Effervescing on the band's return to outstanding fine fettle to anyone granting him airtime, he fine-detailed his satisfaction *ad nauseam*, the recipient of his outpouring either beguiled by the edification or dying to get away fearing his chronicle going on *ad infinitum*. Even Marlon Yardley sprouted as reluctant to extend the welcome mat on the monologue for too long. Instead, he preferred to discuss the band's prodigious appetite for groupies in the 1960s.

"I heard Jagger and Richards each rogered 240, Brian Jones 330, and Bill Wyman a colossal 400 plus," Marlon recounted.

"Hogwash!" Gavin rolled his eyes scornfully. "Divide the summation by two, and you might have the reality. Anyway, what about Charlie Watts?"

"Apparently, Charlie has been monogamous since finding his true love back in the early sixties."

"Where did you get all this salacious info from?"

"Hah, you'll like this." Shouldering a masterful penchant, he revealed, "I eavesdropped on a conversation my father had with a guy he works with at Granada; Tony Wilson, presenter of *So It Goes*."

"*Ohh*, a tremendous entertainment. I distinctly remember the installments featuring Patti Smith, Van Morrison, Costello and John Cooper Clark."

"Yeah, but after Iggy Pop's expletive outburst, it's been axed."

"Shame. Anyway, I gather Tony to be the fountainhead of the info?"

"Yep."

Folding his arms, Gavin volunteered, "On reflection, I'd concede the Stones rumpy-pumpy count could well be true. Undeniably, the band had the means, the motives, and the opportunities, but I didn't dig Bill is such a shagmeister."

"Definitely, or that Charlie is so virtuous. Must have taken some willpower to say no to all the legions of groupies tendering it on a plate."

* * *

After a series of talks with his father and the Kings School career master, Gavin decided on a calling in process engineering, a branch of chemical engineering. Excelling in all the sciences, chemistry enthralled him more than physics or biology, the facet responsible for his vocation preference. After gaining eight GCE O Levels and three A-Levels, he left Christleton in his 1975 1.3 Ford Escort for the University of Edinburgh, to embark on a chemical engineering with business management degree.

Loaning him the money to purchase the car after completing his A-Levels, his parents replicated what they had also done for brother Donnell, Gavin frothing with joy the day he picked up the car from the Ford dealership in Chester. Though subsequent to his induction at Oulton Park he continued to drool over vintage sports cars, and 1970s supercars the Lamborghini Miura and the Chevrolet Corvette, pragmatism coupled with gratitude quickly made him fall in love with the treasured Escort.

By his late teens, Gavin had grown into a handsome rake with a roguish glint in his eye and an ulterior resolve in his stride, his attractiveness not lost on Chester's young fillies' brigade.

Though he had fooled around with girls in his mid-teens, experimenting with how far they allowed him to go in the sex stakes, whilst at Edinburgh he had his first serious relationship with Gail Needham, a stunning blonde from Ripon, studying philosophy and English literature. Both new undergraduates, in the autumn semester they met at a campus dance held in the student's union building, Gavin immediately taken by her jaunty bearing, and summoning up the courage to make an introduction. Responding favourably to his overtures, Gail suggested they left the dance for somewhere quieter, where they could get to know each other, Gavin taken aback by her boldness. After retrieving her checked-in clothing from the concierge desk, his astonishment grew when she tossed him a crash helmet, then led him across a car park to her Vincent Black Shadow motorbike.

"*Jesus*," he gibbered. "Ownership of a classic bike is the last thing I envisaged from a philosophy student."

"Oh, you know about classic bikes then?"

"I'm a car man, but some years ago, I did delve into motorcycle lore in parallel with my fascination for vintage sports cars." Casting an inquisitive eye over the Black Shadow, he blathered, "How on earth do you come to own this beauty? I mean, they're very rare, aren't they?"

"I inherited it from my grandfather. He bought it new in 1952, and fewer than 1,700 were hand-crafted."

Blowing out in esteem, the behaviour's celebrated inference not lost on Gail, he congratulated, "Very impactful." Blinking at her, he submitted, "So, beneath the academic veneer, you're a motorcycle chick?"

"Just let's say, there are many strings to my bow, philosophy and motorbikes are just two of them."

"Well, Gail Needham, where are you going to take me?"

Grinning, shrewd his expectation to be somewhat different, she itemised, "The castle, to take in the panoramic view over the city."

"Oh, *how* disappointing," he responded, hitting her with a mischievous smile. "I fancied you were going to take me back to your room at Pollock Halls."

"Ha, ha." Radiating disarmingly, she moved closer to him. "You're very presumptuous."

"Yes, it's one of my many failings."

She gazed into his eyes, as if probing for integrity. "Your

conjecture might arise," she teased. "Let's see if you survive the ride up to the castle."

Predictably, the happening tarried sex free for the nascent couple, but the relationship soon matured into full-blooded amour, Gavin spending some nights at Pollock Halls, Gail reciprocating at his shared Kincaid's Court flat. Come the Christmas recess, he trailed her down the A1 to Ripon, where she introduced him to her parents, before the couple carried on in the Escort to Christleton to meet Gavin's family. Staggered by their tangible partiality, both sets of parents endured fretful about their offspring's ability to stay focused on their studies.

They need not have worried. Both Gavin and Gail graduated with upper-second degrees. Waning by way of exposure to life's opportunities, their relationship came to an end on graduation, neither party wanting to conduct a long-distance *affaire d'amour*, Gavin going on to a career with petrochemicals giant Scale UK at the Ellesmere Port Oil Refinery, less than ten miles from Christleton, and Gail jetting off to London to join the DTi in the civil service fast stream.

During his time in Edinburgh, he cosseted in all the routine undergraduate pastimes and pranks, incorporating sinking yards of ale, and abseiling off Castle Hill into Princes Street Gardens by the side of Edinburgh Castle, only to be apprehended by castle security personnel, and told not to be so bloody stupid. More outrageous capers and larks followed, nothing too severe, necessitating an interview with the dean and being excommunicated. All part of finding the self in an unrestricted environment after the relative discipline of domestic and school life, his mischief tendencies burnt themselves out before commencement of the all-important final scholastic year.

Some aspects of his studies came harder to him than he had foreseen, fluid dynamics in year two and advanced thermodynamics in year three proving to be constant stumpers in the shape of applied mathematics derivatives needing supplementary diligence. Cementing his understanding of the two topics persisted as central to landing a good degree, his perseverance coupled with some in-depth endeavours with his tutor, seeing him conquer the tribulation. Conversely, his cognizance of general engineering mathematics presented no insurmountable problems, and his appreciation of the business management side of the degree course came to him naturally, his grade-A O-Level business studies attainment providing a solid springboard to branch out into every twist of management studies, without stretching the grey matter.

Constantly craving a music fix, in his second and final years, he revised for his examinations to the soundtrack of the Stones latest albums, *Emotional Rescue* and *Tattoo You* billowing out from his stereo system. Neither a *bona fide* heart stopper, let alone a game changer, he comforted himself the occasional track hit the same apex of excellence as perennial frontrunners *Stray Cat Blues*, *Love in Vain* and *Sister Morphine*.

Spring 1982 saw an announcement in the popular music press regarding the Stones pre-European tour warmup gig at the Edinburgh Playhouse. Trying for tickets for Gail and himself, his postal application failed to be among the lucky 3,000 winners from a pile of over 15,000 applications. Consoling himself the event clashed with his finals, he took the disappointment philosophically, deducing winter could proffer an opportunity to see the band. Little did he know a hiatus of seven years would pass before the Rolling Stones toured again.

Reviewing the no tickets anti-climax with Gail, he told her, "Luck and games of chance have never been benefactors to me. If I chose heads, invariably the flipped coin conspires to be tails, and on the rare occasion I've drawn what *prima facie* is a winning poker hand, some other blighter tops it."

"Are you saying good fortune and you are not devoted allies?"

"I am. I can't recall a single instance of triumph relying on fortuity."

"How do you account for it?" Cocking her head to one side and provocatively placing a finger to her cheekbone, she issued him a teasing air. "Born under a bad sign?"

"Could be. Apparently, when I materialised, a full harvest moon shone overhead."

"Such a celestial coincidence is adjudged to be a good omen for a newborn," she argued.

"Is it?"

"Well—" Sidling up to him, she gave him a peck on the cheek. "Your birthday is 26th September, right?"

"Yes."

"Spiritually speaking, falling well after the equinox, a harvest moon occurring in October is known as a Hunter Moon or a Blood Moon."

"Just remind me, when does the equinox occur?"

"The moment the Earth's equator passes the centre of the Sun's disc. It occurs twice a year, 23rd March and 23rd September. Some believe a harvest moon plummeting in October heralds a bad omen."

"So," he audited, "being born under a September harvest moon means a good omen?"

"Yes, but there are always exceptions. Plus, if you are an astrology advocate, which I'm not, there are other celestial factors discriminating which side of the good and bad luck divide you fall into."

"So, I could be irrevocably doomed."

"Only if you buy into the rhetoric, and for most, it accounts for the vast majority of taken-for-granted good and bad circumstances coming true."

"You mean—" Musing, he squinted. "If you think it, it will happen?"

"Yes."

"I need to assume a dogmatic vibe then?"

"It won't be fool proof but enacting an idealistic bent mellowed by what you perceive to be the odds," she prescribed, "should induce more success than disappointment."

"Gail Needham, I'll never pour scorn on philosophy students again."

She wrapped herself around his torso. "Yes, you will, but I'll forgive you."

A major hill to mount, calling for both invention and steady command, his final year project centred on chemical engineering design and implementation. Choosing a branch of polymer science and membrane separation processes, his goal hinged on identifying a low-cost process for the separation of hydrogen, oxygen and carbon compounds, by comparing the solution-diffusion and hydrodynamic model alternates. Like for many undergraduates, after defining his project blueprint with delivery milestones, his foray into the world of results-founded projects constrained by money and time factors, soon ran into technical snags necessitating extra finance and additional hours put in to conserve the project schedule. An epiphany moment, it taught Gavin about contingency management, particularly the need to add in a sum to address incidental costs when constructing a project budget.

* * *

Proving to be a good take-off pad for his occupation, Scale provided the immersion in process engineering he craved, his acquired knowledge of oil refining into a multitude of commodities bracketing the ensuing chapter of his progression; petro carbons search and mass production. After two mightily successful years at Ellesmere Port, Scale transferred him to North Sea oil and gas exploration, and thereafter onto Oman for the same purpose. Ellesmere Port had toughened him up to the rough and tumble of working with distillation crews, and the prevailing dirtiness of an oil and gas refining plant. Under harsh North Sea oil rig sea and weather conditions plus the blazing Gulf sun fruiting temperatures over 100deg Fahrenheit, the trials intensified, sensational pay compensating for minimal pleasures of the flesh.

Before heading out to Oman, he went for a drink with his brother at the Boathouse Chester, Donnell, returning from New York after a temporary assignment as a business fixer. Following university, Donnell had joined the investment banking sector, currently occupying the industrial mergers & acquisitions manager position for Bryant Zenon, an enterprise-scale investment house with European operations headquartered in London.

"So," Gavin tabled, "how did you find the Big Apple, big brother?"

"Fast and furious, real seat of the pants thrust. The pace never slackened. I'll be glad to revert to the relative tranquillity of London."

"And there's me cerebrating with your ever-increasing ambitions, you'd elect to stay at Bryant Zenon's New York HQ."

"No, Caroline and I will marry next year, and the prospect of living in New York holds no allure for her. She's joined at the hip to her Richmond veterinary practice, so, in a fit of rapport, I'll now be climbing the professional ladder in our London office." Stopping, Donnell smiled at Gavin. "Hah, here's me back into the fold for a few days, and you are off to get a suntan. Mum and Dad will have to get used to neither of us being permanently resident at Christleton."

"Yeah, though they don't say anything, with Knockton & Garwell consuming most of Dad's time, I know Mum will feel it more. She'll be rattling around the house reminiscing about our childhood and teenage years."

"Well, at least she's been getting used to it since we both left for university."

"True, but when I secured my job with Scale at Ellesmere Port, I sensed she thought I'd reversed to the nest. I also divine with me going to Oman, she detects it will be the start of my everlasting withdrawal from the family abode."

Resigned to the inevitable as an integral part of their chosen careers, the brothers agreed to visit their parents as much as possible and call them on a regular basis.

Still needing a daily fix of his beloved Rolling Stones, Gavin never went anywhere without a portable cassette player he had procured before quitting Ellesmere Port. Even in the austere accommodation of a North Sea oil platform or a desert prefab unit, he listened to albums transferred to tape back in Christleton, including 1983 release *Undercover*, and *Still Life*, a live album released a year beforehand.

Hard to take for Gavin, the incipient 1980s saw the emergence of puerile dance-pop and the new romantics slushy soft rock, Jagger keen to keep the Stones current with the trends. Howbeit, Richards lingered unyielding about continuing with their blues and hard rock roots. Consequently, *Undercover* never found focus, friction and tension between The Glimmer Twins flowering a farrago of oddly truncated ditties, torn between Euro-disco influences and post-new wave shred guitar, leaving the listener aggrieved in the expectation stakes, the confused mix of fads only convincing on *She Was Hot*.

Bad enough, the album's resonance appalled Gavin even more, it's new digital transcription technique originating an overly harsh reverberation, making Charlie's drums twang like tin cans, with Bill's bass diminutive and too far back in the mix. Nearly every album he bought in the 1980s suffered from the same lack of authentic musical instrument ring, until Steve Albini bucked the ridiculous trend with an improved reproduction method for analogue inscribing on the Pixies *Surfer Rosa* album, succeeded by Butch Vig's awesome sound rendering on *Nevermind*, Nirvana's landmark masterwork.

Precariously floating in a contradictory time warp, after listening to *Undercover*, the magnificence of *Beggar's Banquet*, *Let It Bleed* and *Sticky Fingers* felt like distant memories to Gavin. Balancing the criticism, he persuaded himself few recording artists maintained par throughout their careers, even Bob Dylan moulding the occasional turkey. Unlike the Beatles ability to create limitless, immaculate yield in the same ballpark as peerless monuments *Rubber Soul* and *Revolver*, until they disbanded amongst recriminations and squabbles, the

Stones studio output lasted as variable, nothing released after *Some Girls* drawing near to *magnum opus* status.

Live shows abided as the Stones bedrock, Mick and Keith seeing no wit to retire from the rock scene when the band stayed cohesive and solid onstage, with an ever-growing worldwide audience. Though in Gavin's opinion *Still Life* paled before the Stones 1969 *Get Yer Ya-Ya's Out!* spectacular, it did suit to cement the notion they endured as a premier live attraction.

* * *

Approaching mid-1987, Gavin's courtship with process engineering field enterprises had petered out. Put in charge of sundry projects, initially at Ellesmere Port, then off-shore, he had assimilated project management skills into his CV and wanted to return to Scale UK in a management role. Receptive to his hankering, and recognising his successful contribution to the firm, they made him deputy head of projects and technology in London, a business group responsible for big-league projects and technology innovations across Scale's upstream and downstream activities, worldwide.

"Well, Gavin," Head of Projects and Technology Everett Sidwell began, on his inauguration day at Scale's Nexus House, "no doubt after your field occupation, being office based will come as a bit of a cardinal change."

"I'd not go that far agreeing with the dictum. You see, even on North Sea rigs, I spent a lot of desk-time on project planning and making reports."

"I heard you were involved in the Endeavor Platform blow out in the Cromarty Field."

"Yes." His torment obvious to Sidwell, he confessed, "An unnerving event, still troubling me."

"We never got the full story here at Nexus House. Is it true a blowout preventer problem caused it?"

"Indeed," he confirmed, licking his lips, his mouth drying, recalling the episode. "I acted as the offshore operations engineer. We were pumping between 15,000 to 18,000 barrels per day, near to the maximum limit of the rig operational specification, but it shouldn't have been a problem because the blowout preventers were regularly tested." Hesitating, he embraced a wretched countenance, his pulse rate quickening. "Then we hit a new seam, instrumentation annunciating a step change of pressure in the upload pipe. Nothing we hadn't seen before, but this time, a valve failed on one of the subsurface wellheads, causing a massive rush on the main upload pipe. When the preventers partially failed, the well stream spewed between the setback and the casing head, gas and oil flying upwards and spontaneously igniting before the preventers struck full-function, cutting off the well stream."

"You were blown off the rig, weren't you?"

"Yes." Gaping at the recollection, he endorsed, "Luckily, I had my back to the derrick, and wore thick overalls, hard-hat safety helmet and safety glasses protecting me from the eruption. The blast sent me clear of the lower deck, so instead of hitting metal, I ended up feet first in the sea, cushioning the impact. Fortunately, it occurred on a very calm day, and soon Scale emergency services personnel rescued me."

"Must have been a traumatic occurrence?"

"It happened so rapidly, I didn't fully take in what had happened for days. We were fortunate the preventers did eventually kick in. If the escaping oil and gas plume had mushroomed out to the flare, the whole platform could have gone up."

After Gail Needham Gavin horsed around with other girls, none making a star connection with him, until he spied a stunning brunette in the Longitude Bar at the Le Meridien Hotel Piccadilly, a cherished watering hole for Nexus House managers after using the hotel's squash and swimming pool facilities. In a fit of blithe abandon, he sauntered up to his mark, boldly introduced himself, and proposed dinner together in the hotel's Terrace Grill. Bowled over by his confidence and winning smile, his target, Francine Landymore, accepted.

"Do you ordinarily invite strange ladies to dine with you?" she probed, as the couple settled at a table with panoramas of bustling Piccadilly below.

"All the time," he joked, tongue-in-cheek.

"Frequently I get rejected, but I perceived you might be susceptible to my meagre charms."

"Why?"

Pouting, he qualified, "because you looked *very* hungry."

Lighting up the restaurant with a scintillating smile, she crooned, "Jeez, I've had some unhindered, full-on approaches in my time, but none as explicit as yours. Tell me, where do you get all this self-confidence from?"

"Ahh." Settling back in his chair, her sparkling cinnamon fading into tawny tinted eyes, pale complexion, and ruby-painted lips framed by a mass of shoulder-length, wavy, chestnut-brown hair riveted him. "I must say, I have never done that before. It's just—" He flashed her a capricious dial. "I seemed to be tugged to you."

"Like a ship to a wrecking siren?"

"Yes. I went for an all-or-nothing tactic. You see, I've dabbled with variations on the traditional subtle slant in the past, only for some other guy to waltz off with my intended quarry." Opening his hands almost apologetically, he divulged, "I didn't want to stand the chance of one of those ultra-rich dudes frequenting Le Meridien spotting you, and me losing out again."

"So, you're not rich, Gavin Anderson?"

"Not yet, but I've got an apartment at Swiss Cottage, run a Lotus Turbo Esprit, and I'm fashioning a portfolio of investments."

"Very grandiose. What do you do?"

After summarising his Scale CV, the couple talked about the usual introductory subjects; family, education, vocation. The daughter of a stockbroker, it betided Francine hailed from deepest Surrey, had gone to Girton College to read natural sciences, and currently biotech Chromium Solutions employed her as a database administrator and application programmer.

Unlatching his receptors without any reservation throughout dinner, Gavin absorbed more of the magnetic aura she threw off, her dexterous eye movements used to emphasise the themes she made, and her abundant charisma making him tingle. After his initial ascendancy, she dominated the conversation, him happy to listen, smile, and prompt in the right places.

"By the way," he began at a suitable juncture, "What's your taste in music?"

"Oh, pretty much anything having a tune to it, but I do have a fondness for the Rolling Stones."

"*Really!*" he burbled. "Oh, this just gets better and better."

"You're surprised?"

"Oh no, it's not a jolt, it's more a case of kismet."

"How?"

"I've been a Stones devotee going back to before my junior school tenure. To stumble upon someone else attuned into their undoubted majesty, and who is—" He ceased abruptly.

"Yes," she prodded.

Chortling, he predicted, "You'll accuse me of being very brazen."

"Go on."

"Well," he began, enrapture roosting into his lineaments. "You have appreciably affected me and coupled with your liking of the world's greatest rock n' roll band, it makes you a very desirable playmate."

"Oh, and there's me fantasising," she smoothly surmised, "it's first blush adoration, and you were going to profess your undying love for me." Deliberately fluttering her eyelids to buttress the kitsch assertion, it left Gavin hugely impressed by both her dapper retort and her appropriate kinesics.

"Wow, you are a really hip operator." Nodding approvingly, he judged, "You have a full house, looks, personality and a wicked sense of humour. Oh—" Surging into a cavalier manner, a fiendish grin permeated his phiz. "What paramount event happened in 1492?"

"If memory serves, Columbus discovered the Americas."

"True, but more significantly, it underscored the Rolling Stones preparatory worldwide tour."

She laughed profusely. "I do like your sardonic wit. Suits you."

By the end of the evening, he had set his sights on marrying the vivacious Francine Landymore.

* * *

Soon inseparable, come June 1990, the couple attended a Rolling Stones concert at the *Estadi Olimpic Lluis Companys* in Barcelona. Part of the band's Urban Jungle Tour, the last with original bass player Bill Wyman, as well as dishing out Gavin-agreeable jewels *Midnight Rambler*, *Dead Flowers* and *Ruby Tuesday*, they also covered numbers from the recently released *Steel Wheels* album.

Deciding to take a holiday in the inclusive week of the concert, appointed for a Wednesday, Gavin and Francine arrived at Barcelona's El Prat Airport the preceding Saturday, hired a car and joyfully toured the Catalonia coastline north of Barcelona. Recommencing the venture after the concert, they headed south, sublimely unaware of something unexplainable happening when they booked into the Hotel Catalunya, a small hideaway in the old part of Castellon de la Plana.

Clutching sangrias, they relaxed into lavish chairs on the hotel balcony overlooking the Med at dusk, the sun near to setting behind them.

"Well, I'll be…" Francine blurted, her attention lured by a far-off entity.

"What is it?"

"There's a figure on the shoreline."

Craning his neck, Gavin distinguished a dimorphous shadow, moving slowly along the space between the rising hill leading up to the hotel and the lapping waves at the extremity of the shore. "Odd. Must be a trick of the light, or heat rising off the sand sculpting an *ignis fatuus*."

"No," Francine contested. "Inspect again. There's a facet more solid than you conceive under her swirling, scarf-like headgear."

"So you think it's a she?"

"Moves like a she."

Standing up, Gavin peered at the silhouette again.

"Strange. I must say, it does resemble a living person wandering towards the sea."

Momentarily distracted by a waiter collecting glasses from an adjacent table, when they rejoined to observe the effigy, it had vanished.

Afterwards, when Gavin went into the hotel to book a table for dinner, virtually as a throwaway remark, he told the hotel proprietor about the revelation. Spooked by the rejoinder, he went back to the terrace perplexed and goggling.

"What's up with you?" Francine enquired. "Have you been given an insoluble problem to wrestle with?"

"Yes, I have." Gazing out into dark space where they saw the likeness, he advised, "I told Senor Mendez about our baffling apparition."

"And?"

Still flummoxed, he advised, "He wants us to leave the hotel."

An hour later, they checked into the Gran Via Hotel, neighbouring the Hotel Catalunya. Relaying on their fix to Gran Via owner Senor Delgado, he told them Mendez had suffered a tragedy a few years heretofore. Disenchanted with life, his wife Isabella had lapsed into acute melancholia then suicidal tendencies, ultimately walking into the sea and drowning. Shortly after, local newspapers reported numerous sightings of a being wearing a long flowing scarf, making from the shoreline to the sea, then disappearing. Engrossing the prominent media nationwide, correspondents bombarded Mendez, breaching old wounds and making him relive his wife's suicide again.

"He must have thought you were journalists masquerading as tourists," Delgado proposed. "It's why he wanted you to leave."

"So, what we saw," Gavin tentatively advanced, "could be categorised as a chimera, a ghost."

"Yes, if you believe in such things." Staring at the sea, he solemnly proclaimed, "I prefer to gauge such findings as tricks of the light."

Whereas Francine took the touchstone in her stride, it continued to plague Gavin after they backtracked to England. As a scientific man with an incisive logic fixation, as both he and Senor Delgado had deduced the provenance of the imprint to be, he strived to explain the bogey as an indisputable trick of the light. During his time in Oman, he had driven from Al Wasil to Wahiba Sands at the peak of the summer season heat, witnessing shimmering mirages over the desert sand dunes. Encountering Bedouins, they told him ocular distortions were fairly frequent, and when travelers were debilitated by the intense heat coupled with sand storms, the phenomena often took on illusory proportions. Did the Castellon de la Plana manifestation fall into the fictitious category, or a much more spectral classification he considered?

Before his O-Level year at Kings, he had voraciously depleted the handiwork of Edgar Allen Poe and M. R. James, their vivid narratives of the supernatural sparking his imagination. Applying the cold principles of science put the other-worldly substance into perspective, Gavin capping the writer relied upon autosuggestion for the reader to lapse into premeditated feelings of dread. Purely an induced state of mind, he had dismissed the concept of ghosts as fanciful, a rigged motif making for trenchant stimulation, but nonetheless an illusion.

Revisiting the shoreline unveiling, his assuredness diluted. True, heat rising from the beach sand as the sun descended could have created a mirage-like hallucination. However, mirages tend to hover and remain static, whereas both he and Francine had seen the phantom moving in favour of the sea. A happening he could not account for, the conundrum resided with him as an anomaly to be periodically reassessed in the light of more data on the prodigy.

* * *

Two years of mutual felicity passed, then after a short engagement, Gavin and Francine were married at St Mary's Church Shalford, the undivided Anderson and Landymore families and intimates like Marlon Yardley present. Slightly before the happy day, Gavin sold his Swiss Cottage apartment, and bought a four-bedroom, detached house at Borehamwood, the newlyweds making it in their image after their homecoming from a honeymoon in the Azores.

Taking to married life like a duck to water, Gavin marveled at how the union somehow forged an even greater and everlasting bond for him with Francine, their symbiotic love continuing to grow. Rarely exchanging harsh words or falling foul of fundamental differences, domestic life in the Anderson household flourished.

Whilst offering relative quiet compared to the constant fanfare and ballyhoo fabricated by revelers in Swiss Cottage, Borehamwood had been chosen because of its proximity to central London. It also furnished a refuge away from the noise and pollution bred by an increasingly, jam-packed-to-the-rafters London city centre, a disruption escalating from a milieu nuisance into a vehement irritation, both husband and wife keen not to spend the largest portion of their lives submersed in its fatiguing effect.

Summer weekends saw Gavin and Francine either regale guests, notably Donnell and Caroline, or lose themselves in the Chiltern Hills or the Thames at Marlow. Winter dispensed an altogether different regime, neither party keen on bucolic adventures in the snow, mulled wine with friends gathered by the fireside, or watching a *film noir* movie on a VHS player, more to their liking. Seasonal variations apart, the Andersons feted their Borehamwood habitat, never lacking for a lively indoors activity, or a diversion in the community to keep them stirred or entertained, going to local repertory theatre spectacles and playing mixed doubles tennis at the Rowley Club strong preferences.

On the career front, after nigh on twelve years with Scale, Gavin left to join global pharmaceutical Oxalite as operations director at their Welwyn Garden City plant, expanding his upward mobility *vis-à-vis* a generous remuneration package. Whilst at Scale, the Andersons holidayed in the Caribbean and the Med. Now they went much further afield, staying at five-star hotels in South Pacific paradises and exotic, cultural locations such as St Petersburg and Kathmandu.

Still an avid Rolling Stones record harvester, Gavin invested in just about everything they released, and over the years, he completed his personal Decca Stones releases agglomeration by investing in the albums brother Donnell had loaned him in his nascent years. Though a plethora of other bands had been attached to his church of top-ranking rock artists, the Stones upheld the *numero uno* spot. Additional to blues-rock pioneers Cream, the Jeff Beck Group and Led Zeppelin, he had dabbled with the jazz influenced rock donations of King Crimson, the extraordinary cadre of New Wave voyagers' Joy Division, the post-punk unorthodoxy of the Pixies, and the blistering grunge of Nirvana. Lucidly, with no evident end to the innovation and invention blossoming from derivative rock artists, their variations in mode and delivery on the baseline theme constantly astounded him. Though nothing equaled the pioneering craft of Presley, the Beatles, Dylan, the Velvet Underground and the Stones, many made scratches on the immensely high wall of excellence.

By Gavin's forty-third birthday, Francine had given birth to two offspring, Michelle and her younger brother Wyatt, both at junior school, and the Andersons had moved to a very large house situated in three acres on the outskirts of Potters Bar.

Behind schedule, when Michelle eventually came into the world, an ecstatic with beatitude Gavin shared with Francine, "My mother told me I was a late arrival, so I assume it's a family tradition."

"Family tradition or not," she countered, "I hope any future ones arrive on time. You've got the easy part in the precreation business. It's me who has to do all the heavy-lifting!"

"Does this mean," he facetiously voiced, "we are going to add to our progeny upstream?"

Beaming at Michelle, she answered, "Oh yes. Next time I want a boy."

Amidst all the elation in the Anderson domicile, Mick and the boys were still rolling on. Mellowing compared to their seminal years filled with controversy, excess and debauchery, England's renegades had at least part-transformed into pro-establishment doyens, rubbing shoulders with royalty, presidents and prime ministers, the world over. With retreat into calmer waters, the Stones album releases in the mid to late eighties and the entire 1990s cascaded into self-parody bailiwick, bereft of the *avant garde* cutting edge synonymous with the holy triumvirate, *Beggar's Banquet*, *Let It Bleed* and *Sticky Fingers*. Albeit an element of unwavering accumulator mentality, Gavin adjudicated them to be better than most artist releases, the band still capable of applying the hook with the occasional sizzling canto, and unique, even landmark song arrangement.

He noted after the sonic craftwork of Cream, Blind faith and Derek and the Dominos, the same thing had happened to Eric Clapton. Succeeding a stretch of sustained heroin addiction, when he pined for Patti Harrison, wife of Beatle George, Pete

Townshend aided his advent from the mire, Clapton's thereafter albums mediocre, and when Patti belatedly joined him, often happy to the brink of banality.

His measurement verified the maxim; musicians make their best designs when they are in their formative period, living in a garret on the wrong side of the tracks, and hungry for success, and food. Despite coming from middle-class environments, Mick, Keith and Brian Jones certainly underwent the baptism, living in various not-far-from condemned London basements and existing on meagre rations, whilst making a name for themselves on the blues-club gig circuit. Seen as a prerequisite for authenticity, integrity and respect, possessing such scar symbol credentials before success became the difference between manufactured pop artists and the genuine article, Gavin flatly subscribing to the axiomatic wisdom. How can you possibly sing about being lonesome, impoverished or crossed in love, if you've never been in those places, he argued with those seeing no difference between plastic, synthetic pop and roots-inspired rhythm and blues.

If the latest Rolling Stones studio tokens left his palate still famished of delight, conversely, as a live act, the band kept on hitting the gold criterion achieved on the 1969 US tour yielding *Get Yer Ya-Ya's Out!* arguably with the Who's *Live at Leeds*, rock's two supreme live albums.

Predictably, Gavin and Francine went to Rolling Stones concerts in the nineties and the early years of the new millennium, typically the Rose Bowl Pasadena, as part of a fly-drive vacation on the West Coast. Backed by the Red Hot Chilli Peppers, the Voodoo Lounge Tour concert proved to be a notable moment for Gavin because the Stones performed one of his bookmark darlings, *The Spider and The Fly*, B-side of the single *Satisfaction*, a song keeping him spellbound since brother Donnell played it to him just before his first day at Christleton Junior School.

Copenhagen's Parken Stadium contributed the venue for a Bridges to Babylon Tour concert, the Stones abetted by Seahorses, a band hatched by John Squire when the Stone Roses eventually fragmented. Having acquired all the Stone Roses albums, Gavin had bought Seahorse's debut album, *Do It Yourself*, and wanted to see them live, their function as a support act a big bonus for him. A year on, the Andersons made their way to Wembley Stadium to see the Stones, Sheryl Crow also on the bill, and August 2003 beckoned them to Twickenham Stadium to watch the band perform a crowd-pleasing selection mainly from their 1960s catalogue.

Coming out of Twickenham Stadium, Gavin heralded, "You know, these days, the Stones only play huge outdoor stadiums, where you need heavyweight binoculars to actually see them at close quarters."

"Mmmm," Francine uttered, her mind more fixed on finding their parked car.

"They played the 100 Club 1982 and 1986, but for one reason or another, I couldn't get tickets." Cultivating a broad smile, he disclosed, "Boy, what I'd give to see them play at the tight, sweaty 100 Club, or The Marquee before it shut down, where you can actually behold Keith performing guitar magic and Mick blowing harp without the aid of a telescope."

"Why don't you book the Stones for our tenth wedding anniversary?" she gibed, then copiously attuning herself with the proposition decreed, "They could play in a marquee in our back garden."

"Now you're talking, girl." Sobering up from his pipedream, he asked, "How much do you estimate it could cost?"

"Oh, at least a million," she ordained.

"Blimey." Wobbling his head, he confided, "I can't see either our parental families or our children being best pleased with us blowing a million, even on a good cause."

"By the way, before I forget, Gavin," she began, "what's your schedule for the week commencing 15th September?"

"Well let's see. Monday I'm in Juarez, Tuesday Tierra del Fuego, Wednesday it's Dar es Salaam, Thursday Singapore and Friday...Batley in glorious Yorkshire."

"*Hah*, joking apart, keep the evening of 20th September clear. We've been invited to a reception at Gilchrist Sanders."

Completing ten years of service at Chromium Solutions, Francine had moved on to enterprise-scale, investment banking house Gilchrist Sanders to run their Java program development department.

"Salivating over even more trillions of profits, are they?" he taunted.

Exposed to the world of investment banking via his operations director role at Oxalite, Gavin had never been unreservedly convinced of money market inner beauty or industry stability. No matter what risks Oxalite took on resultant from new merchandise advancement, as far as he could make out, by contrast, funding supplied by investment banks always seemed to be riskless, and milestone investment repayments invariably met before his firm saw a penny of profit. Worse still, he noticed investment banks had mutated into casino-style gamblers, pushing vast amounts of money into supposedly lucrative investment stocks, principally derivatives such as commodities, currencies and interest rates, often hallmarked by flimsy business plans and administrative recklessness, the wholesale investment capital made on the back of solid companies like Oxalite, and by raiding idiots and widows retail banking accounts.

Grinning at the catty retort, she chastised, "Stop being cynical."

"Well, it's bad enough my brother being in financial services," he went on, "but your employer in unison with the rest of the investment banking fraternity make gargantuan profits, and evidently, greed is their byword. Every time I interact with someone from Canary Wharf, they seem to infer they are doing Oxalite a big favour." Scowling, he slated, "Swanning everywhere in their 911s, endlessly talking about their country estates, and five-star weekend jaunts to St-Tropez and Monte Carlo, also sticks in the craw." Tapping her arm, he prescribed, "A little modesty wouldn't go amiss."

"You're not doing so bad in the wealth stakes yourself, and you do invest in the stock market."

"Both true," he had no hesitation in admitting, "but at least I'm involved in an occupation benefitting mankind."

"A fine distinction," Francine claimed. "*Au contraire*, don't forget, without investors, benefitting mankind, as you so grandly call it, could not be consummated."

"Yes, I will concede to your assertion. It's just—" Glaring with vitriol, he cited, "They must fancy themselves to be the Lord God Almighty, the way some investment house execs parade to and fro, bestowing gratification on the needy, apropos to the Pope giving benediction."

"What are you going to do if Oxalite contact Bryant Zenon for investment funding, and you have to interface with your brother?"

Making a gainsay phiz he superficially reiterated, "I've already told Donnell never to darken my office door."

She giggled, then planted a big kiss on his cheek. "Oh, Gavin, you still have the capacity to make me laugh with your somewhat idealised world view."

"Well…" he griped, before sniggering at his hypothetical foibles of extending the moral compass to the investment banking sector. "Though they have limited conversation beyond bits and bytes, I don't mind your I.T people. Just *don't* introduce me to anyone on the broker side of the Gilchrist Sanders business at this latest shindig. They always see me as an investment opportunity." His venom coming to the boil, he complained, "The last time we went to one of their receptions, some spotty, East End, barrow boy oik collared me, and I ended up spending the evening fending him off and wanting to throttle him."

* * *

Oxalite presented more challenges to Gavin than he had foreseen at the outset of his term of office. Pharmaceuticals spend £billions on drug discovery, testing and certification before the medication goes into production, his operations director responsibility, to ensure efficient manufacturing to recoup the capital investment in the fastest possible timescale before the firm went into profit on the venture. An integral part of his job, licensing patented inventory preparations for third parties to fabricate in the UK or overseas, necessitated a substantial amount of travel.

One trip to Sumatra exceptionally tested both his negotiation skills and his abilities to outlive an unanticipated incident. Headquartered in Palembang, Koto & Bodi the fourmost Indonesian pharmaceutical requested a contract to turn out a variety of Oxalite remedies, Gavin dispatched to tend to the business. Finding a mutually satisfactory pact between the two parties proved laborious, Koto & Bodi not accepting all the terms specified in Oxalite's standard licensing agreement, or the price, Gavin entered a logjam tract. He had successfully dealt with impasses in the past, but after several parleying conferences, he settled regardless of Koto & Bodi's keenness to conclude the deal, the gap between their aspirations and Oxalite's requirements lingered as leviathan.

Travelling to his hotel after one mammoth confab, as he alighted from a cab, a massive explosion in a flanking skyscraper brought about a torrent of masonry and glass crashing on bystanders, many people slugged by granite pieces and pane shards, Gavin inclusive. Visibly shocked by the blowup, the hotel concierge rushed him into the foyer, the hotel doctor fixing up some minor cuts.

With Indonesia blighted by terrorism since the 1960s, originally the hotel management hypothesised a nearby bomb had gone off. Afterwards, police confirmed a gas leak had been responsible for the blast, killing scores of people inside the building and severely injuring many more. Considerate for Gavin's welfare, Koto & Bodi sent personnel overseer Mister Caniago to ascertain he had survived the affair intact. Though Gavin assured Caniago he just needed a few shots of scotch to regain his nerve, the Indonesian insisted on informing Oxalite and Francine about his distressed status.

Like most Scale employees installed in the potentially dangerous environments of North Sea oil rigs and Oman, he had stiffened his resolve to tolerate the risks, and serenely deal with them if and when they happened. Though he never expected to be put in such hazardous provinces again, the resolute attitude stayed with him at Oxalite. Calling on the inclination subsequent to Caniago telling him to get a good night's sleep and departing, he noted the accident gave him more palpitations than he foresaw.

Whereas petro carbons exploration warranted an aptitude to undertake the unheralded, the gas leak explosion fell into *force majeure*—act of god realm, an out-of-the-blue phenomenon, not possible to envisage in advance. As per the Castellon de la Plana spectral sighting, the inability to either prepare for, or evade a life-threatening, abrupt occurrence troubled him. He soothed his anxiety by applying the probability law; lightning only strikes once in the same place, and it is exceedingly unlikely to happen again. However, recollecting lightning can kill, he recoiled at the theory.

Inflaming worries for his family's wellbeing, should he expire from another explosion or accident whilst on business, unbeknown to Francine, on return to Blighty, he took out a comprehensive life insurance policy, lodging it with his solicitor. Determining the unpredictable can materialise without any warning, for the first time in his life, he began to grasp how fragile life sustainability could be. Typical of Gavin, his analytical mind number-crunched the probabilities of chance factors culminating in another life-threatening escapade whilst on business. In the end, he certified anything could happen by pure circumstance, exhaustive forward planning not mitigating an unscheduled meeting with mishap.

* * *

Later in the year of the Stones Twickenham concert, Gavin met up with old school pal Marlon Yardley at Chelsea Arts Club, a convivial haven for the creative corps, prominently filmmakers.

Neglecting his innate rebelliousness, Marlon had not wanted to end up on the scrapheap of life due to prematurely dropping out of the educational system. Diligently applying himself to his studies, he left Kings with three A-Levels, and went on to the University of Warwick to study film and literature, before treading in his parent's film industry footsteps, joining Shepperton Studios as a camera production assistant, before transferring into production management, at the outset as a production coordinator then production manager. Head-hunted by Pinewood Studios about the same time Gavin moved to Oxalite, he reverted to the creative process as director of photography on feature films, joining Chelsea Arts Club soon after.

"I used to conceptualise you were like Michael Travis from *If*," Gavin recalled as the pair devoured very large Havana Coolers. "But with hindsight and the accumulation of know-how, I now recognise you were much more like a mixture of Dean Moriarty and Holden Caulfield."

"What a teaser!" Throwing his head back, Marlon beamed at Gavin. "Given the choice, back at Kings, I'd have gladly taken the Moriarty peg."

"Because the Kerouac character is hipper than Salinger's creation?"

"*Absolutely*," he proclaimed. "The name Marlon Yardley lends itself to a 1950s Kerouac hipster."

"True."

"Tell me—" Styling a searching kisser, he interrogated, "are you still a Stones aficionado?"

"Definitely. Things may come, and things may go, but the holy Rolling Stones roll on forever. Since I found my feet and voice, they've been the soundtrack to my life. A tumultuous fount to accompany good times celebration, and an old familiar friend in times of trouble."

"Yes," Marlon agreed, his modulation ringing with philosophical content. "We all need constants in our lives, and third-party allegiances to movie stars and rock musicians alike provide faithfulness and fidelity, especially when personal relationships fail."

"You're still bitter about your divorce?"

"Huh, I used to be, but not anymore." Sliding down in his seat, his repose an indication of his consent, he outlined, "Temptation is a perpetual spook in the world of film, solid relationships often wrecked on the rocks of temporary bilateral affinity. When Jenelle had her infatuation with a well-known actor, whose name I shall not mention, I gauged it to be dispassionate, and a passing phase. *Wrong*. She waltzed off with him, and we got divorced. Ironically, she didn't stay with him, and ended up with an editing assistant, ten years her junior."

Lowering his head, Gavin reacted, "Yes, I remember you replaying the gory tale when you invited Francine and myself to the BAFTAs when *Sense and Sensibility* won the best film award."

"Dreadful film," he criticised, "though I did like Alan Rickman's performance. If it hadn't been the sugary Jane Austen adaptation, *The Madness of King George* would have prevailed. I didn't value that either. In fact—" Indignantly, he curled his upper lip. "There's not much to admire in 1995 film apart from *The Usual Suspects* and maybe *The Quick and the Dead*." Getting into his stride, Marlon delineated, "When the bean counters took over the uncut industry, every film proposed for shooting had to be safe, meaning low risk, meaning appealing to the lowest common denominator. It has led to widespread mediocrity and the unstoppable dominance of the insipid blockbuster. Crikey—" Proliferating a wry smile, his condemnation sped up. "You mentioned *If*, directed by your namesake Lindsay Anderson. Mavericks like Anderson have practically been culled from the roster and substituted with middle-of-the-road puppets. Even Ken Russell's unparalleled, eloquent wings have been clipped in recent times."

"*Quite*," Gavin acknowledged. Figuring his comrade's hackles were rising to storm grade, he changed the subject. "How's your relationship going with Claudette, is it?"

"Indeed, it is Claudette. Fine within the borders of what is possible on a film set, but I can't see it lasting."

"How many has there been since Jenelle?"

Marlon cranked his head up, Gavin clocking his lips moving as he mentally enumerated them. "Nine I make it." Catching his buddy taking in a sharp intake of air, he granted, "Yes, I know it's a lot, but after what happened to my marriage, I'm unable to press the commit button just in case history repeats itself." His profound bent rejoining, he itemised, "Due to infidelity, there aren't many long-term relationships in my world, and those enduring intact, are often blighted with other tragedies. The only exception I can table is John Mills. Miraculously, he's managing a near-to, life-long relationship with his wife, Mary Hayley Bell, though admittedly, his previous marriage did fail."

"Why don't you scout outside of the film industry for a soulmate?"

"Difficult. The job is intensive, with virtually no time to hunt elsewhere for a life partner. Besides, the film industry is saturated with pretty girls, and there's no guarantee a relationship with someone not connected with film fairs any better." Pitching a disillusioned port at his ex-schoolmate, he confessed, "I'm damaged goods, Gavin. I have a jaundiced take on life. Until Miss Right comes along and demonstrates total fidelity, I will continue to play the field. You've been very lucky with Francine. She's an unconditional corker, and unequivocally she loves you."

"True, albeit when we met, I didn't even weigh long-term loyalty as an essential facet for relationship success. It kind of thrived between us over the years. We trust each other implicitly." Neutrally raising his eyebrows, he revealed, "Other men have often come on to her at social events, but she has always left with me. And for my part—" Unlocking his hands, the gesture intended to convey credence, his voice tone enveloped complete sincerity. "I could never hurt her or foster the hankering to go off with another woman." Sitting back in his ritzy armchair, he declared, "We're happy, and the children have bound us even closer together."

"Yes, you are very lucky, Gavin. I'm glad at least one of us has gained happiness and contentment. Hah—" Forging inquisitive lineaments, he probed, "Did you ever review how your life might pan out when we were at Kings?"

"Never crossed my mind. Even in the sixth form, apart from the latest testament from the Stones, and the occasional fling with a long-legged blonde, primarily I focused on attaining good qualifications for university."

"Step by step, hey?"

"Yep. I didn't survey over and above the forthcoming year. Long term designs only arrived in my cognizance when I decided to marry Francine on the day we first met, then when I left Scale for Oxalite."

"Yes, you've told me about the former before." Briefly contemplating, he shifted his gaze to an adjacent window affording prospects over Old Church Street. "Do you know…" he began, his concentration still absorbed by sundry passers-by, "…I often ask myself, when do you grow up? Is it in your late teenage years, or perhaps never? When do you become aware, you've made the transition from fun-time frolics into the coterie of worldliness and responsibility?"

"You mean, when do you stop growing up?"

"Pardon," Marlon mumbled, his engrossment still part immersed in the doings of local street life.

"I said, you mean, when do you stop growing up?" Gavin parroted.

Turning his undivided diligence to his ally, he confirmed, "In my case, regrettably, never."

"You know—" Percolating a studious mien, Gavin imparted, "aged fifteen, I thought I'd be fulsomely grownup by way of the required obligations at twenty-one. When I got to twenty-one, I questioned life and myself much more than I did at fifteen. Here I am at forty-three, married with children, and I remain persuaded I am still in the process of growing up." Sniggering, he then sincerely expressed, "It's kind of funny, even ironic. When I left for Edinburgh, I presupposed I knew things, and had a feel for how the world functions, but—" He gave Marlon a knowing sideways ogle. "I knew very little, and I'm sure I don't know a hell of a lot more now." Pausing to assemble more judgments, he then avouched, "I've had some narrow escapes and inexplicable escapades. The Endeavor Platform blowout, Sumatra gas explosion, and the eerie business at Castellon de la Plana I've told you about, all come to mind. Although projecting a grownup outlook, scrupulous planning and examining the chapters in the cold light of day, they could all fall into the category of being in the wrong place at the wrong time. Simply put, purportedly, luck or ill-luck plays an influential element, overriding all responsible and solid scheming. Good god!" He laughed. "Whilst at

Edinburgh, I posed the luck issue to my old flame, Gail Needham. She got me to appreciate independent of understood good-luck or ill-luck factors, if you think it, it will happen. From an optimism standpoint, over the years, on average, the maxim has held good."

"Yep, I'm on the same page *vis-à-vis* the destiny tally, but revisiting your growing up theme, in retrospect, it's incontestable the learning process, and it does take in dealing with chance possibilities, never ceases. You never get to the end of the information and experience rainbow, no matter how much you try. It's endless."

"You're right. It's just like the holy Rolling Stones. They'll still be blazing a trail across the skies for decades to come, endlessly touring to the threshold of metamorphosing into a nomadic tribe."

Thereafter, as Gavin strolled back along Fulham Road towards South Kensington London Underground Station, he reflected on his definitive dialogue conclusion with Marlon, contemplating how far he had travelled along life's freeway since vacating Christleton. Pondering if growing up merely entailed relinquishing flightiness for both self-responsibility and responsibility to others, he poured over the changes to his *modus vivendi* and major standouts occurring to date. Priding himself he had long since crossed the demarcation meridian, mindful of societal demands in toto, nevertheless, it had not extinguished his faculty for larks and merriment. He saw no need to curtail the latter, if the preceding persevered uncompromised. If it were so, did growing up equate with the competence to put the two complementary strands into perspective, knowing when to be steadfast, and when to be the entertainer?

Such juxtaposed shades of life continued to perplex him through the years to come. Testing the concept on Francine, brother Donnell and others, nothing solid ever came out from discussions.

As time passed, Gavin Anderson deduced, growing up to be a frame of mind, evident from minute to minute circumstances, as they arose. Keeping the vantage fulcrum in his memory forefront, it never bothered him beyond the occasional introspection.

DEATH OF A RADIO TALK SHOW HOST

DEATH OF A RADIO TALK SHOW HOST

Renata Lapham had become increasingly agitated by Radio Islington talk show host Jarred O'Gara. She took great exception to his constant disparaging of English society and his unbridled support for certain holy cow, untouchable groups O'Gara thought should have dominion over the English, and their lives feather-bedded at taxpayers' expense. Her frustration boiled over to the point whereby she threw things at her DAB radio, the futile gesture a metaphorical action to shut him up.

She had also developed a strong impression about his dictatorial character, noticing that if callers agreed with his views, they were given unfettered airtime, whereas those vehemently disagreeing with his PC rhetoric became subject to his call-in cut off button within seconds. Her loathing of O'Gara grew. No matter how much she tamed her rage, promising herself not to become agitated, every tuning into his programme brought about a viperous reaction, Renata unable to sustain calm. Culminating in a final solution to her adversaries incessant haranguing, she imagined gunning him down, the shot going straight between his eyes and instantly terminating his subversive bombast.

* * *

Following the usual lead-in routine to his three-hour morning show on Radio Islington, Jarred O'Gara stated, "I'm looking at a report stating that two in three babies born in Slough are not white. Why should we be concerned about that?" Going on to produce a highly pro-biased sermon justifying why the English should not be fretful about their country becoming dominated by foreigners, he completely sidelined the impact of unchecked immigration on social, housing and transport schemes, let alone the prospect of the country being irreversibly changed forever in their favour. During his diatribe, his assistant watched as inbound telephone calls racked up to maximum on the programme switchboard. Closing his lecture, O'Gara gave callers a chance to voice their views, most immigrants and trendy lefties praising his polemic, the vast majority of English telephoners questioning his one-sided attitude.

Chomping at the bit to get her two-penneth worth in, Renata finally got through pulling apart his one-sided tirade and quizzing, "And you think it is perfectly acceptable for our country to be swamped by immigrants offspring to the point of chronic bedlam?"

Dismissing her objection in a broadside of PC clichés designed to belittle those disagreeing with him, O'Gara completed his demolition job saying, "Anyone objecting to England being populated with non-whites is a blatant racist and should be banned from expressing their xenophobic views."

Before Renata could reply, O'Gara did his usual 'next-caller' trick, cutting her off the airwaves. Infuriated by the putdown and the discourtesy, the DAB received more rough treatment and a kitchen chair got a sound kicking.

When Renata's husband Ridley returned from his office to their Epsom home, invariably she let fly about her latest radio duel with O'Gara, Ridley sitting down and listening to his wife's familiar philippic about whatever had upset her that day. On this occasion he got the full, unadulterated SP relating to how from Renata's standpoint he had insulted her when she challenged his angle on the Slough report, and why O'Gara was a closet traitor betraying the nation who had fed, housed and educated him.

"He's worse than the moralistic, liberal-left-loving BBC," she proclaimed. "How he gets away with it, I don't know. It's criminal. By allowing him to clog the airwaves with his flighty, pinko proclamations, Radio Islington are being irresponsible."

Having absorbed her latest complaint, Ridley petitioned, "You really shouldn't let this radio chappie get to you. As I understand it, Radio Islington is a commercial station and thereby dependent on advertising to bankroll its programme schedule. In turn, advertisers will only use a given radio station if it can prove they have a sizable and regular listening audience."

Perplexed by the rationale, she queried, "What are you driving at?"

"Well, it's a known fact that controversy gains listeners, thereby ensuring advertising revenue continuance."

"So?"

"Have you considered O'Gara might be purposely being controversial to incite people, such as yourself?"

"You mean, it's all an act, a ruse to trap listeners into tuning in, in the hope the talk-show host upsets them?"

"My dear—" He hit her with a temperate mug. "There are no limits to which the commercial media will stoop to both sustain and attract new advertising revenues. It's their life blood. Declining audience figures means declining advertising revenues. A placid approach to transmitting current affairs views might captivate an impassive core audience, but to nail the big advertisers, large and growing audience numbers are required. Usually, that means fire and brimstone coupled with unpopular rhetoric forming a whirlpool pulling people in."

"So, you're implying I'm falling for the bait?"

"Well, you'd have to make a subjective judgment in respect of O'Gara's credibility. Does he practice what he preaches? If not, then most probably it is an act, designed to lure in listeners. And by the way, why are you tarnishing 'Auntie' with the same brush?"

"Oh, *Ridley*, if you actually listened to what the holier-than-thou BBC are broadcasting instead of burying your head in microbiology papers and golf magazines, you'd detect they have the same 'starless and bible black' to quote Dylan Thomas, anti-English manifesto O'Gara gushes every day on his radio show."

Surprised by the condemnation, he uttered, "Mmmm,

I must start scrutinising BBC programmes more closely."

Taking her husband's analysis as gospel, Renata set about finding out everything she could about O'Gara. Rifling through various government and tittle-tattle websites, she discovered O'Gara was born 12th January 1972 in Hackney to Irish immigrant parents. Educated at Cardinal Wiseman College and the LSE, he then worked for the print media and was a panellist on the television show *The Left Stuff* before first appearing on Radio Islington in 2002 as a relief presenter, going on to become a fulltime anchorman a year later. Regularly making headlines for his pro-immigrant, anti-conservative broadcast opinions and fabricating moral judgements on prominent people in the public eye consequently scuppered by the victim, he gained a reputation for alienating most people apart from his cherished minority sects and fellow members of the PC brigade bolstering his radio show ratings and buying his sinister far-left, highly opinionated nonfictions. Including the raving, loony Liberal Democrats, Guardinistas and the left-wing pressure group Momentum, the faithful wet themselves silly at his anti-English sentiments. According to O'Gara, anyone who voted to leave the EU and voted for the Conservative Party and UKIP were racists, the guillotine division ignoring the many shades of traditional conservatism not necessarily being anti-immigrant, those in the castigated ring accounting for sixty-one percent of English voters. Recording a further thirty-two percent, he also criticised most English working-class Labour Party voters as anti-immigrant and thereby were also racist. What infuriated the stigmatised, particularly steadfast loyalists like Renata Lapham, lay in the irrefutable fact, O'Gara made his hallmarking from his rich and opulent castle in the sky, the draconian effects of mass immigration never touching him or his family.

Renata had a middle-class upbringing in Royal Tunbridge Wells, her parents instilling in her the work ethic and self-reliance in all matters. During her late teenage years she rebelled, dabbling in left-wing politics whilst at art college, but soon saw the clique she ran with as plastic pretenders pontificating Marxist precepts before going home to their bourgeois well-off parents. By age twenty-one, when she went to work for an advertising company, she had ditched the leaning in favour of pragmatic reality. She met Ridley via mutual friends a few years later. Soon marrying thereafter, the happy couple settled down in Epsom before the union brought two children into the world. By Renata's forty-fifth birthday the offspring had left home for higher education and she had become a home-based, freelance commercial artist with an enviable roster of clients.

Her introduction to the *Jarred O'Gara Show* came about quite by chance. During working hours, she usually listened to background music of her own choosing or tuned into Radio Four taking in the drama, comedy and history programmes. After investing in a DAB radio, she used the tuning control to see what stations were available, briefly catching a Radio Islington heated dialogue between the radio presenter and an irate caller before continuing her scan. Curious to know the subject of the verbal clash, she backtracked to the Radio Islington frequency, the dialogue still raging. From what she could gather, the telephoner was opposing the presenter's insistence that the Labour Party could only become effective if it adopted an extreme left-wing leader with a radical agenda centred on state-ownership, the caller, by all accounts a Labour Party member, vigorously disputing the charge and insisting the party had always been democratic and encircled a wide array of policies benefiting the lower stratums of the social structure.

Captivated, not by the content of the disagreement, but the sheer uncompromising and bombastic tone of the presenter, not allowing his opponent any leeway to contest his stance, she decided to hear some more. Additional listeners called in to protest the show host's—one Jarred O'Gara's intransigent perspective, Renata increasingly intrigued and disgusted in equal measures by his obvious abuse of the airwaves to transmit his scriptures and belittle anyone opposing them. So began her daily tuning into the *Jarred O'Gara Show* for his three week days slots, every week.

Meanwhile, judicious and logical Ridley got on with his business and love of golf.

* * *

One evening at Banstead Golf Club, Ridley Lapham ran into an old acquaintance in the bar, he knew to be involved in the broadcasting industry. Deliberating the chance encounter could be used to test the veracity of his wife's Jarred O'Gara loathing, he engaged Floyd Hamer.

"Floyd," he called in an open, inviting manner. "I haven't seen you here for a very long time."

"Ridley," Hamer replied, "Good to see you again."

"It must be over seven years since I last bumped into you in this den of iniquity."

"Yes, my penchant for golf took second place to work demands long ago." Recognising the longevity of his absence, he queried, "Is it *really* seven years?"

"I'm afraid so."

"These days, I rarely have any time for anything apart from my work and home responsibilities. The business in particular consumes a lot of cycles."

Segueing into his purpose, he threw Hamer a sideways look. "Forgive my apparent impetuosity, but do you mind if we change the topic of conversation?"

"Certainly not," he replied.

"I want to talk to you about a troubling matter."

"Oh."

Clearing his throat, he deftly proposed, "I'd like to tap into your understanding of the media."

"Well," Hamer acknowledged, "I'll do my best. What is it you want to know?"

Recalling Renata's reproach of the national broadcaster, he tentatively asked, "What erm… impressions have you formed about the BBC's loyalty to the nation?"

"Ahh," he began, "I left the BBC six years ago."

"Oh, I didn't realise," Lapham declared. "I'm obviously way behind the times. Who are you with now?"

"Sky."

"Really." Fleetingly cogitating, he then reflected, "You must have been with the BBC for over twenty years?"

"Indeed yes, nearer twenty-five actually. Joined at age eighteen, straight after A-Levels."

"I always thought jobs with the BBC were for life. What made you leave?"

Pursing his lips as if bothered by the question, Hamer scanned around the bar. "Come on. Let's find a quiet spot on the terrace. There are too many prying ears around here."

Lapham and Hamer gathered up their drinks, made for the French doors leading out onto the clubhouse terrace, and strolled to the extremity of the terrace east wing. Dropping anchor at a scrolled wrought iron table and chairs set, they continued their conversation.

"You were saying," Lapham prompted.

Taking a deep breath, Hamer exhaled noisily before answering. "When I joined the BBC productions department as a fledgling trainee, 'Auntie', as she is colloquially known to the nation, was a bastion institution for English traditions and culture. At that time, Sir Ian Trethowan ran the corporation, and to a large extent it still fitted the pro-establishment mantle, though many of the senior staff I worked with made no bones about their left-wing leanings, and desire to re-shape the BBC in their image. Being young and ambitious to get on, my only focus became career attainment objectives."

"You seem reserved in your recollection," Lapham observed. "Did something happen or change to contest your pro-establishment view of the BBC?"

"*Huh*, you could say that," Hamer confirmed. "The whole ethos changed when Alasdair Milne succeeded Trethowan. Suddenly, the reds really started to reveal themselves and dominate the programming schedule and content. It got even worse under the stewardships of Checkland, Birt and Dyke. Anybody who openly opposed their left-wing dictum found that their careers faltered, or they were set up to be fired on the dubious grounds of *not* fitting in!"

"What about you?" Lapham questioned. "You are hardly the type to lie down and take it from behind without protesting."

"Hah, thanks for the accolade, but I'm afraid I kept my head down. You see, Sky still looked shaky even after the merger with BSB, and de-regulation of television broadcasting services was yet to stabilise, and I needed security of income for my family and to pay the bills. Recognising the productions department had become inundated with crazed left-wing programme makers, I transferred to BBC Finance and Business, becoming responsible for franchising. Compared to productions it was a safe haven populated by business-minded people. Besides, it became quite clear I was the wrong colour and religion to progress in programme making. Forced quotas ensured my ilk was being systematically eradicated in favour of darker skins and non-Christian faiths."

"Mmmm, I recognise the security driver," Lapham admitted, "but what about ITV and Channel 4?"

"Independent television was going through a severe trade meltdown. Many network providers were ceasing operations or merging with bigger players."

"Yes, I remember the demise of Thames and London Weekend, but what about Channel 4?"

"Like the BBC, Channel 4 are part-funded by the Government and were just as bad as the BBC when it came to pro-left-wing party lines. They still are."

"So, you decided to tough it out with the BBC?"

"Yes, until Sky came calling and offered me a post as head of business." Tarrying, Hamer became inquisitive. "But what is driving this questioning about the media?"

"Huh," Lapham began, "My wife Renata has a huge bee in her bonnet about a Radio Islington talk-show host. Apparently, this person has an extreme anti-English agenda, and seeing you, I thought that you might be able to bring some clarity to the impression."

"Jarred O'Gara, is it?"

"Why, *yes*. Renata gets so agitated by him. I've told her it's probably an act, the self-same ruse employed by many presenters to gain audience share. Am I right?"

"You mean, some intentionally embrace a controversial approach as a means of increasing audience ratings?"

"I do."

"Let me try to demystify O'Gara for you." Knowingly smiling, Hamer divulged, "He has an omnipotent reputation for hamming up the airwaves. Whether it is put on to generate controversy luring both like-political advocates and detractors like your wife to swell ratings and thereby entice advertisers, or whether he is genuinely an unbending leftie, is a matter of conjecture."

"So, it could be an act?"

"Well, just let me say, it's a well-known admission that radio and television often encourage viewer and listener centric employees to err towards the controversial."

"What about this O'Gara chap? Has he been chivvied up?"

"Ostensibly, he's a fully paid up member of the anything that is politically correct supporters club."

"Oh, so Renata might have a point?"

"Yes. O'Gara has gained a reputation for irritating and winding up people. He's so PC, I swear to God his arse squeaks. True, a lot of the commercial media go out of their way to be contentious, but O'Gara really means it. Because his show pulls in a huge national and international audience, Radio Islington has allowed him to run riot." Becoming philosophical, he put forward, "It's human frailty that we are all stimulated to react when a broadcaster raises our hackles with a pro-Johnny foreigner, anti-English rant. O'Gara has capitalised on this to boost his Radio Islington ratings and...make a lot of money for himself. Though O'Gara comes from a privileged background, he is a staunch leftie. Even the left-loving BBC told him to tone down his oh-so-obvious anti-England bias before they'd allow him to present *Newsnight*. It's not just show. He is a nasty zealot. His baseline persona is obnoxious. He will play Renata until she goes loopy. Best she tunes into another radio station."

* * *

O'Gara continued to draw Renata's displeasure. Every mid-morning when she tuned into Radio Islington, he took great pleasure in dissecting conservative fraternities and as she told Ripley, 'Licking the rear-ends of his chosen people like they dripped honey'. Mounting on a daily basis, her vexation finally erupted over the airwaves when O'Gara tagged anyone who intended to vote to leave the EU as racist, the gibe guaranteeing immigrants phoning in to his show supported his distinction and English people vehemently opposed the label.

So incensed by the pigeonhole, she called O'Gara's phone-in number and became selected to air her view.

"Hello, you're through to the *Jarred O'Gara Show*," O'Gara welcomed. "Who am I talking to?"

"My name is Renata Lapham."

"Ah, I recognise the name."

"Yes, we've previously crossed swords."

Neglecting the pugnacious riposte, he got straight down to business. "What's your take on those voting to leave the EU, Renata?"

"I think they are quite within their rights to vote either way, and I strongly object to you labelling those who choose to vote out as racists."

"Oh, I see. May I enquire which way you intend to vote?"

"I will be voting out."

"May I ask why?"

"Simple economic realities."

"Go on."

"If you add our annual EU membership bill to the value of EU imports into the UK and subtract the value of UK exports to the EU, we have perpetually been in a monumental deficit, meaning in the red on the deal since Heath foxed the nation into EEC membership in 1973."

"How do you know?" he stubbornly interrogated.

"Because I got the data from the Office for National Statistics covering the period from 1973 to the present. Add up the total deficit to date and it amounts to over £1000 billion. It's a con on a massive scale which needs to be stopped and the only way to accomplish that is to vote out of the EU. That £1000 billion could have been used to improve the lives of English people instead of being squandered on foreigners abroad."

"Don't you believe in the fellowship of mankind?"

"Liberal-minded poppycock," she convicted, "fashioned by those who do not live in the real world. I believe in what is best for England and her indigenous people, as does every other autonomous nation on the Earth strive for what is best for them. We have been royally conned by politicians on both sides of the political divide into accepting multiculturalism, and those same pariahs are milking our EU contributions to feather their own nests."

"So I suppose you support UKIP and the views of Nigel Farage?"

"As a matter of fact, yes. He is the only sane voice telling the truth about the liberal-fascist EU and their desire to subsume England into an EU-wide federal state."

"Don't you think the EU has done a lot of good with harmonising laws and regulations allowing the UK to trade with our continental neighbours?"

"Claptrap, Mister O'Gara. England had long established trading links throughout Europe going back centuries before the infernal EU lassoed them."

"So, is this why you intend to vote out?"

"Yes. We want our sovereign independence reinstated. We want the ability to make our own decisions without having to consult the blessed EU."

"Would that include who you would allow into England?"

"Yes, and it's not just EU immigrants wanting to take advantage of our social support systems and the NHS. In point of fact, it's mainly immigrants arriving from outside of the EU. The latter group form at least ninety percent of immigrants and asylum seekers allowed into England and economically speaking they contribute very little to nothing."

"How do you know?"

"Because again I consulted ONS. As an example, their analysis shows Britain is sinking under unproductive Muslims, costing £13billion a year. Sixty-three percent of Muslim men and seventy-eight percent of Muslim women do not work. Muslims have also changed the face of the country with clear ambitions to make it into an Islamic province. There are twenty-eight Muslim mayors, over 3,000 mosques, 130 Sharia courts, fifty Muslim councils and Muslim-only-go areas across the UK."

"Don't you think we should help these people to find jobs?"

"That's *precisely* the point, Mister O'Gara. In the main they have no skills and they don't want to work. They prefer to milk the State. It's the only reason why they come here."

"Some people say they are discriminated against for jobs and that explains their dependence on the welfare system. Surely, we should bend the rules to make it easier for them to find jobs?"

"If they're unqualified to do any jobs, why were they allowed into the country in the first place? And I think you'll find most English people do not like positive discrimination, quota allocations and everything about political correctness."

"Why?"

"Because these socially engineered instruments have been the axiomatic elements behind the rise of the mediocrity into positions of influence, power and authority in England for the last twenty-five years. In the process, standards have declined in every walk of life, all to make these non-English people feel inclusive, even if they are inadequate, lamebrains and misfits incapable of doing the job. It has spawned the downward slope and degradation of English culture and values."

"That's just your opinion and the government statistics you quote are biased. Any set of figures can be manipulated to present the required argument."

"Well, how about this one, and it comes from your fellow PC addicts at the BBC. According to them, by the year 2100, the white race may not exist."

"So what!"

"*So what*," she echoed with venom. "If it had been one of your chosen races set for extermination, you would be up in arms."

"Are you a racist, Renata?"

"How *dare* you. You label anyone who does not relish the prospect of our country being swamped with immigrants and irreversibly changing the face of England as racist. All sovereign countries want to preserve their national identity and that includes your cherished African and Asian federations. They don't allow multiculturalism, so why should England be subjected to it?"

After dismissing her charge with all kinds of fashionable, off-the-shelf soundbites, O'Gara finished with, "you are definitely a racist, Renata. Next caller, please."

Infuriated by being cut off, she slammed down the phone, her DAB radio also coming in for more punishment. Meanwhile O'Gara continued to soft-soap oh-so-obvious immigrant callers to his programme supporting his vote out of the EU allegation and denigrating anyone opposing his demarcation as racist. Over the succeeding few weeks, O'Gara sustained his anti-English rhetoric, Renata phoning into his show on multiple occasions but never selected for airtime. Her discontent amplifying, she grew to detest O'Gara to the point whereby she planned to do him the ultimate harm.

* * *

One morning immediately after Ridley had left for work, she walked to Epsom rail station, bought a one-day zones' one and two travel card and caught the seven thirty to Waterloo.

Descending into the bowels of the London Underground, she then jumped on a Jubilee Line train, exiting at London Bridge and changing to the Northern Line conveying her all the way to Islington Underground Station. Surfacing into busy Highbury Station Road, she established her bearings and made for Laycock Street, home to Radio Islington. Outside the radio station, she checked her wristwatch. It read 9:12 a.m.. Spying about knowing his radio transmission began at 10:00 a.m., she checked for O'Gara's arrival. Sure enough, before the time reached the bottom of the hour, he appeared carrying a briefcase and looking extremely smug. Tempted to race up to him and give him a piece of her mind, she managed to apply self-restraint and merely glared at the radio presenter. She knew his show finished at 1:00 p.m. and soon thereafter he'd reappear, make his way to Islington station and return home. She didn't quite know what she was going to do, other than track his movements.

At 10:00 a.m. she logged onto Radio Islington on her IPhone for the commencement of the *Jarred O'Gara Show*, listening through a connecting earpiece. As usual, O'Gara praised anything pro-left-wing and decimated opposing views. Periodically, she blurted something in response to his biased rhetoric, sometimes attracting the attention of passersby. Kicking her heels after 1:00 p.m. when his programme finished, she waited for him to materialise outside the radio station again, then followed him to Islington station.

He made for the Victoria Line southbound platform, Renata less than twenty steps behind him. Boarding a train, she followed suit. Riding the Victoria Line all the way to Victoria rail station, O'Gara then changed to the Wimbledon District Line west, eventually disembarking at Fulham Broadway and walking to a plush four-storey townhouse in Musgrove Crescent with outlooks over Eel Brook Common, Renata never losing sight of him. Stopping on the common side of Musgrove Crescent opposite the townhouse O'Gara had entered she took in its opulence thinking, *here is yet another pious social commentator with 'a do as I say, not as I do' credo*.

Backtracking to Fulham Broadway, she boarded an eastbound District Line train, changed at Embankment for the Bakerloo Line alighting at Waterloo, then caught the 4:10 back to Epsom, arriving home well before her husband returned from his day's labours.

Repeating the process for the next two consecutive days, she made sure she had O'Gara's schedule off pat. On day two, whilst listening to his usual anti-English diatribe, she noticed four other people, three men and one woman, milling around the area immediately adjacent to Radio Islington she thought she might have seen the previous day. Thinking nothing more about the discovery, on day three, once again the same set were present, not in a mutual recognition of friends, but in a loosely-connected collaborative circle, eyeing each other surreptitiously.

On day one, the coterie had moved off before O'Gara sprung from Radio Islington, making for Islington Underground Station, the same action occurring on day two. By day three, knowing where O'Gara headed after his show, she followed the faction, noting they entered Islington Underground Station and hung around the ticket area awaiting his arrival. Then in the hustle and bustle of travelers scampering for the two underground and two over-ground lines, she lost sight of them when O'Gara arrived and followed him to the Victoria Line. Leaving Fulham Broadway, instead of training her vision exclusively on O'Gara, as she had done on the previous two days, whilst walking at a discreet distance to Musgrove Crescent behind him, she scanned about, clocking two of the four patrollers on the opposite side of the street.

During her return journey to Epsom, an almost cinematic scene unfolded in her mind. Could it be she postulated the loosely-connected cartel were on the same mission she had adopted?

Buoyed up by the possible determination the following week, Renata repeated her O'Gara surveillance, noting the same four people milling around Laycock Street. Though she listened to O'Gara's transmission on her IPhone, her attention became more drawn by the collective. They never seemed to exchange a single word, their eyelines purposely aimed so as to avoid eye contact with each other, albeit each was certainly aware of the others' presence.

Tempted to take the initiative, Renata considered making an approach to the gathering, but with what objective in mind? If she asked the question, 'Why are you here every day during the *Jarred O'Gara show*?' she became concerned about what the answer might be. Still not totally sure why she continued with the three-times a week pilgrimage and vigil, and what her intentions were with respect to the exasperating radio talk-show host, she struggled for coherence. Topping the in exactitude, she hypothesised she might be shocked by her fellow watchers possible designs.

So as to keep her husband out of the picture and prevent him asking tricky questions, Renata crammed her usual five-days commercial artist work into two weekdays and the weekend hours when Ridley played golf. If he knew what she was up to, it would lead to a showdown. Whatever she was going to do, she didn't want him implicated through knowledge of her intended actions. Knowing him to be perpetually consumed in microbiology drivers when at home, the subterfuge worked, Ridley merely going through his 'how was your day' carry-out on return from work, Renata making her usual complaints about O'Gara and telling him about her commercial art labours.

* * *

Come the following weekend, whilst reading the Sunday newspapers with Ridley in their capacious conservatory, Renata came across an article in *The Observer* examining the impact of Jarred O'Gara on the airwaves. Including in part an interview with the bothersome radio host, O'Gara made no bones about his confrontational approach to goading what he deemed to be 'right-wing, reactionary bigots' and reinforcing his belief that it should not be an issue if England were to be completely dominated by immigrants and asylum seekers, especially those of Third World origins.

"*Unbelievable*," she blurted.

"Something got your goat, dear?" Ridley enquired.

"This piece in *The Observer* about O'Gara. He just can't resist the temptation to impugn the English nation on every media occasion, with accusations that anyone who does not support England being overrun with immigrants is a right-wing, reactionary bigot. And what's worse is the cornerstone on which O'Gara operates has been instituted by the new cross-party establishment founded by Blair. It has put loaded paraphernalia in place to give the impression we participate in a majority vote democracy. But that's just a front, an illusion to disguise the fact that we live under a benign dictatorship where we are told what we have to accept and that set of constructs is instituted in subjective law."

"So are you saying O'Gara is a symptom of the regime?"

"Indeed, I am."

"*Oohh*," he began, collapsing the broadsheet he read and near-to exasperated by her continuing anti-O'Gara crusade, "though I appreciate your justified denunciation of this fellow, can't you find something else in the vast media spectrum to absorb your intellect and dilute conspiracy suspicions?"

"All the Sundays seem to be full of the same platitudes," she retaliated, "their sense of integrity expunged from the editorial itinerary by an adherence to the PC agenda. We are wallowing in the ever-expanding maelstrom of the second reformation, where witch-finder generals like O'Gara purge the country of anti-PC heresy. The parochial doctrine is more deep-seated than McCarthyism intolerance, has greater acidic properties than communism or fascism, and its consequences are vastly more far-reaching than the Spanish inquisition."

"Why?"

"Because the PC crowd have hitched their evangelising chariot to the potency of the internet revolution to instantaneously report transgressors and brand them without recourse. Unlike the bludgeoning utilities harnessed by latter-day tyrants, information technology is not transitory. It becomes more ubiquitous with every passing day, reaching into everyone's consciousness via the ever-enlarging usage of computers and mobile devices, hitting users with contentious news generated by the indulgent moralists. Taking more and more latitude without redress to subjugate the nation permanently into accepting their dogma, they will not stop until everyone has been mesmerised by their credo or...we fight back and restore our nation."

"You know—" In an attempt to diffuse her anger, he paused to smile at her. "Just regressing to your previous priori, *integrity* is an abstract concept," he argued. "Majority vote does not necessarily equate with right, but I will admit if the minority view is upheld, it merely becomes a whim, a conscious driver of the minority they subject the majority to. In many ways the dichotomy has been born out of the absurdities and excesses of party tribalism producing an artificial middle-ground of consensus in Parliament that satisfies nobody in the electorate."

"That's what I find so galling, Ridley." Rising from her chair and taking a few paces forward to superficially rearrange some magazines on a coffee table, she then recounted, "Not so long ago, I read a piece in *The Spectator* saying the chattering metropolitan classes have subjected rural man to PC pap and when he reacted adversely, they bound him and supplied the spoon for him to gulp down the enforced orthodoxy whilst they watched. It's as if ordinary, normal, taxpaying people already spinning to the tune of work and family demands have additionally been sucked into a vortex created by this new elite and are expected to sing and dance to their sanctimonious melody, knowing full well it is harming them."

"Okay," he conceded, hoping her complaint had become exhausted, "I'll grant you, you make an unarguable point."

Reversing her trek to sit down, then rustling her newspaper, she did not respond immediately. Then her recently gained impetuous nature got the better of her and she blasted, "Independent of apparently being granted the mandate to run roughshod over the English by his preachy and puritanical overlords, O'Gara is just another woolly-headed, liberal-elitist do-gooder playing God. A traitorous fool sponsoring the destruction of our country by the invading hordes. Is there no limit to his treasonous fulminations?" Dwelling, she issued her husband a grim lour. "There are parallels with Hitler's Third Reich happening here. Hitler and the Nazis first gained limited power in the media then in the Reichstag, before enacting schemes to ensure the acquisition of unopposed power. Though only a minority clique, through careful manipulation of the media and wholesale indoctrination, they branded the entire German nation as dedicated Nazi followers in the perceptions of the outside world. Clearly, not all Germans who fought in World War II were devoted Nazis. They had no choice, fight or be shot. Certainly, Hitler succeeded in destroying much of Western Europe and the

Russian hinterlands and killing hundreds of millions of people, but his regime did equal harm to Germany and his own citizens."

"You're intimating the PC camp is doing the same thing in England."

"Well, Ridley, there is irrefutable proof published virtually every day in the dailies and on the internet. People inadvertently saying the wrong thing sent back to correction school for a solid dose of 're-education', anyone questioning the probity of the PC blueprint castigated in public and fired from their jobs, opposition groups either forced into disbanding or jailed. It has the same resonance about it as Hitler's brown shirts applied to anti-Nazi factions in the 1930s. Just goes to show, a minority group can brand an entire nation in the perception of the outside world and have them believe we are all good, little, conformist PC freaks."

Crunching her assertion, he then responded, "You might consider there's a hall of mirrors effect going on here."

"How do you mean?"

"A confusing or disorienting situation in which it is difficult to distinguish between truth and illusion or competing versions of reality."

"Sounds like you are giving O'Gara the benefit of the doubt."

"On the contrary, I'm attempting to bring some brio to this on-going conflict."

"How?"

"Last time we spoke about O'Gara at length, you conceded his apparent anti-English act could be a front, a ruse, to generate resentment and thus gain airtime market share."

"I did, but there's just too much vitriol in his manner to suggest he does not believe in anything less than he is saying. There is no tongue-in-cheek delivery to soften his trenchant words. If anything, he gets more stringent and immovable with each passing broadcast, his self-belief in the PC bile he spouts, boundless."

"Even if he does mean what he says, put his position into perspective. He is a radio talk-show host with no consigned or legitimate muscle. Such agencies lay in Westminster with the majority-elected government. Now—" He leaned forward to give elan to his argument.

"Do you really think a government would allow immigration to get to the point whereby the indigenous population is slowly but surely eradicated in some form of passive ethnic cleansing?"

"Ridley," she launched, a sliver of verve in her timbre, her vitality kindled, "You seem to forget there is a very cosy relationship between the left-wing of any party elected to office and the media, and…many left-wing media pundits end up in politics."

"That is true, but can you really see this caucus applying the politically correct dogma to the extent they endanger their own wellbeing?"

"If I'm reading the ONS figures right, extrapolating the inward migration trend rate which is doubling year-on year since Blair first took office plus the procreation pace of those already settled, the lefties will be overrun and subsumed by the very people they put on a pedestal and sponsored their rise in society to positions of dominance."

"Ohh, Renata, that's a bit fanciful," he chided. "It takes a tremendous leap of faith to even consider this grand old country of ours will end up with immigrants taking absolute power and the English wiped out by fair means or foul. I mean…the one aspect you have got right is plainly, the vast majority of immigrants into England, certainly those from Eastern Europe and the Third World do not possess the intellect, invention and insight traditionally associated with English people going back at least ten centuries. Thereby, if this foreign camp were to be assigned key positions via positive discrimination and quotas in industry, commerce and the civil service, the house would quickly tumble down."

"Well, you might consider that is *exactly* what they want!"

Astounded by the claim, at first Ridley fell silent, then engaging his logical brain countered, "But they'd be killing the goose laying the golden eggs, meaning private sector English taxpayers funding the benefits system, that the vast majority of immigrants rely on."

"Mmmm, I think you may be too consumed with microbiology and golf to appreciate what is really going on."

"Explain."

"Immigrants congregate in ghettos, achieve majority votes in a ward and vote in their own kind as councillors and mayors. Irregardless of what political flag immigrant candidates fly, their own kind tend to vote for them. It's laid the path to authority open to Muslim and black extremists. Once they achieve a population majority, such fanatics could turn England into an Islamic dominion run by mullahs or a satellite colony in the Central African Republic."

"Again, it's hyperbole, speculation…worst case outcome."

"Yes, but nonetheless a possibility, and PC freaks like O'Gara are instrumental in laying the ground for the takeover." Glancing at her laptop, she then shared, "I did some research into the effects of the literal-minded intolerance of the social justice brigade. Did you know Twitter and other social media platforms have become weaponised, and those in the public limelight are self-censoring and withholding their true opinions for fear of being ostracised by this prudish set and consequently forced into resigning or being sacked?"

"I'm not a social media fan, so no."

"Apparently, you're entitled to hold any opinions you like, so long as they're the *'right'* opinions. Cancel culture or call-out culture is a modern form of excommunication, whereby someone is thrust out of social or professional circles, either online on social media, in the real world, or both, for contravening the 'right' code. Those who are subject to this banishment are said to be 'cancelled.'"

"You don't say."

"More seriously, the social justice junkies organise cultural combat events where the likes of Caroline Lucas, Will Self, Jarred 'O'Gara of course, and other prominent lefties pronounce judgment on those earmarked with breaking their self-appointed moral code by doubting the tenets of positive discrimination and quotas in favour of certain pressure-group untouchables. It warrants the question, why can't the holy cow faction placed on high just be offended and upset, as opposed to being offended and upset and seeing it as their right to obliterate the offender?"

"I must say, such a disfigurement of the social media and the creeping threat of cultural policing does not bode well for the future. It reeks of liberal-fascism."

"Precisely. Perfectly sound and reasonable people are treading tentatively across the new-media firing range, as if nervous about stepping on a troll-mine."

Meditating for a few instants, he then recapped, "Interestingly enough, I recently met someone on the financing side of the microbial systematics camarilla. He told me, when he's at work, it's like Orwell's *Nineteen-Eighty-Four*, and when he's at home, it's like Huxley's *Brave New World*. Huh, I must admit, that gives some credence to your research."

* * *

Resuming her Radio Islington patrol, additional to the principle four she had previously seen, Renata clocked more people hanging around Laycock Street during O'Gara's transmitted radio show. She questioned herself as to if they had been present on previous occasions, and she had failed to detect their presence because of being so consumed with scanning for O'Gara and listening to his programme. She wondered if they had the same harm planned for him she intended to carry out. Now fully cognisant at least nine others additional to herself milled around outside Radio Islington, she tried to remember their faces.

On the following day, like taking a class register, Renata mentally recorded the same nine faces she had previously clocked. Unlike when she detected the original four, intermittently they stared at each other, and her, but no one ever spoke or made body language signals. Like Renata, they remained lone hunters, stalking their prey but aware other predators might make the kill.

By the third day of the week, she also recognised the two of the original four watchers who had pursued O'Gara all the way to his Musgrove Crescent abode, as she did, no longer initiated their Islington to Fulham trek. Like the rest of the voyeurs, having seen their quarry board the southbound Victoria Line train, they remained at Islington Underground Station, fixing the carriage containing O'Gara and herself until it disappeared into the blackness of a connecting tunnel.

Unremittingly, the status quo went on for another two weeks, the lurkers inclusive of Renata following the same daily ritual, waiting for O'Gara's arrival and following him to Islington Underground Station after delivering his show. She desperately wanted to communicate with at least one of her fellow gawkers to verify they were on the same mission, but something inside told her none of them would salute her, just like they did not acknowledge each other. Instead of pursuing O'Gara to Fulham, she decided to remain on the Victoria Line platform at Islington Underground Station and scrutinise them.

When O'Gara left Radio Islington, walking without rush, looking his usual smug self and apparently without a care in the world to the tube station, as always he remained oblivious to his followers mingling in the crowded Islington streets and the equally crowded station, Renata following suit. As he stood on the platform awaiting his train, she noted all nine gogglers fixed him with fierce consolidation, sustaining the blaze until he boarded the train. Then the intensity seemed to slacken, the sentinels dropping into a sullen order, they merely eyed the departing train.

After the penetration exercise waned, the nine looked away, absorbed themselves with other stimuli, then like Renata, boarded the next train. Presumably, she imagined, like her, making for their homes.

Engaging the same discipline twice the next week, Renata observed the nine perusing O'Gara with venom on the Islington underground station Victoria Line platform. On the third occasion, remarkably, after O'Gara's train had departed, she felt their biting gleam on her. Compelled to return their stares, she eyeballed each of the nine, some sort of symbiotic communication occurring, light-headedness overwhelming her and opening her mind up to suggestion. Intrinsically, she knew what they wanted her to do.

Back home, she cascaded into delirium, images of O'Gara and

the nine floating about in her mind. She figured nine was not enough, but ten might be.

* * *

When Ridley returned home from work, he found his wife to be unusually prepossessed, her customary greeting nondescript, her habitual tendency to engage him in some issue or another surfacing during her day, vacant. To all intents and purposes, she appeared depleted of her everyday personality. Puzzled and concerned, he questioned if something had happened to cause her apparent befuddled disorder. Temporarily rising above her rapt in inertia shape, she faked she had a headache, the excuse only partially placating her husband's anxiety. Querying if she needed a doctor, her vigour grew, Renata assuring him the encumbrance would pass. Nevertheless, during the course of the evening, he detected no improvement in her condition as she again lapsed into lassitude. Retiring for the night, Renata's torpor still bothered Ridley.

A sound sleeper, he did not awake when his wife got out of their bed after several hours of tossing and turning without achieving the same blissful state. Peering through the bedroom window, her note became drawn by a solitary fox meandering across the front lawn, nose down, scavenging for food scents. Fascinated by its foraging, she began to see herself as the fox and any tasty nugget it might find and devour as Jarred O'Gara. She imagined the radio host slept soundly in his Fulham mansion, totally unaware later in the day he would meet his maker. Wrecked with indecision regarding her participation in the quest, her mind drifted, settling on the first occurrence she had come across his show whilst frequency hopping on her new DAB radio.

Before that watershed happening, she had been a normal-everyday person, sound in her thinking, steady in her actions and not easily aroused by scurrilous cant. During her time at art college, she had developed a detached emotional discipline granting her the ability to engage her studies with an objective attitude, her invention with painting materials enabling her to originate strong subject matter themes in response to course topics, the ability making the transition into the world of commercial art well within her talent spectrum. Capitalising on the precepts, her career and personal life had flowered. It was only in relatively recent times concomitant from her Jarred O'Gara Show entanglement that she had succumbed to tetchiness and an inability to control her sensibilities. She wanted to get back to her previous sanguine, calm and collected identity, a desire only achievable if O'Gara could be obliterated from the airwaves.

During breakfast the next morning, Ridley noted her preoccupied mood still persisted. Revisiting the option to call for a doctor, she waved aside his disquiet, insisting she'd be fine by the time he came home from work. Trusting his wife's previous impeccable track record of delivering on promises, Ridley left at his usual time.

* * *

Following in her near-to-daily footsteps, Renata wound up on Laycock Street to find the nine were already present and dispersed at irregular intervals outside Radio Islington. As she passed them en route to her usual station, she felt their glare upon her personage, their message clear, their calling resolute. When O'Gara materialised, the nine faded into the procession of passing people going about their business, Renata also adopting measures to disguise her picket until the talk-show host went inside the Radio Islington building. Though wanting to see the demise of the infuriating O'Gara, throughout the morning, she experienced cold sweats and had multiple qualms about joining the nine. In the cold light of day, disposing of someone, albeit merited, remained a heavy duty, duelling with O'Gara voice-to-voice child's play compared to wielding the terminating axe.

She remembered a juncture from her junior schooldays, when a school minibus she travelled in coming back from a hike in the Brecon Beacons collided with an out-of-control flatbed lorry, the minibus forced into a ditch after the lorry impaled itself into the minibus driver side. In charge of the school party, a teacher got the children out of the stricken conveyance, then dragged the unconscious minibus driver from his seat and well away from the crash site. Trapped in his cab by the impact of the collision but still alive, the teacher then attempted to extract the lorry driver, the school children, watching the endeavour from cover.

During the impact, the minibus fuel tank became ruptured, petrol seeping onto the hot engine of the lorry. Catching alight, the schoolchildren recoiled as the teacher fought to unlatch the lorry passenger door, jammed consequent from the smash. When the fire bloomed to engulf the lorry cabin and the driver screamed, the rescuer became consumed in discordant contentions.

If he sustained his action, when the petrol tank exploded he might be killed, if he receded to safety, the lorry driver would meet a grisly end. As the fire thrived, the attendant heat forced him to back away. When the fuel tank detonated, the resultant blast blew him off his feet, the lorry driver perishing in the flames. Shocked by the incident, subsequently the schoolteacher underwent psychiatric examination. He blamed himself for not having the strength to rescue the lorry driver, the thorny admission nettling his thoughts day and night.

Analogously, Renata put herself in the schoolteacher's role and cast O'Gara as the lorry driver. Could she watch as he met his end?

As the morning relentlessly ticked by, her queasiness increased, her misgivings amplified. She listened to the *Jarred O'Gara Show* on her IPhone, as did the nine on their listen-in devices, his hobbyhorse that morning being ethnic transgenderism and why this group should be given singular preference in the jobs marketplace. As usual, minority proponents were allotted unlimited airtime and any caller objecting to the forcing of round pegs into square holes summarily castigated as a bigot and cut off, the offensive partition buttressing her hankering to see the defamatory radio presenter's reign permanently ended.

Caught in a maelstrom of indecision, she rocked between her squeamishness at his demise and the desire for his terminus.

Then, at ten-after-one, O'Gara exited Radio Islington, his physiognomy wrought with customary smugness. Like soldiers facing an imminent battle, the nine riveted their vision on his movement, Renata also transfixing him. Striding away, as ever completely unaware of his trackers, O'Gara quickly reached Islington station and headed for the Victoria southbound line, standing near to the edge of the platform and staring at the advertisements on the opposite wall he usually gawped at while waiting for the train.

Moments later, the nine took their usual places behind him, Renata hanging back on the passenger tunnel steps above the platform, still unsure what she intended to do. Then something clicked in her mind; a positive action, disposing of the thorn in her side meant radio listening without being made to feel like a bad apple in her own country. Gathering her wits, she stepped forward onto the platform, some fifteen feet away from O'Gara. Instead of clocking her fellow beholders as per previous occasions, like them, she focused her mental competencies through her peepers at O'Gara. As if drawn together through joint-collaboration, the nine and Renata then moved to form a close-knit cohesive unit, collectively concentrating their mental energies on the radio host in a unified power beam.

After a minute of concerted mental telepathy, O'Gara swivelled from looking at the advertising. Gazing into their midst, he seemed mesmerised by their commonwealth coercion. Out of his cognizance, the station visual annunciator displayed VICTORIA TRAIN 30 seconds, travelers hearing the distant woosh sound of its approach. Reaching a crescendo, it burst into the underground station, its transit creating a draft making platform commuters cling onto their hats and belongings.

Like Wyndham's *Midwich Cuckoos* drilling a victim to submit to their will, O'Gara felt the full-force of his accusers' penetrating dazzles, their missive clear and unrelenting. Unable to prevent losing his balance, he toppled off the platform and into the path of the on-coming juggernaut, his skull splitting between the nearside rail and the train's leading wheel, sending little rhythmic arcs of blood into travelers yet to fully comprehend what had happened.

JOURNEYS END

JOURNEYS END

Tired and sticky, Kory Farnham arrived at the Fort George Hotel mid-afternoon, heading straight to the bar. His flight from Houston into Belize City had been ghastly, excessive passenger pandemonium, a surly steward and inedible food proving to be overwhelming factors propelling him nigh into despair. By the time he had quenched his thirst and reached his room, an extended bathing session became his only desire.

Sliding into the bath and resting his head against it, he began to feel more human again. Luxuriating in the soothing water, he retraced his foremost impressions of Belize. Just like he had seen in movies set in 1940s South America, locals had danced to samba music on the roof of the small airport building. Unlatching his bags and summarily rifling amidst their contents, the customs official looked disappointed not to have discovered contraband. As he meandered across the arrivals concourse, a dapper man dressed like a New York pimp had sidled up to him, enquiring if he needed a senorita for the night. Taken aback, he replied in the negative waving the ponce aside. When at last he emerged from the arrivals exit into the sweltering heat of the ex-British colonial territory, his immediate covet centred on a long, thirst-quenching drink. He figured heat to be a constant companion needing subduing for the visit to be a fruitful endeavour. Adding to his discomfort, the taxi carrying him to the hotel had no air conditioning. Wanting a breeze to take away the furnace-like temperature, he wound the windows open, only to find the outside atmosphere even hotter. Attired in a Carman Miranda rig, an effervescent black lady welcomed him at reception with a beaming smile, entreated him to call her Mama Celeste, and gave him directions to the hotel bar where he drained a Belikin in one.

Leaving the taps running, as the tub filled, he part-floated, his arms breaching the surface, his feet bobbing up and down against its base. His nausea quelled, he entered cogitation mode wondering what else lay ahead in his stopover.

Adrift in an arduous and demanding literati landscape, his second novel elaboration had stalled, leaving him in rudderless disorder. Back in Canterbury, it brought on a brusque temper, and had him arguing with his wife Candice. Since quitting his job at the *Telegraph* to concentrate on private writing, she had become the main breadwinner, covering all domestic bills, including the mortgage. Additionally, after good reviews and early adopter sales, revenues from his prior published book had faltered, Candice left to involuntary take care of his personal luxuries as well, mainly the *Courvoisier* brandy he drank when invention deserted him. A pivotal principle for her, rather than a practical absolute, she pressed him for results. They were hardly on their uppers, but she felt if not corrected soon, the revenue deficit might become unstoppable, spiralling into a critical economic issue and causing renewed friction. Sustaining her onslaught, she wanted him to park his alter ego, return to journalism, and forget about composing novels.

Worse, and a juxtaposed dichotomy, his agent swearing a second book was imperative to sustain momentum, only aggravated the complication and the pressure. Farnham had struggled with the task, without either cogent inspiration or lucid imagination coming to the fore to relieve professional necessities, and thereby household axioms. He resided bereft of innovative ideas, and those writing constructs which did come, were glacially slow, taking hour upon hour to coalesce into tangible and coherent text.

Lying naked on his bed listening to crickets chirping outside the window, and gawking up at a whirring ceiling fan, its downdraft drying traces of moisture from his lithe body, he replayed the thorny issues but came up short in terms of resolutions. Still to be combed, his dark hair splayed on the pillow, Farnham disinclined to appear well-presented should he receive an uncalled-for knock on the door from a hotel maid wanting to turn back his bed sheets. Irritated by a chin bone itch, he scratched the offending area, finding the five o'clock stubble begun at Heathrow had thickened. Self-conscious of his bedraggled state, he made for his electric shaver, but abruptly stopped, deciding to keep the facial growth. Falling in tune with his new surroundings and geographical placement, he recalled Hemmingway had grown a beard when he used Key West as a winter shelter from the snow-bound wastes of Wyoming, to compose his stellar undertakings. Acting as a trigger, the recollection reignited longings about the need to write, and the requisite to placate Candice.

* * *

Beautiful Candice, bright and dazzling Candice, worthy of stupendous love and life-long devotion, had bowled him over the instant he saw her standing in line at a general store's post office facility in Old Dover Road, Canterbury. A game changer moment, she took his breath away. After both had transacted their postal business, he summoned up all his courage to speak to her as she perused birthday cards in an adjoining part of the store.

Now, in the entirely heterogeneous milieu of a Belize hotel, he could not remember what he had said, but whatever the nucleus conveyed, it did the trick. He'd found himself gazing into her enormous grey-blue eyes and planning, I'm going to marry you one day.

That happy event happened less than a year afterwards. With things bordering perfection on all fronts by means of shared agreement and fulfilment, the Farnhams enjoyed a bountiful and rewarding lifestyle. Early in the burgeoning relationship, they had a kind of simpatico happening between them, *inter alia* the unmasking of a reciprocative love of cricket, both having inherited the interest from their respective fathers. While Candice abided as a spectator and avid records keeper, her future husband played for the Pilgrims Way Club in the Canterbury & District Cricket League. Both attended county cricket matches at the St Lawrence Ground, unfailingly witnessing Kent demolish all comers with consummate verve and aplomb.

Fulfilling idyllic qualities with trivial effort, the status quo lingered for two years, then his private scribing ambitions began to bite, neither he or Candice realising it would culminate in broken harmony and ultimately, discord and a cracked union.

His earlier oeuvre, *Vanquish the Bold*, the often heart-rendering story of a society discarded, battlefield-weary Falklands War veteran, and his subsequent salvation from drugs and self-harm, had come easy for him to write. Inwardly accumulating story marrow for years, his craftsmanship evolved into a matter of transcribing from the mind into the written word, then polishing and fine tuning the primer to achieve the finished article. When the book started to sell, he reasoned his decision to quit the *Telegraph* had been vindicated. Then pressure arrived from his publisher via his agent for a second work.

Wrestling with the brute for three months, he wrote over 50,000 words but edited most of them out, nothing of any *bona fide* or noteworthy consequence arriving in his consciousness, worthy of advancing the thesis spirit, or appending secondary elements to the baseline notion.

Tensions grew between Candice and him, at times, pals and family picking up on the jagged atmosphere fabricated by their impasse. It led to fragmented social occasions, steeped in the tapering of eyes and the throwing back of heads, onlookers not knowing whether to diplomatically retire, or furnish support and sympathy. Torn between appropriate husbandly responsibilities, and the craving to leave his stamp on the bookish world, Kory Farnham avalanched into debilitation caused by trying to simultaneously address the opposing poles.

Although the Farnhams had estimable investments, most were tied up in long-term bonds. Those available for instant withdrawals were on the wane and hammering zero-bound if they sustained their nowadays rate of spend exceeding essential costs. As a means of helping cover habitual expenses, Candice encouraged her husband to at least do some freelance assignments for the *Telegraph*, but his focus weathered on the second novel exertion, his mind staunchly irreversible on the singularity. Obstinate she called it, when house guests enquired into the belletristic verses the utilitarian deadlock.

Decisively, the wordsmith announced if she continued to badger him about home economics, he'd need a change of stage to progress his new treatise. Though usually exhibiting a tolerant demeanour, Candice tarried adamant, refusing to withdraw what she appraised to be rational entreaties. Inevitably, the meltdown led to a critical reaction, he maintaining he had to get away for a while, Candice unambiguous she'd not stand in his way.

With their normal sanguine personas disengaged, they had not parted on good terms. Candice seething with resentment, Kory left under a cloud.

God, it's excruciatingly hot, he comprehended. No sooner had his body dried from bathing, perspiration reformed again. He wanted to sleep, but knew it roosted as impossible until night descended, his insomnia requiring pitch black even before sleep could be attempted. Deciding to make a stab at the folio, he unpacked and fired up his laptop, quickly finding the draft and staring at page one, a miscellany of disjointed wording displayed on the unforgiving screen. Scrolling the introductory chapters, he randomly read speech and connecting paragraphs. Nothing staggering or astounding, it cruised like flimflam, inadvertently architected to engender a mishmash of visions hanging without crystallised determination, and essays impoverished of wit and coherence. Farnham had come to Belize in the hope a divergent vista might provoke a deluge of paradigms. Nothing came, the page he weighed dwelling blank of new stanzas.

Frustrated and deflated he went to the window, gaping out on the cafés and bars on Marine Parade, and beyond, the eternal Caribbean. Hearing the hustle and bustle of late afternoon revellers intermingling with the strains of mestizo and kriol music drew his attention to the Fort George jetty, venue for a local street festival endpoint. Leaning out of the window to catch a better reckoning, his nose picked up the enticing aroma of garnache, tamales and conch fritter dishes soaring up on thermals from nearby kitchens.

Everything he beheld depicted the New World, with its adroit irregularity, uninhibited splurge into spontaneity, and complete retraction from rule obedience, a far cry from the restrictions and conformity of post-millennium England, labelled by a salute to political class pomposity, ostentatious PC piety, and finely tuned hypocrisy.

Kicking himself out of despondency, he pondered about Hemmingway, and how his sojourn to the south had kindled fresh energies and tangential trends in his writings. Belize represented his Key West equivalent, the place where he'd find his own *To Have and Have Not*.

* * *

Come the following day, Farnham donned a lightweight, off-white, two-piece suit and a cream coloured panama to shield his head from the fierce mid-summer sun. Hands in pockets, outwardly edgy but expectant, he ambled to the harbour, past the Baron Bliss Lighthouse and into the relaxed, laidback world of the pueblo. Seeking motivation, he gazed out on pleasure sailing vessels bobbing on their sea moorings, and cormorants and gannets amongst a host of extraneous seabirds coasting above them in a cloudless, brandeis blue sinking into translucent sky. At the promenade's extremity, he observed port-bound fishermen with their snapper variants and yellow tail jack catches, their tiny boats skipping over the surface like waterskis. Others on the beach prepared their larger craft for more heavy-duty activity, their quarry, tarpon and barracuda. Sparked off by the seascape composition, he conjured up Hemmingway's Santiago preparing his slender boat, before seafaring into the Caribbean to do battle with marlin. Continuing to scour for impulse distilled from the industrious quayside scene, still nothing came.

Thereafter, he sat in an old colonial chair on the veranda of a bar, sipping a cold Belikin whilst brooding again on the troublesome circumstances carrying him to Belize, until he heard the firm footsteps of someone crossing the wooden flooring of the bar before springing onto the veranda. Peeking to his left, he saw an extremely sun-tanned man, dressed in brilliant white apart from sable designer sunglasses, come into his field of regard. Attracted by Farnham's presence, the man removed the sunglasses revealing piercing blue eyes, then made his way over to him.

"Good morning," the stranger greeted. "It's not often someone else is in the Calypso Bar before noon. Do you mind if I join you?"

"No, not in the least, please pull up a chair."

"My name is Gerald Chaplin," he enlightened, submitting his right hand, Farnham rising to take it.

"How do you do, I'm Kory Farnham."

"Have you just arrived, Mister Farnham?"

"Came in yesterday from Houston."

"But you are not American."

"No, English. I'm from Canterbury."

"Canterbury, hhmm. My daughter studied at the University of Kent in Canterbury. She got the top honours in astrophysics. Are you a university man?"

Chortling at the remembrance of his degree years, Farnham replied, "Yes, but not in the study of astrophysics."

"Oh, what then?"

"Journalism at Birkbeck College."

Sitting opposite Farnham, Chaplin probed, "What brings you to Belize?"

Without exposing his soul totally, Farnham explained the motives for him being in Central America, Chaplin reciprocating with accomplishments from his own life CV.

Originally from Haslemere, and a Belize resident of ten years after retiring from the Foreign Office, he had bought a house on Hudson Street, not far from the US Embassy. Posted to the British High Commission in country capital Belmopan back in the 1970s, Chaplin and his wife had fallen in love with Belize, deciding to settle in the country on his retirement. Their conversation unfolded ancillary brass tacks, both men exchanging credentials and proficiencies before Farnham reiterated his principal focus for being in Belize, emphasising his objective to address his writer's block and finish the troublesome second novel.

"If it's a place of calmness for lettering you are tracking," Chaplin critiqued, "then Ambergris Caye is the location for you."

"Where's it situated?" Farnham investigated, his curiosity escalating.

"On a remote headland, thirty-five miles north, north east of Belize City. Maya Island Air runs a commuter flight every hour, seven to five, from Belize City to San Pedro, the only town on Ambergris Caye."

And the flight time?"

"Oh—" Chaplin beamed. "Fifteen minutes. You will be hither and yon before you know it. I recommend you to stay at Journeys End. It's quiet but elevating. Just the setting to make the words flow out effortlessly again."

"Could just be the right ticket for me."

Finalising their dialogue, Chaplin gave Farnham his contact details, insisting when he regressed to Belize City, they met again.

Miraculously, when Farnham got back to the Fort George, he felt inclined to write, the backdrop change coupled to his conversation with Chaplin and the anticipation of going to Ambergris Caye fully opening the creative valve. Charged up, he gushed off a new chapter.

* * *

Next day, Farnham took an early morning flight to San Pedro. Demonstrating the informality of the service, the twelve-passenger Cessna Caravan operated by Maya Island Air had been overbooked, last aboard, Farnham solicited to take the trip in the co-pilot's seat. Willingly accepting, he was thrilled at the prospect of a front aspect panorama of the flight, distinguishing such unpredictable bargains were only obtainable in England at the advent of commercial passenger flights, when Imperial Airways ran services from Croydon Airport in the early 1920s. Shaking his head he fleshed out, *in comparison modern commercial flights are sterile, tedious, and banally regimented from inception to finish, airbuses aptly named.*

As soon as the light aircraft hit 1,500 feet, the pilot made his descent into San Pedro. Ahead, Farnham made out the airstrip, not tarmac but hardened sand. Reinforcing the fancy Ambergris Caye held the astonishing and the unforeseen gained from Chaplin, he fervently prayed whatever thenceforth came equally spurred on his aesthetic bent.

Farnham had been booked into the Journeys End Resort by obliging Fort George Hotel Receptionist Mama Celeste. Grasping the Englishman had been enticed by the headlands' mystique, she told him Ambergris Caye had become a refuge for many Europeans and Americans. Backing up Chaplin's soft-sell, with a winsome smile she convinced him the trip held both amazement and spirit arousal.

Apart from narrow streets in San Pedro, there were no roads on Ambergris Caye. Located north of the town, on the east coast of the caye, Journeys End prevailed as only reachable by sea. Climbing aboard the hotel motor launch, its only passenger, once again Farnham marvelled at the trek's uniqueness in his occurrence log. As it sped over the seascape surface he foraged out to shore, seeing the jungle measurably thicken from the outskirts of San Pedro. Above the weird and wonderful tree line, distant hills bobbed up between the azure firmament merging into the greens and browns of the landscape. Breathing in deeply as sea spray splattered his facade, he took in the ozone like newly discovered nectar. Invariably, the fresh Canterbury rural countryside climate and the sea breezes at Herne Bay braced his nostrils, but both paled compared to the purity of the off-shore Caribbean Sea atmosphere.

As the cruiser slowed and its bow dipped, Journeys End came into sight. Comprising small to large beach-standing guest rooms, with an extensive administration and services centre, all cocooned and interwoven between palm trees and engrossing foliage, he esteemed it to be more like a tropical paradise than a hotel complex.

Thoroughly absorbed in his surroundings, the vessel's crew had to draw his notice before passing him his bags on the jetty. Padding along rafter-walkways to reception, he checked in, then wandered to his accommodation located no more than fifty yards from the Caribbean. Gazing out of a window at the waterfront, palm tree leaves and shell-coloured sand framing the foreground, he assessed what a terrific architecture, straight out of an equatorial Matisse invention. Though the Farnham's house on the south side of Canterbury boasted an excellent spectacle over adjacent fields and the rolling hills of the North Downs, the sheer unfamiliarity of waves gently breaking into ripples crawling up the shoreline, a kaleidoscope sky filled with cobalt and sapphire, and oddly grown palm trees with ripe coconuts and flayed out branches devising an umbrella effect, simply mesmerised him. He likened it to heaven falling on the Earth in the form of an idealised precinct, each organic element carefully selected by the creator to fuse into a matrix of hues and shapes most pleasing to the eye.

Spending the remainder of the day exploring the Journeys End geography, he got to know each gentle curve in the sand's geometry, noted the random spouting of palm trees in the most extraordinary places, dipped his bare feet in crystal clear water along the shoreline, and most essentially, inspected the landscape immediately to the front of his beach lodge. A cathartic phenomenon, his mind surged exhaustively into absorbing the rapture, all worldly concerns quenched and filed to the back of his memory. Merrily ambling along, he grinned involuntary, the effect sequent from his new ambience fabricating a pacifying and stress-relieving antidote to his tricky domestic baggage and vexing qualms.

After a light breakfast, very early the subsequential morning, he activated his laptop and began assembling new chapters. Chaplin had been right. Ambergris Caye generated the stimulus for a torrent of words, the day flashing by in a series of formulations, edits and fine tuning the copy. His productivity had not been as good since he had got into the swing of compiling *Vanquish the Bold*. Beginning to feel reinvigorated, at the helm, and unusually in recent times even pleased with his efforts, he concluded the day's endeavours were prolific, and ascribed his authorship abilities had flip-flopped, a watershed he privately feared had deserted him permanently back in Canterbury.

Emanating an aura of confidence, Farnham retired to the resort bar for well-earned refreshment. Gregarious during his brief conversation with the barman, he then sipped on a Rum Punch and jiggled his fingers to backcloth calypso music, whilst venerating the bar décor and smiling at the other patrons.

"You're comparable to the cat who's just had the cream," a fellow barfly venerated, detecting Farnham's sparkling mood.

"*Yes*, I'm on top of my game," he reported.

"Well, that's just fine and dandy. There's not enough positive vibe in the world." Converging on Farnham holding out his hand, he introduced himself. "My name is James Carter, but people usually call me Jim."

"I'm Kory Farnham, glad to meet you, Jim."

Carter told him he hailed from Westchester in upstate New York and had property developer credentials. Growing into a seasoned Belize visitor, he had struck up good relationships with local businessmen and government officials, resulting in two beachside resort initiatives to date. Now scouting loci for new five-star hotel developments, he'd acquired a comprehensive insight into the Belize economy and business *modus operandi*. Like many Americans, he possessed an eggs-over-easy, natural salesman approach, charming customers and buddies alike. With his playful facial expressions, scintillating repartee and a burgeoning waistline, to Farnham he epitomised a colourful Hemmingway character. Promptly acclimatising with his new comrade, the fictionist explicitly professed his rationale for being in Belize, Carter's empathy for his situation cementing the thriving friendship.

"I morphed into a work junkie whilst in the newspaper business," Farnham admitted. "But in more recent times, my embodiment of the occupation status quo as a fundamental has diminished, fast expanding into a visceral hatred of everyday monotony, systemic failings and conformance archetypes."

"Well, in my experience, it happens to a lot of compulsive people," Carter assured. "I believe it to be a temporary status, with any causal consequences swiftly put into perspective and forgotten." Lingering, he threw a snooping mug at Farnham. "Tell me, Kory, what do you put your writing hindrance, or perchance, impediment might be a better word, down to? I mean, how did the artistic engine become mired and fatigued?"

"Dammit!" Farnham blurted, his phiz evincing vacancy. "I thought I had it sorted out." Pausing to constrict his eyes in self-contempt, he wisely added, "Now I'm not so sure."

"There must have been a provocation."

Embarrassed by his failing, Farnham divulged, "Back in Canterbury, I tried to be overly forensic about the uncut blessed thing. But like a restrictor in a water pipe, little dripped out apart from the odd, partially-defined nugget."

"And presumably, you were petitioning for jam tomorrow?"

"More the case, it should have been exceptional ambrosia, a step jump by way of writing excellence, exalted way above the dash of my maiden yarn." Ogling blankly at Carter, he lifted his arms, letting them flap against his sides. "My exertions floundered, explaining why I hitched my wagon to Columbus's juggernaut, and made my way to the New World."

"Oh, I see," Carter verified. "You know—" Deliberately sniggering to act as a breakpoint, his intonation moved into a lighter register. "There are no infinitely duplicatable certainties in any walk of life. Sometimes, getting lost and vanishing from the terrestrial Earth is a good thing. It rejuvenates the spirit and cleanses the psyche, washing out fractious ambiguities, thereby enabling the unfortunate to go full-circle."

"Yes, I've observed the adage in practice already. Only today, I had my most fertile bout in many months, even managing to come out with some worthy aphorisms and epigrams to add richness to the story."

"You mean, pithy banter and articulations of cleverness?" he tested.

"Ha, ha, quite."

Farnham and Carter continued to reconnoitre each other's

lives and justifications for being in Belize, before the American turned the subject matter to amusements.

"Kory, I don't know if you'd be interested, but some of the other businessmen and I have got a trip to the Great Blue Hole tomorrow." Shooting a prize-winning grin at Farnham, he suggested, "Why don't you come with us?"

"Yes, I'd *like* to," the Englishman imparted.

"By the way, can you scuba dive?"

"As a matter of fact, I can. I learnt a few years ago when my wife and I were in the Windward Islands. What's the Great Blue Hole all about?"

"Oh!" His unbroken being lit up with relish. "I promise you won't be disappointed. It's a sea life delight."

* * *

By mid-morning the following day, Farnham, Carter and other scuba divers were on a large cruiser, heading south-east from Journeys End into the Caribbean for the Great Blue Hole, forty miles from shore. Farnham felt good. Before they left, with his expressive bent renovated, he had blasted off two-thousand words just after daybreak.

Hovering slightly behind him, Carter queried, "what's your new book about?"

Peering out of the boat stern, Journeys End dissolving into the horizon, he ignited a sparky aspect. "It's about a man perceiving he is being eaten up by the modern world but realises it's just a perception. He had always been told, the world is big, and he is small, meaning learn to stomach your place in the grand scheme of things. He had gone along with the edict for decades before he suddenly rebels, breaks out of his constraining domain, and finds himself."

"Sounds like it's about you."

"You're very sharp, Jim. It is, partially. From the age of twenty-one onwards, I spent fourteen years nose to the grindstone in the newspaper business, being a cog in the machine before I conclusively broke out. It caused a rift with my wife, Candice. I unconditionally love her, and she knows it, but I just had to do this. You see—" Leaning against the stern rail, he made a sardonic mien. "I don't want to be knocking on heaven's door, and St Peter asks me, 'What did you do with your life?' and I lamely answer, 'It was largely unfulfilled in terms of individual jubilation.'" Twisting away from the American, he gaped into the vacant seascape. "I must make sense of the world, try to indent it with my stamp, and not let the machine consume me from the cradle to the grave. Somehow, I've got to demonstrate the world is small, and I am big. My only route to carry out the precept is by way of penmanship. It will render the attainment I'm pursuing." Vacillating, his kisser dropped into fretfulness. "Do you understand what I am saying, Jim?"

"As a matter of fact, I do." Navel gazing, as if he too had been a candidate for an import of truth cleansing, he explained, "For me, the breakout involved getting away from hotel management. I made some property development investments, speedily coming good. Then I got on a roll, made a lot of Franklins, erm, dollars to you, from an investment in Puerto Juarez Cancun, quit my day job and instigated a property development operation." He rippled his brow as if the self-review shocked him. "During the succeeding thirty years, I've hit multimillionaire status, met my wife to be, had children, and dovetailed my energy into implementing what I wanted." Resting, he beamed at the Englishman. "Ostensibly, they are credentials itemising how I will leave my imprint on the world. So yes, I understand what you mean. I too broke out, and in doing so, proved the world no longer ran me."

"Superb recap, Jim. You're already there. I feel my junket has only just begun."

"You'll get there."

"I hope so."

"Incidentally," Carter pushed, "what's this new handiwork entitled?"

"Aahh…I've struggled to come up with an apt moniker encapsulating the sum-total ethos of the enterprise in a single phrase. I tried multiple titles, none hitting a sonorous note. Then benightedly, I came up with the probationary title, *The Finding of Life*."

"Yep, seems representative of the summary you delineated."

"The thing is, my preliminary submission resonated with mainstream reader determinants. Hence, my agent easily found a publisher. *The Finding of Life* will not be witnessed as being appealing to the same demographic. It's more a piece of literary fiction than commercial fiction."

"Are you saying, the difference could introduce some issues regarding publication?"

"Definitely. Publishers seek blatantly mercantile fruit. Any tilt at adventurism in root and provision outside the prescribed box is perceived to be too challenging for Joe Public's obsolete or pre-programmed intellectual equipment and thereby deemed to be too commercially risky." Agitated by the admission, Farnham emitted frustrated features. "But I'm damned if I'm going to write to a formula, and be template coerced. Pure coincidence played a hefty part in *Vanquish the Bold* happening to meet the mass market criteria. *The Finding of Life* is a parting from convention, its…it's not a judgement of elected folkways and habits, but much more of mood cast of mind." Dwelling, he eyeballed Carter enquiringly. "Do I make sense?"

"Yes, I understand what you are saying," he confirmed. "Art genres shouldn't lend themselves to a production line mentality. If they did, we'd still be reading Chaucer replicants, and flattering Botticelli impersonators, the likes of Huxley and Picasso never darting off the starting blocks. What we crave as a reader or a beholder, is the singular, the special, or perhaps a litmus test challenging our preconceptions and sensibilities. Not many people indulge an artist, a filmmaker, or a writer, who merely replicates the same thing every time, just because it triumphed once." Stepping back, he emanated a mature air, reminding Farnham of his yesteryear university lecturers casting an informed standpoint on an undergraduates' conundrum.

"Oh, I can see variations on a gist have credence, and thereby achieve eyewitness satisfaction, but the conviction of merely changing the protagonist and antagonist names and the setting, whilst retaining the basic story, is crass, even exploitative. In no way does it foster the genus in terms of stretching the possibilities. In point-of-fact, it shelves it in the disrepute bracket, relegating novel writing into boorish pulp fiction."

"Your analysis is spot on," Farnham enthused. "However, it is also the axiomatic rider why this second origination has given me so many sleepless nights and caused so much discord with my wife."

"You're wrestling with the contradictions between artful credibility and commercial conformance. Somewhere between those two poles, you'll find a compromise."

"Precisely."

Soon, the craft came to a standstill, dropping anchor on the inside of the Great Blue Hole, a large submarine sinkhole, about 1,000 feet in diameter and less than 400 feet deep at its midpoint, in the centre of the Lighthouse Reef, itself a small atoll. Awarded world heritage site status, and made popular by marine ecologists such as Jacques Cousteau, on first sight, it astounded Kory Farnham. He and Candice had seen some fascinating submerged coral reefs off St Lucia in the Windward Islands, but the Great Blue Hole levitated on a much more majestic plane of specialness. A remnant from the Quaternary glaciation period, and fused from karst limestone formations metamorphosing to coral, tourists flocked to the offshore attraction, like for Farnham, its nimbus customarily having them in slack-jawed awe.

On this day, the cruiser occupants had the Great Blue Hole to themselves. Donning scuba diving gear, Farnham and Carter tipped over the side of the gleaming white vessel into gemstone, crystalline water. Having become a haven for marine life over many epochs, immediately shoals of upper-water swimmers came into their view. Across from the anchorage, along the periphery of the hole and just below the surface, angelfish and blue parrot fish nosed into the coral reef crevices. Lower down, surgeon fish and midnight cowfish filled the mid-water level, and groupers scoped the reef gullies in pursuit of small fry.

Empowering universal movement in the lateral and azimuth planes, Farnham became utterly liberated in the fluid environment. He had forgotten how a medium providing support in three planes made scuba divers feel as if they were flying, his spiralling somersaults forming a flurry of bubbles, the playfulness taking him back to childhood memories of frolicking in the sea off Herne Bay. Waving to Carter, the American stared at his ballet-like manoeuvres, startled by the spontaneous parade of exuberance. Already new certitudes flooded into Farnham's mind to progress *The Finding of Life*. As soon as they returned to Journeys End, he'd busy himself banging the laptop keys again. Comprehensively adapting to the liberty-enhancing medium, Farnham shot off to sightsee the circular edge of the hole, Carter residing static below the surface, slowly treading water and still taken aback by his newly acquired chum's antics.

Back on deck, Carter quipped, "Well, Kory, you really resurrected your vivacity amidst the dive."

"Yes, I'd forgotten just how emancipating scuba diving can be."

At noon, the scuba divers and crew lunched. Overhead, a Van Gogh yellow-coloured sun subdued them, its intensity moreover increased by reflections off the sea surface.

Seeing Farnham lost in cognition, Carter petitioned, "Before you meander away into writer's heaven completely, tell me about your impressions of the Great Blue Hole."

"I'm overwhelmed. The Windwards were remarkable, but this —" He spread his arms to encompass the seascape. "This is way beyond reasonable expectations, its impact as an inspirational agent, bigger, better. I began to unlock in Belize City, by Journeys End words were streaming again, but the Great Blue Hole has driven me to a strengthened plain of self-actualisation. Now, I've got enough substance floating in my head to write another few chapters."

Breaking into an approving grin, Carter then gazed at the white fading to dark green coral contour of the Lighthouse Reef's perimeter dancing below the sea's surface. "You know, people come here for all kinds of accounts. Evidently, even for writers, it conjures up its magic."

"Let's do another dive," Farnham implored.

Ruminating on the request, he then advised, "I'll have a word with the captain. See what he thinks."

As the gentle rocking motion of the boat floated him higher into bliss, Farnham watched them talking. Shutting his eyes, he cerebrally revisited the travelogue moulded in his mind in the course of the dive, pronto establishing creation had come about resultant from the sheer therapeutic by-products of the ethereal rendezvous. Accrediting retreat into an otherworldly dimension paralleled such an obvious antidote to unchain his writing inhibitions, stimulating artistic juices to flow again, he questioned why on Earth he had not called upon such a releasing force back in Canterbury. It did not have to be an exotic location for the witchcraft to fashion its spell. He could easily have gone scuba diving off the North Kent coast, with Candice by his side. Why had it taken a 3,000-mile flight and a change of continent for the notion to occur to him? While still pondering the poser, he heard looming footfalls.

"Afraid not, Kory," Carter relayed on. "The captain says, soon it will be feeding time for sharks, and there are tigers in this area."

"*What*!" Flowering his eyes to their extremities, he bolted into full alertness again.

"I computed if I had told you about the sharks before we came, you might not have wanted to scuba dive."

"Damn right."

Twinkling at the boomerang, Carter supplemented, "I also determined you needed the Great Blue Hole, and I fancied I'd scare you off with tales about sharks, barracuda and octopus."

Farnham's dial released from anxiety, a cheerful countenance overcoming his shock. "You were right. It's worth the risk. All the same, if you had told me, I'd have probably declined scuba diving."

"If we had dived below a hundred feet, you'd have seen blacktips and bulls, maybe even hammerheads, towards the bottom. At this time of year, they don't come into the upper layers until late afternoon. So, we were unreservedly safe."

Seafaring to Journeys End, Farnham and Carter saw a fifteen-foot tiger shark, its dorsal and tail fins skimming the sea surface, as it made its way to the Great Blue Hole.

"If I had seen a man-eater on the way out," Farnham murmured, "there's no way you'd have got me in a wetsuit."

Laughing and slapping Farnham on the back, Carter proclaimed, "me neither."

* * *

Back in his beach room, Farnham transcribed his brainwaves into new content for *The Finding of Life*. He had projected staying at Journeys End for just a few days, before reverting to the Fort George. Now he felt compelled to stay on Ambergris Caye until he perfected the new story. Making a call to Candice, he explained his writer's block had gone, and he intended to be back in Canterbury by the end of the month. Not exactly pleased, nevertheless, she bought into the plan.

Carter had business back in Belize City finalising a property development deal for a hotel and resort complex on Long Cay, part of the Drowned Cays islands just off the mainland. Leaving, he said to Farnham he'd be inbound to Journeys End by Friday next.

Replenished with a plethora of postulates, Farnham furiously went to work on his draft with renewed vigour. Able to vision out its unmitigated architecture, he had it subliminally mapped out as an end-to-end narrative, replete with cohesive main thesis, intriguing sub-plots, and fully-formed personalities. All the basic ingredients were there. Now he had to knit and splice the whole thing together into a range of interconnecting themes and premises, before fine tuning the entire text.

Composing four new chapters and a substantial re-write of the earlier chapters written in Canterbury, categorically the book came together. With his output approximating the same rate he had set himself on his previous novel, he adjudged the effort might be finished ahead of the timescale calculated and given to Candice, enfranchising him to be Blighty bound ahead of schedule. Radiating at the possibility, he readily appraised he had been the prime mover behind the discord with his wife. He could not wait to hold her close and make profuse apologies for his tactless and insensitive behaviour.

Over the days, when the heat thickened into overbearing territory, he took a break from authoring, roved to the shoreline, waded into the welcoming water chill, and swam out to sea for a few minutes before backtracking. Throughout the brief aquatic jaunts, images of the Great Blue Hole flashed around his mind. Several times after swimming, he sauntered along the jetty, gaping at small octopi and starfish basking in the shallows, their mottled skins part-camouflaging them against the speckled beach sand. At the wharf's frontier, he extended both his hands to his forehead providing relief from sun glare, and scoured eastwards into the Caribbean, the Great Blue Hole entering his deliberations again. Appreciating its significance in regenerating his composition capacity, in his mind, he planned another trip to the atoll when Jim Carter arrived back on Ambergris Caye.

Chuffed with his wording accomplishments, in the evenings he went to the Journeys End bar, ordered a very large rum-based cocktail, and retired to a hammock tied between two palm trees on the beach, just yards from his lodge. Gawking at the fathomless Caribbean night sky from the gently swaying crib, he mentally audited the days' product, and considered the novel's ensuing segments.

Friday soon came, and with it the big American property developer birthed at the Journeys End jetty, Farnham immediately engaging him, enthusing about his words' proliferation, and more commandingly, his desire to revisit the Lighthouse Reef locale. Pleased to see a dramatic reversal in the Englishman's fortunes and frame of mind, Carter endorsed the proposed trip.

Early the postliminary morning, they embarked for the famous atoll, another flawless day in paradise unfolding ahead. Marvelling at a cerulean sky mirroring off the water, and the sun shining an even fiercer shade of Van Gogh yellow, both ideal for making a dive, Farnham anticipated fathering more highbrow-induced material for *The Finding of Life*.

Anchoring in a different part of the Great Blue Hole, the

divers made their preparations for the sub-sea adventure, then tipped over the side of the cruiser. Soon they were pouring over the reef again. Staring in astonishment at the panorama of nature's best coming into perspective, Farnham's mind segued into creative mode, trawling images and harvesting meditations to be transposed into words. Once again performing underwater aerobatics, he began memorising new tenors and story board edits for the conclusion of his book.

Sensing the Englishman's confidence, Carter indicated to him they could venture deeper than on the foregoing occasion. Reflecting in the few days he had been away from Journeys End, Farnham had changed from pensive apologist to full-blown thrill-seeker, ready to take on the Caribbean's treasures, the American felt vindicated in introducing him to the wonderment. Often meeting people refreshed after immersion in the releasing lifestyle accessible in the Belizean Cays, the about-face in Farnham's persona did not stun him.

As the divers headed downwards, more of the atoll's subsurface secrets were revealed. On its rim, coral had coalesced into stalactite and stalagmite-like edifices, eternally hanging or thrusting up like giant Roman candles. Turtles and rays gracefully moved between its endless nooks and crannies, carved into the karst limestone superstructure by subaquatic currents. Moving in regular rhythmic patterns, shoals of squirrelfish and diamond blennies occupied the mid-water at the coral reef periphery, the divers so enthralled by the spectacle, they failed to notice a second shoal of squirrelfish zip past. It signalled the onset of something unanticipated, something sinister.

The tiger shark hit Farnham like a train. Initially imagining he had been whacked by a ship's anchor descending from above, he then caught sight of a huge dorsal fin as he slid and spun along the shark's hard body. Twisted and rolled in the perpetrator's wake, as if entangled in an invisible snare, he gulped air, dazed at the realisation, before coming to a jarring halt against the reef. Then he saw Carter frantically gesticulating upwards. Immediately he kicked into action, making for the surface.

Sufficiently switched on to examine for the predator's

whereabouts to ensure avoiding a further attack, he stopped and scanned the seascape. In the distance, he spotted his pursuer slowing and turning. Glimpsing up, he saw the bleary outline of the vessel's hull above and kicked hard. Moments later, the crew hauled him out of the water, his assailant coming back for seconds and narrowly missing his legs. His heart pounding, he spiralled into shock. Already aboard, Carter began stripping off Farnham's scuba diving gear, crisply sucking in air as a nasty gash in the small of the author's back became exposed.

Peeling away the wetsuit, the wound blossomed, blood spurting over the deck. Farnham lost consciousness.

Turning to the captain with an agonising mien, he blared, "If he doesn't receive medical attention quickly, he will bleed to death."

* * *

Unsure of his surroundings, for the succeeding few days, Farnham drifted in and out of comprehension, obscure recollections about the Great Blue Hole haunting his psyche. He gauged a disturbing happenstance had occurred but could not convert his remembrance into identifiable formulations and idiosyncrasies to crystallise specific conceptions. Incessantly trapped between semi-sleep and semi-awake, he perpetually trembled between the two poles, never achieving either exhaustive sleep or cogent nimbleness.

At some juncture in his apparent timeless trek, he sensed the warmth of someone's hand on his, the tactile bond making him emerge into an elevated register of awareness.

"How are you feeling?" he heard someone say.

With effort, his eyes flickered open. In due course focusing, the finely chiselled, high cheek-boned visage of his wife came into view. She squeezed his forearm.

"*Candice*," he uttered.

Though appearing tired consequent from worry and a spontaneous excursion across the Atlantic, Candice had lost none of her inborn fluorescence, her golden hair flowing loose and bouncing around her shoulders, her plumbless hazel eyes shining with kaleidoscope brilliance. Swinging into a much more *compos mentis* condition, Kory Farnham marvelled at his gorgeous wife. In the months predating the Belize sojourn, and until the moment he saw her again, her natural beauty had paled from his cognizance. With his writer's block now released, she distilled into his attentiveness as she truly transpired; a breath-taking woman.

"I thought I'd lost you," Candice volunteered, her voice smooth and silky, like honey dripping with neat velvet.

Managing a half-smile in response, he then cringed, the measure causing him pain. Reactively trying to find comfort in his prone position, he clocked Jim Carter behind Candice.

"Hello, Kory. You had us worried for a while."

"Jim…where am I?"

"You're in Belize City Hospital."

Trying to square the mind-boggling information, he then asked, "What's happened to me?"

"Oh, we'll talk about it downline."

Additional sentiments were exchanged between the threesome before a doctor joined them.

"You'll have to let him rest now," he declared. "Mister Farnham is still weak and needs sleep, but he'll be fine."

Making their farewells, the visitors prepared to leave, Candice turning to goggle back at her husband. "By the way, I like your moustache and beard."

Her compliment made him remember the commitment he devised whilst lying naked on his bed at the Fort George on his prefatory day in Belize City. Since, his facial hair growth had significantly grown, founding a dark moustache and beard.

Saluting his wife's praise with a wave, he winced at the derived torment caused by the slender movement. *Whatever has happened to me*, he meditated, *my body feels like it has been trampled on.*

After a few days, he felt better and able to sit up in bed. Candice and Jim sat by his side, their locutions optimistic on seeing some colour imprint the writer's complexion.

"You are a very lucky man, Kory," Carter credited. "Candice has not left the hospital since she arrived nearly a week ago."

She sparkled at her husband, her devotion to him unmistakable.

"Yes, you are right," he agreed, reciprocating her jaunty mannerism. "I am a very lucky man."

Detecting the connection, Carter nurtured a playful smirk. "You two need to be alone. I'll come back in a while."

Withdrawing from the Farnhams, he strolled out of an ajar pair of French doors and into the Belize City Hospital gardens.

Make up time for husband and wife, Kory apologised for his blindness to conceive the wrench his penning ambitions had levied on their marriage. In turn, Candice dispensed contrite regrets for her intolerance of his need to create using the vehicle of fiction writing. Beholding each other, as per the first time they'd met at the Canterbury post office, Candice wide-eyed and pouting, her luscious mouth marginally cracked, Kory left breathless by her splendour, they mutually recognised each other's folly. She leant frontwards and they embraced before breaking into a long and succulent kiss.

"*Boy*, did I need the physical," he remarked. "In my self-induced, insular drop into lettered abstraction, I'd clean forgotten just how invigorating a kiss from you can be."

"We should do this more often," she posed, her siren's voice even more breathy and seductive.

"Yes, you're right." His self-recrimination heightening, remorsefully, he shook his head. "My dear girl, it's all contingent on me. What a *stupid* fool I've been. In my blinkered attempt to satisfy my alter ego, I've managed to alienate you and put our financial stability at risk."

"Nothing is irretrievably broken yet. You are allowed one major misdemeanour." She wagged a cautionary finger, then cast a semi-menacing glower at him, Kory interpreting it as a terminal warning. "But just one, mind you."

"You're very generous, Candice. This must have been said by millions of men to their wives…I don't deserve you."

Flagging receptiveness, she puckered her lips. "This is not a time for counter charges. Right now, the most vital thing is for you to get well."

Flashing an endearing simper at her, he prudently commented, "There you go again, bowling me over with your compassion, when most gorgeous women would have moved on to a more deserving case. One without conflicts and insulating them from money worries for life."

"I didn't marry you for money." Blooming, her eyes grew larger than ever, her mouth curving into a coquettish trim, her sexuality lush and blazing. "I married you because I fell for you, and I knew you were a decent man."

After a suitable period of privacy had elapsed, Carter re-entered to find the Farnhams entwined in each other.

"Well," he began, "clearly you two have sorted out your differences."

Rising to her feet, Candice gave Jim a peck on the cheek. "Thank you for taking care of him."

Breaking into a broad grin, the American confessed, "He had me worried for a while, but I distinguished the picture of making up with you would pull him through."

An essence of relief permeated the threesome, and not just because Kory Farnham had outlived an underwater assault. More importantly, two loving people had come together again.

"What went on back at the Great Blue Hole, Jim?" asked the patient. "My memory is somewhat vague. Maybe I'm in necessary denial, but I know I had a narrow escape."

Carter recounted the precursor to what had happened before moving on to the tiger shark incident.

"When the brute homed in on you, I fancied you were a goner. You see, it's most unusual. They are normally night hunters, but that fella must have had his body clock out of kilter. I saw him coming at the last moment when those squirrelfish were on the move. You had your back to him. Before I could reach you, he ploughed into your side. You must have revolved just as he struck, and he got a mouthful of compressed air cylinder, then jolted you onto the reef. It's what slashed your back, not the shark's teeth. By the time he turned, I had you back to the surface, and the crew yanked us aboard, before he nearly got more of you. The captain made a mayday call, and we bandaged you as best we could while racing back to Journeys End. We'd only gone a few miles when an air sea rescue chopper came into view and took you off to Belize City Hospital." Gunning the Farnhams with a semi solemn comportment, tongue-in-cheek he annexed, "You had a lucky escape, Kory. You shouldn't let wild colonials like me get you into such outrageous trouble!"

Candice broke into laughter at the laconic wisecrack, Kory trying to join in but restricted by his restraining flesh wounds.

"Anyway," Carter continued, "the sawbones say although you lost a lot of blood, and will be sore for a while, you will fully recover, though you will have a scar on your side as a memento of the incident."

"He came here to write a *To Have and Have Not* type epic," Candice recapped. "It nearly germinated into *For Whom the Bell Tolls*."

* * *

Released from hospital at the weekend, Kory took Candice back to the Fort George Hotel. Casually picking up a copy of the Belize Times in the lobby, his eyes widened as he took in the headline, 'Englishman survives shark attack'. Tapping Candice's shoulder, he enticed both her attention, and consternation.

From her receptionist station, Mama Celeste bellowed, "We kept it for you, Mister Farnham."

Smiling at the affable Belizean, he approached reception. "Hello, Mama Celeste. How are you?"

"Oh, I'm fine. More to the point, how are you?"

"Still shaken but improving all the time."

Checking in and retiring to their second-floor quarters, the Farnhams' captivation with the newspaper coverage intensified. Going out onto the balcony, they read the Belize Times account in full. It still seemed unreal for Kory, like he read about someone else's cataclysm rather than his own. At the *Telegraph*, he had been used to reporting the news, not making it. Feeling remote from the description, as if ascribed third person status, he reckoned the article to be more graphic than the reality of the incident, though he conceded Carter had underplayed what happened. Made him comprehend, had he similarly embroidered the truth as a correspondent for his past employer? Or conversely, did he now wallow in self-denial, his fate hanging by a thread, and for reasons still to come to terms with, he had yet to accept the possible irrevocability of the dangerous carnivore onset.

Turning away from Candice, he recalled in a dull tone, "I had some risky escapades when I covered the Middle East in my journalism days, but nothing budding as a life-threatening moment. This story reads more like a fanciful oddity happening to someone we'd read about over Sunday morning breakfast back in Canterbury."

Defending her bewildered husband, Candice assured, "It will take a while to bite the bullet about what happened at the Lighthouse Reef, and I discern you are reticent to talk about it." Draping herself around him and hugging him affectionately, she advised, "Try to classify it as a providential escape. You were very fortunate, Kory."

"Yes, after Jim filled me in on what happened, it began to sink in."

"What?"

"Just before the raider offensive, a slight shift into the wrong path could have spelt curtains for me."

Much later, as the sun coasted into the Caribbean and after an extensive love-making session, Kory and Candice lay in bed gawking up at the gyrating ceiling fan, it's downdraft providing a welcome stream of cooled air.

"God, I needed that," he blathered.

Nudging his elbow with hers, she teasingly tested, "Hungry for love, were you?"

"Ohh...much more than sex." Raising his arms aloft in a token of sincerity, he then let them flop by his sides. "It provided an affirmation of just how much you mean to me, an avowal I'd unintentionally sidelined back home, when my creative juices stopped flowing and I plunged into a woeful pit." A new notion springing to mind, he queried, "By the way, did Shanon Minter and Ruben Fricker hassle you, when I left for Belize without telling them?"

During the course of his journalism career, Kory had met Shanon Minter saying he plotted to write a fiction novel when a fitting crossroads presented itself, Literary Agent Minter contending she could provide a route to market when the event occurred. Fricker represented Overton & Gilpin, a seasoned publisher of prose literature and biographies, responsible for publishing *Vanquish the Bold*. When progress of the sequel faltered, Fricker put increasing pressure on both the author and his agent, Minter taking it in her stride, Kory Farnham telling him his coercion made his composition task even more problematical.

"Shanon telephoned the day after you left, and every third day thereafter."

"What did you tell her?"

"Only you were taking a break in Belize to help replenish your authoring skills."

"What about Fricker?"

"Oh, he tried to schmooze me with flattery before parading the crux of his call."

"Where's your damned husband?"

"Right."

"Well—" He sniggered almost contemptuously. "Most likely both will be pleasantly surprised when they see what I've been doing."

Jim Carter came to see the Farnhams at the Fort George before returning to Westchester to take care of the stateside end for the Long Cay hotel development.

"How goes it, Kory?"

"Apart from some physical discomfort, I feel fine."

Moving closer, Carter inspected the Englishman for signs of modesty in his claim. "Without doubt, you're much better than when you were admitted to hospital." Squinting at Candice, he solicited, "How about you, good-looking? Have you recuperated from your ordeal?"

Navel gazing, she safeguarded in her most serenely soft voice,

"Oh, I'm still descending from the mad rush to get here, then finding Kory laid up with a ghostly white expression."

Caringly tapering his eyes, Carter attested, "Fatigued by the upheaval, you're in need of some TLC yourself." Turning to Kory with a knowing idiom, he counselled, "Look after this angel, Farnham. She's your biggest asset."

"Unconditionally," he confirmed. "When are you coming to Belize again, Jim?"

"Oh, not for four, maybe five weeks. Planted on the rate you are breeding your novel, it will be complete by then, and you will have left for England."

Both parties exchanged contact details, with a pledge to get together again in the future. Carter left secretly discriminating that Kory had still to grapple with the Great Blue Hole shark ambush, and Candice to truly grasp she could have been made a widow.

* * *

Within their ever-needing air-conditioned room, Kory resumed his drafting task whilst Candice either monitored him writing or cruised the Marine Parade Boulevard waterfront exploring the local cultural allurements. A few pleasant days went by for the Farnhams before Gerald Chaplin telephoned the Fort George inviting them to dinner the following evening. Walking the short distance from the hotel to Chaplin's Hudson Street house, Candice took in the white-painted, colonial buildings and the glory of Memorial Park, saying they reminded her of similar spectacles in Charleston and Savannah the Farnhams had seen on a trip to Georgia to see her elder brother and his family, the observation stirring Kory to propound they made another visit to the Southern state in the new year.

Chaplin's wife Abbigayle made the Farnhams welcome, the foursome tucking into a traditional Belizean meal, Gerald Chaplin continuing in the gregarious genre Kory had formerly encountered at the Calypso Bar and filling in Candice as to how him and his wife had pitched up in the ex-British colony.

After more customary kick-off meeting dialogue, and with the diners nicely spaced out on a particularly rich rioja, Gerald gave Kory a sideways glint, then twisted to petition his wife.

"Do you know, Candice," he began with a weighty aura, "I feel at least partially responsible for your husband's unfortunate contretemps. You see, I suggested he went to Ambergris Caye."

"Oh, you do yourself a disservice," Kory insisted. "The tiger shark incident could have happened to anyone. On the contrary, your recommendation had an uplifting influence on my scribing predicament."

"So, you were able to overcome your problem?" Abbigayle put forward.

"Absolutely. To say Ambergris Caye had a beneficial affect is an understatement. I'd not shaped such prodigious quality text since I spliced together *Vanquish the Bold*." Making an emboldening gesture to the Chaplins, he specified, "What happened at the Great Blue Hole comes under the guise of a rare mishap, a by-chance occurrence that could have happened to anyone."

"Well, I must say, you have surmounted the trauma with remarkable resolution," Gerald enthused. "Many have perished under similar circumstances."

"Yes, I'm finding things out about myself I never knew existed," he declared. "Before Belize, if someone in Canterbury had promoted diving in shark infested waters for the buzz, I'd have recoiled at the impulse. Ambergris Caye definitely had a favourable impact on my standpoint, and in the process, has rejuvenated my inventive skills." Lowering his eyes, he sheepishly augmented, "The only thing is, I am yet to comprehensively take in and come to terms with what happened."

"How do you mean?" Abbigayle canvassed.

"I'm still in denial, or at least in partial denial, about the shark attack. I guess Jim Carter, someone with ken of similar onslaughts, thinks I am yet to let go of what might be still inside of me."

"Denial masking off fright," Gerald offered.

"Yes, if you like. I presumed Jim foresaw me coming to my senses screaming, but I didn't. I knew a dreadful episode had happened, but even when he filled me in on the details, I couldn't see myself in the eyeline of a hunter, as it made its charge at me and came back for seconds."

"What are you going to do next, Kory?" Abbigayle enquired.

"I'm going to take Candice out to the Journeys End, so she can see what a marvellous place it is."

* * *

Like her husband, Candice became amazed by both the brevity of the flight, and the improbable sand runway at San Pedro when they arrived on Ambergris Caye.

"The same as landing on a beach," she corroborated, gazing back at the Cessna Caravan, as they made their way to the quayside. "Undeniably, Belize is saturated in the mind-blowing. I can see the attraction."

"Indeed," Kory supported, "the more the clout of the revelation, the more mercurial the valuation appreciation. It's the kind of thing you expect to read about in a Hemmingway plot."

She laughed. "Well, if the unusual is an Ambergris Caye trademark, it bodes well for the Journeys End Resort."

By the time the water taxi had the Farnhams at the retreat resort, all signs of stress had left Candice. Refreshed with zest, her plenary deportment blazed with excitement and energy, Kory witnessing the change in his wife and recollecting the identical dash across the sea had the very same fallout on him over three weeks earlier. As fortune had it, the Farnhams were allocated the same lodge he had for his prior stay at Journeys End.

Like meeting an old familiar friend, when they made their way from reception to the accommodation over the shell-coloured sand and between a maze of palm trees, a zing of sanguinity ran through him. Tendering to his wife, it represented a second domicile, and he fizzed with joy, recounting his previous time in the room to her.

Spending a few days wandering about the resort complex, cavorting in the sea and shopping in San Pedro, the couple jetted into a blissful fettle of repose. Though Kory Farnham had to attend Belize City Hospital to have his stitches taken out, nevertheless, he'd been briefed by the doctor in charge of his case to take as much light duty exercise as possible to kindle the healing process. In the meantime, they planned to do nothing apart from having more fun, and him nailing *The Finding of Life*, Kory keying in the closing chapters whilst Candice slept or read the local information guides. She now sailed as altogether relaxed with her husband's campaign to make a lasting dent on the artistic world, and he had agreed on resumption of their domestic life in Canterbury to freelance for the *Telegraph*. Behaving like newlyweds again, they brimmed with optimism and buoyancy.

When he initiated the ultimate check over his new creation, Candice sat contentedly on the bed, browsing a history of Ambergris Caye she had bought at the San Pedro tourist centre.

"Kory."

"Yes, darling."

"What are you going to call this new book?"

"Oh, I had the interim title, *The Finding of Life*, but now I'm pondering *The World is Small. You are Big* is a much more apt title."

"Why?"

"Because—" Ceasing abruptly, he swivelled his chair to rubberneck her. "Now I have the ensemble sussed out, I've appraised it is not about the finding of life." Rising from the table used to platform his laptop, he sat beside Candice on the bed. "It's more a realisation of how an individuals' lifestyle is much more meaningful, than being overwhelmed and defeated by visualisations of a feverish world, where we are infinitely small cogs keeping the machine going, for the sake of it."

Chuckling, she lay back on the pillow. "A bit of a mouthful, isn't it?"

"Yes, you're right. Let's see if I can précis it into a simpler summary." Studying for a moment, he then acclaimed, "It's about breaking out from self-imposed constraints."

"You mean conformity?"

"*Huh*, precisely what Jim intimated I banged on about…yes."

"But we all have to conform to some extent," she proposed.

"You're right, but it's the ever-increasing grade and gradient that profusely disturbs me. We are creatures of the herd in our developmental years, needing to be approved, and not wanting to be left out in the cold. Most of us never grow out of the mentality. It is literally what the in-office rubber johnnies' want the status quo to be."

"Sheep?"

"Yes, sheep. Dim-witted, comatose, obedient sheep. Sheep playing the required game from the cradle to the grave, making no waves, or exacting scope to exist outside the prescribed box. Non-conformists and oddballs are deemed by those in power to be a distraction at the very least, those in the forefront of primary bodies, fearing the discontent will diffuse into the core. They don't like non-consensual, rampantly individualistic will. Consequently, they will do anything to stop it, including reducing basic prerogatives and implementing draconian laws. Sound familiar?"

"Yes, I'm afraid it does."

He rested back, his eyes only inches away from hers. "Way back in the mists of time," he eulogised, "when I was a youth finding my way."

"You mean in 1066, when Bill the Conqueror took digs in Canterbury?"

Cheering at her punchy humour, he replied, "Quite. Back then, and I acquiesce it might have been an illusion, I felt totally uninhibited regarding what I wanted to do, and when I wanted to do it. I don't mean paying bills or doing necessary chores, or any let's call them, life maintenance actions. Ostensibly, the comprehension linked to an inobtrusive frame of living reference. I'd been born into an egalitarian country, in many ways the template and envy of the rest of the world, especially those countries trying to attain democratic rights." Lifting his head, he scrunched up his lineaments at her. "Do you know what democracy means?"

"Of course, the will of the majority."

"Yes." Settling his head back on a pillow, he propositioned, "I don't know when or even how it happened, but such a fundamental keystone, central to consensus politics, does not exist anymore."

"You mean, the will of the majority is not observed in the political process and its institutions?"

"Definitely. Hence, the awareness could even be fact, we are no longer mapping out our own destiny. It has become predetermined for us, the machine I referred to making all our decisions and pushing us into submission." Swiftly halting, sullenness overcame him. "I don't recognise the England from my teens anymore." Gimbal eyed and patently confounded, he advanced, "It's gone in its totality. At best, it's been deconstructed into a benign dictatorship, run by autocrats to ensure their phantasm of how the undivided world should function is sustained and maintained by the machine they have created. The machine dictates every aspect of our lives and has been designed not to tolerate detractors by the introduction of subjective laws."

"And your book is about breaking out of the machine's grasp?"

Sculpting an admiring dial, he complimented, "There you go being astute again…it certainly is. You see, in many ways, machine conformance is an adherence to compulsory temperament. But, we are not yet at the Orwellian-come-Huxley demarcation, where there is no option but to obey and participate. We still can choose to jump off the ride. Those who rule still sanction it. Howbeit, here's the rub." Levering himself up on his elbows, he proclaimed, "Jumping off, means dropping out. It's what I began to do back in Canterbury, engendering the kernel behind our troubles, and I candidly admit to being the instigator. I couldn't see a way of finding the self without submitting at least in part to the machine."

"Going back to the *Telegraph*?" she posed.

"Yes, right again. But now—" Euphorically, he whirled an up-thrust hand about in an encompassing fabrication. "This whole Belize affair, notably Ambergris Caye, has shown me a contrasting way to not be wholly devoured by the machine. Principally perception, it's about turning the tables and using the machine to fulfill the self, meaning earning a crust to bankroll a given way of life, whilst concurrently, and this is a mental perspective, pulling the ripcord and divorcing the self from being consumed."

"I understand where you are coming from," Candice verified. "There are parallels in Solzhenitsyn's *One Day in the Life of Ivan Denisovich* with what you are saying. Though Denisovich is physically confined in a Siberian labour camp, in his mind, he is a free man."

"An excellent comparator," Kory extolled. Propping himself up on his elbow again, he stared at her, his physiognomy serious. "So, you see where I am coming from?"

"Yes, I do."

* * *

Once Candice acclimatised to Ambergris Caye, Kory asked her if she'd like to go out to the Great Blue Hole. At the outset, hesitant, her reluctance resultant from his subsea bushwhack and a sensation foretelling he might dissolve if confronted by a man-eater again, he persuaded her lightning never strikes twice in the same place.

Joining a group of scuba divers aboard a cruiser bound for the Lighthouse Reef atoll, they stood in the stern watching Journeys End melt away over the horizon, just as he had done for his inaugural trip to the world heritage site.

Heeding a wary mode on her kisser, he perceived, "You're perturbed about my carnivore waylay, aren't you?"

"Under the circumstances, it's impossible not to be."

Encircling her waist, he guaranteed, "I didn't even get a good look at the beast, though on the first occasion Jim and I visited the Great Blue Hole, we did see a fifteen-foot tiger shark whilst reversing to Journeys End."

Recoiling from his hold, she blasted, "And despite the identification, you *still* went scuba diving!?"

"As Jim told us at the hospital, tigers are normally night hunters. What happened to me could be categorised as near to unprecedented."

Still electric with recrimination, she examined, "So you have no qualms about being out on the Caribbean?"

"No. Only yesterday, we were swimming off the Journeys End shoreline. There are more frequent shark attacks in the shallows than in the depths of the sea."

"Goodness." Her eyes widened. "We must have swum half a dozen times off the shoreline. If you'd told me about the likelihood of shark ambuscade to begin with, I'd have not gone anywhere near the water."

Sniggering at her admonishment, he then rendered, "It's just a matter of probabilities. There are shark assaults all over the world. Hell, Great Whites have even been seen off the Cornish coast."

"Well, you won't get me snorkelling or scuba diving off Herne Bay again."

Breaking into laughter, he warranted, "They don't come as far as the North Sea. It's too chilly for them."

Grinning at his barbed remark, she censured, "It's all very well being blasé, but if another mishap occurs, I don't relish the prospect of becoming a hospital visitor again."

"Candice, I'm not going into the water at the Great Blue Hole. I just wanted you to see the Lighthouse Reef locale. It might be a once in a lifetime experience."

An hour into the travel, the vessel came to a halt on the inside rim of the Great Blue Hole, once again, the sky ceaselessly cloudless under Vincent's yellow sun.

Peeking at the scuba divers making their preparations, she probed, "Are you tempted to join in?"

"Phew," Cory groaned, whilst gently caressing his wife, "I might believe in lightning not striking twice in the same place, but no, tempting fate too much could equate with a titanic mistake."

Very pleased with his response, she burst into a warm smile and drew him into her, their bodies melding into a gapless fusion.

"Did you ever consider the hotel name to be profound," she catechised, "even prophetic?"

"You mean, Journeys End?"

"Yes. As soon as you told me, my propulsions massed on Dante's Inferno."

"As in, *abandon hope, all ye who enter here?*"

"Correct."

"It did cross my mind when I initially heard the name, and again when I finally got back my cognitive powers at the hospital. But then the Chaplins re-entered my cognition. They have found their journeys end in Belize as a place for peaceful retirement, so I'd put a positive spin on their heavenly breakthrough."

"Yes, I see what you mean. Maybe after what happened to you, I'm being overly melodramatic."

Agape at the divers having their pleasures in the depths of the Great Blue Hole, he pleaded, "The other purpose for wanting to come out here again is to defy my demons. I didn't want to get back to Canterbury and have nightmares about marauding sea hunters. I figured if I could make the voyage to the reef, and gaze into the Great Blue Hole without going crazy at the supposition of another shark raid, it'd effect closure, and I'd file the event deep in the backwaters of memory."

Wrapping herself tightly around him, Candice beamed at her husband, her anxieties quelled.

Sipping on rum cocktails, they continued to re-discover each other under Vincent's matchless sun and sky. The tiger shark never reappeared. Kory Farnham had proven he was big, the world was small.

THE BALLET MEISTER'S
CALLING

THE BALLET MEISTER'S CALLING

Wondering if any of the nascent ballerinas he assessed might graduate to Company status, Emile Chevalier reposed on his trusty staff, carefully studying them wheel and pirouette through their daily drill routines.

Not unattractive for a man in his late-forties, he had managed to keep his body supple by adopting an unfluctuating fitness regime. Though his jet-black hair had thinned and become wispy, his eyes persisted magnetic, entrancing his charges and transfixing their willpower, the dancers unable to do anything but obey his every command.

As the ensemble continued to weave their graceful rhythms, Chevalier drifted back thirty years to a time when Margot Fonteyn and Rudolf Nureyev graced Covent Garden, and he roamed in the backcloth as an aspiring *danseur*. As a boy, he had seen *The Red Shoes*, a Michael Powell film centered on a prima ballerina, unable to resolve the conflicts between the competing demands of love and the ballet. She jumps from a balcony and is killed, though he concluded the theatre to be emblematic of the contradiction, rather than real. Extremely compelling and passionate, the film inspired the adolescent Chevalier. The son of French parents owning an up-market bistro in Kensington specialising in Aquitaine cuisine, they expected Emile to become a

Michelin chef and run the business, but he had other ideas after seeing the Powell classic.

Enrolling at the English National Ballet in 1956, he quickly blossomed, and within a few years challenged for premier *danseur* roles. Then an unfortunate car crash resulted in a leg injury, wiping out his burgeoning *ballerino* career.

Soul-crushed, Chevalier descended into a decimating pit, near to broken and inconsolable. Then Vivien Kendall entered his world, her no-nonsense approach to solving life problems refreshing his vigour and imbuing him with new-found purpose. Just the antidote to rejuvenate him, he took up the ballet again, taking stage director and associate-impresario professions. Though failing to compensate for the loss of his dancing dreams, he still contributed to his beloved art form, finding solace and satisfaction in seeing his schemes discharged by the success of those he managed and guided. Eventually, he graduated to chief choreographer, a.k.a. ballet meister for the Henderson Ballet Ensemble, also occasionally acting for affiliated companies in Europe and America. Empowering him with daily exposure to the dancers, he considered the prized occupation to be his personal comfort zone, teaching others his art, his teenage ambitions fulfilled by proxy.

Back in London again, instructing the latest HBE intake after a brief engagement with the Vienna Ballet Company, he still pondered about what might have been. Complimented by Nureyev in his seminal years, the praise enriched Chevalier's confidence and added to his verve, his craving for triumph burning brightly. In his imagery, he saw himself going on to the Royal Ballet, the Bolshoi and others, winning accolades and international acclaim, audiences warming to his skillful rendition of the great ballets. But it was not to be. Though his personal tragedy had long since been put into perspective, nevertheless, often witnessing the achievements of his proteges only served to amplify his misgivings *vis-à-vis* being cheated of the approbation. Managing to contain his frustrations, he had kept them undetectable to collaborators, his *de facto* dazzling and approachable personae masking internal hurt.

The warble of ballet shoes squeaking on wooden flooring brought him out of daydream, his attention enticed by *nouveau* entrants at the *barre* refining warm up exercises whilst squinting at their images in an opposite wall mirror, each diminutive blemish in the workout magnified by an unforgiving reflection.

"Julia," Chevalier cooed, lifting and pointing his staff at her.

One of the hopefuls in the training session turned to peep at him.

"Julia, just what is that curious swirl you are attempting to execute?"

Embarrassed by her flawed movement, the immature swan hung her head. "It's the pirouette sequence in *Sleeping Beauty* Act 2, when Princess Aurora appears as the Lilac Fairy to Prince Desire."

Throwing her back an encouraging smile, Chevalier entreated, "Best to walk, my dear, before you attempt running…understand?"

From foregoing classes, he had already cottoned onto Julia's special aptitude, but she needed to be carefully nurtured and honed to eliminate error and imperfection.

"Yes, ballet meister," she meekly muttered.

"Good." Clapping, he created a ringing clang heard everywhere in the practice studio. "Now, let's see those *pas de valse* and *pas de chat* from all of you."

Assembling into a rectangular matrix formation, the attentive mavens assumed the lead-off position awaiting instruction.

"And one and two, and one and two," Chevalier began. "Keep those toes straight out, and one and two and one and two."

Loaded with zeal, the dancers went to work, Chevalier monitoring their every movement whilst tapping the floor with his staff in metronome fashion. Lightly admonishing their failings and praising their accomplishments with economy of gusto, he smoothly orchestrated the praxis, the trick being to realise a disciplined underpinning, without them becoming audacious about their talent and transitioning into flair too early in their development.

Pleased with the dancers' progress, Chevalier's concentration partly broke when he caught sight of the practice studio entrance doors beginning to move about their hinge sockets, the Company's musical director, Meredith Gray, a tall, elegant, well-groomed man, dressed in an Armani suit, entered, and walked by the dancers casually observing their enactments, before joining him. Replicating the ballet meister, in his teens he had also seen *The Red Shoes* and been impassioned by Anton Walbrook's portrayal of the charismatic but ruthless impresario, Boris Lermontov.

"Any budding Fonteyns or Bussells in this intake, maestro?"

Glowing at the inevitable question posed by all HBE executive managers, Chevalier wavered playfully about his staff. "There is always such a possibility, and I know you are being intentionally sardonic, *mon amie*."

Reciprocating Chevalier's facial gesture, Gray begged, "Do forgive me, Emile, I occasionally lapse into satire after decades of being disappointed by fledgling swans."

"Yes, the incidence of locating a genuine pearl gets remoter with each passing year." Lingering, his swaying on the staff exaggerated. "Or is it, as I get older?" Twinkling at Gray, he proposed, "What once hit the requisite apex of excellence, is now a run of the mill requirement, and increasing hungers have become unobtainable."

"True. I referee we subconsciously upgrade the bar year on year, never totally gratified with what we see. We harbour yearnings of finding someone extraordinary, and undertaking the wish, we constantly hoist standards above the stratospheres." Making a repeated up gesticulation with his arms, he emphasised the point.

"Yes, you are probably right."

Gazing back at the dancers, Chevalier motioned. "You see the tall girl in the light-pink leotard, fourth from the left in the front row?"

Gray's eyes traversed the ballet line. "Yes."

"Julia is her Christian name. I have colossal hopes for her. There's a touch of the Fonteyn about her propagation and poise." Careening his head positively, he credited, "She could be the one."

"Well, categorically we could do with a new prima ballerina, someone to get the audiences' juices flowing again." Grimacing, he complained, "It's all a bit stale and stilted at present." Casually eyeing Julia again, he mentally noted the precision parabolic arc of her body concurrent with an *emboité* execution. "So, you appraise she could be our new superstar?"

"Patience, Meredith, it's early days. Identical to the rest of them, Julia needs to be given time to mature both physically and mentally." Marginally retreating, he fabricated a weighty expression. "Burgeoning talent is never enough." Gaping at Gray with pride, he stipulated, "They are all talented, but what will separate those graduating to the *corps de ballet*, from those we send to variety theatre, will be grit and determination notwithstanding hard labour and pain, and more pain."

"And Julia?"

"She will make it to the Company," he predicted, tapping his forehead. "I've seen enough to date to forecast with conviction she will do anything necessary to be on the right side of the cut."

Perpetuating their inspection of the entrants, whilst discussing the latest events in world ballet, Gray took the opportunity to segue into the recruitment of the season's chosen prima ballerina.

"By the way," he prompted, "did you know Madame Blanchard has asked for you?"

"Christelle Blanchard?"

"The very same."

"Seymour did hint he's about to sign a big name." Pensively, the ballet meister informed, "I've not seen her for over ten years." Frowning, he conveyed to Gray the tang of trepidation. "Not quite long enough to muse about her fondly."

"Well, Seymour has got her agreement to be our guest prima ballerina this season for *Le Corsaire*."

"She must be virtually as old as me," Chevalier scoffed, simpering with scepticism at Madame Blanchard's apparent hankering. "Is she trying to supersede Fonteyn's record?"

Smirking at the suggestion, Gray conferred, "I did hear she injured herself at the *Teatro alla Scala* whilst performing the lead in *Giselle*."

"*Oh*," he responded, uplifting his eyebrows.

"She remembered you from her days at Covent Garden and the Coliseum. She has it in mind, you can somehow help her back to fine fettle."

"Back to fine fettle?"

"Yes. Allegedly, she esteems you can provide the physiotherapy essential for her to discharge her best in *Le Corsaire*."

* * *

After telephoning fellow ballet meisters in Milan, Paris and Berlin about their recent experiences with Madame Blanchard, Chevalier went to see HBE Company Director Seymour Henderson, his door forever unbarred to him. Notably, Henderson revered Chevalier both as a ballet professional and as an honourable comrade. Over ten years Chevalier's senior and approaching his sixtieth birthday, they first met at the English National Ballet when Henderson operated as a stage director. In his late twenties at the time, he possessed a quintessential film star semblance reminiscent of Stewart Granger. Young starlets worshipped him, lured like a moth to a flame by his vibrant constitution and grandeur. Inevitably, he married one of them, Magdalene Bouvier, an adept ballerina, and proceeded to raise a family. Always a worrier, the whims and quirks of the ballet world had taken their toll on his facade. Though he retained his rooted idol likeness, now his skin shone sallow, his once square jaw had the beginnings of jowls, and his luminous eyes had dulled. Albeit, over the intervening years, his personage had not changed, his amiable and scholarly frontage maintained.

Along with Meredith Gray, Chevalier and Henderson had formed an impresario triumvirate, successfully staging superior-caliber ballet productions in a plethora of international theatres for over two decades. Impeccable reputations and intimate relationships had been forged, coupled with the necessary skills to supervise the most temperamental of principal men and women, the threesome able to administer the right proportions of carrot and stick to extract optimum feats from their stars. In the process, awards had been showered on them from the uppermost echelons in world ballet.

Chevalier and Henderson settled into easy chairs to discuss the *Le Corsaire* opus and Madame Blanchard's central role, Henderson well aware of the history between the ballet meister and the prima ballerina.

"Tell me, do you have agonies about Madame Blanchard, Emile?"

"Yes, I do, Seymour," Chevalier admitted. "Much as I'd enjoy jousting with Christelle—" He cultivated a tongue-in-cheek phiz. "It's a matter of wills you'll understand, and her reputation goes before her. She has become famous, or should I say infamous, for her bad temper and discourtesy. My concern is for the *corps de ballet* and the Company at large." Furrowing his brow, he conceded, "Indubitably, we want *Le Corsaire* to be a winner, but not at the expense of the HBE as a whole," then rubbing his chin cautioned, "an injured Madame Blanchard could be a very vexatious beast."

"I take your point," Henderson concurred, "but she is now under indentures. If we cancel her gig, she will sue us for breach."

"But surely the appointment sealing occurred before we knew of her injury?"

"Not quite," Henderson confided.

"*Oh!*" Chevalier blurted, agog the Company Director had permitted himself to be sold damaged goods.

"Her manager Cesare Bartolini did give me the full nine yards relating to her injury, but I still elected to proceed to contract signature."

"But why?"

"No doubt Meredith has shared his longings with you about needing a spark to incite public interest for the forthcoming season?"

"He has."

"Well, Blanchard at her best remains unsurpassed, and a mystique has bloomed about her personality, creating curiosity, especially for embryonic ballet aficionados. She meets Meredith's prerequisite, and as soon as her lead in *Le Corsaire* is announced, it ensures a sellout in advance for every rendering in the early weeks, and thereafter, for most nights of the season. Adding to the justification, I've had a plethora of enquiries from corporate and private sponsors to part-cover *Le Corsaire* running costs, making her engagement just too lucrative a business break to turn away."

"Sound business strategy, Seymour, but it will not be totally riskless. According to my European congeners, an ordinarily fit Madame Blanchard is difficult enough to control, but one in pain will make everyone else suffer with her." Pausing, Chevalier let his words sink in, then supplemented, "Is there a get out clause allowing for cancellation, when injury might impair performance?"

"No. Such an aspect is protected via insurance for both parties. We are obliged to take dear Christelle."

"Very well," Chevalier accepted. "I just wanted to explore the possibilities, but you have my bond, I will be accommodating and cordial with Madame Blanchard at all times."

"I never doubted you, Emile. Now let's get Meredith in here, and we'll toast to the success of *Le Corsaire*."

A few weeks went by before Madame Blanchard arrived in London to a fanfare of newspaper photographers and television interviews at Heathrow Airport. Like Chevalier, with marching years, she had worn well by averting drugs and tobacco, her only indulgences; champagne and husbands, the latter, many. Fifteen years her junior, the new incumbent Gerhard Friedmann, a Swiss investment banker and an avid *balletomane*, trailed her like a toy poodle ministering to her every whim.

Her starting stint with Chevalier had been inaugurated by Seymour Henderson, Christelle wanting it to be a near-to private liaison, just the two of them, and her manager. Going out of his way to make her feel welcome and at ease, Henderson escorted the already attired in a dance costume Madame Blanchard and her entourage to the *foyer de la danse*, where the ballet meister awaited. Swinging the studio doors to latch them against restraints, he saw Chevalier in discussion with his support team.

"Emile," Henderson crooned in his finely cultivated voice.

Turning in the direction of the oncoming party, Chevalier affectionately greeted, "Madame Blanchard," as the prima ballerina made her way into the hub of the practice studio, her head held skyward befitting ballet royalty.

"Maestro Chevalier," she warbled, a rich, sensuous smile virtually leaping from her finely chiseled features, reminding him of a smoldering Marlene Dietrich at her very best.

Embracing in the traditional artist's manner, cheek to cheek, they kissed fresh air.

"How are you, my dear Christelle?"

Peevishly blowing out, Blanchard replied, "I've seen better days, Emile."

"Well—" He took her in again. "You look stunning."

"So kind of you to say so. Still the faultless gentleman, I see. Tell me, how is your exquisite wife?"

"Vivien is fine."

"Such a regal name, and your children?"

"Philippe is now twenty-three and running the family restaurant. Camille passed twenty-one last year. She has graduated from Queen Mary College with a cinematics degree and is driving everyone crazy with fancies to become a cinematographer."

Mindful she had no children, Chevalier refrained from asking Christelle about her private life. Under advisement from Henderson, he also did not enquire about husband number four, Herr Friedmann, Christelle ceaselessly unsure how long she'd keep her current spouse. Besides wanting her to reside focused on dispensing an imperial *Le Corsaire* enactment, Chevalier wished to evade unnecessary domestic complications and the vagaries of prima ballerina ego drive.

"Oh, Emile, I'm being rude, I haven't introduced my manager to you." She swivelled to salute a slender man with raven hair and a thin mustache, decked out in a two-piece pinstripe suit, bow tie, and holding a homburg in both hands. "This is Signori Cesare Bartolini."

Expansively grinning like a Cheshire cat, the trim gent stepped forward. "Monsieur Chevalier, it is my supreme pleasure to meet you," he gushed in a falsetto Italian accent.

"Signori Bartolini, *Il piacere è tutto mio.*"

"Oh, you speak Italian."

"A trifle."

"The pleasure is all mine as well," Bartolini warranted.

Madame Blanchard coughed fractiously, Chevalier glancing at her, heedful she expected to be the centre of attention at all times, her fuse often mightily short.

"Shall we begin?" Chevalier broached, waving to the studio centre.

Sneering indignantly at Bartolini, Madame Blanchard spat, "Yes, lets," a trace of dark menace in her tenor.

Snapping her fingers, Madame Blanchard's cortege hurriedly made their way out of the studio, Chevalier amused at the quickness of their departure. Wheeling to shine at his backing staff, he artificially mimicked her stern demeanour, making them snigger. He nodded and they too left at pace. After parting civilities to Blanchard and Bartolini, Henderson went off to resume his management duties.

Avoiding Blanchard's eyes, knowing he had exceeded the very narrow margin granted to acknowledge his introduction, Bartolini took up a post on the periphery of the studio, nervously kneading his hat. Meanwhile, Blanchard and Chevalier gazed at each other like gunfighters about to conduct a duel.

Beaming graciously, Chevalier instructed, "To begin, we will loosen on the *barre*, and then proceed into *battement.*"

Gliding to the *barre*, Blanchard undertook a preamble deportment, Chevalier inspecting her carriage.

"*Seconde*, if you please," he requested. Actioning the required posture, the dance master mentally noted her wrist, elbow and chin attitudes. "Fine, and now let's move into some loosening exercises."

Taking Christelle through the warm up patterns, he judged her *batterie* and gauged her *frappé*, *glissé* and *tendu jeté* executions, before the drill progressed into a series of more exacting demands, Chevalier logging the prima ballerina had trouble balancing amid *piques* and *pirouettes*, *rond de jambs* and *sissonnes*. Suspecting the twist mentioned by Gray affected her undertaking, he abruptly clapped, stopping the ritual, Madame Blanchard coming to a rapid standstill and anxiously eyeing him.

Eternally tactful, he ventured in an empathetic inflection, "Christelle, you are exhibiting slight signs of maneuvering impediment."

Modulating into circumstantial nervousness, Madame Blanchard ripened a wan dial. "Emile," she spluttered out, "there is a hindrance, but I presumed you knew about it already."

Casting a dominating pout at Bartolini, she indicated for him to make an explanation. Striding frontwards, still subconsciously abusing his hat, a doleful veneer covered the Italian's face. In as delicate words as he could muster, he told Chevalier about how the prima had strained the muscles encircling her left knee during the penultimate night's performance of *Giselle* at *Teatro alla Scala*. At the outset, her attendants were phlegmatic, but the dull pain did not relent, and a doctor had to be called. Subsequent to his examination, he prescribed rest after finalising her Milan commitment.

"Of course, by then, my commitment to *Le Corsaire* had been sealed," Madame Blanchard interjected. "Bartolini had agreed to the contract terms with the Henderson Ballet Ensemble, and I have my reputation to consider." Professedly distraught, she beseeched, "I cannot let the audience down, Emile." Dissolving into sorrow, her *de facto*, hard, shell-like persona crumbled. Near to tears, she divulged, "I am so worried I might not be able to perform. Ballet has been my life since childhood. I just cannot conceive of a future without my craft."

Hurrying to a chair, she sat demonstrating anguish and incapacity, then cloaked her phizog with her forearms as if trying to blot out her terror.

Caught between compassion and reproach, Bartolini gawked at her, then at Chevalier, almost pleadingly. At times he could willingly strangle Blanchard, but conversely, felt a chasm of empathy for her prevailing predicament.

Sitting beside her, Chevalier consoled the despondent prima. "Come, come Christelle, it can't be so bad."

She flashed him a melancholy mien. "Maybe, but I do feel discomforted, Emile?"

"Well, you are not exactly in traction, are you? You are moving, not normally, but nonetheless the restriction is not sizable." Shooting an encouraging smile at her, he cajoled, "Let me see the knee."

Obliging, Blanchard stretched out her left leg, then folded it about the knee while keeping the foot straight to fully expand the knee sinews. Fastidiously probing the affected area with his digits, Chevalier mentally stored each irregularity in the muscle tone.

His own wound of nearly three decades had taught him a lot about outwardly inconsequential, minor injuries limiting ballet technique. Dancers knew of his misfortune, and his successively acquired skills to analyse and heal injuries. Often, they consulted him for advice and therapy, Chevalier having a faculty to pinpoint the problem, and prescribe an exercise regime to complement medical advice. In advance of Madame Blanchard's arrival, he guessed her injury to be the crucial reason why she coveted his ballet meister services.

Pressing the perimeter of the affected area, he solicited, "does the pressure hurt?"

"It's tender."

Moving his thumbs to the inside of her knee, he depressed the tissue. "And here?"

"Ooohh, yes it does hurt."

Persisting with the scrutiny, he gently moved his fingertips over the knee's contours, searching for irregularities and inflammations. "There is some damage."

Alarmed at his diagnosis, she sharply sucked in breath.

"Calm yourself, Christelle. It is not permanent," he contended. "You will have to rest before we can resume recitation and—"

"But what about rehearsals, Emile?" she interrupted.

Holding up a heartening hand, he declared, "there's plenty of time for preparation. To make the swelling desist, you'll need to keep your left leg higher than your waist for at least a week, maybe more. Then and only then, can we begin building strength in the knee muscle and ligaments again."

"But Emile," she bleated, "*Le Corsaire* begins in less than four weeks, and I will need to rehearse with the rest of the Company." Rubbernecking at him imploringly, she confessed, "I'm having major trouble sustaining the *ballon* and the *deboulé*, and my *en dedans* are collapsing. Worst of all, once seen to be my *piéce de résistance*, my *grand pas d'action* is incomplete."

She swooned with consternation.

"As I say, there is plenty of time, if you heed what your doctor and I prescribe."

* * *

Ten days passed with the irritable prima in the prone position, her husband playing the whipping boy to her frustrations. Visiting their Bayswater apartment every other day to check on Blanchard's injury, Chevalier also comforted the hapless Friedmann.

"Emile, she has me at my wit's end and in the jaws of desperation," Friedmann bawled, his intuitive sense of *joie de vivre* drained. "No matter what I do to comfort her, it's wrong."

"Gerhard, let me assure you, the baptism will soon be over," Chevalier promoted, his voice wittingly soothing. "The doctor tells me Christelle is on the mend."

Engrossed in his own qualms, Friedmann hardly took in the words. "I'd just hit thirty-three when I met her, and we were married less than three months thereafter." Pitching a wry, convulsive glare at the ballet meister, he complained, "Now, in less than a year after the nuptials, I feel like I am twice my age. My forehead is prematurely wrinkling, and my hair is going grey."

Uncertain he had convinced Chevalier, the part-time investment banker showed him a photograph of Christelle and himself on their wedding day. Sure enough, when Chevalier peered deep into the image, it revealed a healthy and still youthful groom. Goggling at Friedmann using his peripheral vision, he noted his once billowy walnut hair and vivid green blue eyes had both dimmed.

"I know what you are deliberating," Friedmann bemoaned, "'He's losing his looks.' Moreover, I am thinner than my age thirty-three physique. Usually, people gain mass with age, but Christelle's constant tension plagues my nerves, hence the weight loss, but I doubt she has even noticed. All she talks and meditates about is her blessed ballet workouts and theatre performances."

Much to Friedmann's relief, at length the doctor gave the all-clear, Chevalier's own inspection revealing the troublesome knee to be fit enough for light ballet exercise.

Back in the practice studio, Chevalier began Blanchard's ballet recovery process. Primarily, the exertions were gentle, her mentor meticulously testing the tormenting knee after every session, ascertaining it had not become inflamed. As confidence built between ballet meister and prima ballerina, the auger intensified, Chevalier taking Blanchard through a succession of dynamic movements to test the knee's robustness. Lastly, satisfied unimpaired mobility had been accomplished, he sanctioned her to dance an act from *Swan Lake* with musical accompaniment, Madame Blanchard still intact at the conclusion of the exercise, and wanting to do more.

With her comprehensive dance repertoire restored, Henderson, Gray and Chevalier mutually agreed to her now being capable of performing *Le Corsaire* in its entirety. Assembling the orchestra and the *corps de ballet*, full rehearsals got underway, Blanchard astounding the HBE with her majestic display. Thankful for the respite from her haranguing, Gerhard Friedmann paid homage to all those involved in his wife's recovery.

Platformed at The Royal Opera House Covent Garden, the HBE production of *Le Corsaire* cascaded into a raging hit, Madame Blanchard receiving rave reviews from media ballet critics, dispelling their assumption the prima abided past her best. Flower tributes filled her dressing room nightly, and she collected a host of congratulatory telegrams from counterparts across the spectrum of world ballet.

With the generous acclaim, happiness and zest returned to

Christelle Blanchard, but as the season wore on, her impulsive bordering on obnoxious trait surfaced. She began to live up to her reputation as a fiery dragon, criticising her fellow dancers and finding fault in how the HBE were handling her engagement. Taking his fair share of the vitriol, Friedmann surged into an overwrought vein again, telling Chevalier whatever he does, it's wrong, Christelle constantly bombarding him with complaints and gibes. Exasperated with her constant bitching, eventually, Gray and Henderson also threw in the towel, as did Signori Bartolini. In an effort to contain the stress caused by his client's barrage of grievances, he had taken to tranquillisers. All of them shied away from Madame Blanchard, jittery she could erupt on the spur of the moment dishing out bitter pills to anyone in her firing line. Chevalier anticipated nothing less, knowing once the beast had the thorn extracted from its paw, its predatory instincts would ignite. He had seen it all before. Little dazed the ballet meister.

By mid-season, the London ballet scene had erupted, awash with excitement and praise, capping in *Le Corsaire* ticket sales going sky high, ballet addicts once more in awe of a fabulous dancer. Needless to say, when the occasional spat materialised in the entertainment columns of the broadsheets, her adoring legions largely lingered oblivious to it, or glossed over Blanchard's loopholes as artistic bent. Indifferent to the constant headaches, Bartolini persuaded the HBE to extend the *Le Corsaire* season for a further two months, telling Henderson, 'It's just too good a commercial opportunity to spurn.' Only too willing to make a substantial contribution to covering costs, in trade for their brand or family name being associated with Madame Blanchard's victories, more corporate and private sponsors lined up to become part of the circus. Though abiding as a pain to everyone she came into contact with, particularly Chevalier, the HBE management team deemed it a necessary torment to undergo, explosive revenues compensation dulling the grief.

On the terminating night of the germinal *Le Corsaire* season, a tangible aura of enthrallment pervaded the Company, everyone charged up about the ballet's season extension. Happy sponsors sat alongside Seymour and Magdalene Henderson and Emile and Vivien Chevalier in the front row of the stalls, lapping up the audience adulation of Madame Blanchard, in yet another breathtaking carry out from the veteran prima ballerina. Then it all changed.

Out of nowhere, whilst fulfilling a *sur le coup-de-pied* followed by a *sontenu en tournant* in act two, Blanchard's knee gave way, sending her tumbling with a crash to the floor, the other dancers coming to a brisk halt, open-mouthed or sighing at the shocking calamity.

Conducting for the evening enactment, Meredith Gray brought the orchestra to a shuddering stop, the audience leaning forward in their seats gasping at the explicitly distressed prima ballerina. Stage Manager Kendrick Tremblay darted to Blanchard's aid, his eyes out on stalks and hunching his shoulders up at Henderson and Chevalier as he went, the pair exchanging disconcerted glances. Speedily appreciating she'd be unable to continue, Tremblay made a signal of regret to the HBE management, then gesticulated to a sceneshifter. Amidst the roaring clatter of ballet lover speculation, the man brought the curtain down, press columnists hastily leaving their seats to phone in the breaking news to their editors.

After Tremblay had briefed Henderson, Gray and Chevalier, the company director promptly took to the platform, the melee diminishing as he held an arm aloft and politely petitioned for quiet.

"Ladies and gentlemen," Henderson began, an air of gloom in his modulation, "I regret to inform you, Madame Blanchard is unable to continue." An increasing-in-volume murmur rose from the audience in response to the somber statement, Henderson reacting by holding an appendage up again. "Consequently, as a mark of respect, we shall not be resuming tonight's rendition of *Le Corsaire*. Please accept our most sincere apologies the evening's entertainment has had to be curtailed. Thank you, and goodnight."

Still gripped, the audience brattle reached crescendo

proportions as newspaper men made for the exits, keen to update the stop-press news for the next day's first editions.

Over the ensuing hours, the HBE management frantically made calls to booking agents and personal managers worldwide, trying to find a seasoned campaigner to replace Madame Blanchard. With all contenders committed elsewhere, their efforts tarried in vain, leaving Henderson *inter alia* beside himself, the Company Director saturated in visions of impending financial disaster.

In a week, the succeeding season of *Le Corsaire* commenced, every ticket sold in advance on the strength of the prima ballerina's extraordinary bulletins.

Party to the management's replacement crusade, Chevalier maintained remarkable cool, even when it emerged no suitable nominees were available. Seeing his unambiguous well-being, Gray wandered over to the ballet meister, likewise noting his sanguine even serene forbearance in the jaws of disaster.

"Emile, I've known you for more years than I care to remember," he accredited. "Everyone is running around like scolded chickens, yet you remain placid." Ceasing, he revisited Chevalier's mien. "What is it you know, we apparently don't?"

Glittering back at his old buddy, Chevalier voiced, "Meredith, do you recall the entrant ballerina we were watching when you told me about Madame Blanchard's imminent arrival?"

"Vaguely at least seven months ago." He mused for a few seconds. "What about her?"

"I've been busying myself with her ever since. She is the exceptional candidate in her class, and since you last saw her, she has perceptibly mellowed into a wonderful dancer."

"You're not planning…" Grimacing, the thunderbolt sunk in. "…to propose this girl as a substitute for Christelle, are you?"

"Ordinarily no, but I waited to see if another prima came to the fore before tabling the suggestion."

"Ohh, Emile, you cannot be serious. There must be other more accustomed ballerinas in the Company we can use. What about Suzanne Elliott or Barbara Kemble? At least they are in the *Le Corsaire corps de ballet.* "

"Ah yes, both are very competent for the *sujet* and *coryphée*, and I could also nominate a few others, including Helen Graves and Monique Estler, but right now, they do not have the essential spark mandatory to make the conversion from ballerina to prima ballerina."

"And you evaluate this girl *does?*" he pressurised, his voice rising an octave brought on by skepticism.

Shooting one of his knowing smiles at Gray, Chevalier invited, "Come to the *Foyer de la danse* tomorrow at ten, and I'll have her go through her paces. If you judge she is capable, then we'll take it to Seymour."

"What's her name?"

"Julia Huxley."

* * *

Prim, proper and swimming in dreams of becoming a prima, Julia Huxley had attended ballet lessons since the age of five, her mother entering her at the Hampstead Junior Ballet School, more resultant from certitude her equals deemed it to be the chic thing to do, rather than any ambition to see her daughter in the national ballet. An unequivocal natural, Julia quickly found her dancing feet, her talent steadily flourishing as she grew into her teenage years. Aged sixteen, she joined the Henderson Ballet Ensemble Company as a junior, whilst in parallel completing the balance of her education. Three years thenceforth, she had amassed sufficient potency in her lissome body to fruit outstanding poise and control. For Chevalier, only the acquisition of passion and emotion dawdled to be added to her canon. She had to learn release from glacial aloofness and let herself go.

Howbeit, during her early period as a hopeful ballerina under his tutelage, Chevalier had categorised she stood out, her temperament and execution nearing the acme, her interpretation of prototypical ballet pageants noteworthy and singular. Sensing the ballet meister's recognition, Julia realised she controlled a very rare touchstone. In the context of cutting-edge ballet steps, she jetted into ambition, hence Chevalier's instruction to learn to walk before she ran.

Since, her development had been eye-popping. As part of the training, some junior ballerinas were allowed to dance with the senior members of the Company, even taking onboard prima ballerina protagonists. Julia had *Le Corsaire* off pat. Additional to Chevalier, the *corps de ballet* and her contemporaries articulated the neophyte dancer shone beyond her tender years. However, with the nature of the ballet world being so competitive and racked with jealousy and envy, no one went on the record. Besides, any official assessment lay within ballet meister Chevalier's remit.

He had planned to inaugurate Julia as an understudy, either in the second season of *Le Corsaire* or the befalling ballet, *Swan Lake*. Nevertheless, with Madame Blanchard unable to affect her appearance, and with the lack of other prima ballerina availability at such short notice, affairs overtook Chevalier's plans for Julia.

When Gray arrived at the practice studio the sequent morning, Chevalier's charges were already loosening up at the *barre*.

"Good morning, maestro."

"*Bon jour*, Meredith."

"So just remind me, which one is she?"

"The one with her blonde hair in a ponytail, second from the right."

Twisting his gaze into the path of the budding dancers, Gray immediately picked out Julia Huxley.

Clapping firmly, the dancers came to rest awaiting Chevalier's instruction. "Right, ladies, let's go into *The Sleeping Beauty* Act 1. Julia—" Instantly, she peeped at him, her eyes blooming, her lips parting, her yearning lucid to Gray. "You will take the part of Princess Aurora."

After Chevalier's assistant slid *The Sleeping Beauty* CD into the studio player, Tchaikovsky's passionate music filled the chamber. As the rendering took hold, Chevalier peeked at Gray's reaction to Julia's eloquent Princess Aurora construction.

Seconds later, he blinked at the ballet meister. "She's good," he commended, "she's very good."

"Good enough to play Medora in *Le Corsaire*?"

Studying Julia for a few minutes, he pronounced, "Well, she's certainly got poise and elegance, and technically she is virtually faultless." His mug hardened. "But this is a practice studio, Emile. How do we know she can make the transition to a live audience at Covent Garden?"

"We don't, but we never know, do we." Delaying, he momentarily took in Julia's matchless portrayal. "Regardless, there's a more crucial dynamic."

"Go on."

"Perfection is not just accomplishing command and technical distinction. It is also about the ballerina losing herself in the role, astonishing both cohorts and audiences alike. It has to approach and even surpass transcendence to merit the thunderstruck wow comeback."

"Yes. Pavlova, Fonteyn and Bussell all had it. Even Blanchard." Hesitating, a questioning purview grew on Gray's kisser. "And you calculate, Julia has it as well?"

"There have been occasions when her spirit has dignified her discharge above the generally approved vocational excellence footing. As to whether she recognised it or not, I'm hesitant. The upshot being, it has become an indigenous asset, a force emanating from her very being, setting her apart." Swaying on his staff, he eyeballed Gray. "*That, mon amie*, is very rare."

"Well yes, and the measure is will the audience receive the sorcery, becoming transported by the dancer's presentation?"

"Quite."

"Mmmm, I suppose the first thing does give rise to the second."

"Absolutely. But the overriding factor in her favour is being so young, she is fearless. She doesn't think about it, she just dances." Enacting a show of splendour, he inflexibly delineated, "I believe it's the central ingredient enabling her to make the transformation from surfacing novice to prima ballerina, with very limited time to spare."

"Some proposition." Gathering his ponderings, he asked, "So how do you want to play this, Emile?"

"Let's get Seymour to see her at a *Le Corsaire* rehearsal in the Covent Garden main arena."

"Well, we don't have any other alternatives, but can you get her ready for the inception of *Le Corsaire's* second season? Bear in mind, you have just seven days before the cardinal landmark."

Grinning, Chevalier moderated, "She's already there. All she needs is the repeated holistic ballet enactment under all-inclusive rehearsal conditions, with lighting, orchestral augmentation and act to act costume changes."

Having circumscribed choice as to rescuing the *Le Corsaire* second season, and by implication sustaining the HBE's reputation, Henderson agreed to examine Julia Huxley. Similarly amazed by the maturity of her representation, the outcome blossomed as affirmative, Chevalier authorised to get Julia ready for initiation night.

When Chevalier told the aspiring ballerina she had been selected to play Medora, Julia jumped at the chance to become a prima.

"Yes, oh yes," she trilled, elation spilling over. "The ballet is all I live for."

"It will mean some very taxing efforts between now and the premier performance of the second season," Chevalier warned.

"I can do it, maestro," she pledged. "I know I can."

* * *

Over the duration of *Le Corsaire* rehearsals, Chevalier's faith in his protege segued into unmitigated vindication, the unalloyed Company management team perusing reverently, as Julia conducted the three-act ballet in not far from a nonpareil exhibition.

Making noises about divine providence, Seymour Henderson could not countenance such a fine gem had come to the fore on cue. Insisting the manner sent from heaven to be proof positive the second season of *Le Corsaire* might exceed the success of its predecessor, his earlier doom-laden motif cracked into auspicious optimism. Equally buoyant, in due course when Julia became revealed to the ballet world at large, Gray and Chevalier could only see more exuberant articles and idolisation ahead.

Persevering with her dance routines, she worked like a Trojan with Chevalier and the *corps de ballet*, fine honing her dance steps to ensure her *Le Corsaire* undertaking equated with flawless appraisal. The day before investiture night, Madame Blanchard made an unscheduled visit to the rehearsal, her damaged knee heavily bandaged, dutiful husband Friedmann pushing her in a wheelchair, Cesare Bartolini in tow.

Whispering in his ear, Chevalier's aide informed him they had visitors. Seated in the stalls, he, Gray and Henderson apprehensively glimpsed in the invalid's direction, not comprehensively indisputable as to how Blanchard might respond.

"Christelle has a reputation for not taking kindly to ambitious pretenders attempting to take her crown," Gray forewarned.

"Yes, not even under the uncommon circumstances seeing Julia Huxley promoted from promising ballerina to principal dancer," Chevalier broadened. "This no-doubt paltry interlude will need treating with kid gloves."

"Leave this to me," Henderson urged. Moving to greet Blanchard, he donated a warm smile to her, the pair participating in the trendy kissing of fresh air greeting, before Friedmann helped his stricken wife into a seat adjacent to Chevalier.

"Christelle, how are you feeling, my dear?" the ballet meister sensitively prospected.

"I've felt better," she reacted, never taking her eyes off Julia dispensing Act Three, Scene Three, the Pasha's palace. "So, Emile, this is my surrogate?"

"Indeed, yes."

Comprehensively scrutinising the *nouveau* lead, Blanchard exhibited a string of expressions ranging from the incongruous to the popeyed, Chevalier monitoring her facial changes out of the corner of his eye.

"How old is she?"

"Nineteen."

"*Huh*, I'd danced the lead in *Coppelia* before hitting my nineteenth birthday."

"Yes, but you were extraordinary, Christelle," Chevalier diplomatically countered, his compliment intending to solicit patronage for Julia from the injured swan goddess.

Beaming with gratitude at the accolade, Blanchard purred, "At least you didn't choose one of my main competitors, someone like Edith Verlaine."

"No, we resolved it ought to be to your liking, if we chose a newcomer," he claimed, the white lie satisfying Madame Blanchard's ego.

"She is good," the fallen star credited. "She's got a superb *arriérre*, and her *cabriole* definitely has the Emile Chevalier eminence."

Swollen with vanity, the ballet meister gently took Madame Blanchard's hand. "Why thank you, Christelle."

At the rehearsal's completion, Chevalier introduced Julia Huxley to Madame Blanchard. Marvelled by the world-renowned prima, the emerging swan hardly concealed her homage, gushing praise by the bucket load, Christelle reciprocating by bidding her cordial regards for the season. Throughout the amiable encounter, the management team exchanged lofty airs, conjointly reviewing it could not have gone better, Christelle adding kudos to Julia with some especially encouraging reassurances. Veteran and novice stretched their conversation, Blanchard advising Huxley about the pitfalls to dodge as her calling progressed, her replacement taking in the advice like tablets of stone bestowed by a sublime deity.

As early evening neared, Madame Blanchard invited Julia to her Bayswater apartment for supper. After Julia had bathed and changed clothing, the pair sat in the back of Gerhard Friedmann's Bentley, with him taking the wheel. Expanding on their ballet experiences, Christelle did most of the talking, Julia playing it smart by hanging on every word and never losing eye contact with her senior. Knowing esteem from Blanchard to be axiomatic to her career advancement, by the end of the visit, the rookie prima had affected a good relationship with her advisor.

After Julia left the apartment, Friedmann commented, "There

is more guile and enterprise to that girl than meets the eye," an estimation the HBE management team soon appreciated as well.

Frowning, Christelle shot back, "Hah, you've jolted me. Did I miss something?"

"Maybe. In my vocation, I often interface with fledgling investors, perceivably behaving like babes in the wood. Nonetheless…"

"What?"

Streaming into a statesman-like demeanour, he continued. "Closer inspection often reveals it is a front, a cover erected to disguise their real intentions."

"And you've concluded Julia has some sort of agenda going on behind an innocent pretence?"

"As I say, maybe. It began as an inkling, thickening as the evening wore on."

Unconvinced by the mensuration, Christelle contested, "Oh…no, you're being too hypersensitive."

"Well, being in observational mode while you two chatted, I had an opportunity to tune into her more subtle nuances, the odd out of place word, and the probing way she dug into your locker seeking guidance."

"You're being paranoid, Gerhard," she upheld, then after reflecting qualified, "no, all I detected amounted to a sweet girl with exceptional etiquettes, trying ever so hard to be courteous."

"As I said, it transpired as an inkling." Neutrally quivering his brow, he qualified, "But I could be wrong."

Mid-morning the subsequent day, Seymour Henderson gathered the Company *en masse* onto the Covent Garden stage to say a few words and toast the introductory night of the extended *Le Corsaire* season. Holding Julia's hand, he led her to the top of an artificial staircase, used in the staging of the ballet, both carrying charged champagne glasses.

"My dear friends," he began, staring down at the assembly with pride, "today we bid farewell to one cherished and venerated supreme dancer, and welcome another into the pantheon of the gods. After being hailed as one of the most celebrated prima ballerinas, and as a corollary attaining worldwide credit and winning many honours, our dear Madame Blanchard has decided to retire from the world of ballet." A hushed gasp went up from the gathering. "We wish her well in her next venture, whatever it might be." He raised his glass. "Madame Blanchard."

Very near to tears, now on crutches and served by the ever-faithful Friedmann, with a bowed head, Christelle acknowledged the surge of applause and toast from her brethren.

"As you all know," Henderson went on, "our own Julia Huxley, a nascent dancer demonstrating remarkable talent and maturity, will take the role of Medora in our rendering of *Le Corsaire* commencing this evening. Please join me in wishing our new star our best wishes.

* * *

After the Henderson Ballet Ensemble issued a press release introducing Julia with a glowing approbation from Madame Blanchard, the *Le Corsaire* protracted season opened with the audience pumped up on adrenalin, their culture cravings sharpened by news of a startling new prima ballerina. When the curtain rose for the outset act and Julia entered, an impromptu round of applause rose from the audience, the ballet goers wanting her to succeed and be uplifted to yield a sparkling rendition.

Delivering on presuppositions, at the ballet finish, lavished in bouquets and plaudits, the new prima swan received a five-minute standing ovation. Acquiring the adulation gracefully, Julia curtsied then blew a single kiss to her admirers, the latter etiquette surprising the HBE management team, the act generally not heralded by a prima ballerina, let alone someone taking their inaugural virtuoso bow. Proclaiming the new sensation's prima ballerina triumph at Covent Garden, the arts media machine gathered pace, Julia's mastery going viral within minutes. Retiring to the company director's office, Henderson and his senior staff made a toast to extracting success from the jaws of near catastrophe.

Supercharged with vim and vigour, night after night, *Le Corsaire* notched up incremental glory, aghast ballet partisans and happy financial backers basking in Julia Huxley's conquest. News of the HBE's latest discovery winged its way into the wider world, often translating into newspaper headlines and the topmost story on television news channels, Julia germinating into a branded commodity ballet aficionados hastened to idolise, and commerce signed to endorse their merchandise. Soon after the extension finished, the HBE awarded Julia the paramount character of Princess Odette for their vanguard interpretation of *Swan Lake*. Another delirious hit, drawing sell-out crowds and wildly enthusiastic reviews, the HBE management team could not quite digest they had stumbled on pure gold.

Trophies and worldwide stardom eventuated for Julia, ballet meisters and impresarios from the world's uppermost ballet companies paying tribute to her. Talked about in the same rarified terms as the legends, her ascension to the zenith of international acclaim charged towards a certainty. As the season ensued, word about Julia's talent spread around ballet performer management agencies like wildfire, inducing a feeding frenzy by switched-on personal managers.

In secret, she confided to Quentin Zuckerman, a manifestly iniquitous predator, the HBE had signed her until the end of the *Swan Lake* season. Telling her, he could fix a very lucrative deal for a worldwide tour of international ballet companies in the capacity of guest prima ballerina, she signed with Zuckerman, only informing Henderson about the deal after the event. Henderson took the news philosophically, knowing primas' invariably become snared by personal management agents, in place of tying themselves exclusively to a single ballet company.

"I know I said the ballet had dulled and needed some fresh life, but I never foresaw anything like this," Meredith Gray enthused at a reception for Julia held at the Savoy after her final *Swan Lake* performance.

"Yes," Chevalier favoured. "She has exceeded even my wildest benchmarks."

"Mother of god," he wailed. "If it had not been for Madame Blanchard's unfortunate accident, Julia Huxley could still be a fledgling dancer in one of your novice classes, possibly on the verge of a minor role."

Smiling at the kismet inference, Chevalier wisecracked, "I guess sometimes, a bit of good fortune comes out of unpredicted upheaval."

Hearing his compatriots discussing the Company's luck, Seymour Henderson joined in the eulogy. "It puts me in mind of when Fonteyn broke in the profession, and immediately wowed the ballet world. My, my…such a historic threshold value had not been achieved since Madame Pavlova arrived on the English ballet scene in 1912." Lingering, as if lost in the momentous happening, he recollected, "I remember being at the Royal Academy of Dramatic Art when my mentor, John J. Preston, revisited attending Pavlova's first-ever show at Covent Garden." Reciting the story, he virtually swooned.

"Do you gauge Julia is good enough to be pigeonholed in such an eminent coterie?" Gray drilled.

"To my mind, if a dancer can perform prima idols in front of the most discerning audiences without fault, then I do. Unquestionably, she is destined for fame," Henderson established. "You'd agree, Emile?"

Chevalier beamed at the accolade. "Unequivocally, I do. It gives me immense satisfaction to agree with you, Seymour. And of course, she has the additional precious gift of transcending the audience."

"My point precisely," Henderson endorsed. "To find the asset in one so young is extremely rare."

"True, albeit there have only been two English ballerinas elevated to the exalted rank of prima ballerina *absoluta*."

"Dame Alicia Markova and Dame Margot Fonteyn," Gray bracketed.

"Yes," Chevalier confirmed. "But it's far too early to frame Julia in the aforementioned illustrious sorority. As Seymour says, she is very young, and the incumbent pressures on a prima can change personality and standpoint." Rippling his brow, he recounted, "We've seen it before, so I will await with reservation to see if Julia retains ego control."

Briefly considering the caveat, Henderson responded, "Very perceptive, Emile. But—" Chuckling, he waggled a baleful finger. "I did hear the personal manager who signed her has instituted a rigid disciplinary regime. I wonder what effect it will have on her ego control?"

"Probably make her command astronomical fees," Gray mooted.

"Probably," Chevalier agreed. "I've never met a star yet who does not milk her talent in terms of justifying towering payments. Moreover—" Consternation began to engulf him. "What I am much jumpier about is, she's becoming head strong."

"You mean," Gray determined, "she is beginning to enlarge her ego already?"

"There are signs. Sometimes her butter-wouldn't-melt mask drops, and she lapses into stubbornness, redressing the balance before too many commentators clock her crown slipping."

"Well," Henderson began, "let's hope by the time she returns to the HBE, they will have burnt out."

* * *

Julia Huxley went on to success after success, her notoriety facilitating her to pick and choose prima ballerina demigods on the international dais. After a few years, she regularly slipped into global front page news, but not always for the right motives.

While at Milan's *Teatro alla Scala*, she had a violent argument with her leading man, Enrico Di Maria. A much more proficient and lauded dancer, he threatened to walk if the headstrong prima prolonged her personal insults. Her engagement at the New York Met brought reports of conflict within the *corps de ballet* about Julia's dismissive attitude to her fellow cast in *Paquita*. While in Rio de Janeiro, the prima took tremendous delight in telling everyone involved in the realisation of *Don Quixote*, they had it completely wrong and demanded substantial changes to the cast and arena scenery.

Abiding unabated in virtually every ballet rendezvous she performed at, her infamy catalogue drove ballet company directors to despair, leaving the habitually tough and intransigent Quentin Zuckerman regretful about his thirst to sign Huxley. Not lost on the HBE management team, the international news delineating her moodiness had Henderson, Gray and Chevalier streamlining, but for Zuckerman's greed, they could have been endlessly subjected to Huxley's intolerable behaviour.

Regardless of the pain she created for others, her magnificent form weathered, Huxley enthralling audiences wherever she danced. If there were reservations about her being tricky to administer when out of the public's gaze, perennially she sailed as fireproof onstage, spectators mesmerised by her genius-like depiction of ballet principals, and financial backers ignoring the duress as the box-office receipts flooded into their coffers.

Her victories lit up a ticket to wealth, her ballet career income significantly supplemented by endorsement and sponsorship deals, making her a multi-millionaire before her twenty-third birthday, Huxley indulging in riotous utilitarianism, her buying power incorporating opulent domiciles in Tuscany and upstate New York, a fleet of executive cars and a wardrobe containing all the latest *haute couture* creations from Paris and London.

As the years flew by and her prominence grew astronomically, beyond the exit doors of the theatre, Huxley also demonstrated most of the typical, indecorous traits of the modern, cosseted celebrity artist, whetting them to new summits of intolerance from her peers, and those involved in her personal management. With her ego unchecked, her temper riotous, and her requirement of others to fit her mould exceeding the reasonable, she had no pals and only transient lovers.

In contrast with courted desire, people dealt with Julia Huxley out of necessity. Always welcome at *beau monde* functions, her very presence swept in the curious, and ensured a froth-filled account of A-list opulence in the society columns. All the same, those making the summons were constantly on guard for Huxley's indiscretions, explicitly her tendency to insult the great and the good, when they failed to agree with her viewpoint. Eternally cast in the social pariah vein, many saw her as someone captivating to have on a celebrity invitee list but tolerated as opposed to loved.

Despite being surrounded by people, mainly sycophants and hangers-on, paradoxically, Huxley distinguished an innate sentiment of loneliness and alienation, intrinsically knowing it flourished of her own making. Those gravitating to her either wanted to laze in her emitted grandeur or sought to exploit her illustriousness for ulterior purposes. Never able to forge lasting camaraderie with ballet confederates or people she met outside the world of ballet, she often cut a lonely figure, hugging a cup of coffee in a deserted café after the midnight hour. Those good eggs persevering against the baseless abuse she invariably gave them, were often brushed aside, Huxley instantaneously suspicious about their motivations for befriending her.

Just like Madame Blanchard in preceding decades, Huxley's reputation went before her, ballet companies procuring her services more impelled by commercial determinants, than any overwhelming appetite to work with her. Huxley's frosty and often conceited disposition resulting in many bothered impresarios and enraged ballet company managers wishing they had never set eyes on her.

* * *

Having gained recurring sell-out seasons in Moscow, New York, Paris, Milan and a host of other ballet centres of honoured excellence, after a nine-year absence, Julia Huxley reverted to the Henderson Ballet Ensemble. Whilst away, she had outgrown her old confidants and colleagues at the HBE. Even her erudite mentor Chevalier and once cosy compadre Madame Blanchard had faded from immediate memory.

She had changed her *nom de plume* to Madame Julia Dubois, sacked Quentin Zuckerman on grounds of incompetence he did not contest, accepting compensation payment for the residual of his contract whilst breathing a sigh of relief, employed a plethora of superfluous admin staff and personal services providers, and engaged a lawyer with attitude to negotiate her professional contracts.

Seymour Henderson informed Chevalier and Gray about Madame Dubois agreeing to take the lead in *La Bayadère*. Since her previous season with the HBE, Chevalier's hair had become even thinner, and he had put on weight, relying more on his staff for support. Henderson's legendary film star facade had declined, and even Gray's elegance had been superseded by the onset of his twilight years. Conversely, the teenage Julia Huxley had mushroomed into a stunningly, beautiful woman, her cobalt-blue eyes, generous mouth, flowing, wavy blonde hair and unblemished complexion combining to spawn divine attractiveness.

Notwithstanding the physical by-products of the passage of time, all three men still conferred total dedication to the ballet, remaining enthusiastic about the unfolding of new talent, and invariably seeing every HBE performance at Covent Garden, the London Coliseum or Sadler's Wells. They had heard from colleagues at the Kirov, Ballet de l'Opéra national de Paris and the Staatsballett Berlin about Madame Dubois's outrageous conduct, and how she treated underlings with disregard and derision. As usual, it came as no bombshell to the three wise men, preponderantly Chevalier. He had seen it all before, nothing alarming or fazing him, all revelatory news assessed without astonishment.

With her entourage of functionaries, inclusive of her latest manager, Roland Spencer, and a cavalcade of hangers-on in tow, Dubois made her imperious entrance at the Coliseum auditorium, the chosen venue for the *La Bayadère* season, Seymour Henderson escorting her to the stage where Chevalier awaited, the ballet meister seeing he appeared bruised and bashed, presumably by a blitzkrieg from her wicked tongue, his indignation evident as the group walked towards him.

Gazing at her past ballet mentor, Dubois cattily jeered, "Why, Emile, is that *really* you?"

"Hello, Madame Dubois, yes, it is me."

"You've grown so old." As a perplexed larrup took root, she furrowed her brow. "I'm staggered you have not retired."

"With age, comes tolerance and a thick skin to ward off the

indelicate and the tactless," he confidently retorted. "This is what sustains me, keeps me going."

His rebuttal floated over the prima ballerina's head, Madame Dubois implicitly immune to light sarcasm.

"And you still train the entrants?" she spitefully hypothesised, as if small talk came as an adjunct new to her vocabulary.

"What else?" he queried, withdrawing one hand from his trusty staff, and bearing his palm in a complementary token. "It is what I do best for the HBE."

Unrestrained, the gauche dialogue progressed, Henderson increasingly perturbed at the extent of Dubois's gripes and moans. No matter how courteous Chevalier responded to her issues, she abided obnoxious and haughty, constantly denigrating the esteemed ballet meister and scrutinising for fault. Not rising to the bait, Chevalier tarried tranquil and unflustered, decades of accruing an aura of impregnable control enfranchising him to deflect insults without descending to her obtuse and patronising equal.

Belatedly, Dubois addressed *La Bayadère.* "I understand Savrosav is to be my *ballerino.*"

"Indeed, he is," Chevalier validated. "Viktor Savrosav is our guest premier *danseur* noble for this season."

"I met him at the Kirov." Emanating a sulky scowl at the remembrance, she criticised, "He's very arrogant."

"Then you will be exquisitely matched," Chevalier counter charged.

Grimacing, Dubois's nostrils flared, but she did not react. Instead, she walked about the Coliseum's platform, peeking out into the stalls, then the upper circles, as if scheduling where to make her curtsies to safeguard maximum impact at the ballet's conclusion. Already wondering what imprudent peccadilloes, she had in mind to make life difficult for the Company, Henderson and Chevalier watched her actions with suspicion.

When Meredith Gray entered the arena, he welcomed the prima ballerina with chivalrous felicitations, but like for Henderson and Chevalier, the waspish Madame Dubois treated him with equal discourtesy, the Company's musical director patently psyched out by the savagery of some gibes, but refrained from contradicting, his mind rightly fixed on the money.

"Well, I can guarantee, Madame Dubois," he began to assertively challenge, after she had cast doubt on the proficiency of his orchestra, "every musician has been meticulously chosen. They all have impeccable reputations, as tried and honourable orchestral players."

"May be so, Meredith," she contradicted. "Just warrant they come in on-queue when I make my entrances."

Bewildered by the incredulity of the unjustified petition, Gray sniggered then acquired Henderson, the company director befuddled but gesturing to take the censure without rebuke.

Coughing to relieve the tension in his vocal chords, Gray genially solicited, "Please be assured, Madame Dubois, I will do everything within my power to secure the orchestra is metronome precise with your entrances."

"What about the score?" she enquired, further stumping him.

"The score," he gingerly replicated, his countenance steeped in agitation and, increasingly, bemusement.

"Yes, the score," she authenticated. "When I danced *The Nutcracker* with the Chicago Ballet Company, Edvard Weismann changed Tchaikovsky's original score."

"But…but I know Weismann," Gray cajoled, aghast at her claim. "He's a top-notch orchestrator." Baffled, he bonded, "He'd not change Tchaikovsky's score."

"Well, it didn't sound right to me. I want you to keep to the Ludwig Minkus composition, when you conduct *La Bayadére*."

Left partly flummoxed by the unprecedented decree, Gray uttered, "You have my word, the musical accompaniment will be literally as composed by Minkus."

Whilst Dubois ceaselessly persisted in her hatchet job, now pillorying the HBE management team for their choice of the Coliseum to stage *La Bayadére* and dismissing their legitimate replies from the left side, Viktor Savrosav entered with the *corps de ballet*. Hovering in the wings monitoring the thorny dispute, he gauged the accent of the conversation to be mounting cordiality, so tentatively decided to join the group.

Out of the corner of her eye, Dubois saw him approaching. Momentarily adopting a civil tongue, she lavishly saluted, "Viktor, how good to see you again."

"Hello, Julia," he greeted in a capacious Russian accent.

Reverting to type, she snapped, "Still haven't learnt to speak English properly, I see."

Narrowing his eyes, he brusquely let rip, "Have you learnt to speak Russian yet?"

Sensing the re-acquaintance descending into fiery affray, Henderson intervened. "Emile, can we please commence the rehearsal?"

"*Bien sûr*," Chevalier responded. "*C'est mon plaisir.*"

Glaring at each other, Madame Dubois and Savrosav retired to their dressing rooms, the former with her circus in attendance. Re-entering within minutes and already warmed-up from a pre-rehearsal practice, Savrosav made a few movements to ensure his muscles resided supple, then nodded to the ballet meister, indicating his readiness to perform. Whilst Gray primed the orchestra for the beginning music with some descants from the overture, and Chevalier assembled the *corps de ballet* for the first act of *La Bayadére*, Henderson stood in the wings praying for the *entente cordiale* to prevail between the prima ballerina and everyone else. All waited for Madame Dubois to make her usual ostentatious ingress replete with her cortege, but she failed to show.

"The d*amned* woman is throwing tantrums already," Savrosav complained. "She was just the same at the Kirov."

"Please, Viktor," Chevalier beseeched, leaning on his dependable staff. "Give her a few more minutes."

Making a dismissive nod, Savrosav grilled, "Do you imagine it will make any difference?" Goggling to the heavens, he acrimoniously tested, "What devil on Earth dominated to let the HBE talk me into taking the *ballerino* role?"

"As I recall, the remuneration bargain agreement had a lot to do with it," Henderson quipped.

Tapping the polished brass surround on the conductors' podium with his baton, Gray brought the musicians clatter to a stop. Ogling dolefully at Henderson, then Chevalier, with a speculative visage, he catechised, "Are we going to begin?"

Chevalier made an apologetic shrug but lingered tight-lipped.

"Good lord, this is intolerable," Savrosav scorned.

As the minutes ticked by, the dancers delighted in light gyration to keep their limbs warm, and the odd violin and cello tuning rasp flew out from the orchestra pit, everyone registering a distinct overtone of anti-climax.

Inevitably, Henderson turned to Chevalier. "Emile, be so kind as to see what is keeping Madame Dubois, will you?"

"Gladly," he granted, his modulation charitable.

Finding her diffident brigade clustered by her dressing room door, mumbling and glum-faced, he took Spencer aside. "What's happening?"

Blowing out and gyrating his head, his nonplussed ailment instantly connected with Chevalier. "No sooner had we entered her refuge, she threw everyone out."

"You included?"

"Me included."

"Aahh." Smirking in a consoling fashion, Chevalier investigated, "How long have you been Madame Dubois's manager?"

"Just a few weeks. I perceived it could be a good career move. Now I'm not so sure."

"Don't worry," he emphasised. "In time, you will learn how to get over the barricades. Persevere, *mon amie*."

"You think so?"

"I know so." Sighting Madame Dubois's inner sanctum, he propositioned, "Perhaps, if I talked to her?"

"If you can perform the miracle, Monsieur Chevalier, you'd have my eternal gratitude."

Laying a comforting hand on Spencer's upper arm, he mellowed a festive smile. "It's Emile. We all use Christian names in the HBE family."

Gently rapping on the prima's door, he tattled, "Julia, it's Chevalier. May I come in?"

Hearing a laboured, "Yes," he entered to see an addled

Madame Dubois, staring at her beleaguered image in her dressing table mirror, tears forming in her eyes.

"The Russian peasant is insufferable, Emile," she whimpered. "He must learn that the audience comes to see me, not him."

"Julia—"

She cut him short. "Needless to say, I didn't envision anything less. His manners to me at the Kirov were disgusting."

"Julia," he attempted again.

"I will not tolerate any—"

"*Julia*!" Chevalier bellowed with force. It got her attention. "Have you come to the Coliseum for a feud, or to dance?"

Soberly eyeballing him, her diatribe abruptly dried up, then she candidly avowed, "To dance, maestro," her timbre suddenly conciliatory.

"Very well then, can we please have your presence at the rehearsal?"

"By all means, Emile," she sheepishly verified, her mug softening from offended into accommodating.

"Good, then dry your tears, and let us return to the amphitheatre." Espousing a blithe mode and grinning, he announced, "Meredith has the indivisible orchestra awaiting your grand entrance."

"Ohh, Emile," she chimed, almost breaking into a weep. "I am so glad your humour has lasted the ravages of time."

For those on the receiving end of Madame Dubois's vicious tongue, the truce persisted as a welcome interlude. Albeit, over the ensuing days, tension grew between the two crowning protagonists, Dubois accusing the Russian of not bolstering her ballet displacements properly, and Savrosav grumbling the prima ballerina never arrived on time. Affecting *corps de ballet* members, the orchestra, and the Company's support and backroom staff, the continual fracas left many on the verge of dismay, Henderson's door constantly knocked on by aggrieved dancers, jittery musicians, and irritated stage crew, the Company Director using all his persuasive skills to allay their anxieties and frustrations.

Often approximating bedlam proportions, Chevalier took the daily debacle in his stride, knowing artistic differences nearly always brought out the best displays in major players. Contrary to his designs, the more latitude he accorded Madame Dubois, the worse she became, infuriating Savrosav beyond distraction, the Russian often storming away from dress rehearsals, threatening never to enter the Coliseum again.

As initiation night loomed, Henderson petitioned Chevalier to quell the inferno, Dubois the instigator behind all the uproar, Savrosav merely responding in kind.

Armed with mediation skills, the ballet meister visited Madame Dubois at her hotel suite. Trailing his mollifying line, she promptly served up hostility and rebuke in reaction.

"How can you possibly expect me to compromise with that poor excuse for a leading man?" Dubois whined, walking smartly from the lounge into the bedroom to comb her mane of rolling golden hair. "I've seen schoolboy entrants with more intuitive talent than he will ever hold sway over."

Pursuing her, Chevalier corrected, "It's simply not true, Julia, and you know it. Viktor Savrosav is one of the top three *ballerinos* in world ballet. He has racked up nearly as many awards as you have."

"Huh, if it were true, then he must have bribed the allotting committees."

"*Ohh!*" Chevalier exclaimed, rolling his eyes in disbelief, his typically ultra-calm hackles beginning to rise. "How can you possibly say such an untrue thing? The integrity of such committees is sacrosanct. They are conspicuous for their impartiality." Astounded by her false viewpoint, he retarded from her. "Why, Seymour Henderson himself has sat on numerous attributing caucuses, and no one accuses him of succumbing to a bribe, do they?"

"Of course not," she conceded. "Seymour has unparalleled integrity. I got carried away without regard for the clout of my words."

"Yes, you frequently do," Chevalier admonished, nearing her again. "You know, Julia—" Blinking at her, he tried for the right degree of dogmatic tone. "A little modesty and composure would not go amiss."

"What do you mean?" she shyly polled, twisting away from him.

"Madame Dubois!" Holding her shoulders, he rotated her to confront him head on. "Do not vex me. You know perfectly well what I mean."

"Emile!" she blathered, her eyes screwed up in an incredulous puss. "Are you admonishing me?"

Glooming, he unreservedly informed, "Julia, there comes a time when diplomacy and turning a blind eye no longer accomplishes the end objective." Dwelling, he let his words sink in. "We have surpassed the artfulness point. First night is four days away, and still, you cause disquiet across the collective ballet ensemble, especially with Savrosav."

Shocked by his sincerity, Dubois dawdled silently, his frankness permeating her consciousness lashing home truth.

"Talent coupled with modesty and self-effacement, I find irresistible," he passionately attested. "You had it in plenty when you initially came to the HBE, but since, you have indulged in some of the worst ego excesses I have seen in over forty years in the ballet business."

Agog at his unfluctuating bluntness, she stared at the ballet meister, solemnity devouring her soul. Lowering her eyes, she admitted, "You know, they call me the black swan, don't you? The perpetual black swan, doomed to be alone forever." Shrinking into herself, she moved away from him and sat on the edge of her bed, her bottom lip quivering. "People despise me. Oh, they say the right things, but I know what they really think."

Sitting beside the distraught prima, Chevalier told her, "You've brought it on yourself, Julia. You must change, revert to the sweet girl so impressing me all those years ago. There's no need to be so aggressive and temperamental all the time. It's not a prerequisite for a prima ballerina."

"Madame Blanchard taught me," she defended. "She said to be a successful prima, I'd have to build a ring of steel around me."

"Madame Blanchard took over twenty years to drive people away from her, and she regretted it." Pausing, he flatly told her, "You've achieved the same belligerent notoriety in just nine."

Chevalier's crushing criticism hitting the bull's eye, she dropped into a crestfallen condition. "I will try to govern myself, Emile," she pledged. "I promise you, I will try."

* * *

Madame Dubois kept to her word, making peace with Viktor Savrosav, the *corps de ballet* and everyone else she had miffed. Light-heartedness prevailed after rehearsals and shows, the untouched assemblage enjoying a fortuitous new age of placid contentment. Meanwhile, *La Bayadére* received ecstatic reviews from enraptured broadsheet ballet correspondents, sponsors baying for a season extension, the HBE management team watching the treasury swell.

Then old habits and an unruly ego got the better of the principal dancer. Accusing Savrosav of trying to outmaneuver her, Dubois also reignited her curtness with other members of the Company, and generally made life difficult for the management. One grossly malignant outburst occurred sequel to yet another noteworthy transcription by the entire *La Bayadére* cast. After the final curtain call, she stormed off to her dressing room, threatening never to dance for the HBE again.

Fraught with premonitions of being sued by both the HBE and the Coliseum, Roland Spencer ran after her, his purpose to try for peace and reconciliation. Not far behind, the HBE management team followed, grim tints adorning their kissers. Catching up with the prima ballerina, they congregated in the vicinity of a dejected Madame Dubois, intent on trying to put her complaints into perspective.

Sitting at her dressing table, her back to them, she venomously pronounced, "Savrosav has insulted me for the last time. I will not dance for the HBE again until that Russian peasant has been dismissed from the Company."

"But Julia," Spencer pleaded, "he just cited you were slightly late coming in for the second scene of the third act, an observation from a fellow virtuoso, rendered free from any malice." He swivelled to face Chevalier. "Tell her, Emile."

Endeavouring to compile the right words to placate her, the ballet meister evaluated the solicitation before expounding. "You know, Julia, not even Fonteyn retained superiority all the time. It is ingrained for Company members to bring up issues and discuss their fellow dancers. In your case, customarily, they are incandescent tributes."

"It's not just the Russian, it's the whole cast, it's Seymour, Meredith, and even you, Emile." She bore at him, then the rest of them accusingly. "You all hate me, the eternal black swan. I know it's true."

Panting with rage, she held her head, cascading into a suppurate mess.

"Julia," Spencer gabbled, genuinely alarmed for her wellbeing, and extending a soothing hand she gratefully clutched.

Henderson and Gray glanced at Chevalier, signifying for him to cheer the prima.

"Julia, you are wrong," Chevalier refuted in a soothing voice. "No one hates you. But you are your own worst enemy. Your lack of professionalism, and the unwarranted attacks you make are unbecoming for a masterful and idolised dancer. Not even Pavlova dared to behave like you do, and she is still heralded as the very best of the best prima ballerinas."

Craning up her neck, semi-refreshed by the mention of Pavlova, she whispered, "Do you suppose I could be as good as Madame Pavlova?"

Taking over, Henderson answered, "Anna Pavlova conclusively endures as the greatest prima the ballet has ever seen, the World's utmost exponent of poetry in motion. My father saw her in *Cygnet* at Drury Lane in 1920, dancing opposite Vaslav Nijinsky. He endlessly talked to me about it." Consumed in sincere reminiscence he paused, then eyed her with foremost conviction. "Julia, if you are to become a truly preeminent dancer, like Pavlova and Fonteyn, you must learn civility and to curb your ego. Being a dazzling dancer is not enough."

Ashamed and embarrassed, Dubois recognised her self-seeking posture had been the central cause behind all her woes. Making remorseful flags to everybody, she begged them to forgive her inadmissible attitude, her contrite repentance moulding empathy from those yearning to guide her. Rationalising a notable bridgehead had been attained, Spencer and the HBE management left her haven. Finally, Madame Dubois had seen the light.

A modicum of normality percolated into the Coliseum, Julia requesting a gathering of the undivided *tout ensemble* and making abject apologies for her improper behaviour, the regret accruing pleasant smiles and good wishes from the cast and crew. As she spoke, relief came over Spencer, his inbred wherewithal for optimism refreshing features becoming anguished after weeks of unabated discord. Driving fingers through his thick auburn hair, as if drawing out troubles from his mind, his plumbless russet eyes lightened. Noting the scales had similarly been lifted from Henderson's, Gray's and Chevalier's eyes, as if a new dawn had arrived, he made an optimistic wave to them, the HBE management team reciprocating the formality. Afterwards, the four men gathered together and made a toast to the future, convinced Madame Dubois had her paranoia and ego firmly under control.

Serenity survived for a week, rehearsals and recitals a sheer pleasure for all concerned, then on a no-evening-show day, after being held up in traffic, Savrosav entered the auditorium late for an afternoon rehearsal. Zooming in on the prima ballerina to make his apology, before he could begin, Dubois tore into him with one of her brutal onslaughts, the *ballerino* stupefied by the intensity of her vitriol. Gathering his wits, the Russian responded in kind, the eruption intensifying, Spencer vainly trying to pour oil on troubled waters, but to no avail, and told in no uncertain terms to beat it by his client. Exasperated by the latest contretemps, Henderson and Gray threw up their arms in irritation. Frowning and fuming, they absorbed the slanging match for a few minutes, then left the rehearsal with Madame Dubois still plastering Savrosav in insults, both principal dancers oblivious to their departure. Loitering in the wings, evidently in a trance trying to vanquish himself from the affray, Spencer knew it could be the terminal straw breaking the HBE's back. Abiding relaxed throughout the animosity, Chevalier leaned on his staff, waiting for the kettle to quit boiling.

After subjection to a particularly malevolent barrage of abuse, a maddened Savrosav shouted back, "You're certifiable, Julia. You *are* the perpetual black swan."

She drew in breath and held a forearm to her chest at the piercing indignity, like she had been cut to the core. Perusing the *corps de ballet's* dropped heads and the silent musicians in the orchestra pit, she also clocked Henderson and Gray had left before spotting Chevalier. Marking the ballet meister's unruffled physiognomy, Dubois decoded it as contempt and burbled, "I surmise you judge I'm acting like the black swan as well?"

"Madame Dubois, what I think is immaterial," he piped up. "It's how you see yourself, you should be scrutinising."

She pursed her lips to make a malicious retort, then thought better of it. Instead, not knowing what to say, she paced the platform, generating a series of pent-up, staccato motions, the *corps de ballet* besotted by her angular movements, the stage crew mesmerised by the real-life drama. Coming to a halt and near to snorting like a runaway bull about to make a charge, she scowled and muttered obscenities in an act of defiance. Then, unusually, consideration overcame her congenital tendency to go on the offensive. Realising a watershed juncture approached, and she hung precariously on the limit of her compatriots' tolerance, self-preservation took over her mantle. She had to be careful not to push too far.

Assuming a contrite air, she scoured the ballet meister. "But Emile, I…I do try, but everyone is conspiring against me."

Chevalier brought his trusty staff down hard on the stage floor, its impact making a grating crack, ringing far and wide in the theatre. "*Not* true, Julia. Your overactive imagination is making excuses for your own indiscipline," he reprimanded, his voice potent, inflexible, but measured. "You know it to be fact, as well as I do. This is the only time Viktor has not arrived on time, and in response you throw a massive fit. Contrast your flare-up to his understanding on the myriads of occasions you have shown up late, justified on some fictitious or flimsy excuse."

Stunned by his forthright condemnation, Madame Dubois dovetailed into incandescence, her neck veins swollen and eyes bulging. Infuriated by what she knew to be the truth, she bleated, "If you are going to have a go at me, you can chase Seymour and Meredith, and leave as well." Shaking, she gawked at Chevalier, a mixture of indignation and anger written into her hyper-emotional mug. Wavering on the brink of tears, she barked, "Go on, *get out*, and take that poor excuse for a manager Roland Spencer with you. Go and join your co-conspirators, Henderson and Gray." She flashed a penetrating blaze at Savrosav and the *corps de ballet*. "Go on, all of you, get out."

"Very well," Chevalier loudly declared. "We will leave, but don't beg me to take you back in the morning."

Last to retreat from Madame Dubois's savage tirade, when Chevalier and Spencer reached the connecting corridor leading to the back-stage door exit, the doorbell rang. Louring at each other, the ruffled men wondered what fresh bait lay on the other side of the door to incur Madame's resentment. The bell pealed again.

"I wonder where the doorman is?" Spencer posed.

"Must have gone off to fetch a pail of water to put Madame Dubois's flames out," Chevalier jeered. "We'd better see who it is."

Releasing the door's security catch, Deborah Hardy, an HBE entrant dancer exhibiting colossal potential and totally bewitched by Madame Dubois confronted Chevalier.

"Deborah, what are you doing here?"

"*Oh*, Monsieur Chevalier," she blurted, not envisaging her mentor to open the back door. "I brought these corsages' for Madame. They were left behind when the others were amassed from Thursday night's reception for her at the Savoy." She gaped lovingly at the cuttings. "They are beautiful, aren't they?"

Surveying the buds, Chevalier commended, "Yes, Deborah, they are beautiful." Peeking at Spencer, then back at her, he instructed, "Careful when you give them to Madame, she might wither them with a single glare."

Taken aback by the caustic remark, Deborah cried, "*Oh*, Monsieur Chevalier!"

"You'll find her onstage. Good afternoon, Deborah," Chevalier icily wished her, as both men crossed the exit gulf, straight away, ledgering relief from the earlier stifling set to.

Puzzled by their odd swing but unperturbed, the unseasoned dancer merrily moved along the corridor, eager to make her encounter with the famed prima ballerina. Nearing the arena, she called out, "Hello, Madame Dubois. It's Deborah Hardy from the Company."

No response.

Illuminated by two spotlights, Deborah proceeded onward to stage centre raking a space where she expected to see Dubois, but the malcontent had retired into the shadows to lick her wounds.

Floored not to see her, again Deborah ambivalently murmured, "Hello."

This time, Dubois heard. Emerging from her lair, she saw someone ogling out into the amphitheatre wide-eyed, as if about to take a bow. "Who are you?" she bayed.

Sharply revolving about, Deborah subserviently cawed, "Oh, Madame Dubois, I'm from the Company…Deborah Hardy."

She eyed Deborah suspiciously before moving frontwards and circling her like she inspected a prize-winning sculpture. Parking her aggressive nature, she decided to address Deborah with delicacy. "Oh yes, I know you. You're in Chevalier's entrant *corps de ballet*." She spied the teenage dancer carried a wrapped package.

"What have you got there?"

"Bouquets of beautiful red roses for you, Madame Dubois, left behind after Thursday night's Savoy reception." Breaching the wrappings, she unveiled the vibrant, scarlet flowers.

Acquiring Deborah *mano a mano*, Dubois acknowledged with a dull, almost dismissive air, "Oh, I see." She gawped at the novice dancer, apparently making deliberation capping in a decision. "You can put them in my dressing room with the rest. Come with me."

Intoxicated by the prima's rare aegis, Deborah nearly swooned. Walking side-by-side to the star's refuge, her adoration increased as she fantasised about what the opportune happenstance might induce.

Inside, Dubois gestured at a small mountain of corsages, Deborah tracking the line of her directive.

"Over there, please."

"Yes, Madame Dubois."

Delicately placing the bouquet, Deborah then revolved, twinkling gleefully at the prima. "Can I do anything else for you, Madame Dubois?"

"Yes. Get my gown from the wardrobe, the one with the lilac trim."

Scurrying away, she resurfaced with the garment to find her idol sat at her dressing table ministering to her hair. Glowering at the starlet's reflection in the mirror, Dubois noted she had developed into a very pretty girl.

"As per the rest of them, I suspect you've labelled me as a nasty black swan."

"Oh *no*, Madame Dubois," she contested, her mien swelling with admiration. "I've always regarded you as wonderful. I want to be just like you one day."

"You mean, you want to be a prima ballerina?"

"Yes, oh *yes*," she cooed. "The ballet is all I live for."

Caught off guard by her candour, Julia recollected she had spoken the very same words, nine years ago.

"So you want to be a principal dancer. What does Monsieur Chevalier say about you?"

Avalanching into shyness, Deborah hung her head navel gazing. "I can't be specific, Madame Dubois. Sometimes he praises me, sometimes he corrects me, but never says I could go on to be a prima."

"My dear girl," Dubois retorted, critically browsing her. "You'll have to get used to the non-committal. It's routine, but you need to seize the day, *carpe diem*, make a preamble for yourself, or be ready to fill in at short notice. Madame Blanchard's accident led to how I got my chance." She tossed her head in the air. "And since, I have never looked back."

Deborah's cavernous blue eyes brightened. Propagating their conversation, she moved close to Madame Dubois, secure the prima ballerina had patronised her.

* * *

Much to the HBE management's wonderment, the next day, Dubois arrived for rehearsals ahead of time. Saying nothing about the preceding day's heated words, she loosened up at the *barre*. When Savrosav landed just before the due start time, he came over nonplussed at the sight of the prima warming up. Precipitously drawing in breath in amazement, he ogled Chevalier, his gaze soliciting an explanation. Fanning out his digits, the ballet meister indicated he had no idea what had impelled Madame Dubois's early arrival, and prominent eagerness to undertake dance practice.

With Meredith Gray at the conductor's rostrum, and the *corps de ballet* assembled, Chevalier guided the dancers through *La Bayadére* in its totality. Stood in the wings, Deborah Hardy's eyes never left Dubois during the course of the performance. In the breaks between each act, Chevalier and Gray appraised Madame Dubois picked out Deborah to talk to, their mutually flattering body language denoting a kinship being forged. They also recorded Dubois had lost the everyday, put-upon pout she habitually wore at rehearsal breaks. She smiled at Deborah, even occasionally laughing and touching her, the tactile link inextricably binding the two dancers and consolidating the connection.

Tapping Chevalier's wrist, Gray besought, "What do you ruminate is going on there?"

Chevalier beamed back at him. "History repeating itself."

Blinking at the bizarre statement, he recoiled.

"Whatever do you mean?"

"Come with me, Meredith." Channeling the company's musical director into the auditorium front stalls, he voiced, "Do you remember Madame Blanchard befriending a young Julia Huxley?"

Thoughtful for a jiffy, Gray affirmed, "Why yes, I do."

"Well, it seems Madame Dubois has befriended young Deborah Hardy in the same way," Chevalier speculated, breaking out a slight laugh under his breath.

"You mean, our dear, sweet, butter-wouldn't-melt Deborah, is going to follow in Julia's footsteps?"

"She has the talent, but is not quite ready yet," he advised. "But what I am saying is dear, sweet, butter-wouldn't-melt Deborah, as you call her, could well become our latest large-scale headache as a prima."

Dumbfounded by the pronouncement, Gray prattled, "You *really* credit so?"

"Madame Blanchard launched the trend. Julia Dubois has taken it to new heights, and maybe, just maybe, behind all the specious innocence, coy, demure Deborah might have it in mind to follow the same trajectory." Wistfully, he appended, "After you and Seymour left yesterday's incendiary rehearsal, she brought a garland for Julia. This morning, Roland Spencer told me Julia invited Deborah back to her suite, and she stayed for at least three hours. They had supper together."

"*Wowzers*. So what you are implying is Julia could now be acting as her confidant and mentor."

"Exactly *mon cher vieil ami*. Gone are the halcyon days of Pavlova, Fonteyn, and even Bussell, forever. There is an incipient, new breed of prima ballerinas. To stay out ahead, they presume they need to grow a thick layer of impenetrable skin to shut out the world and have to appropriate a caustic persona to survive."

"Yes, I can see your explication, and as long as they sell out ballet houses, impresarios like Seymour Henderson and personal managers like Roland Spencer will continue to pander to them."

"Mmmm." Scratching his head and blowing out his cheeks, he positioned, "It's not an appealing notion, is it. Maybe we should ponder about retiring."

"Unquestionably. You, me and Seymour should go to Harrogate or Bath, take in the waters and just melt away."

"Ah, what a pleasant picture. No more prickly primas."

"No more having to act as referees and arbiters."

"No more late nights mending fences and splicing deals."

Sustaining their reverie, ballet meister and musical director settled back into their seats. With eyes resting, their whimsey deepened until Chevalier felt a pat on his shoulder from one of his support staff.

"Monsieur Chevalier, you'd better come quick. Madame Dubois and Maestro Savrosav are squaring up to each other again."

Both men spluttered out of daydream.

"That's *your* domain, Emile," Gray upheld.

"Yes," Chevalier confirmed. "It appears to be the eternal ballet meisters' calling."

I DREAM IN TECHNICOLOUR

I DREAM IN TECHNICOLOUR

Gene Fogerty felt his right eye cornea swell and bow in response to a high-intensity, pinpoint light source. He'd had sight examinations before, but this one heightened his sense of foreboding. "Relax, Mister Fogerty," Dr. Cribb instructed. "This will only take a few moments."

"*Jesus*," Fogerty murmured, his hands reaching up involuntary, the gesture automatic, a reaction to protect his eyes.

Fogerty had seen Dr. Cribb, an eminent neurologist with a speciality in sleep disorders on numerous preceding occasions. Each time Cribb prescribed a remedial treatment to counter his increasingly restless nights, but nothing worked, the combination of recommended lifestyle and drugs failing to redress his imbalance.

Pushing his left eyelid up, Cribb probed with the light source, Fogerty's retina shrinking in response to the photon beam.

"Hhmm, as usual," Cribb reported, "there is nothing obviously wrong with your eyes."

"That's what I keep on telling my GP."

"Quite." Thoughtfully, Cribb moved away from the patient, a perplexed expression spreading across his lined face, a legacy brought about by over forty-years of often demanding medical practice. "Regarding the dreams you are having recently, what do you experience?"

"Anything and everything, ranging from cinematic phantasmagoria to the downright frightening. Three nights ago, it began with wolves sniffing around a decomposing carcass. Wolves nurturing me as a baby. Wolves running by my side as I head for school. Black branches dripping blood. A highway littered with severed tongues on legs, running into a wormhole infinity. Nondescript creatures performing hideous dissections on live animals."

"A nightmare escapade, and then?"

"After the unsettling opening chapter, it got murky with brief glimpses of mist-laden mountains surrounded by dense parakeet green forests. Then I'm stood by a ladder plummeting into a ravine, by its side, an old sage, mirroring Jimmy Page in the *Dazed and Confused* video, replete with a long white beard and bony hands, thundering out a warning. Couldn't hear it though. Sometimes I can, but not that night."

"Who is Jimmy Page?"

"The guitarist in Led Zeppelin and that video is from the Zep film, *The Song Remains the Same*."

Flicking through Fogerty's case file embossed with Patient Number 174697, he then remarked, "You often dream about real people."

"Yes. Why is that?"

"Oh, the appearance is quite normal. Often manifested figures representing wisdom neutralise the bad elements. However, what puts you in a matchless classification revolves around your ability to distinguish colours and hear sounds." Halting, he dipped his spectacles. "Just remind me, for how long have you possessed the capacity?"

"As I've told you at countless sessions. It's now close to fifteen-years. Before then, my dreams were soundless, monochromatic affairs."

Ignoring the irked reprimand, Cribb persisted with his grilling. "And you believe the more graphic instances have intensified subsequent to the watershed juncture you first told me about?"

"Put it this way. I dream every night without fail. Some are prophetic, meaning whatever my mind conjures up, comes true. It might be a phrase someone or myself thereafter says, a setting I subsequently enter in the real world or a person's features that transform into an actual human being. A second set are reflections of past events and people, and a third, phantasms and nightmares often depicting journeys I take and convoluted buildings I can't escape from."

Pausing, he viewed the specialist with an expectant demeanour, ever hoping for a resolution to his encumbrance. "Does that answer your question? It should do because I have frequently recalled the episodes to you. Why is it the medical profession makes identical enquiries, knowing what the answers are in advance?"

Unflustered, Cribb smiled. "It's all part of the process. Conditions often change. We have to check for certitude. Tell me some more."

Pondering, he then proposed, "I'll recap two dreams about my ex-wife Cherilyn."

"Go ahead."

"I'm in a hospital waiting room. It's so brightly lit, everything looks washed out. I have the impression Cherilyn has been taken ill. I'm there for days, first sat on a chair at a desk surrounded by other seated people, then hunched down in a darkened corridor. I see someone, possibly a nurse approaching me, but she evaporates. Next I am in the woods and for some reason I think Ian Negus, an old colleague of mine, is coming to visit me and I have to wash and clean my Cooper to make it presentable. The woods deepen and I see a hospital bed with a girl in it, presumably Cherilyn, stretching out her arms to me." Briskly stopping, he grimaced at the recall.

"And the second materialisation?"

"I'm with Cherilyn in Tarvin Sands, where I grew up. She wanders off. Then I find myself in Dana Coupland's house waiting for Cherilyn. Dana is the mother of an old flame of mine. She tells me, 'Cherilyn really loves you and she will be back.' Later, I'm sitting on a coat of many colours laid out on a bed in a bedroom where the walls are shape-shifting from rectangular to rhomboid form. I glance down at the scarlet floor covered in what I presume is my underwear. Then I pick up some bits of something unrecognisable off the carpet, leave the bedroom and enter into a landing with at least five connecting doors. I select one door, go through into a kitchen where Dana is with other women milling about. I put the bits in to a giant-sized, silver waste disposal bin."

"Is that it?"

"Yeah, like so many of my jigsaw puzzle dreams, it ended abruptly like an incomplete story."

"Tell me about Cherilyn."

"I've told you before. You must already have enough material in my profile to compose a volume of novellas."

"Please."

"She's the most stunning creature roaming the planet. Hah—" Agonisingly, he simpered, Cribb forewarned about the usual dichotomy. "But she never knew when to stick. She was constantly in twist mode, thinking the grass is always greener, but in the end she got busted. I still love her, but for a book-smart, street-wise operator, she's terminally harebrained. She has lemming behaviour. Can't resist going over the top, even when she knows slaughter awaits. She thinks her God-given beauty and charisma will overcome the odds, but in practice, faced with an insurmountable challenge, they are neutralised. It's why we split."

"You resent her shortcomings?"

"At the time, it resembled admiring a perfect stone, then after a while noticing a slight flaw and when the stone is cut, instead of producing sub-sections to be made into smaller gems, it shatters and is obliterated. My job was to reconstruct the jewel, but there are so many times that can be performed before the jeweller quits."

"Tell me about the dream you had last night."

Closing his eyes to aid concentration, he outlined, "I'm doing my finals at university. The lecturer says, 'As well as computer sciences, the examinations will also cover history, philosophy and a whole host of other disciplines.' I get the impression there is little time to study the unforeseen supplementary curriculum. Then I'm on a coach with other students. It stops at a very large building. We all pile out, go inside and investigate. After a while, I find myself with just one other student. Somehow, we both know we are late for the return coach trip. The other student disappears, and I run down a very long passageway with daylight visible at the other end.

"Emerging into a garden, I see the coach parked on the road opposite the building's main entrance. I realise I have come out of the wrong exit. As I head for the road, the coach pulls off. Instead of stopping to let me board, it carries on, the driver shouting he will wait for me at a petrol station around the corner. I run to the petrol station, but the coach is already pulling out. Then I'm at Marconi, my first employer, sitting at a desk next to manager Dave Silsby, with a large unopened folder before me. He hands me a brightly coloured journal. I push the folder aside and open the journal, its pages saturated in artistic contours in every hue of the rainbow. I get up with the journal and go to a different desk. Rubbernecking up, I see students heading for a hall and a voice calls 'Examination time.' I leave to join them. Realising I have left the mesmerising journal behind, I turn to retrieve it, but it's gone."

"Scanning through your mental health biography as you spoke, I clocked you've had similar nocturnal visions in the past."

"Yes, university examinations have arisen in multiple dreams."

"Why do you think that is?"

"I haven't the foggiest. That's your realm of expertise. You tell me."

"It is a symbol of anxiety. Did you have this dream whilst at university?"

"No, only in recent times."

"Well, this is conjecture, but recurrence of the same theme often equates with an unresolved issue."

"You *know* what my unresolved issue is."

"Indeed, I do. Now seems like a good time for a summary review."

And so, the analysis went on…

* * *

Previously, Cribb had scribbled in Fogerty's case notes, 'Prone to autosuggestion, an adoration tempered with acute realism complex about his ex-wife, and an enmity towards the girl who applied the final *coup de grace* sending him down the psychiatric well.' Convinced the patient had a hyperactive imagination and let rejection play on his mind, resulting in his melancholia, he had suggested to Fogerty the characteristic was at least partly responsible for his restless nights. Recalling many cases similar in nature, Cribb ascribed he should put his failings into perspective and recognise they were by no means without equal. Unconvinced, Fogerty countered, saying he had researched the field and had discovered his symptoms were commonplace with people suffering from enforced abandonment. Agreeing though mentally strong and he had no prior history of slipping into the despondency mire, regardless, he came back to the axiomatic point that his breakdown came about because the final straw had been laid on his back. Furthering the argument, he insisted every man had his limit and his had been surpassed.

Cribb had also minuted, 'The patient talks about getting through life as he puts it, as if there is a reward on the other side!' Discussing the oddment with other colleagues, they agreed Fogerty's otherwise positive creative mind had conjured up all kinds of supposition resultant from his wretchedness. Accordingly, they agreed he was attempting to give rationality to the unfortunate state overwhelming him.

During his career, Cribb had seen thousands of people with mental challenges, the commonality between cases in terms of the stimulus activating disturbance overlapping to a very high degree. Fogerty was different. Though the same stimuli applied to him, he exhibited some singularities. He possessed an X-factor, something new to the annals of psychiatry. At first, Cribb and other psychoanalysts placed his apparent originality by way of his ability to accurately retread his dreams in such vivid and believable terms, his skill with words making for bringing sleeping visions to life.

Albeit, during the multiple sessions Fogerty had attended at

Sevenoaks, he had recounted hundreds of dreams, their content and the unexpected way most developed into film-like sequences covering perhaps hours of sleep time was the real unique. Cribb had appraised it resembled having a cine-projector in the back of his head, his frontal cranium acting as the display screen, whilst Fogerty sat in the mid-stalls observing the ludicrous theatre enacted to his front. After further analysis he updated the facsimile, suggesting instead of the back to front projection, four laser beams conspired to conjure up 3-D images, Fogerty at the epicentre of their combined focal point show, observing the drama or participating in the goings-on happening all around him.

* * *

Gene Fogerty had gotten in deep with Cherilyn Wagnell, her feminine allure unlocking his defences. Marrying her, he found out she couldn't have children, but the revelation did not chasten his love for her. When they forged the nuptials union, he didn't really know her. He only saw what he wanted to see; her warts made hazy by his undying love for her. Then it went sour. She messed him around, his tunnel vision broadening to sense her imperfections. Enduring it for nearly a decade, he then exploded, telling her enough was enough. She cleared out.

He had a couple of girlfriends after Cherilyn, Barbara Simmonds, a Cherilyn clone, then Gabrielle Young, a girl twelve years his junior with a craving for hot love. He'd known Barbara before he and Cherilyn split. She tended to his gaping wounds, the affair lasting eighteen months, as did the one with Gabrielle. Both wanted to get married, but having gone there and been roasted, Fogerty shied away from the commitment.

Then one day he got a call from Sabina Rainville, a girl he'd met whilst doing an evening class A-Level sociology course twenty years earlier. She was married at the time, but they had a short-term affair. She told him she was still married to the same guy, but she had never really loved him. Fogerty agreed to meet Sabina by the muddy banks of the Medway in Aylesford. She still looked terrific, much the same as when he first knew her. She told him her woes, admitting she'd been down for an awful long time, the recall making her tearful, her head swaying onto his shoulder.

Sensitive to her troubles, he comforted her. She lightened up, stroked his face, thanked him for his understanding. Compelled to preserve her newfound fettle, he invited her to see his house in Hempstead. She accepted, he leading the way in his beamer, she following in her Passat. Further seeking to dispel her blues and spark some cheer, he showed her the prints adorning every wall of his house. Whilst in the library explaining why Van Gogh prints had been selected for the room, her rapture hit the acme and she wrapped herself around his torso. Feeling a sense of unfinished business from the earlier venture, he wanted to see more of her.

They got close, very close. She divorced her husband and the pair flitted between her Rainham house and his in Hempstead, engaging in lovers' fun and games. Blossoming into bilateral love over the next few years, Fogerty seemed all set for nonstop happiness. Then she told him, old work colleague Leo had seen them in the Black Horse at Thurnham appearing very content, the idyllic picture stimulating his want for her. Soon after, he contacted Sabina. Before Fogerty first knew her, despite her being engaged, she always had a thing for Leo, but it never came to anything. Now he declared his love for her. She'd always wanted to test him out, so she told Fogerty it was over. Married Leo left his wife and moved in with Sabina.

Shocked by the disloyalty, it proved to be the final unwarranted betrayal breaking Fogerty's emotional fortitude. He had done everything within his power to make Sabina's life wonderful, yet it decoded as insufficient to attract her loyalty. She knew it, but she still applied the terminating blade. He went downhill fast, his profession suffering and his social life halting. Becoming a recluse, he shied away from people he knew, isolation his only companion outside of the work domain.

Ironically, it didn't work out for Sabina, Leo not the man she idolised in her teens. Soon she asked him to leave, Leo backtracking to his wife. She contacted Fogerty, her aim to rekindle their relationship but irreversible damage had been done. He told her he felt a sense of acute depression and failure consuming him resulting in many physical ailments. He had learnt to cope with the loss of Cherilyn and the Barbara and Gabrielle washouts, but the shock of her dumping him for a whim became the tipping point, a regular societal move causing an unpredictably large and sudden reaction because of the cumulative effect it added to lesser actions.

She had changed as well. Gone was the damaged girl he'd met in Aylesford and whom he had repaired, nurturing her into a kind and considerate being. In place of those positive qualities, she exhibited a cold, callous detachment. Though she wanted to know him, she was standoffish, as if she recognised she had been very nasty to him and wouldn't permit herself to refresh the love connection.

Taking in his obvious poor state of health, she said he should get his doctor to channel him to a psychiatrist. Doing so, his GP scheduled an outpatient's request with the Kent NHS Mental Disorders Board and prescribed Drinamyl to combat his sense of spiritual apathy.

Fogerty met with Dr. Heiren at the Medway Mental Disorders Clinic. Employing the routine trick cyclist's artifice of first regressing Fogerty to his childhood, Heiren then forwarded to major events happening in his life. Amongst a plethora of recollections, Fogerty told him about the loss of his parents, what had happened to his marriage, his linkage with Sabina and the stresses and strains of his high-powered job.

"You're like a coiled spring, Mister Fogerty. If the tension is not released, it will cause you a great deal more mental distress and physical pains."

"So, what precisely can you do for me?"

"Ideally, you need to be put into a stress-free environment where you can get away from your problems."

"You mean an institution?"

"Not necessarily. There are NHS units specialising in short-term care for the disturbed. However, places on such schemes are far and few between. I will put your name forward to the register, but don't expect inclusion to happen overnight. It could take up to six months. In the meantime, since you reported to your GP the Drinamyl he prescribed had no effect on relieving your symptoms, I'm going to provide you with a stronger dosage of the amphetamine. Nonetheless, please understand Drinamyl might relieve your symptoms but it is not a cure and can only be prescribed for a limited time. And by the way, your self-imposed estrangement from social interaction is not helping. You need distractions, and that means becoming involved with people. Mental strength is the greatest antidote to desolation. If you can achieve that, your dejection will lessen and the aches you are experiencing will go away. The longer the recovery remedy takes, the higher the probability of sustaining long-term physical ailments."

"So, what's the worst case?"

"If after you have attended the short-term care unit, whilst upholding the amphetamine intake during this period, there is no improvement, you should consider a spell of intensive care in an NHS facility." Casting an authoritative mien at him, he pleaded, "Please take these recommendations seriously. If the infirmity is not controlled and reversed, your general health *will* dilapidate further. In that respect, consult your GP regarding resultant physical complaints. Best not to let them fester."

Soon after Dr. Heiren confirmed his blue funk, Fogerty started to get red-top newspapers through his letter box on Saturdays and Sundays. He also received multiple calls to his mobile and landline numbers, the devices displaying 'no caller ID'. Each time he answered the call, the line quickly went dead. It went on and on, almost as if the caller checked to see he was still alive.

Curious about the source of the red-tops, he approached two local newsagents. They knew nothing about anyone paying for the newspapers to be sent to him and suggested the supplier came from outside the Hempstead locale. Placing the curio on hold, he cerebrated whoever the benefactor was, it would fizzle out, as would the mysterious calls. Wrong on both counts, the newspapers persisted for eight years and the puzzling calls went on for eleven.

Soldiering on, despite the increased Drinamyl dosage, Fogerty's malady deteriorated. Then, unexpectedly, less than a month after seeing Heiren, he received an invitation from the Darenth Neurological Care Centre to attend a two-week residential assessment at Sevenoaks Hospital, commencing the following fortnight Monday. Not wanting employer Logic Solutions to find out about his ailment, he elected to take a fortnight holiday from his entitlement.

Arriving at the centre, a nurse took him to his bedroom, told him to unpack, then report to the group therapy room. Having never been hospitalised before, Fogerty felt a sense of numbness as he swept his vision around his room, nothing from his past qualifying him to make a considered judgment on his current surroundings. They were just there, like immovable objects encapsulating his predicament, a characterless, disinfected confinement, designed to accommodate with the bare essentials. He felt like a test-tube baby, his very existence cocooned in narrow hibernation. Swiftly, he recognised he had self-detached from the regular world, forfeiting the ability to manipulate his volition, his future now determined by external forces deciding on which side of the sane-insane barrier he fell into.

Finding his way to his appointment, he passed along near-to deserted, starched corridors before knocking on a door marked Therapy Room and entering. Inside, he scanned to and fro, dialing two nurses murmuring to each other at the top of the room. Not acknowledging him, he switched his focus, settling on a set of patient occupied seats arranged into a semi-circle, one vacant presumably for him, he surmised. Nobody said a word, everyone gawping with hollow eyes to infinity. Instinctively, he wanted to at least say hello. Regardless, he sensed his attempt at communication would go unanswered. They appeared to be preoccupied, some in a comatose state. At least he hadn't slipped that far into the listless swamp. Compelled to take the spare seat, he sat assimilating the all-white décor and sealed windows, the same setup as in his assigned room, then counted twenty persons including himself. Seconds later, the door opened and a man in a white doctor's coat entered with a clipboard.

Striding to the top of the room, the chatting nurses, also dressed in white, stood either side of him.

"Good morning, I'm Dr. Montgomery, Head of the Darenth Neurological Centre Sevenoaks clinic." Scouting around those seated, he empathised, "I'm sure you all have a lot of questions regarding your individual complaints, nevertheless, can I please ask you to bear with us until we have completed our assessment programme. You are going to participate in some studies enabling us to gain a broad view of your infirmities."

Like the other sufferers, Fogerty did not react or say anything.

"Over the course of the next two weeks, we will be analysing your symptoms, subjecting you to studies and measuring your responses to medications." Holding out his clipboard, he informed, "First of all I need to confirm our register of participants." Reading out names, he combed for acknowledgements. Some raised a laboured hand, others uttered a jagged 'Yes', Fogerty confirming, "that's me."

During his intern at Sevenoaks, Fogerty had little interplay with his fellow brethren. Some seemed to be totally zonked, spaced out on tranquillisers. Others scuttled away when they sensed another inmate was about to speak to them. That left a small coterie, including himself, who exchanged the odd word, nothing approaching a conversation, more an acknowledgement someone had addressed them, and they felt a mannerly compunction to at least say a few words in return.

Daytime and night-time analytical monitoring encompassed delving into subjects' backgrounds, their symptoms, prescribed drugs and their responses to stimuli, Fogerty submitting to all the intrusions without reservation.

One procedure involved sensors attached to his body to measure his heartbeat and biorhythms as he slept, a low-level light camera logging his movement as dreams percolated his consciousness causing motor stimulation. After the first session, Dr. Briscoe, one of Montgomery's assigned lieutenants, set up a review with the patient.

"I'm going to show you the sleep pattern for a man not laboured with any mental stresses and strains."

Selecting a file on his laptop, Briscoe ran a speeded-up rendition of the video recording and sensor loggings, Fogarty noting over the eight-hour cycle, the dummy specimen hardly moved.

"You will notice, as well as remaining mainly static, his heartbeat and biorhythms remained constant." Fogerty nodded. "Now, I'm going to run your sleep cycle for last night."

Comparatively speaking, Fogerty witnessed his sleep cycle was like an out-of-control mime artist, the observer wincing at his jerky and frequent motions, whilst his heartbeat and biorhythms readout fluctuated. He also clocked at the top of the video, 'Patient Number 174697', an identification becoming synonymous with him over the years to come.

At the termination of the show, Briscoe ventured, "You'd agree you are moving around quite a lot."

"Uh-uh."

"I'd like to see your elbows and toes."

Obliging the request, Fogerty bared the identified components.

"Both your elbows and big toes have friction burn marks resultant from you thrashing around whilst sleeping."

"Yes, I know."

"For how long have they been burnt?"

"From the time I entered into melancholia. I assumed they were resultant from my volcanic dreaming."

"What did you dream last night?"

"In dreams, the fantasiser always experiences what is happening as a viewer from inside their own mind acting as an amphitheatre. So, if you accept that definition, I'm with three other people in a train carriage. We're watching a metropolis flash by backgrounded by a yellow and red sky through a window. When the scenery becomes static, they leave the carriage. I trail them onto a rail station platform, the carriage door slamming shut behind me with a clatter, but they vanish. Next, I begin to ascend stairs, turning into a ladder to reach an upper platform. A second train carriage is so near the upper platform I have to edge round it to get onto the platform surface. It's almost as if the carriage is trying to deny me access. Somehow I fumble around the restriction and emerge onto the platform surface. Then I hear a shrill whistle, the carriage moves and I go searching for the three people."

"And then?"

"Nothing, and I have no concept of how long in real time the vision lasted."

"Probably, it wasn't the only figment you had last night. It's just the one embedded in your consciousness."

"But what do these sound and light shows mean?"

"Ahh, that's a colossal question, Mister Fogerty, the answer still in its infancy despite over a century of acquired psychiatry knowledge. According to Freud, dreams are the way the brain relaxes itself of the stress accumulated during conscious hours. Further, dreams are manifestations of deep desires and anxieties, driven by unconscious wish fulfilment. It works infrequently because dreams have both manifest, meaning 'superficial and meaningless,' and latent, meaning 'deep unconscious wishes or fantasies' content. Manifest composition often masks or obscures latent content, that being the key reason for the irregularity of desired dream material. Jung contested Freud's perceptions, insisting dreams were messages to the dreamer, and argued dreamers should take heed for their own good."

"Hah," Fogerty reacted, "the dream-come-nightmare landscape seems indeterminate, imprecise and unpredictable, no theory exhaustively accounting for the demonstration content, or the external factors energising them."

"True, but unlike the physical sciences where reactions to a given stimulus yield the same results every time the experiment is conducted, our perceptions about the brain and sleep behaviour are largely empirical-based on observation of habits, documenting feelings and registering recounted dreams."

"I see, but what do you make of my last night's exhibition?"

Considering for a trice, Briscoe advised, "Often, nocturnal disturbances centred on disrupted travel indicate anxieties about domestic and career ambitions."

"Well, that certainly applies to my domestic situation."

"Yes, that is what you are here to resolve." Inspecting his burnt appendages again, he promoted, "I think we'll bandage your toes and elbows before you sleep tonight."

"So presumably, you can confirm my abnormal sleep behaviour is typical for someone with mental health problems?"

"Indeed, Mister Fogerty."

"So, what can you do to alleviate the wretchedness and thereby presumably prevent excessive motion as I sleep?"

"Mmmm, we'll come to that later."

Miffed by the forestall, irrespective, Fogerty accepted the decision on the basis at completion of his stay, the medics would set out a prescription to combat his debility.

Crushingly, disappointment followed. Despite the extensive trials, measurements and interrogations he complied with over the two weeks, all Montgomery recommended at the end of the exercise was to steer clear of stressful booby traps and keep on taking the Drinamyl. Feeling distinctly short-changed by the time investment, he returned home in the same mental state he arrived in.

Immediately thereafter, Sabina contacted him, wanting to know about the Sevenoaks retreat. Instead of being a praxis aimed at a cure, he told her, it much more resembled a data gathering drill on twenty chumps to be used in a paper published in the British Medical Journal or one of the psychiatry periodicals!

"That's the key as to why I was allocated to the Darenth Neurological Care Centre so quickly," he insisted. "When Montgomery said, 'studies' in reference to why we had been selected, I should have twigged."

"You're saying the practitioners were using the twenty as guinea pigs?"

"Yes."

Cogitating, she then briefed, "*The Glass Menagerie* is being performed at the Apollo with Jessica Lange in the Amanda Wingfield lead role. You like Tennessee Williams, so why don't we go to see it. It'll take you out of yourself."

Startled by her invitation, howbeit he felt obliged to be courteous. "Okay. There's a Gilbert and George retrospective on at Tate Modern Bankside. We could visit the exhibit as well."

On the day, he found Sabina to be very buoyant about what she perceived as his temporary mental condition. Somehow, whether by pretence or misinterpretation of what she knew, she assumed he'd soon return to his normal sanguine self. Whilst walking south over Waterloo Bridge to Tate Modern, she was still high, extolling about his shape being transient, when abruptly, he turned her to face him.

"This is not a fleeting malfunction, Sabina. The all-in-white-clad brigade have made it perfectly clear no one gets off melancholia scot free. There is always a residual and the attendant physical effects can be lifelong."

Deflating her ebullience, her peepers widened, her mouth opening involuntarily. He got the impression having burst her bubble, she resigned herself to his fate.

Over the coming years, nearly every infrequent time she contacted him to enquire about his health, they ended up visiting historical retreats such as the castles at Chilham and Sutton Valence to 'take him out of himself', but he could tell it was forced on her behalf, something she did to ease her sense of guilt, and always in the back of his mind he felt guarded resentment.

Resigning himself to no instant cure to his mental incumbrance, Fogerty adhered to Montgomery's prescription. Albeit, not akin to taking a couple of paracetamols to combat a headache or Rennies to settle indigestion, swallowing a daily intake of Drinamyl and attempting to circumnavigate stress proved to be wholly inadequate to diffuse his dumps and the attendant physical pains it caused. Assuming the condition would relax, in truth it worsened, outside of work time, Fogerty facing the daily battleground of cascading into a numb and anesthetised state.

Spending his evenings and weekends trying to absorb his concentration on music and videos, he quickly found he'd drift away, meditating on his dilemma and insensible to whatever he listened to or watched. After registering openings, subsequently whole albums and films passed him by, their rousing content failing to ignite his interest. The same inability to focus occurred when he performed domestic chores. His mind so littered with melancholia fragments, often after realising he had left a bottle of ceramic cleaner in the bathroom, by the time he reached the landing, he'd completely forgotten why he had ascended the stairs. Short-term memory loss became a daily home environment occurrence. Setting himself some regular mondaying task, involving getting from A to B throughout his premises, either inside the house, the double-garage or in the gardens, by the time he'd completed the short journey, his goal had been forgotten. Staring about, asking himself 'Why am I here?' invariably he couldn't figure it out, then hours or days later, the objective of the trek came to mind.

* * *

Soon after another session at the Darenth Neurological Care Centre, fifteen months after the first, coincidentally, Sabina contacted Fogerty. Tabling her usual enquiries about his health, he told her about the recent trek to Sevenoaks, she wanting to know the outcome of the consultation. Arranging to pick her up, they travelled to Harrietsham, taking in the bucolic sights whilst they walked and conversed.

"This time around, amongst a plethora of tests, they checked for normality of social life."

"What does that entail?"

"Clinicians as the term implies, are clinical, unsmiling robots. I'm not even sure they have a heartbeat. To use a musical expression, their *modus operandi* revolves around a kind of call and response idiom, but binary in nature and devoid of any emotion. Anyway, I tell you this to set the stage. Social life check-lists identify to what extent the puppets are engaged in everyday activities, those not afflicted by mental illness take for granted. Social engagement is a measure of normality, an asset psychoanalysts view to be crucial for good mental health. My mother used to tell me, 'No man is an island,' meaning humans are social creatures needing constant interaction with their own kind. Some people get withdrawal symptoms if they are out of contact with their most immediate kin for more than a few hours.

Others crave solitude, but it has to be with a purpose in mind. Solitude without an intent or enforced seclusion is a slow killer." Eyeing her semi-accusingly, he detailed, "According to the shrinks, I fit into the last category, living my life on the periphery of the margins."

His accusation penetrating her psyche, she remained even-tempered and tight-lipped, guilt swallowing her natural tendency to defend the indefensible.

"One of the questions asked," he continued, "was 'When did you last have Sunday lunch?' Shrugging my shoulders, I responded, 'Generally, I have something to eat on a Sunday lunchtime.' Erring into a more precise mode, the inquisitor updated, 'I mean, a traditional Sunday roast.' Huh—" He shook his head. "It now seems odd, but at the time, I had to ransack my memory. In the end, I narrated having roast lamb with all the trimmings on a Sunday at Gabrielle's mother's house at Bexleyheath in 1999."

"What did the consultant say?"

"Oohh, they never comment. They just record the response."

"We had roast for Sunday lunch when we were together."

"Did we? I don't recall."

"You also emailed me when you had a vague recollection of our long weekend trip to Suffolk."

"Yes. I don't know what prompted it, but a nebulous impression of a village church and roaming about by the side of a river came to mind."

"The church was at Bacton and the River Stour ran beside the old mill at Flatford. You wanted to visit Constable country and we went to Dedham Vale as well as Flatford."

"Yes, you might be right."

Returning to Hempstead after he dropped Sabina at her home, he realised he remembered little of the events occurring during his years with her. Intrinsically, he knew he had taken her to London and Canterbury to see plays and they had dined at hundreds of restaurants, but he couldn't detail any of them, the stretch September 2000 to March 2005 bereft of content enacted with her. Before that time slot, he could recollect virtually everything he did with Gabrielle, Barbara and even a short fling with Anju, an Indian girl with huge eyes who had sidled up to him in The Churchill Arms in Kensington Church Street, declared she fancied him, and they should engage in an Anglo-Indian summit. Reaching further back, he could still remember hundreds of happenings during his iconoclastic Cherilyn phase, and beyond their significant meeting, a passel of girls entering his life all the way back to school. Of course, since March 2005, he recapped his social calendar remained blank, the only entries made in his private diary relating to medical appointments. Concluding his time-travel trawl, he realised he blanked virtually everything from his liaison with Sabina, her betrayal acting to shatter the times they had together.

* * *

After what had happened with Sabina, Fogerty swore he was through with women. They had formed a central part of his life since his first adolescent fumblings with schoolgirls. Now he intended to live his life without another come down resultant from a failed romance and all its attendant humiliation and wreckage debris.

Finding isolation and loneliness to be unforgiving companions, apart from work, he'd spend hours enrapt in absolutely nothing, his lack of inertia adding to the inherent tiredness associated with depression. Not bargaining for an inability to control the decimating frailty, it took all his inherent will and motivation to prepare himself for the business world. Once engaged in the daily goings-on of the solution-provider to client and business partner connection, his natural businessmen vent surged into automatic, his vivacious aura effectively neutralising the hollowness and body spasms he felt commensurate with the ailment taking off. Conversely, the spell became progressively broken after working hours when he returned home from London or an overseas destination. By the time dinner finished, the spectre had once again enveloped him.

Over the course of the next few years, Fogerty went further

downhill, his ability to conceal his suffering from employer's Logic Solutions waning. Though clients and business partners never suspected behind his convincing regional sales director's mask lay a tormented man, sometimes his concealment fractured when out of their eyelines. As the disconsolation pressure built, his defences weakened, some board level officers making inquiries as to his health, Fogerty putting the out-of-character malaise down to tiredness. A common symptom for ever-under pressure line managers, they thought no more about it.

Then one day, after a meeting with a client team at Logic Solutions London offices, he felt light-headed and in need of fresh air. Stepping outside onto Charlotte Street, he exchanged felicitations with a colleague about to enter the company then collapsed, an ambulance summoned by the workmate to take him to St Mary's Hospital. Becoming compos in the ambulance, he insisted he was alright, but the onboard medics advised a full examination.

Diagnosed with acute nervous exhaustion after an ECG and other life function appraisals, he was then allowed to return to work on the proviso he took a holiday to relax and rejuvenate his body. After consultation with alerted HR Director Wendell Lomax, as per company practice, Logic Solutions sent him to see Dr. Purcell, their appointed medical practitioner in Harley Street.

Examining Fogerty at length, Purcell then delved into the distress problems itemised on his NHS medical record. Fearing for his career longevity with Logic Solutions, Fogerty assured the inquisitor he had the complaint under control via Drinamyl tablets and that his keeling over episode had resulted from a number of pressure points. Endorsing the St Mary's Hospital staff holiday advice, he viewed getting away from work and domestic strains would be a boon to Fogerty's wellbeing.

"That's what I am going to recommend to your employers," Purcell told him. "And you needn't be worried about me divulging your mental problems. Patient-doctor confidentiality applies even when a third party is picking up the bills."

With a great deal of expectancy, Fogerty jetted off to Bangkok to visit long-term friends Lawrence and Christine Mole. When

Logic Solutions were embroiled in business with Bechtel Incorporated where Lawrence worked as a building systems design manager, the pair met to discuss business systems requirements capture. Striking up a social relationship based on their business amity, they partied in the West End's best clubs and restaurants and went out as a foursome when Fogerty was still married to Cherilyn.

The Moles lived in East Sheen but had domiciled in Port Elizabeth and Singapore when Lawrence was engaged in extended off-shore secondment for Bechtel. Two years further down the track, Bechtel offered Lawrence the post of running Bechtel's South-East Asia operation headquartered in Bangkok. Jumping at the opportunity, the Moles planned to stay in Bangkok until Lawrence retired, then head back to Port Elizabeth. Over the intervening years, Lawrence had returned to England twice on business, Fogerty tying up with him for a few precious hours.

Since his session at Sevenoaks Hospital, for obscure and irrational reasons, Fogerty had rarely taken any days off from his holiday entitlement. Now he looked forward to spending some quality time in Thailand with Lawrence and Christine, and in the process ridding himself of his damned melancholia.

Producing the desired effect, being with his friends and participating in their lifestyle in a location radically different from London and Hempstead calmed his inner maelstrom, for once his nights much more settled without extreme motive movement or crazed nightmares. During the sojourn he took a short trip to Kathmandu with Lawrence, the therapeutic benefit of being amongst the sadhus and Buddhist pilgrims further pacifying his tortured mind and soul.

During the return flight to London Heathrow, he still felt good, the tranquil property lasting for a few days after he got back into the swing of work. Nonetheless, for no apparent reason, the bugbear of Sabina's betrayal ignited thorns in his mind sending shivers down his back and he lapsed into deep gloominess again. Over the course of the subsequent week, he began to take on an extremely strained visage. His work application lapsed, and uncharacteristically he became short with his sales team, his behaviour detected by fellow senior managers, the churlishness reaching boardroom ears. Moreover, he sustained another keeling over episode, this time in his office at Charlotte Street, again an ambulance called to ferry him to St Mary's Hospital, the medics diagnosis repeated as acute nervous exhaustion.

Holding a key position for the company, the board could not let Fogerty's quandary go on unbridled. Taking measures, they had Wendell Lomax tell him he was clearly ill and under the circumstances, they couldn't be responsible for something far worse happening to him in the workplace. After much consideration, the board decided to put Fogerty on extended furlough for six months, his number two taking on the regional sales director role.

Diminished by the decision, Fogerty receded further into his homelife hermit's existence, never socialising with local friends and rarely speaking to his neighbours, his days mostly spent sitting on the side of his bed staring out of glazing at the back garden, his nights a proliferation of disturbing dreams and renewed friction burns. On the upside, he distinguished being away from the stresses imposed by his high-powered job resulted in improved physical health, however dismay and out-on-the-rim expeditions into bad never-never land during his nights continued. He began to realise work and downheartedness were mutually incompatible. If he could get rid of the mental hang-up, he could work. If not and he worked, then more keeling over occurrences would certainly happen. Testing the prognosis on Montgomery for validity, the specialist concurred with his take.

Ancillary visits to his GP resulted in a change of amphetamine from Drinamyl to Benzedrine in the hope a shift of 'pep pill' would subdue his inner demons and bring him into the realms of tranquillity. More psychological than actual, at first Fogerty persuaded himself the Benzedrine worked. Howbeit, after the new drug settling in span, concretely he still felt the same, his existence one long meandering trek to the pit's bottom. No matter what he did to try and budge himself out of the malaise, nothing worked. Like an engine failing to burst into nonstop life independent of how many times the starter motor is engaged, he lolled about, shoulders hunched up, his gait unsure, his physiognomy plastered in a doleful consternation.

Unremittingly, the plight persisted to the six-months mark when he was scheduled to return to Logic Solutions. Receiving a telephone call from Wendell Lomax regarding his restart date, Fogerty surprised the HR Director by saying he did not intend to return to the company. Justifying the stance, he confessed to not feeling well enough to combat the stresses imposed by a sales director role, and if put to the test, he'd collapse again. Bowled over by the unexpected rejection and knowing until his mishap Fogerty had an outstanding track record of achievement with Logic Solutions, he played for time saying, he'd call again when perhaps Fogerty was in a better frame of mind.

Sure enough, a day later, Fogerty got the call, not from Lomax but Company Chairman Harland Swales.

"Hello, Gene."

"Harland, I expected a call from Wendell Lomax."

"The board deemed it far too important a matter to leave it with HR, so I agreed to talk to you. You've got us all worried you really meant what you said to Wendell."

Taking a deep stuttering breath and then exhaling, he replied, "No disrespect intended, but I did mean what I told him."

"Oh, come, come, Gene," Swales extolled with vim, "we know you've been unwell, suffering from shall we call it executive burnout, but there is no need to bring the guillotine down on your career with Logic Solutions. You have a bright future here." Expecting a swift response, the line seemed to go dead at Fogerty's end. "Hello…Gene, are you still there?"

"Yes, Mister Chairman. I…I thank you for your support, but my decision has been made. You see…I don't think I'm in the right frame of mind to address business anymore. I've crossed over into no-man's land where I seem to be stranded. I'm no longer an active participant in society."

Shocked by Fogerty's trenchant admission, Swales finally acquiesced to his angle, saying he'd make arrangements for Logic Solutions to settle his final months' salary.

When sitting on the side of his bed meditating became all

played out, Fogerty began to tackle long-outstanding jobs around the house and re-read Bukowski and J.G. Ballard novels plus the poetry of Ted Hughes and Ezra Pound, the literary adventure stimulating him to examine the poetry he had composed for Cherilyn way back when and published in *Poetry Monthly* and a plethora of other journals, some no longer in existence.

Finishing the stopover in past glories, he realised he had not written anything since Cherilyn and he had parted. Sitting in front of his laptop, he ran Word and pulled up a blank page. For quite a while, he stared at the white rectangle, thinking, then a flood of ideas and notions began to coalesce in his mind.

Spending the next Sunday to Sunday interval furiously converting partially-formed conceptions into prose, he realised with his mind centred on the creation task during the workout, he didn't revisit the thorny circumstance first driving him into the doldrums. Albeit, once keystroke action stopped and his thought patterns went into neutral, the aberration quickly returned, decimating him again, the two-part cycle-maintained *ad infinitum*. In an effort to absorb all his waking hours in the founding exercise, he relentlessly hammered away at his laptop keyboard. Notwithstanding, he could not control his nocturnal clock, the eerie dreams taking off concurrent with his lapse into anguish still filling his sleep time with troubling visions and wholly impossible, not improbable, mini-operas in which he held stage centre observing the ludicrous dramas unfolding before him.

In quieter moments, he got very emotional, certain memories, screen images and sounds igniting tears and a quivering lip. Amongst the litany of flashbacks triggering disintegration, he found he couldn't listen to Bruce Springsteen anymore. Every heartbreaking and tragic song he wrote had parallels with Cherilyn and himself, the awareness cementing regret and remorse. Shrinking further into himself, he rationalised, there's no salvation, no release, only degrees of fate acceptance. Concurrently, he grew to despise Sabina, judging God would never allow her into heaven.

* * *

One Saturday morning Fogerty awoke with severe abdominal pain. Assuming acute food poisoning, he tried to ignore the misery and get on with his daily routine. By Monday morning the irritation still persisted. Thinking the worst, he consulted his GP. After some trials, he was sent to see an abdominal consultant at Medway Maritime Hospital. Finding no physical abnormality and explaining the stomach is closely aligned with the nervous system, the specialist concluded stress to be the culprit behind the hindrance and he was suffering from irritable bowel syndrome. Though pleased with the diagnosis not being life-threatening, nevertheless as predicted by Dr. Heiren five years earlier, it brought home the recognition his mental problems had led to physical ailments.

Around about this time, out of the blue he got a call from Cherilyn.

"Hi, darling. How are you?"

Astounded to hear her satiny-smooth, sexy, midwest voice, for a moment his vocal chords failed him.

"Cherilyn."

"Bet you didn't expect to hear from me again."

"No."

"How do you feel about us getting back together?"

He gasped. "What!"

"You're mine, Gene. I'm claiming you back."

Stunned by the proposal, he finally responded, "I'm not sure there's an awful lot to claim back."

"Listen," she petitioned, "Uncle Ambrose is coming over to England next week on business. He'll talk to you about how I see our future."

"But…"

She carried on regardless, deflecting his protestations with her charm and guile. Before he knew it, he'd consented to Ambrose staying with him for a few days.

Way back at the lift-off of his career, when Fogerty conducted business on behalf of Apollo Systems at Forrester

Wardle, an industrial conglomerate on Long Island, he'd met Ambrose Buchanan, their VP of Futures. A southern gent hailing from the Carolinas with a gravelly, commanding voice, he took a shine to Fogerty, offering advice to the young Englishman regarding how to deal with the American market and suggesting if he ever got to Indianapolis, to look-up his niece, Cherilyn Wagnell. As it happened, Fogerty was due to visit Cleaver Inc, another industrialist in the Indiana state capitol three weeks later, as part of his coast to coast selling tour. 'She's beautiful and charismatic,' he ascribed, pride in his articulation. 'A handsome devil like you should get along with her just fine.'

Meeting with Cherilyn at the downtown Hilton Embassy Suites, they hit it off big time. One thing led to another, love blossomed and eventually Cherilyn joined Fogerty in England where they married.

Fogerty met Buchanan at London Gatwick, immediately the elder man noticing his protege exhibited none of the brightness and zest he exuded when they first met.

Over the course of the ensuing few days he stayed at Fogerty's house before going on to conduct his UK business, they dined at local restaurants, went for extended walks, talked into the wee small hours and drank Glenfiddich. Constantly monitoring for a spark indicating Fogerty's melancholia could be extinguished by a reunion with Cherilyn, it never happened.

Before leaving he called Cherilyn, Fogerty overhearing their conversation. Always a restless being, Buchanan liked to saunter, hands in his trouser pockets as he talked, so he had the landline on speakerphone.

"He's not the confident man you used to be married to anymore, and he's certainly not the hotshot, magic-bullet firing, high-flyer I pointed in your direction."

"Why not?"

"It's complicated, Cherilyn. Since you two split, he's been subjugated to some goddamn awful experiences."

"With women?"

"Yes."

"He's more resilient than that. I've seen him mount insurmountable odds and prevail. He's a winner."

"I think he loves you so much that he doesn't want to disappoint or burden you with his troubles."

"Ohh, Ambrose, you've really taken me by surprise."

"Surely you got an inkling when you spoke to him?"

"I was so caught up in trying to make him believe I wanted him back that any undercurrent passed me by. When he said, 'I'm not sure there's an awful lot to claim back,' I thought he was being his usual modest self and that underneath he is still a go-getting, raging spitfire."

"Honey, I'm afraid the fire has gone out and I don't think even you could re-light it."

A few days later, Cherilyn called Fogerty again, pleading with him to give it another go.

"Cherilyn darling, I've not worked in over two years, and I don't expect to earn a crust ever again. I'd just be a burden to you."

"We used to be able to live on love."

"I'm not so dazzling in that department, either. I don't think even with your feminine graces and caresses you could stiffen me to make love to you. It's all dead down there."

"Ohh, Gene, won't you give me a chance to prove you wrong?"

"You are the love of my life. I couldn't even countenance you seeing me in the state I'm in. Believe me, Cherilyn, I would fail you in every way you can imagine. You deserve better."

"So, you're going to play the Sidney Carton role?"

"It seems that's where my destiny lies."

No matter what she said to sell him on the reconciliation, he declined the approach. When they said their goodbyes, she was in tears. As soon as he put the receiver on its cradle, he broke down, sliding from standing and slithering onto the kitchen floor, a mass of broken pieces symbolically scattering here, there, and everywhere.

After the heartrending interlude, he sunk much further into the decimating pit, his waking periods filled with sorrow, his sleeping patterns worse than ever.

* * *

Another five years passed, Fogerty making further visits to the Darenth Neurological Care Centre but on each occasion, as per the first, they merely recorded his symptoms and subjected him to appraisals, but never prescribed a killer solution to his depression.

"Tell me about these near-to nightly disturbances," Dr. Ansell requested. Another member of Montgomery's team, Ansell claimed to be a dream analysis expert.

"Okay, I'll play the game," Fogerty sarcastically responded. "Here's a selection. Dream one. After dressing in work attire, I leave the house but register I have forgotten my reading spectacles. I see a bleary calendar with Saturday written in fire-engine red and realise it's not a workday. The scene changes to me scrutinising small nuns by the side of a road, not dressed in black but white, before I start playing cricket. A hooded figure tosses a ball at me. I hit it and as it rockets away and disappears, someone shouts, 'Not out, only dozing.' Waking up twitching, I felt very hot with itchy legs, and I had to scratch them repeatedly, drawing blood to the surface. That has happened quite frequently over the past ten years. I have to apply Nivea moisture serum to my legs and sometimes my forearms to combat the itchiness. It's all in my case notes."

"Affirmative."

"Dream two. I'm in a small plane, probably an Avions Robin DR100, doing circuits and bumps at Rochester Flying Club, but the aeroplane has no engine. Peeking up, expecting to see the sky, all I see is the blackness of space with no stars, but when I peer down, the ground is a profusion of radiant colours. The plane dissolves, but I'm still flying like Superman. I veer away from the airfield and have a bird's eye view over Rochester High Street and the River Medway. Dream three: a similar theme."

"Just a moment." Rifling through Fogerty's patient file on his laptop, he then notified, "You reported a similar manifestation in 2012. What is the significance of the Avions Robin DR100?"

"I learnt to fly in a DR100 at Rochester and Headcorn."

"Do you analogise flying with escape?"

"Escape from what?"

"Your troubles."

"I hadn't considered it."

"Go on with dream three."

"I'm with an old schooldays girlfriend watching shiny flying objects when I hear a voice say, 'Richard Shenton will be joining you.' I turn to the sound of the call but cannot see anyone. It then switches to me floating in deep space with dimorphous figures rushing past me, some transparent, some melded into pewter grey statues."

"Who is Richard Shenton?"

"Someone I met at high school. The next morning, I tried to recall his features, but nothing came. I'd forgotten all about him until I heard his name in the dream."

"Next."

"Dream four. I'm viewing some sort of light array power unit source projecting red, blue and green spikes of light. People I at least half recognise are randomly milling about. Some want me to join in. One of them takes off in a helicopter. It hovers over the top of me. The pilot loses control and the helicopter tailplane crashes into the power unit. Then I turn around to see a line abreast set of people at the top of a front garden descending on the house I am in. I try to turn off the lights in the lounge and the lobby, but they stay on. I see a figure resembling my father at the top of the stairs. I think he is coming down to disperse the attackers." He rested. "Is that enough material for you to crunch?"

"Who was the girl in hallucination three?"

"Could have been Sharon Boyd. I had a big thing with her at the time. With my adult private life not working out, I've often thought I should have stayed in Tarvin Sands, gone to work for UKAEA at Capenhurst as a systems designer, married Sharon and had a brood of rugrats, instead of leaving home for university and staying in Kent. Might have been far less exciting, but at least I'd have found long-term happiness."

Ignoring Fogerty's wish, Ansell designated, "There are recurrent themes of flying. How do you account for that?"

"Okay, I do know."

"Go on."

"Subconscious desire to escape from my waking world."

"Yes, but in dream…" He scoured his scribbles. "…four, the helicopter crashes. That could indicate an alternative world on the other side of the fence is not always serene, if you take my meaning."

"True, but equally couldn't it indicate, as you and others of your profession have repeatedly told me, I am living in the margins of society, an outsider viewing proceedings from the sidelines?"

"Possibly." Squinting at Fogerty, he beheld him for a good minute, then tabled, "What *will* satisfy you? By that I mean, what in your mind will bring you out of your chronic melancholia?"

"How about a large dose of normality?"

Taking the desire with a pinch of salt, Ansell did not reply, Fogerty once again leaving Sevenoaks thinking, what's the frigging point! Apart from writing and domestic chores, taking trips to the local supermarket filled his schedule once a fortnight. During one expedition, he ran into strawberry blonde, Emily Rushworth, an old friend from his late teens. Following the usual salutations, Fogerty felt the need to tell her something, cogitating he might not have the willpower to do so on a future occasion, if indeed such a happening occurred.

"I've always adored you, Emily, right from when we danced at Anthony Musgrave's housewarming party back in 1982, your future husband observing suspiciously."

"I never realised."

"Yes, you did. Women can always tell."

She blushed. "Okay, I did know, and I did fancy you. Still do, but I was tied to Daron at the time and now I'm tied to Woodrow. In the meantime, you've been married and have had a string of girlfriends."

"True, but it didn't diminish my feelings for you." Taking her in, he praised, "You're just as gorgeous as when we first met all those centuries ago. We've never had an argument and I've always enjoyed your company. Often when we hugged at the beginning and end of a social affair, I wanted to kiss you."

"Yes, I know."

"You did!"

"As you said, Gene, a woman can always tell."

"Perhaps we should have done something about it before you met Woodrow."

"If we're being honest, I hoped you would."

"*Hah*—" Stung by the admission, he rolled his eyes. "On reflection, those times when you came to my house for drinks and a buffet were ideal, but I was so cut up after what happened with Sabina, in practice my body was with you, but my mind floated elsewhere."

* * *

During further sessions at Sevenoaks, additional to analysis, Fogerty recounted more nocturnal apparitions to Ansell. Though very personal, the former had become a forum for Fogerty to admit his innermost fears without embarrassment, something he struggled with earlier in the treatment.

"What is it that plagues you the most?" Ansell inquired.

"Can't get a damned thing to work."

"What in particular?"

"Life."

"How do you deal with making others aware of your condition?"

"I don't. I'm good at covering it up. Apart from the medical profession and Sabina, no one knows about my fragility."

"What are you good at?"

"Lying. I'm a salesman."

"Are you lonely?"

"God, yes. Stupid question. The answer is obvious."

"True, but I had to get you to admit to it."

"Why?"

"Because once the subject admits to their feelings, they are in a position to tackle them."

"*Really.*" Enigmatically, he bent forward, derision adorning his features. "And how would you tackle my situation?"

Blustering around to arrive at an unconvincing retort, he uttered the usual platitudes Fogerty had heard from him and other clinicians a thousand times before.

"In other words, you don't know!" He paused. "Well, I know. A resurrection of how my life used to be before Sabina fucked me. Can you do that for me, Mister psychiatrist man?"

"I'm afraid I can't."

"Then why on Earth am I sitting in this chair?"

"Let's turn to your latest dreams," Ansell counselled, completely sidestepping Fogerty's plea. "Can you summarise a few instances?"

"Why not? It's always fun chronicling something to shock you, but you never display any physiognomy reactions, do you. You remain placid and aloof, either recording what I say, or penning commentary in my file. You're just like an audience member who won't laugh, no matter how funny the onstage comedian is. *Huh*, I've worked with computers that have more personality and heartbeat than psychoanalysts."

Sitting back and folding his arms, he beefed, "This is just a lab experiment for you people, isn't it? An opportunity to gather patsy data to populate the endless psychotherapy thesis. But you know, in my commercial world, for a business system to have credibility, as well as inputting information, it has to output solutions. That was my stock in trade. It doesn't seem to apply to your profession."

"First account, please."

Shaking his head at Ansell's academic stance, he became tempted to walk out, then thought, no, this is a rare time I get to talk to somebody, so I might as well oblige him. "Very well. I'm in an office with other people. The walls are cracked and painted green. I'm reading a pastime magazine at a desk. It's cover portrays a man free-falling through space. I put on my trainers and walk down the office with the intent of finding an official document to explain the magazine cover. I never get there. Three men and one girl bundle me into the back seat of a small car. Then we're walking around a packed high street splattered in a kaleidoscope of colours. I guide them inside a pub for a drink. They all sit on a bench. They want wine. I go to the bar then it fades to nothingness."

"And the next?"

"My lifelong friend Hector Mcintyre comes to visit. I'm embarrassed because the house is untidy. I have to go out to buy something. I'm dressed in a shirt, tie, dark jacket and some old brown trousers I recognise that would never hold their crease. I wander into a shop. Later, I'm with the actress Greta Scacchi in her *White Mischief* guise, as guests in someone's house. The owner sits at the head of a long table in a dining room. He says to me, 'Put the radio on. It's in D16.' I search a set of wall cabinets for D16, but I can't find it. Then Hector walks in and finds D16."

"Why do you think Greta Scacchi appeared?"

"Simple, she plays a selfish bitch in the film."

"So presumably, Greta is analogous to Sabina?"

"Even I worked that out."

"Next dream."

"I'm walking along a spent riverbed with someone else I don't recognise. From a very tall brick bridge, two people are throwing solid seagulls at us. We duck and dive to avoid the missiles. Then I'm in an indigo blue corridor containing an infinite number of brilliant red doors. I unlatch one door, sit down at a desk, read some papers, open a notebook and proceed to copy down their contents. For some unknown reason, I think the originals belong to Jose Mourinho."

"The football manager?"

"Yes. Someone opens the door and I rapidly gather together all the papers."

"No concluding scene, then?"

"No, the majority of my sleeping mirages are open ended like watching snippets of next week's soap opera."

"Next dream."

"I'm on a golf course with Graham Thomas, an old buddy of mine." Stopping, he quailed. "I've had this one before or a variation on it."

"You mean with your friend Graham Thomas?"

"Yes. We are about to tee-off on the first and it starts to rain.

We take refuge in a hut, then I find myself lying down on the ground covered with a sheet and staring up at a cloud formation in the shape of a broad spear which appears to be manmade, coming in from right to left. The scene changes to a shopping centre, possibly Bluewater. I go inside a cinema probing for seats to accommodate four people. I am standing at the front right side of the amphitheatre, making for a poor acute-angle to view the screen. There's a picture being shown in brown and white, but I can't make out what it is. All the seats in the middle are empty but cannot be used. The cinema melts into fragments, then I hear the sound of something heavy falling. It woke me, certain the sound had been real. I checked around the house, but nothing had fallen off the walls or from the cupboards."

"The free-falling and missiles symbols indicate you have a threat complex."

"I don't doubt it."

"Were you bullied at junior school?"

"Everyone is bullied at junior school. You've already tried on that cliché for size."

"True, but sometimes patients are inaccurate with their recalls."

"You mean they lie?"

"Yes. Are you lying?"

Smiling sardonically, he said, "I'm just playing your game."

* * *

Skirting amongst the usual governance and execution of mental health care, occasionally a humorous nugget materialised. As well as trips to Sevenoaks, sometimes Fogerty had to attend the Medway Mental Health Clinic at Newhaven Lodge for a brief check-up. Unlike the Darenth Neurological Care Centre inextricably linked to heavy duty cases, Newhaven Lodge dealt with minor mental problems, including those resultant from the aging process.

On one occasion, whilst sitting in the waiting space, he marked a couple of old dears dressed like Dickensian characters with flamboyant scarfs and mittens exposing their fingers. Both of East End extraction, the man muttered in cockney rhyming slang, his wife responding, in a similar verbal inflection, their Darby and Joan persona a touch of light comic relief amongst the usual down-in-the-dumps whackos and timid coo-coos either sloped up against the walls looking vacant or slumped in a chair bent over navel gazing. Clearly not predisposed to seeing a mental health clinician, the octogenarians griped to each other about the enforced imposition. Finally called into the consulting room, their session only lasted a few minutes before they burst out into the waiting chamber, their dander ignited, their indignation on overload.

"Wot a *fackin'* liberty!" the woman loudly blurted, as the pair trundled to the exit. "Wot do they think we are, a couple of fackin' nutters?"

Though such amusing incidents were far and few between, Fogerty welcomed them, the milk of human intolerance to authority interrupting the monastic propriety of deadpan mental health buildings.

Since Sabina did the dirty on him, she still called him every year or two, he thought, just to make sure he was still alive.

During one linkup, she asked, "Are you still going to Sevenoaks?"

"Yes."

"What did they have to say at your last session?"

"They view me to be a Robinson Crusoe like-character marooned on my own deserted ocean island, the difference being, though I am surrounded by other households and passersby when I go to the supermarket, they are impervious to my senses. Because I am no longer involved in society in any capacity, they might as well not be there."

"Would you like to come over for dinner? We could also watch a film."

"Yeah, why not."

When they met at her house, she usually told him about her adventures in America and Europe. On this occasion, he decided before she launched into world traveller mode, to tell her about the newspaper deliveries and the phone caller who always hung up after he answered, also recapping, that in the opinion of Dr. Montgomery, they were the acts of someone with a very guilty conscience.

"It was you, wasn't it?" he laid down.

Shaken by the unforeseen accusation, she furrowed her brow, her jaw simultaneously dropping. After licking her lips, she reluctantly admitted, "Yes."

"Why did you do it? What were you hoping to achieve?"

As usual, her body language became defensive.

"Were they attempts to absolve yourself of the foul deed?"

She dropped into a pensive deportment, her reply cloaked in semi-justifications for her selfish move leading to her lame attempt at making amends by having red tops delivered.

"It went on for seven years, then without notice I received a bill from Claymore Newsagents on Woodside in Rainham," he briefed. "I went to see the newsagent. For confidentiality reasons, he wouldn't tell me who had paid the bills but said the person in question had stopped paying the monthly account." Abiding forthright, he scrutinised her. "Woodside is less than a quarter mile from your house, so I knew it was you."

"Why didn't you say anything nearer that time?"

"Didn't want to embarrass you."

"But you do today."

"Ohh...it has been long overdue for confirmation, same as those phone calls." Gyrating his head, he sought, "What were you hoping to achieve by calling, hearing me say hello, then ringing off a few seconds later?"

"I just wanted to make sure you were..."

"Still alive?" he supplied.

"I suppose so."

"Why did you stop the redtops and the fake calls?"

"Because your health came across as better in your manner and speech when we met up."

"*Hah*, that was an act, put on for your benefit." Bewildered by her apparent naivety, he coaxed, "Incidentally, did those two futile actions cleanse your conscience?"

"No, not really." Seeking to change the subject, she solicited, "What would you like to watch after we've eaten?"

"Anything not solely reliant on CGI. Something classic. A film *noir*."

During their meal, she spoke in glowing terms about a trip to Yellowstone Park she'd made the previous year, the American recollection triggering Fogerty to tell her about Cherilyn wanting him back and why he was unable to fulfill her want.

"When did this happen?"

"Back in summer 2010."

"Like for the redtops discovery, you never said anything at the time."

"No. Behind the benign façade I projected for your benefit, I hid enormous pain."

I guess I'll never stop paying for the inconsiderate Leo indiscretion."

He didn't answer her. No point. The damage done, irreversible. Then a sense of charity overtook him. "If you're ever in the US again, don't venture into Indiana," he advised. "She'll have you killed. In fact, she could have you killed over here. If I were you, I'd be careful. She's very strong on vengeance."

* * *

..."So, Mister Fogerty," Dr. Cribb continued, "we've established your dreams can be categorised as manifestations of deep desires and anxieties, in your case driven by melancholia. Some are superficial and meaningless. Others reflect real people and situations you've been through or will happen at a later date. Certainly, your overnight illusions exhibit unconscious wishes and fantasies, but you've regurgitated nothing to suggest your mental state is anything other than a disorder from your breakup with Sabina."

"Yes, I've heard all this from your colleagues over the years, so frequent, I can almost recite it verbatim. And as usual, you soft-peddle what happened with Sabina. As I have gone on record repeatedly, we didn't break up, she fucked me."

"Quite. However, and this is a cardinal point. It is clear since the outset of your illness, Cherilyn enters your subconscious much more than Sabina." Dwelling, he allowed the diagnosis to sink in. "Do you miss Cherilyn?"

"Huh, I remember an instance when she was still in Indianapolis and I stayed at the Hyatt House. After she exited my room, I found a scrap of paper on one of the bed pillows. She'd written on it, 'Miss Me?' I still have the scrap, but I left missing her behind me long ago when I entered the undefined regions."

"Well, we're all in some kind of hell, even psychoanalysts."

"Oh, for sure. My own 'season in hell' to quote from Rimbaud has now been in play for fifteen years. It's a madhouse, filled with the inversion of everything I once held dear."

"Why do you say that?"

"Because for me, Dr. Cribb, the sun only shines when it's raining."

"So, you're saying your current world is occupied by the antithesis of all the components inhabiting your world prior to your breakdown."

"I am."

"That's extraordinary."

Staring to the heavens, Fogerty felt a sense of high release. "*Don't* you know?" he thundered out. "I'm unique, a freak within the annals of psychiatric history. I dream in technicolour with quadraphonic surround sound and three-dimensional prospecting. There have been more pages devoted to Patient Number 174697, than any other study case over the past decade and a half. I am truly in trance as vision, peeping over the other side of the wall, wanting to participate in an alternative parallel universe where I can find some everlasting peace."

KASHMIR: A VISIONARY'S TALE

KASHMIR: A VISIONARY'S TALE

Ever inquisitive academic Mikhail Bulgakov never shied away from the unknown. Amidst his trek into making *The Master and Margarita* a literary fiction of uniqueness and wit, he had explored the tricky highways and byways of inspiration, spending endless hours poring over ancient documents and artefacts, and visiting a plethora of heritage sites, all in an effort to satisfy his goal. Nonetheless, nothing he read or dissected met his needs. He cerebrated he had assigned himself an impossible task, until he entered an outlandish, backwater antiques shop.

Crossing its threshold, he heard the doorbell clink, the chiming resulting in an unexplained, light-headed sensation. Dismissing the occurrence as autosuggestion brought on by the emporium's old-world transcending atmosphere, he moved into its midst. Moments beforehand, he had seen an enticing jewel-encrusted casket in the shop window, experienced its magnetism, and became besieged by the dominance, unable to resist its faculty for persuading him to enter the premises.

Silence reigned after the bell vibration faded. Scanning about, he awaited the owner to materialise from one of the many crooks and passages he saw at the back of the establishment. A minute passed without anything happening. Not unusual for an antiques shop, their owners tended to the eccentric side, focusing more on collection at the expense of commerce. Bulgakov concluded the owner must be in an ante chamber serving another client, or perhaps at the back door accepting receipt of goods from a seller.

Crammed from floor to ceiling with all manner of furniture, bone china, cut glass and fabrics, the interior held his application beyond the beckoning box. An avid accumulator of figurines, taking his fancy, he spied an array of Russian Imperial Porcelain pieces in a glass display cabinet, but the irresistible enchantment in the window lasted as his primary bibelot.

Becoming annoyed no one had still not responded to the doorbell, he nosed into the forefront of the outlet, even squinting over the counter to see if the owner hid beneath its top, unwilling to participate in banter with yet another supposed pesky curio hunter, only window shopping. Adding to his increasing bitterness at the lack of customer service, his quest revealed nothing. Then the odd force emanating from the casket resumed, his concentration despatched to the window display, Bulgakov compelled to move towards it. Examining the ornate rectangular object catching his eye and sending out its plea for attention, he suddenly slumped into overbearing dread, the hairs on the back of his neck surging up, his peepers beginning to bulge, a dominating aura sucking at his very being.

* * *

Late the foregoing night, Bulgakov had supper with Elena Shilovskaya, his lover, and a colleague from the University of Moscow. Sitting in front of a log fire, they discussed the forthcoming release of *The Master and Margarita*, Bulgakov confiding he had plans to make the surrealistic volume extraordinary. Began in 1928, but subsequently, seeing no future as a writer in the Soviet Union, he had ceremoniously burned the first manuscript in 1930. Regretting the emotional, self-centred act, he reconstituted the draft from memory a year later, in promotion of making it his *magnum opus*.

Possessing the nimbus of an enigmatic muse, inscrutable and mysterious, coupled with her fine features disguising the unfathomable, scholarly talent within, Elena had come into

Bulgakov's life at a time when his ability to create cogent, convincing narrative had largely vanished.

Intellectually erudite and bookish, her department colleagues lauded her to be an outstanding scholastic luminary, capable of assessing and putting into context the golden age lexicon of 19th century Russian literature giants from Pushkin to Chekhov. She carried her slender, eye-catching shape with poise, her elegance hallowed by many, but her capacity to express judicious and wise deduction intrigued most, setting her apart, people mesmerised by what she said, as distinguished from her physical attractiveness. Somehow, she managed to project a perturbation of acumen through the ether, superseding the listeners' tactile sensors and connecting them squarely to her hyperactive mind, the beauty of its rhetoric far exceeding conventional precepts of womanly charisma. Bulgakov adored her, but paradoxically calculated himself both physically and cerebrally plain in her fellowship.

Though not uncomely for a man in his fortieth year, his youthful looks had waned, and he wore a world-weary mask at times, triggered by too many disappointments in respect of what he premeditated to be reasonable expectations of the human race. Mannerly contemporaries told him he resembled their conceptions of Sherlock Holmes, his angular peculiarities and piercing optics representative of the Conan Doyle invented sleuth.

"You know, Mikhail, your book will get you into trouble with the authorities," Elena warned. "They are already talking about banning it."

"Let them," he taunted, tapping his cranium. "They can't ban what's in here."

Casting him a disapproving gloom, Elena told him, "I love you, Mikhail Afanasyevich Bulgakov." She prodded his arm. "But I fear for you."

"Steady, my dear," he entreated. "Nothing is going to happen. Stalin is more rapt in nailing Leonid Maximovich Leonov for his dissident activities, assassinating Trotsky, and catching that young upstart Solzhenitsyn in the act of sedition, than persecuting a lower order writer like me."

"You are being artificially modest, Mikhail. Along with

Nabokov, you are rightly seen as Russia's current preeminent lights." She threw a scowl of censorship at him before adding, "And…" She wagged a foreboding finger. "…you can't write yourself out of Stalin's gaze, like your Master just avoids the Devil in Moscow. Stalin is real, not imaginary."

Flustered by Elena's words striking him to the core, Bulgakov irritatedly poked the fire, encouraging it to beget more heat. "Just what would you have me do, skulk in a cellar with the rats?"

She did not match his retort. Instead, pursuing a different tack, she solicited, "Do you have inputs for the latest incarnation of *The Master and Margarita* yet?"

"By all that's holy," he quacked, throwing his head back in a depiction of over-theatric artistic temperament. "Suitable footings have become a sore point. I have let it be known in didactic circles, the approaching release of *The Master and Margarita* will be the definitive version, and my agent has been publicising my ambition." Mulishly curling his top lip, he admitted, "But nothing of any significance has come to mind." Hesitating, his body language betokened acute miscarriage had become his constant companion. "Usually when blankness happens, like many writers, I search for an episode, or better still, an icon to galvanise and stimulate."

"And have you found such an icon?"

"No…not yet." Leaning forward in his chair, his demeanour changed to buoyant. "Are you unfailingly swayed I am Nabokov's equal, Elena?"

"Ohh, *Mikhail*, you know you are as good as Nabokov, if not better." Giggling, she categorised, "You are falsely asking me to inflate your ego, when you know you are reckoned by most connoisseurs to be the best from the current batch of modish writers." Fabricating an incisive dial, she chastised, "you should have more confidence in yourself. You are a visionary, a pathfinder, a writer divining unrivalled themes and trends from mere acorns of stimuli. Nabokov is yet to come up with an original to better *The Master and Margarita*."

"You absolutely think so?"

"Well—" She furrowed her brow. "Can you name a Nabokov story hitting the same summit of invention?"

"Maybe not, but he always has a labour on the go, and is revered in international authorship forums."

"Does not necessarily mean he will top *The Master*."

"No, it doesn't." His aggravation intensifying, Bulgakov got to his feet. "If only I could find a spur sparking my invention for the impending edition of *The Master*."

* * *

"Can I help you, sir?"

Conspicuously coming out of thin air, Bulgakov swivelled away from the window display and in the direction of the voice. From behind a Louis XIV cabinet, a bulbous head popped out, accompanied by a well-nourished, rounded body.

Signifying with his faithful walking stick, Bulgakov replied, "Yes, I'm interested in this jewel-encrusted casket."

"Ah, yes…the casket," the proprietor parroted, his plush tone filled with enough mystique to suggest the need for ancillary elucidation, Bulgakov instantly intrigued.

Meandering nearer, the fully rounded man inspected his patron, noting his confident deportment and pronounced command. Pressing his lips together and raising open hands to indicate truthfulness, he confessed, "I must tell you, the jewels are imitation." He shot an ambiguous lour at Bulgakov. "Moreover, real value resides in the casket's contents."

"*Real* value!" Bulgakov retorted, recoiling, his rationality amply alert, his curiosity aroused. "What do you mean by real value?"

Leering precociously, he furtively uttered, "Ahh," as if knowing a big fish had become spellbound by the lure he had laid.

Turning away, and making for the window, he left his prospect seized by bated breath. Delicately lifting the item of Bulgakov's desire out from its exhibit stand and between other scrutiny inducing curios, he carried it with reverence, like he held an entity of singular antiquity, before placing it on the shop countertop.

Eyeing Bulgakov with profound allure, he reported, "The coffer contains a scroll. This is the article holding important merit."

"What kind of merit?" Bulgakov shot back.

"The kind that dreams are made of."

On cloud nine, the candid reply only served to amplify Bulgakov's eagerness. "Can I see it?"

"Ahh," the bulbous man wailed, clasping his hands together in a prayer-like fashion. "To see it, is to own it, and I already have another gentleman sufficiently beguiled to want to acquire it."

"Darn it." Frowning at the setback, Bulgakov deliberated. "How much *do* you want?"

"Hah!" he impertinently scoffed. Gurning gratuitously unmasking an inner glutinous mouth, the shop owner asserted, "More than you can possibly afford, if you need to ask me how much."

Affronted by the rebuke, Bulgakov argued with him for a few moments, saying how could he possibly make a bid without knowing the kernel of the thing under purchasing evaluation. Unremittingly adamant, the proprietor left the potential buyer without success. Furious at his impudence, Bulgakov stormed out, cursing under his breath.

* * *

Continuing to fume, he backtracked to his central Moscow apartment. After multiple shots of brandy quelling his rage, Bulgakov resolved to revisit the antiques shop in the afternoon to continue the battle with its intransigent owner. Lunch came and went without enjoyment. Champing at the bit, he desperately wanted to reengage the dismissive bourgeois, and get the better of him.

By 3:00pm, Bulgakov bore down on the antiques shop, determined to secure the casket, and thereby the scroll. Just as he negotiated the corner leading to his quarry, Vladimir Vladimirovich Nabokov came into view, entering the premises. Stopping abruptly in his tracks and gasping, Bulgakov wondered if Nabokov was the competing client the shopkeeper had referred to.

"For the love of *God*," he angrily spat out, his mug awash with vitriol as he conjured up daydreams of doing unspeakable acts of torture to his competitor. "Why did it have to be him? Of all the intellectuals in Moscow, *why* Nabokov?"

An often trenchant and sometimes prurient fellow in Bulgakov's opinion, he knew Nabokov never lacked for the enquiring streak necessary to provoke good art. An old chum and sometimes academic adversary, even nemesis for Bulgakov, over many years their relationship swung vehemently between harmony and discord, rarely settling at a balanced midpoint where consensus existed. When their views did fuse in consummate agreement, the accord promoted affection and shared intimacy, but more often than not, a collision of juxtaposed standpoints culminated in friction and tumult.

Bulgakov had not seen Nabokov since Christmas. On that occasion, though junior to himself, Nabokov had come across as wearisome and in need of stimulus, his frame thickened due to overeating, his eyelids heavy, and his receding hairline adding years to his semblance.

If Nabokov turns out to be my competition for the scroll, what are his intentions, Bulgakov contemplated? Deciding to wait, he stirred several possible permutations, each coalescing in the same conclusion. Nabokov craved the parchment to aid his penmanship, but what did the relic actually have to offer by way of illumination? Had Nabokov persuaded the shopkeeper to convey its mystery in advance, or weathered as much in the dark as himself, and had decided to risk a speculative procurement?

After a few minutes, craving overpowered prudence. Creeping on, so as to see into the shop window, he unearthed the casket had gone. Disgruntled, he punched the pavement with his walking stick and cursed Nabokov. Then he heard the familiar chime of the antiques shop bell, as the door began to open. Rushing back behind the corner, he monitored the shop, spying on Nabokov as he surfaced, carrying a package, its size and configuration implying a small chest could be secreted within.

"*Blast!*" he bawled, annoyed his procrastination had led to Nabokov gaining the prized basal he so frantically sought. Incensed he had missed out on the casket, and thereby it's hidden cache, he disconsolately tramped back to his apartment and broke out the *Remy Martin* again. Worse still, Nabokov had succeeded, the thorny recognition dilating his sorrows. Brooding on his failure, his bad thoughts about Nabokov strengthened. A few more hours of brandy consumption and inner turmoil passed before he decided to phone Nabokov, saying he wanted to see him on some synthetic but credible pretext. Once in his apartment, he'd dovetail into a conversation about Nabokov's day. Well aware of his challenger's knack for one-upmanship, he knew he'd not be able to resist disclosing his find, the receptacle inevitably forming part of the discussion.

* * *

Feeling sharp in his reflexes and with an air of fortitude, at the appointed time Bulgakov rang the doorbell at Nabokov's nearby apartment.

"Hello, Vladimir Vladimirovich Nabokov," he hailed as Nabokov stood before him. "How are you, my dear friend?

"I am good, Mikhail." Gleaming warmly, he grasped Bulgakov's hand. "Come in."

Much to Bulgakov's surprise, when he took a good gander at Nabokov, remarkably he appeared refreshed, in good health, and more athletic than he remembered. His eyes shone with brilliance, his hair had bounce, his skin smoothed from firm muscles below its three layers. Aghast at the indisputable metamorphosis, Bulgakov appreciated his faultless being resembled a rejuvenated phoenix.

Still perplexed by the physical renewal, Bulgakov trailed his host along a narrow corridor and into his study. Dominating its interior, a vast library of books, partially finished manuscripts and sundry papers occupied every shelf and every flat surface. A trait always staggering Bulgakov, he could never suss how Nabokov located anything, filing explicitly irrelevant to his management system. Cobwebs over curtains never drawn, and windows racked with grime and rarely unsealed, capped the familiar setting.

"How goes it for you, Vladimir? Are you making money? Is your writing progressing?"

"I am doing very well," Nabokov confirmed. "*The Gift* is beginning to sell in Russia and Germany, and I am working on a new novella called *The Enchanter*." Ceasing his comeback, he issued his guest a mischievous glance, Bulgakov detecting it but tarrying undecided as to its significance. "But let's make ourselves comfortable before we bury ourselves in abstract minutiae."

Settling into sumptuous chairs, a blazing fire and *Beluga* vodka adding to their comfort, the two novelists eyed each other, neither wanting to trigger a gambit.

Mindful that he had requested the meeting, Bulgakov decisively took the initiative. "Tell me, Vladimir, what is *The Enchanter* about?"

Styling a sickly, self-conscious smile, Nabokov divulged, "You'll condemn me as the voyeur, Mikhail, but this is a story needing to be told."

"My goodness, sounds singularly extravagant. Please, go on."

"It's about a middle-aged man lusting after a certain type of adolescent girl," Nabokov gushed, the statement's dramaturgic overtones not lost on Bulgakov. "No doubt you know the type?"

"Comprehensively. Someone addicted to hebephilia," he posted. Flashing him a derisive bore, as if critical of the subject matter, he added, "Ooohh, too risky, Vladimir. The authorities will not like such a dissertation."

"Undoubtedly, but I felt compelled to write it. Structured on a draft and stationed on its organic essence, I have a sequel in mind to be entitled *Lolita,* but this will be a screenplay as well as a novel. Anyway—" He took a long pull on his drink, as if at least partially deflated by Bulgakov's censure. "I am still researching for *The Enchanter*, seeking constituents to build the main protagonist's reign over juvenile girls."

"Have you seen anything?"

"Indeed, I have." Eyeing Bulgakov cautiously, he informed,

"Just today, I bought an item already proving to be an invaluable revelation."

Immediately Bulgakov knew it must be the casket. "Oh, what is it?"

Recalling the detail, Nabokov reexamined how he had seen a jewel-encrusted casket in an antiques shop window. Upon enquiry, he discovered it contained a scroll. When he asked about a selling price, the shop owner answered with the same reply Bulgakov had been given. Howbeit, Bulgakov did not intend to come clean about a duplicate forage for the piece. After much conjecture, Nabokov could no longer resist the temptation to possess the baffling curio, post haste going back to the antiques shop and purchasing the gem.

"So how much did you pay for this…" Bulgakov waved his hands about, pretending no cognizance of the article in question. "…this receptacle?"

"More than you could possibly evoke or justify."

"You don't say. So, erm—" Gaping like an immature sapling, his snoopiness worsened. "What precisely is written on this scroll?"

"Ahh…" Nabokov got up and paced around the retreat, his obvious enthrallment not lost on his visitor. Turning to address Bulgakov with a reticent air, he advised, "It is extremely precious, a serum solving all, the equivalent of a transcendental roadmap to Kubla Khan's treasures in Xanadu."

"*Caramba*, a Coleridge comparison. Is it so auspiciously golden?"

"It is."

"Can you tell me what it contains, or better still, can I see this scroll?"

Stalling, Nabokov poured two large *Belugas*, giving one to Bulgakov. Sitting and exuding a show of superiority, Bulgakov judged to be smug, Nabokov fixed his gaze on his probing associate. "To see it, is to own it."

Distinguishing the words he had initially heard from the antiques shop owner echoed by Nabokov, Bulgakov's captivation intensified. Grimacing at the cagey declaration, he held his rancour in check. "Can you at least give me a hint?"

Beaming boastfully, as if he had been bestowed with the Holy Grail's sacred competencies, Nabokov articulated, "Incontestably, there are some things I'm always willing to share with a fellow writer." Lingering, as if deliberately intent upon imparting the melodramatic, he qualified, "But on this occasion, what you ask is impossible."

Inwardly Bulgakov boiled, his hunger to see the scroll inhibiting his composure. "But *why*?" he whined, his shrill tenor betraying his vexation.

"Mikhail, please believe me," Nabokov begged, spreading his arms appealingly. "To see what rests inside the repository, is a one-time only experience."

Tempted to cut to the chase, declaring he knew about the vessel, Bulgakov surmised veracity might persuade his compatriot to share the find. Pondering on the proposition, he suddenly recognised the fatalistic trophy had reduced his accustomed sense of propriety, not only in Nabokov's presence, but from the instant the antiques shop owner had belittled his query. Merely ruminating about the casket overwhelmed him, accelerating the aspiration to unlock its latent secret. Even worse, by negating logical judgment to bystander status, it had him in the grip of intransigence, unable to break free of the spell.

With the realisation crystallised, his customary cool returned. Falling back into his habitual sanguine style, he discerned the object of his obsession had coerced him out of character. *Why*, he mentally queried? *Why has the beatified trinket become a fixating obsession? Why does this superficial bijoux have such an enveloping effect on my psyche?* He shelved the posers.

"Vladimir, it's just simple inquisitiveness," he assured. "We writers get intrigued by the unusual, the unexplained. Odd things adding vital worth to our endeavours become cherished. I—" Wavering, his voice descended into a lower register. "I just comprehended you might wish to share your good fortune with an old buddy."

"*Ahhh*," Nabokov warily responded, the eye glint of

circumspection augmented to his countenance. "Bulgakov plays the kinship card. Well, you know, Mikhail, we have not always been mutually gracious affiliates. I enjoy the cut and thrust, and I concede I find you amicable and congenial at times, but authoring is a competitive venture, subject to the old maxim, keep your enemies close and your friends even closer."

"*Vladimir!*" Bulgakov blathered, effecting an innocent carriage in an act of sincerity.

"Please, let me finish." Nabokov drained his glass. "Yes, we are amigos, but let's be honest. Like with all writers, it's a love-hate relationship, one of convenience perhaps, even necessity, nevertheless—" He laughed at the self-admission. "I do like you, Mikhail Afanasyevich Bulgakov, and I have always admired your oeuvre. In the years to come, *The Master and Margarita* will be appraised as a masterpiece, even if it is now frowned upon by Stalin's henchmen."

Ashamed, Bulgakov knew he had energised too rapidly and too acutely with his comrade, the casket ownership ambition superseding his manners and decorum. "Vladimir, forgive me, if I seemed insensitive and hectoring," he beseeched. "I must confess your find has got the better of me."

"Calm yourself, I'm only playing devil's advocate, if you'll forgive the pun reference to *The Master*." Frowning apologetically, he elucidated, "All I can tell you is, the casket comes from Kashmir."

"I see," Bulgakov favourably accredited, immediately fetching from mind the pantology affiliated with Kashmir, and inwardly applauding the feint and clever citation.

Kashmir, the very word awakened auspices of Eastern mysticism. Bulgakov had journeyed to Tibet in his mid-thirties, keen to tread the same trails taken by Herman Hesse, fourteen years his senior, and a major influence on his composition. From high up in the Himalayas, he had gaped out on the Kashmir valley, its renowned folklore and crimson history enriching his foresight, adding to his writer's canon, and making him accept there could be more to the afterlife than heaven and hell. Beguiling and bewitching, the esoteric exercise had a profound effect, Bulgakov able to solve conundrums unendingly impenetrable before his trip. Once foggy ideas, laden with cryptic evaluation and arcane inference crystalised into irrefutable facts, the scales of ambiguity lifted from his eyes. A transforming occurrence, whilst immersed in the quandary-relieving melting pot of the East, he had been able to see things as they truly were, just as predicted in Blake's doors of perception. On return to Moscow, he found the gift had deserted him. Clarity of thought and lucidity of insight once again evaded his artifices, meditative supposition inescapably annihilated by his draconian social environment, and Stalin's restrictive laws. After the antiques shop interlude, subconsciously he envisaged whatever lay in the shady chest could rekindle the Kashmir happening.

"Yes, Kashmir," Nabokov breezily reiterated. "Judging by your detached aspect, I can see the place has as much significance for you as it has for me." Reclining in his seat, he petitioned, "Tell me, Mikhail, why do you crave to know what is written on this parchment so much? What is it you dream it might enable you to accomplish?

"Hah, you are very sagacious, Vladimir," Bulgakov complimented. "There is no advantage in pretending your casket constituent description has not stirred my fascination."

"Yes, but why?"

"In part, for the same rationale motivating you to hunt for artefacts you hope will boost your crusade to complete *The Enchanter*." Irritably shifting his weight about in his seat, he admitted, "*The Master and Margarita* still needs a compelling yardstick to make it fly."

"How do you mean?"

"Well, let me see—" Wrestling himself out of agitation, he sat back. "After finishing the first edition in 1928, I've been concentrating on various supplementary versions. Currently, I am on version five, and still I feel there is scope for a crucible to set it apart from concurrent psychological plots." Gawking at Nabokov, he buttonholed, "I'm combing for a seed, an impetus childing a new and unusual channel to upgrade the apriorism and the plot."

"I see." Mulling over the purpose, Nabokov declared,

"Palpably, we are both scheming along similar lines. I need a differentiator for *The Enchanter*, and you, an incitement for *The Master*." Quivering his brow, he proclaimed, "What it is to be a writer in need of inspiration!"

"Indeed. So——" Bulgakov pitched a pleading comportment at the repository's owner. "Are you going to help me?"

"You mean, tell you what is written on the parchment?"

"Yes."

Musing on the demand, Nabokov announced, "I'll tell you what I will do, Mikhail. Are you attending the Moscow writers' forum tomorrow at the Dostoyevsky Club?"

"I am, Vladimir."

"Good."

Standing, Nabokov adopted a military-like modus as he moved to his desk then an adjacent cabinet, picking up the odd paper fallen to the floor whilst cogitating, Bulgakov rising from his seat observing Nabokov's actions with expectancy in anticipation of a beneficial proposal.

Twisting to face him, Nabokov promised, "Tomorrow, I will bring the casket to the Dostoyevsky Club. There, I will let you see what it contains." Moving in on his persistent confederate, he tested, "Will my commitment satisfy your prying plea, Mikhail Afanasyevich Bulgakov?"

* * *

Eager to reconnect with Nabokov, Bulgakov arrived early at the Dostoyevsky Club, his appetites magnified by an imminent inspection of the scroll, but bizarrely uneasy about the choice of venue. *Why divulge the casket's secrets in a society colloquium*, he deliberated? Putting aside his reservation, each time the riddle permeated his consciousness, his mind raced away, churning over Nabokov's parallel pursuit of the receptacle independent of his own, and analysing his motivations for granting him access to the matchless document. He wondered what stupendous enigma it held, and why Nabokov plainly weighed it to be a landmark epiphany? Annoyed, he abided unable to judge the heirloom in context, and evaluate it dispassionately, he consoled himself, knowing the deficiency would soon be over.

Reflecting they were both students of life and keen metaphysical explorers, maybe he had unjustly held malevolence for Nabokov's success in procuring the casket. Despite professional competitiveness, and the occasional spat brought on by a clash of egos often engendering artificial disagreement for the sake of it, they had much in common, synergy a usual element binding their intellects together.

Why then did reticence so concern him about the Dostoyevsky Club as a rendezvous location? He had foreseen Nabokov balking irreversibly at the prospect of sharing the scroll's inestimable data, but against all odds, he had readily acquiesced to his request. But why such a public place to put on display a clearly venerated object? Yet again, he perceived the adored box had become the root cause of his over-anxiety, boosting suspicion and blowing up distrust out of proportion.

Each time the club's entrance door opened, he scrutinised to see if Nabokov came into view, but no, only fellow writers and patrons entered. Some he acknowledged with a wave of his walking stick or a smile, albeit, he tried to emanate an ambience insinuating he did not wish to talk. Such communal interaction might distract him from Nabokov's arrival.

During his bothersome wait, Nabokov's restored window dressing he witnessed at his apartment came to the forefront of Bulgakov's mind. He had meant to enquire about the refresh at the time, but having become totally absorbed in his casket quest, it had vanished from his query list. Now he made calculations. Could there be any correlation between Nabokov reviewing the scroll and his sequent transmogrification? Certainly, the transition eventuated as too sudden, too phenomenal, to be resultant from conventional medication affects, it's deliverance almost as if Nabokov had been consecrated by a super-deity bequeathing instantaneous rebirth on him. Pondering more about the uncanny renovation, he came to no steady-state determinations.

As the large, gold-plated clock in the foyer ticked on approaching the appointed start hour for the writers' caucus,

Bulgakov's anxiety increased. Had Nabokov played a cruel trick on him, never aspiring to show? Fuming at the inkling, he noticed participants enrolling for their seats in the main salon. Soon he'd have to join them.

With a few minutes to go before the event began, he crossed the foyer, near to exasperation Nabokov had not arrived.

"Your name, sir?" enquired the *maître d'*.

"Bulgakov."

"The writer of *The Master and Margarita*?"

"Yes."

"Oh, we are honoured, sir," enthused the *maître d'* with a warm smile. "My son reads your books. His favourite is *Adventures of Chichikov*, and like me, he has read the latest published edition of *The Master and Margarita*. A remarkable enterprise, it had us guessing as to its ending throughout. We have also read in literary journals, the subsequent edition of *The Master* will be the best yet."

"Yes, it is correct. My agent has insisted publicity and pre-marketing by my publisher will ensure the definitive version earns buyer traction in advance of the publication date and becomes a bestseller."

Ambling frontwards, halting only a few inches from Bulgakov, the *maître d'* enquired, "Tell me, sir, did you make a pact with the Devil to write the book, just like its hero, *The Master*?"

Peeved by the ask, Bulgakov broke into a narrow smile, the same assertion having been proposed many times. "It goes without saying," he reacted, superficially participating in the asinine hypothesis. "How else do you concoct I could have come up with such a fantastical tale?"

Recognising he had tabled a blooper, the *maître d'* made a nervous cackle. "Quite."

His tetchiness blooming at the all too familiar remark, Bulgakov shot off a rebuking cast.

"Oh, I do apologise for the unintentional *faux pas*," the *maître d'* entreated.

Breathing out heavily, Bulgakov's posture softened. "It's

alright. I've become used to answering that indecorous inquiry...repeatedly."

"Yes, I fancied I am not the incipient person to table the assumption."

"No, and probably, you will not be the last." Beginning to lose his patience again, he blasted, "*Now*, can you please escort me to my seat?"

Still in the throes of jittery cachinnation, his foot-in-the-mouth blunder lingering, the *maître d'* took Bulgakov by the forearm. "This way if you please, sir."

* * *

Finding the writers' seminar dull and predictable, its soporific downside made Bulgakov's eyelids heavy, and periodically he yawned. Principally delineated by too many callow careerists trying to make an impression on their seasoned elders, with over-elaborate dissertations on the negative capability of the narrative form, and other such obscure concepts, he became tempted to put them in their place, only lethargy shackling his attack. Swaying between indignation and boredom, at one point, he nearly dropped off in toto when one head-strong writer dispensed an especially lacklustre account of his tedious expeditions to Persia.

In no mood to indulge their fancies, his mindset toppled into increasing commotion. Barely containing his turbulence, he desperately wanted the hallowed event to finish ahead of schedule. Besides, his only objective remained the cabalistic vessel. *Where on Earth is Nabokov*, he subliminally contested? Before the initiatory speaker took to the lectern, Bulgakov had scanned the audience, conceding somehow, he had missed Nabokov in the foyer, but his accomplice did not come into view. Amidst the talks, when not near to sleep or about to challenge a speaker's grasp of his construct, he regularly craned his eyesight at the main salon door, yearning to see it sprung ajar and Nabokov entered. His disappointment persevered.

At the conclusion of the speaking session, he hoped to dodge meddlesome pretenders and sycophants, but regrettably, the prickly ordeal was not at an end just yet. Before heading out into the night, it had become traditional for members to congregate in small discussion groups to review the meeting and make subjective observations.

Pretentiously doing his duty, Bulgakov sat in the conservatory, sipping on a waiter-provided glass of *Château le Fete*, but still steadfast on residing alone. A fallacious yen, sundry society members landed on him, firing off their unsolicited views and seeking his approvals, Bulgakov fidgeting at the polished mahogany table and chair set he occupied, vainly desiring they'd assimilate his unsociable mood, and quickly go. Instead, after dissecting various expositions to the verge of banality, they wanted to know, did the upcoming release of *The Master and Margarita* comprise any significant new angles and themes.

With supreme effort, he made measured replies, his addresses concise and to the point, never diving deeper than necessary to satisfy his inquisitors. Though logged respectfully, he wanted to elude their fussiness and frippery, his interest exclusively dominated by Nabokov's influx. Discontent began to rear up again, Bulgakov becoming snooty with those unrelenting in wanting more explicit responses. *Post factum*, he lost patience, acridly dismissing well-wishers, and sending them away with a waft of his hand, many taken aback and appalled by his discourteous behaviour.

Moments thereafter, ascribing he had been uncharitable, Bulgakov came over guilt-ridden. Abandoning his base, he slowly paced the conservatory, pinpointed those he had aggrieved, and made abject apologies for his boorish conduct. Exchanging polite conversation for a while, he repaired the temporary damage, refreshing his public image, though internally his agitation prevailed.

Having made adequate restitutions, he charted a course back to the polished mahogany table and chair set. Sitting uneasily, trying to govern his inner pent-up frustration, his clenched fists and throbbing jugular signifying his continuing resentment and annoyance at being foiled by Nabokov, he knew the sarcophagus had him in its embrace again. The more the repository and its unknown scroll contents inhabited his machinations, the greater his disturbance wound into turmoil.

Replaying events in his mind, he deduced he had been thwarted in his drive to acquire the quarry by the slenderest of margins. If only he had embarked a few minutes earlier from his apartment, the casket would be his, and he'd not be soaking up a fools' errand, waiting on the treasure's owner.

Then cursorily out of nowhere, Nabokov stood before him, his being radiating a quality of towering magnificence, leaving Bulgakov stricken in wonderment. If Nabokov appeared in the best of health when he had visited his residence, he now cruised as even more resplendent, a halo-like corona surrounding his entire body. Bowled over by the lustrous effigy, Bulgakov rose from his chair, inadvertently jostling aside the table on the conservatory's polished wood floor in his enthusiasm to greet his near-to dazzling compatriot, the ancillary scraping noise created distracting nearby groups from their debates.

"*Vladimir*—" he shrieked with a flabbergasted locution. "You look so well, like you've drunk from the cup of life, or gobbled ambrosia by the bucket load."

"Oh, you flatter me, Mikhail."

His hypnotism increasing, Bulgakov murmured, "I fancied…I fancied you weren't coming." Espousing a conciliatory disposition, the stance targeted to convey authenticity, he attached, "I…I couldn't see you anywhere in the foyer or the salon. I—"

"You must forgive me, Mikhail," Nabokov interrupted. "My publisher delayed me. I knew impatience would be getting the better of you, so I do apologise."

Startled by his spot-on reading of the situation, Bulgakov enquired, "How did you know? Oh…never mind." Shaking his head, he dislodged the imagery, impairing his train of insight. "Do you have it?"

"You mean, the casket?" he wickedly probed, his dial dripping in mockery.

Before Bulgakov could confirm, a waiter drew up, offering refreshment, both men taking a glass of *Château le Fete*.

Contracting his engrossment again, he glared at Nabokov's teasing rebuttal. "*Yes*, the casket," he corroborated.

Plunging into a large briefcase, Nabokov brought out the jewel-encrusted casket, positioned it on the table, sat down and ogled Bulgakov, his fellow writer's intuition readily having him wetting his lips.

"This reminds me of Dashiell Hammett's *The Maltese Falcon*," Bulgakov quipped, surveying Nabokov in an accusing modality. "Heavens, it makes me Sam Spade and you Casper Gutman?"

Amused at the symbolic motif, Nabokov posed, "Do you picture I'm going to drug you, like Gutman did to Spade?" Jolting his head back contemptuously, his frontage smothered in an aporetic smirk, he jeered, "Using the same facsimile, I have the bird already. Why should I want to incapacitate you?"

"Oh, I don't know." Liquefying into self-recrimination, Bulgakov claimed, "I lapsed into a tortured fettle whilst waiting for you. Maybe the Falcon is an inappropriate metaphor."

"Mikhail, Mikhail," he profoundly began, "you are being overly operatic, my friend." Propagating a quirky phiz, as if about to uncover a priceless relic, he instructed, "Relax, all will soon be revealed."

"You are really going to let me see the scroll?"

"Yes," Nabokov silkily avouched.

On the border of delight, and within fingering distance, if his courage could be stiffened, Bulgakov peered at the abstruse holder of secrets.

Laying a sedative-like clasp on his shoulder, Nabokov informed, "I will leave you to unmask the pleasure you covet."

Already transfixed by the enticing casket, Bulgakov hardly felt the contact or heard the words. Forsaking him to his entrancement, Nabokov joined a group of collaborators on the far side of the conservatory.

Waveringly reaching out to the spring of his fixation, Bulgakov carefully cracked the jewel-encrusted lid, his hesitation roused by the revelatory words, 'The kind dreams are made of,' spoken by the antiques shop owner. Compared to its ornate exterior, he ascertained the casket's interior to be plain and unspectacular. Wrinkling his nose in reaction, he then concentrated on its inventory, the alluring scroll. Dipping inside, he drew out the parchment and began deciphering its substance.

Whilst sipping the red wine, Bulgakov never displaced his diligence from the sorcery he studied with his visionary's eye. Amassing what arose to be an inexhaustible repository of prophetic information, he ignored the passage of time and space, viewing the elemental functions to be irrelevant entities. Both sped by with unfluctuating regularity, comparable to the constant modulation of the stars into the infinite void, neither registering on his altered state nor deflecting his concentration. He had never been entrapped in such intense absorption, its intrinsic coercion sapping all his mental resilience. Routinely, he assessed the unknown with a scientists' method, satisfying himself the uncharted could be classified as inert, then continuing the examination with a clinical detachment. On this occasion, he sidelined caution, devouring the data and feeding on its elucidation like a hungry gannet. The more he read, the more the spectacular message pulled him inextricably towards its climax.

Assembled in a corner of the conservatory, a string quartet began to play the allegro from the *Brandenburg Concerto No. 3,* a rhapsody not usually lost on him, but today an earthquake could have laid waste to Moscow, and he'd not have tagged, his submergence in the document immovable, his deafness to Bach's delicate music sustained.

Further digesting the intelligence in acroamatic cynicism of the fabulous illumination held within, a desperate plan began to crystallise in his mind, and as in ancient antiquity, when the lonely time traveller became blessed with a makeup for escapade to the precipice of self-destruction, he to unwittingly trod similar moonstruck footsteps. Breaking off from appraisal, he determined somehow, he'd hide the scroll or pretend of its passing when Nabokov returned, his burning thirst for sole ownership addictive and all-pervasive. Panning the freakish and screwy blueprint, he singled out its drawbacks, but still resolved to have absolute possession of the scroll to the exclusion of all others, to share, he equated with diminished uniqueness.

Riveted at his station, Bulgakov settled into such crazed infirmity he failed to comprehend external events were overtaking him. An intangible force took hold to increase his obsession, its spellbinding effect originating a radiant spiralling sun within a climate of such rare beauty, neither Stalin's henchmen nor a visitation from the archangel Gabriel could interrupt his fathomless ingestion. Instead, he passed on a perilous preoccupation to the other occupants of the conservatory, blinding him to the behemoth enveloping everything within its clutch.

Continuing to investigate the scaly script, his mind sorting and analysing as he read, without obvious explanation, he picked up on a chiming bell, just like he had heard in the antiques shop. As the audible disturbance washed over him, moreover, cementing his concentration, miraculously, the scroll began changing form as he relentlessly decoded its messages. No longer resembling flaking parchment, it transmogrified into a living organism, his unerring application precluding irrefutable accreditation of the vicissitude. Worse, in his beguiled frame of reference, he failed to distinguish mind and matter had become disconnected, the Fohat neutralised, his very existence akin to a time traveller trembling interminably on the threshold leading to the edge of darkness, his regard clueless to the scroll's metamorphosis.

"What is the meaning of life?" he enquired of no one in particular, professedly oblivious to fellow guests in his coordinate system.

They had progressively become impassive to his shrinking presence. Those attracted by Bulgakov, only tendered a blank, perplexed stare at the incredulity of the universal conundrum, writers and aesthetics had wrestled with since time immemorial. Even if they had corresponded, he'd have not filed a single word. Losing muscular control, his reflexes wilting, Bulgakov sunk into a trance-like, plumbless detachment, all sensory perception left behind in a veil of blurred images and indistinct soundscapes. Down he went, descending through real-time frontiers into the bucketing abyss of a spaceless and timeless dimension.

With the crowning drops of the *Château le Fete* resolutely

drained, Bulgakov's fellow patrons began to depart, their audible and visible port fading as farewells were exchanged and vows made for forthcoming meetings. Not able to explain away their evanescent dissolution in touchable terms, he interpreted them as waves of fleeting sea spray knocking against his insular world, but not breaching its impassable barrier. Their functions impaired by the grape haze, he lasted undetected by their sensory systems, his embryonic personage lost in hazy remembrance. The weight of pointed deliberation drowning his attentiveness, Bulgakov's eyelids sluggishly sealed.

Vaguely mindful of the consuming daze he had slipped into, albeit too late to call out to the departing entourage, his vocal chords inhibited to hail for help, his arm muscles persevering listless to signal assistance imperative, in the end he conceived something extraordinary had engulfed him. Alarmed by the cognizance, the transfigured scroll fell from his grasp. Wrestling in vain to disengage himself from captive malaise, he learnt the more he physically and mentally struggled, the tighter the boa constrictor-like grip became encircling his body and entering his cranium via his eye sockets, the bigger the fatigue on his declining energy resources. Belatedly succumbing, a cavernous and toilsome sleep, shackled and entrapped him, his strength spent.

As he slept, the fallen flaking parchment continued to change, its latent mysteries budding and expanding to configure a dense maze. Probing and investigating their newfound domain, unseen and unheard by the occasional entrance of waiters collecting lead-crystal glasses and empty wine bottles, they extended far and wide.

Clocking a still figure in a corner of the conservatory hunched over a mahogany table, one attendant beckoned to his sidekick. "What about him?"

"Let him sleep it off," the second barista warbled.

"He'll go home this evening, when he recovers."

Transparent to the waiters' sight, the scroll's hidden mysteries persisted to weave their swamping patterns overwhelming the conservatory.

* * *

At length, Bulgakov awoke from a disturbing dream, gasping for breath. Disoriented, he squinted whilst perusing about, but did not relate to the environs shrouding him. Needing to establish his whereabouts, he began to harmonise his faculties, flexing his eyelids to unwrap his retinas and jerking his neck sinews to incite his hearing.

Lifting himself off his seat, he stretched his stiff backbone. After fumbling about in the opalescent darkness of his arresting confinement, only partially illuminated by what he presupposed to be outside streetlamps, he secured himself leaning against an exquisitely engraved Georgian dresser. Identifying the piece, he concluded he must still be in the Dostoyevsky Club's conservatory, but why did everything seem out of place?

Still unsteady on his feet from the weighty slumber, he strained to see, trying to spotlight on his silhouette replicated in an ornate mirror located above the dresser. With his inner gyroscope still failing to respond to commands, he pressed his left forearm over his eyes in an attempt to stabilise his body. Finally, he accomplished a modicum of mastery, and rapidly began recounting the day's events.

Rising from bed late morning, he breakfasted lightly, then grabbed his invitation to the afternoon meeting of the Moscow Literary Society, Nabokov promising a surprise to both astound and enrapture him at the event. Making his way through the city back streets, occasionally he peeked into antiques shop windows to see if anything unusual caught his eye. Maybe he envisaged a second jewel-encrusted casket might come into view, negating the need to beg Nabokov to let him inspect his treasure, but no such luck came his way.

Crossing the busy boulevard into the park where he had framed the Master's encounter with the Devil, disguised as a cat, he marvelled at its rustic landscape ablaze with autumn red and mocha leaves blown into his path by the easterly Steppe wind. Stimulated, the bucolic pageant led to the formulation of a new thesis for the volume, Bulgakov placing it in memory to be retrieved and written later in the day.

Latterly, with his longing on overload, he had entered the Dostoyevsky Club, eager to see the cargo inside his colleague's jewel-encrusted casket. They had agreed to meet in the foyer, but there was no sign of Nabokov. When the meeting session bell pealed, the *maitre-d'* escorted him into the main salon. Listening to the speakers with unabated disassociation, his mind irrevocably anchored itself on the vessel. Then out of the blue Nabokov arrived, according him access to its puzzling content. Afterwards, everything else eventuated as unclear and indefinite. He sensed a macabre, even sinister prodigy had occurred in the afternoon hours as he studied the flaking parchment, a crash only he had experienced, whilst the other occupiers of the conservatory lingered indiscriminate to the limped entity, and its flourishing androgynous evolution.

Removing his forearm, Bulgakov's coherent vision began to materialise. He traversed around his image in the mirror, then spied outwardly at the periphery of the oval wall piece. What he saw astonished him, encasing his body with consternation. Where once had been quarters only containing choice quality furniture, fittings, artefacts and decoration, surpassing all comprehension it had been transmuted by the addition of a perfectly formed vine and fungus forest, overgrown, dark and intimidating, with no perspicuous gateway granting a corridor to sanity, he entrusted laid beyond its domain. Stupefied by the relentless parade, a tremor of fear ran up his back. Turning to confront his newfound inner sanctum, he picked out the jewel-encrusted casket, still open on the table and the scroll by its side. Barely seeable, both had become entwined within the recesses of incalculable fungi and perpetual vine.

Then he logged a shallow, murky light emanated from the casket, dimly illuminating the lodging. Only moments beforehand, he had guessed the light fount to be external. Now he realised nothing he knew existed exterior to the forest, apart from eternal darkness. Staring in veneration, scintillation produced by the phenomenon began to regress back into the holder, shafts of light visibly backsliding. Then a strange convulsive voice, he pictured to be Stalin's, began to laugh eerily, then hysterically, it's obvious disgust at his self-imposed predicament ringing in his ears.

Petrified and fearful, Bulgakov digested his unbridled lust for the scroll and his uncontrollable appetite to read its missive had become his undoing. Nabokov had set him up for the ultimate fall, the paramount act of gamesmanship by his hypothetical nemesis. Lunging forward in despair, hungry for the frail light, as if it represented life itself, his reach failed to halt its fleeing retirement. Deep in the casket's chamber, a fiend stirred, breeding a shrill clatter, Bulgakov covering his ears to blot out the decimating acoustic disturbance. Then everywhere about him, the vine and fungus forest began to collapse, as if called back by the clarion call. Retreating into its creator chasm, taking the flaking parchment and him with it, a rush of torrential wind supervened, sealing his fate cognate to the cast of the Medusa's gaze. Not a single shriek of his screams was heard, the regular world happily continuing its many functions as he vanished, crushed unmercifully into the imploding casket. Ultimately, the sticky seclusion of vine leaf and decaying fungi evenly receded to its lair, jamming Bulgakov in his new habitat.

With the gruesome spectacle complete, the conservatory reverted to normality. Outside, a night owl cooed at the moon. Streetlamps once again wrought twisted shadows in a vestibule which only moments hitherto had been a horror theatre.

Next morning Nabokov revisited the Dostoyevsky Club, an obliging waiter ushering him into the conservatory. Shutting the lid of the jewel-encrusted casket, he fondly picked it up from the polished mahogany table, departing the writers' venue with a satisfied smile. Negotiating the park, where years prior Bulgakov had told him about *The Master and Margarita*, he glanced about to ensure he had privacy, stopped walking, then unbuttoned the receptacle.

Smiling at an infinitely smaller version of Bulgakov nestled against the faking scroll and entrapped in the delicate vine and fungus cocoons of his nascent domicile, he smugly informed, "I

KASHMIR: A VISIONARY'S TALE

knew you were after the casket, Mikhail. The antiques shop owner contacted me, saying someone else had shown an interest in acquiring it. I asked him to describe the person, and from the portrayal, evidently my competitor transpired as you. I knew you'd not be able to resist buying the article, so I waited outside your apartment and followed you, knowing where you were bound, the clever bit, deviating from track and getting to the shop just before you. Naturally, I made sure you saw me enter and leave with a package."

Appreciating he'd been kippered and usurped by a skilled artisan, the unabridged bewilderment of his plight embroiled Bulgakov.

"My word, you are so predictable, Mikhail," Nabokov scoffed. "I divined you'd telephone me on some pretext to make a visit, and then, oh so subtly segue into a conversation about exhilarating objects." Grinning at his captive, he boasted, "You made it very simple for me, Mikhail, very easy to entrap you. I had bled the holder before you arrived, appropriating its body and soul renovation potency, and thereby its credentials to act as the master—" He puckered his lips conceitedly at the referral to Bulgakov's envisioned *magnum opus*. "If you'll forgive the pun. Then I baited the trap to eliminate you from being my stubborn, penning competitor forever. The rest you must have worked out."

Pushing his hand into the casket, he stroked Bulgakov with his index finger. "Goodbye, Mikhail, I will finalise *The Master and Margarita*, and credit you with a posthumous salute for the idea."

It became Bulgakov's terminal moment, the last time he'd ever see the cold light of day. Fastening the lid and locking the container, Nabokov resumed his passage across the park, lightly humming the 1812 Overture. Welling up in his mouth, the humming modulated into an arrogant snigger of amusement, then turned into hysterical laughter. Inside the casket, the chiming bell Bulgakov first heard at the antiques shop continued its infinite song.

* * *

"Mikhail…Mikhail."

Bulgakov felt his shoulder being shaken.

"Mikhail, wake up, *wake up*."

Spluttering out of sleep, he coughed and hacked for air. "What's, what's happening?"

"Mikhail, you've been dreaming."

Focusing, he discerned his partner. "Elena—" His jaw dropped. "Where am I?"

"You're still in the Dostoyevsky Club. When you didn't come home, I came to find you."

"What day is it?"

"Thursday, off course. What day were you expecting it to be?"

Reaching inside his waistcoat, he withdrew his pocket watch. "Half past ten." Staring at Elena with a dubious expression, he blathered, "I must have been out for at least five hours."

Scrutinising his dishevelled trim and pallid complexion, she submitted, "Well, you exhibit signs of exhaustion, like you've contested some sort of harrowing ordeal. And what's happened to your clothing?" She pulled his hunched-up jacket down and straightened his tie. "It's creased and stained like you've been wrestling a bear in the depths of the Arctic tundra."

"I think I have." Applying a hand to his aching head, he bellowed, "Oh, Elena," trepidation ringing in his voice. Eyeballing her pathetically, his dismay tapped into her sensibilities. "I had the most terrible dream…at least I fancy I dreamt."

"You're as white as a ghost, Mikhail. Have you had some kind of fright?"

"You could be right," he concurred. "Conclusively, I don't really know."

"Did you have too much to drink?"

"No, er—" He grimaced. "Very little."

Still confused as to what had happened to him, Bulgakov struggled for the rational. His mind unblocking, the scroll came into the reckoning, Elena anxiously ogling at him, gauging his dumbfounded plight to be beyond the realms of too much alcohol intake.

"Where is the casket, Elena?"

"The casket?" she yelped. "What casket?"

"Erm—" His disorderly recollect fractured into disparate fragments. "I know I had it. It rested here."

Searching either side of where Bulgakov sat, Elena's beeline settled on a bright box under the mahogany table. Picking it up, she wondered about its significance. "Is this what you mean?"

Gawping at the sarcophagus, he sprung up in his seat suffering flashbacks, his imprisonment distilling in his mind.

"Yes, give it to me, Elena."

She held out the rectangular receptacle, Bulgakov marking it as if infatuated, but reluctant to take it.

"*Mikhail!*" she exclaimed, a concerned overtone inflecting her voice. "What is it? What is bothering you so much?"

"I don't know."

His apprehension intensifying, he took the funerary container, anticipating it to be locked. Pulling at its jewel encrusted-lid, to his puzzlement, it popped up. With his phobia amplified, he glared inside, but found the vessel to be empty. "The *scroll*," he bleated, dashing his eyes about, hoping to see the sacred parchment. "Where is the scroll?"

"Scroll, *what* scroll?" she rasped nearing the tolerance limit of her sympathy.

Deflated, he beheld her blankly, his aspirations evaporating. Crestfallen, he slumped back into the chair, bewildered, bemused and speechless, Elena left pitying him.

"I had it," he mumbled. "I had it in the palm of my hand."

Sensitive to his melancholy affliction, she babbled, "Mikhail, what are you talking about? What scroll?" She took the coffer from him. "The box is empty." At a complete loss to account for his odd shift, she rambled backwards. "Whatever has happened to disturb you so vividly, must have been part of your dream." Gingerly fanning out her digits, she maintained, "There is *no* scroll."

Dissolving into unexpurgated dejection, Bulgakov's head dropped near to his knees. *Has the whole episode been illusory*, he internally postulated? Unable to justify his sorry fettle, he felt compelled to make an abject apology to Elena.

Sitting up and about to address her, he caught sight of someone tapping on the outside of a conservatory windowpane. Capaciously sneering at him, Nabokov gesticulated at the near-to translucent entity he held up to the window, Bulgakov recognising the casket's flaking parchment. Though he could not hear him, he saw Nabokov begin to laugh deliriously, Bulgakov left agog and hypnotised at his lampooning antics.

Spooked by the symbiotic exchange, Elena gawked at Nabokov's macabre shenanigans, then at the foaming stupefaction on her partner's face, wondering what on Earth had gone on at the Moscow writer's meeting.

In the root of Bulgakov's inner ear, he distinctly heard the tinkling chime of a distant bell.

ME7 WRITERS GO LARGE IN NEW ORLEANS

ME7 WRITERS GO LARGE IN NEW ORLEANS

Forever harbouring ambitions to read their oeuvre to world famous penmanship societies, despite underground acclaim, ME7 Writers, a group of Medway-based scribblers, remained disappointed until they received an invitation from the New Orleans Literary Society to participate in their annual writers' congress.

Word had diffused across the pond that a crazy bunch of English writers were doing thought-provoking things in the Medway delta. Ratifying the request with relish, they prepared to do some missionary work in the colonies, carry the word to the settlers, and reclaim the Americas for the Crown.

Writers Alicia, Natalia, Arron, Gilbert and Stanley saved up their hard-earned pennies and pounds, converted them into nickels and dollars, journeyed to Heathrow, and a big silver bird took them stateside.

On arrival at Louis Armstrong International, two society brass hats met them, all rigged out in fine Southern raiment, including huge white panamas and alligator shoes.

"Well, I do declare, if it's not the Head of ME7 Writers, in the flesh," enunciated one of the dapper men. "How are you today, Miss Alicia?"

"I'm fine. We didn't foresee being met but it's very kind of you."

"Please allow me to introduce myself. I am Alexis Dupree, Treasurer and 2IC to Mister Laurent Fournier III, President of the New Orleans Literary Society." Beaming gregariously at the visitors, a ting of light flashed off his immaculate gnashers. "We are so pleased you and your fellow writing cohorts graciously accepted our solicitation to recite your writings at our annual convention, mmmm, mmmm." Pausing to let the salutation permeate, Dupree dazzled the limeys with his flawless pearlies again. "Oh, do excuse me, I'm being discourteous. In my enthusiasm to welcome you, I neglected to present my illustrious companion." Turning to his left, he felicitated, "Ladies, gentlemen, may I introduce one of the South's finest writers, some say, the best since the late, great Margaret Mitchell, Mister Pierre Rene Bernard."

Taking a bow, Bernard doffed his panama, took Alicia's hand and lightly kissed it. "*Enchante mademoiselle.*"

Unlike the rotund, mid-sized, with porky eyes in a sphere-shaped phizog Dupree, Alicia adjudged Bernard to be well over six-three, with piercing grey-blue eyes, and a handsome deportment. She also observed both men were heavily sun-tanned, suave to the fringe of absurdity, and incongruously, somewhat reminiscent of Laurel and Hardy, though the comparison tarried as tenuous.

"He is such a charmer, Miss Alicia, mmmm, mmmm," Dupree proclaimed, evaluating his companion with an aura of incontestable pride. "If I were to tell you about some of the compliments bestowed on Pierre by New Orleans' finest families, well, you'd be amazed."

Whilst continuing to eulogise about Bernard unabated, out of Dupree's earshot the ME7 gentlemen writers originated a whispered conversation.

"Have you presumed they are an item?" Stanley posed to Arron.

Wincing, Arron cast a critical eye over the bombastic duo. "Naw, I know anything goes in New Orleans, but these boys are bastions of the city's scholarly elite. Any hint of impropriety, and they'd be given their marching orders by the city fathers as well as the guardians of the New Orleans Literary Society."

"I reckon you're right," he conceded, glancing at New Orleans 'Odd Couple' again. "Yeah, scrub the assumption. The Society is far too drenched in conservatism to even contemplate same sex relationships, and no doubt city hall would go ballistic, if it were true."

Overhearing the dialogue, Gilbert chipped in, "Nonetheless, their conduct is suspicious. Better get used to standing with our backs to the wall, just in case."

"Mmmm, mmmm," Stanley jabbed, mimicking Dupree, Arron and Gilbert, facing away to snigger.

"...yes, without doubt, Miss Alicia," Dupree auspiciously promoted, "you will not meet a finer man during your stay in New Orleans than Pierre Rene Bernard."

Unused to such urbane rhetoric and genteel courtesies, Alicia had become part-mesmerised by Dupree's eloquent citation. Regaining her poise, she swiftly presented her fellow fiction travelers to the society dignitaries, the Southerners paying particular heed to Natalia, dispelling the ME7 gentlemen's assertions about possible man-on-man action between them.

"My, my, Miss Natalia, what a fetching outfit you are wearing," Dupree murmured, his tenor brooding like a stalking wolf. "I can see you are going to draw a lot of attention in the Big Easy."

Moreover, amused by Dupree's steadfast, Southern ease, Arron muttered to Gilbert and Stanley, "Bees around a honey pot."

"The *Big Easy*?" Natalia delicately imitated.

"Yes ma'am, it's what we Louisiana folk call New Orleans, because it's an exciting place, brimming with what Edgar Allen Poe called mystery and imagination. Everyone is relaxed and serene, cool I'm advised is the modern idiom to describe it. But er, enough waxing lyrical for the time being." Motioning with an outstretched hand, he arrested Bernard's eye. "Time we got our guests to the Lafayette. What say you, Pierre?"

"*Bien entendu*," his colleague replied.

Making their way out of the arrivals lounge, the Anglo-American party transitioned from an air-conditioned environment into seventy-one degrees Fahrenheit of Louisiana heat, three degrees above the seasonal average, and twenty-seven degrees above London when ME7 Writers departed. Though the Big Easy resided in the depths of mid-February winter, it felt like high-summer to the English. Still talking to Alicia and Natalia about Bernard's mounting studious regard, Dupree wafted a draft over his moistening forehead with his panama, whilst Bernard tried his best to moderate the praise with bashful reserve, his French clichés dampening Dupree's outlandish PR job.

Nudging Stanley, Arron deftly cracked, "They talk like up-market, more softly spoken versions of Boss Hog."

"Yeah, it's the *de facto* standard, the professional trademark for Louisiana citizens."

"You were here before then?"

"No, Baton Rouge, about a hundred clicks Northwest of Orleans, but they talk the same way." Chuckling at the peacock-like, verbal pomp from their hosts, he recommended, "You just gotta get used to these Louisianan ways. It's the same culture throughout the state. They're French Catholics, so they have a cavalier boldness to life, elegant language, and bohemian tastes." Peering at the rich array of finery and elegance to his front, Stanley reflected, with their glamorous dress code, splashy speech patterns and eccentric behaviour, even at Louis Armstrong International, the locals acted like real life personalities from a F. Scott Fitzgerald novel. "This is going to be superb," he enthused.

"Excuse me, Alexis," Gilbert begged.

"Yes."

"Your colleague Pierre, does he ever speak English?"

"Oh yes. Ordinarily he speaks English, but he wanted to enchant you with his foreign language skills," he explained, sashaying into the throng like feigned royalty. "My, my, what a beautiful day, mmmm, mmmm."

* * *

Climbing into a palatial, stretched limousine, taking up two spaces in the airport parking lot, and big enough to erect a tent inside and camp out in, the English contingent persevered with absorbing Dupree's flowery rhetoric glorifying all things Southern, especially his beloved New Orleans.

Browsing them, a huge grin adorning his features, he fostered, "You all will love the Lafayette. It's located in the nucleus of the historical Arts and Warehouse districts and has a classy and colourful history."

"Colourful history. How do you mean?" Alicia enquired.

"Well, let me see." Embracing a benevolent countenance, he then broke into an irrepressible simper.

"Are you folks familiar with the moving picture, *The Cincinnati Kid*?"

The limeys nodded.

"Norman Jewison shot the movie in New Orleans, and the Lafayette provided the backdrop for the big poker game, you know, the one between Edward G. Robinson and Steve McQueen. So, you're going to be breathing in the same fine Southern air these luminaries from Tinsel Town once breathed, mmmm, mmmm."

"Mightily impressive," Arron trilled with a hint of sarcasm.

"The Lafayette is the hub of the universe," Dupree proudly opined. "Everything the Big Easy is famous for is within a few blocks of the hotel, such as world-famous Bourbon Street, genesis instigator of jazz." Holding up a dismissive hand, as if to repudiate any reservations before they were voiced, he neutrally accorded, "I know it has a reputation for being notorious, but I prefer to categorise it as colourful." Casting a reassuring smile at them, he affixed, "The French quarter, where *mon cher ami* Pierre lives, is in easy striking distance, and the Canal Street ferry is just a few minutes from the Lafayette, ready to take the adventurous to Algiers across the mighty Mississippi river. There are other famous centerpieces as well. The Superdome and the Convention Centre come to mind, but we'll talk about them downline."

Suitably affected by Dupree's critique, ME7 Writers settled back in the limo, taking in the city prodigies. Soon they found themselves immersed in *Mardi Gras*, also known as Fat Tuesday in the Big Easy, the carnival beginning with the Feast of the Epiphany, or Twelfth Night, as the locals call it. Signalling the start of the debutante season for aspiring young women to demonstrate their worth at masquerade balls and street parades, the event had flourished into New Orleans' main tourist attraction. Gaping in awe, Alicia and her associates were jarred by the baroque and florid costumes worn by street revellers dancing their way along Bienville Avenue.

"I see you are fascinated by our annual festival," Dupree discerned, clocking the English faction's admiration blossoming.

"Yes, it's quite a tableau," Stanley enthused. "We all knew about *Mardi Gras* in advance of the trip, but actually experiencing it squarely is trippy, staggering."

"Yes, yes," Dupree agreed. "We are very proud of our festival heritage, and in the spirit of the celebration, *Mardi Gras* forms the centrepiece of the NOLS event. Often attendees dress lavishly or attire themselves in the garb of famous characters from American yore. It all adds to the beatification of our illustrious city." Tapering his eyeshot, he annexed, "Not even Katrina could dislodge our resolve to sustain *Mardi Gras* in all its splendour and regalia."

"Wow," Natalia gushed, "so we are going to be in for a treat?"

"*Indeed,* you are, Miss Natalia," Dupree verified. "Indeed, you are."

"How is the city coping post Katrina?" Gilbert investigated.

Turning grave, Dupree confided, "The cursed hurricane evolved as the worst we have ever endured. I cannot begin to adequately tell you about the damage it did, and the heartache it caused." Brightening, he qualified, "But we New Orleans folk are a resilient and robust people. We coped with the disaster, notwithstanding having diminutive financial and resource assistance from the federal government and Washington."

Spreading out in the limo, pleased to be basking in the unfamiliar ambience, the writer's jet-lag began to take effect, Dupree's dulcet tones washing over them also aiding the drift into sheer relaxation under the Big Easy's intoxicating resplendence.

Pulling up outside the Lafayette, Dupree declared, "Well, here we are, folks, 600 St Charles Avenue, mmmm, mmmm, what a place. New Orleans' fashion and lure at its finest. Twenty-four king rooms and two suites." Glowing with felicity, he endorsed, "This is a 1916 historic landmark replete with Old World architecture, French doors, wrought iron balconies, marble floors, polished mahogany and…English botanical prints. The ambiance is pure luxury."

"I must say," Alicia eagerly began, "it is magnificent, even august."

"Ohhh, I can see you have an eye for the finer things in life, Miss Alicia," he flattered. "I swear you will not be disappointed."

Within the opulent and exotic foyer, Dupree and Bernard took care of the registration process, then made ready to leave.

"Well, here you are, all checked-in and ready to go," Dupree confirmed. "Pierre and I will bid you *adieu* for the time being. We will see you at this evening's reception in the William Faulkner suite. Don't forget, ladies, evening gowns, gentlemen, black ties." He broke into playful laughter. "Only joking, wear what you like, it's a tradition at *Mardi Gras.*"

Watching their hosts evaporate back onto Saint Charles Avenue, ME7 Writers then took a casual gander at the foyer.

"Manifestly, the Lafayette has been done up since Steve McQueen's time here," Gilbert commented.

"Yes, but it's too artificial for my liking," Arron criticised. "Too many ponderously polished brass trims and unblemished crystal chandeliers."

"Huh!" Stanley spouted. "*Space may be the final frontier, but it's made in a Hollywood basement.*"

"What?" Arron chirped.

"It's a lyric by the Red Hot Chili Peppers."

"Meaning?"

Holding out his arms, Stanley encompassed the foyer's fabricated decoration. "It's just an illusion, America's way to compensate for lack of genuine authenticity and longevity. There's nothing very old here apart from the indigenous North American Indian cultures. The Pilgrim Fathers, the early Western European pioneers, and a thousand varieties of immigrants have all tried to make America in their image. It's a hotchpotch of competing European and oriental cultures, none dominating from coast to coast. Ergo, because of its gallic heritage, Louisiana is saturated in a bequeathed French blend, but with 21st century American-dubbed gloss and veneer." Taking in more of the hotel's interior, he projected a learned comportment. "Rendering is the order of the day. The Lafayette is more like a Las Vegas themed hotel, with no real attempt to preserve even its recent yesteryear glory."

"Let alone *The Cincinnati Kid*," Natalia seconded.

"You are all being a trifle harsh," Alicia interrupted. "Granted, it has not got the layered radiance of jim-dandy European city hotels, but it has a damn sight more atmosphere than those Lego-like rectangular abominations dominating most American cities."

"She's right, you know," Stanley substantiated. "Compared to the ubiquitous Marriotts and Hiltons flung up in fifty states, the Lafayette is positively stunning."

* * *

As evening budded, and the sun descended over the city's western horizon, ME7 Writers made their way to the society's reception at the Lafayette in their best bib and tucker. Bursting at the seams with flamboyantly attired enrollees, after scanning over a sea of bobbing heads, they picked out Dupree within a gaggle of the New Orleans intellectual elite, all robed in 19th century period costumes.

"Maybe we should have come as Mark Twain or Robert Penn Warren," Stanley quipped.

"Or Caroline Gordon for Alicia and me," Natalia attached.

"I'd prefer Walt Whitman or Emily Dickinson," Gilbert nominated.

"Irrefutably you'd look very fetching in a mid-nineteenth century ladies rig," Stanley jested. "However, Whitman and Dickinson were Yankees, and you don't bring knives to a guns-only reception." He winked at Gilbert. "You follow?"

"I do. Good point."

"Yeah," Arron concurred. "We don't want to get strung-up on our maiden night in the glorious South, do we?"

As the ever-hospitable French-American saw the English troop approaching, he waved summoning them onward, then took hold of the gentleman's elbow hovering adjacent to him, the pair gliding towards them.

"Mister Fournier, sir. May I introduce Miss Alicia and her circle from ME7 Writers," Dupree vivaciously championed.

Emanating old world charm and panache, though older, Fournier's similar form to Bernard made him every bit the archetypal Southern gentleman. Thirty years earlier, tawny brown hair covered his scalp in the swept back manner of Rhett Butler. Time had transformed it to mazy grey, but in no way diminished his lordly, cerebral outer shell.

Meandering forward, he bowed to Alicia. "Laurent Fournier III, mademoiselle. We are genuinely gratified by the attendance of you and your eminent coterie at our annual reading event." Taking in the rest of the limey brigade, he bowed again, accrediting, "Lady, gentlemen, you are most welcome to our famed soiree."

"Thank you, Mister Fournier," Alicia graciously appreciated. "We are very honoured to be invited to your forum."

"Oh, Miss Alicia, we are all on Christian names here," Fournier counseled. "Please call me Laurent."

After completing the outstanding introductions, the American and English writers dropped anchor, collated for commonalities, and fired up the strands of burgeoning kinship, a necessary ritual to engender what both parties hoped to be a lasting relationship. Already, Alicia had it in mind to reciprocate, and invite NOLS back to the Medway delta, to see how the Brits ran a bookish event.

Captivated by ME7 Writers' understanding of the current belletristic landscape, Fournier and Dupree warmed to their newfound arcane disciples. Before jetting off to New Orleans, they had done their homework, concentrating on current Southern writers such as Padgett Powell and Tom Wolfe, so as to be in tune with prevailing tastes.

Decked out in an 1860s Jefferson Davis type costume, Bernard joined the get together. Now exclusively speaking English, he advised, "You know, Miss Alicia, this is a brand-new panacea for us. We have never had a body of like-minded individuals join us from England before, at least not in my lifetime." Turning to Fournier, he sought clarification. "I am correct, aren't I, Laurent?"

Frowning and patently shaky about the fancy, in turn Fournier rubbernecked Dupree, the pass-the-parcel conduit making the Englishmen smirk. "*Is* this the initial time, Alexis?"

"Well, let me see." Issuing the gathering a shrewd frontage, Dupree quantified for a moment. "Retarding the clock many decades to when I joined NOLS, I recall being told we did have some visitors from England. They performed for the society, but not at *Mardi Gras*."

"Oh, when did it occur, Alexis?" Bernard probed.

"If memory serves—" He hesitated, as if double-checking his memory. "My predecessor, the honourable Elwood Lancelot Auberry, told me, the summer of 1919."

"*Really*! A long time ago," Fournier cooed. "Who were they?"

"G. K. Chesterton and W. Somerset Maugham, but the records show nothing formal took place. They just happened to be in Orleans and contacted the society. You'll find their signatures in the guest book from that year. "

Turning his absorption to the English, Fournier congratulated, "My, my, Miss Alicia, you are in distinguished company, mmmm, mmmm."

* * *

Early the ensuing day, the inaugural palaver of the annual New Orleans Literary Society writers' festivity kicked off at the Lafayette. Compared to UK events, tending to be small and bordering on the discrete, the American occasion bloomed with grandiose sonority and spirited energy, at least 350 delegates creating buzz and hum in anticipation of a congenial conference. Constituting a golden opportunity for ME7 Writers to forge new affiliations, shine in their presence, and apropos to this, sell their wares, it represented the axiomatic reason for their taking part.

Creating a befitting theatric atmosphere, the lighting dimmed, the congress hushed, and a cluster of local writers and poets took turns to recite their fables, most rooted in jazz, *Mardi Gras*, the Big Easy, and Louisiana in general. The kind of thing vaunted by the society to promote in their view, 'America's best and most vibrant state', the audience zealously lapped up the provincial donations. Causing amusement amongst the English group, some performers appeared to have come hotfoot from the bayou glades, overflowing with Davy Crockett coot skin attire and shotguns.

Whispering to his comrades, "They're like refugees from *Southern Comfort!*" Gilbert added a defamatory smirk to his witty observation.

"Maybe even *Deliverance*," Arron warily augmented.

With one of the film's more infamous scenes coming to mind, the male ME7 Writers sucked in air and clenched their buttocks, resolute on not getting gang-banged at the New Orleans Literary Society by sexual deviants from the Louisiana backwaters.

Though Alicia and her troupe assessed the bayou renderings as entertaining, a Cajun dictionary and speech decoder would not have gone amiss for those delegates not hailing from Louisiana, some of the swamp's balderdash, unfiltered and raw to the threshold of being incomprehensible. They noticed those delegates from the north-east and north-west United States were equally flummoxed by phrases such as *vieux carre*, meaning old quarter and referring to the French quarter of New Orleans, *zydeco*, a relatively new kind of Creole dance music fathered on a combination of traditional Cajun music and the blues, and *couche-couche*, a popular breakfast food. All flew over the heads of the most erudite gurus, without the slightest connection to Webster's venerated dictionary or coherence of comprehension.

Later in the morning, the symposium content broadened out into a cosmopolitan framework. To those not having French Cajun as their first language, performers from as far afield as New England and Washington State racked up a voluminous note of deference with their universal, topical and rounded cachets.

Champing at the bit, in the twilight of the afternoon, ME7 Writers took to the rostrum stage, each ready to step up to the plate for individual achievement. Acting as the caucus moderator, Fournier inaugurated Alicia. In turn, she briefly reviewed her compatriots' writer biographies, and the material they were about to discharge.

Primary on the rhetorician roster, Arron recounted a short story about his rearing in York, a watershed jumping off division catapulting him to a borderline anarchist tendency.

"Or should it be antichrist status," he wickedly pretended.

Kicking at the old Establishment, his subtle nuances failed to distill on American sensibilities, their antennae not attuned to clever and cunning Yorkshire oratory. As his tale progressed, rather than the story content, conversely, they were more enthralled by his accent, primarily his middle register pipe causing bewilderment. Just as newsworthy, his charcoal, wide-brimmed fedora, never taken off during daylight hours, had them in raptures.

At the end of his talk, Fournier invited questions for Arron. A flock of hands shot up, the not-bargained-for number surprising the session moderator. Perusing the patrons, he designated a sturdy man in the tenth row from the front.

"Sir, your hat has got a lot of us fascinated," saluted the salubrious gent, thumbs tucked into his waistcoat pockets, his rococo garments suggesting he had jetted off the set of *Gone with the Wind* to participate in the rally.

"Perhaps you'd care to share with us the origins of your head gear?"

Narrowing his eyes, Arron then gawked sideways at his abettors. "Sarky bastard," he hissed away from the lectern microphone.

Pulling an impatient demeanour, Alicia ticketed for him to answer.

"I actually bought the hat from a charity shop in Rochester." Breaking off, he revisited the notion. "Or it could have been in London. My ally Stanley calculates it is similar to a Guy Fawkes hat. Most fitting, because I'd like to burn down the Palace of Westminster in London."

Thunderstruck by the renegade-like admission, the examiner tested, "Sir, are you trying to say, you'd destroy the mother of all modern democracies?"

Shuffling on the spot, trying to control his temper, the Yorkshire antagonist pondered. Glimpsing up into the emulsion white ceiling of the auditorium as if trying for uninhibited candour, he then grasped the lectern and propounded, "Democracy is a mirage, a tool used by the ruling upper-crust to give the people a chance to elect a fresh clique of buffoons every five years, but nothing changes. So yes, I'd blow up Parliament."

Completing his forthright proclamation, he made an ironic grimace and wrinkled his nose to emphasise the sobriety of his intent, his acrid declaration igniting assemblage hum, prattles of 'This fellow is joking, he's just putting on a Monty Python act for our enjoyment,' and 'He's not being earnest, he can't be, it's a joke,' accompanied by a few under the breath laughs filling the gallery.

Picking up on the undertone, his bona fide port increasing, Arron quested, *I am earnest.*

Savouring the mood of his fellow delegates, the inquisitor cultivated an empathetic mien. "Sir," he asserted, "you're being facetious. You can't be serious."

"Oh, but I *am*," Arron confirmed. "On average, we have three score and ten years to fulfill our ambitions. The slow slope change synonymous with politics is incompatible for consummating an end objective within the lifespan."

"And just what is the objective?" queried the thumbs-tucked-into-his-waistcoat pockets man.

"To accomplish wide-ranging change." Psyched up, he provocatively puckered his lips. "That needs a step response, a revolutionary creed."

Bringing about increasing aporetic mumbles, Arron's latest incendiary exposé had listeners lapsing into restlessness. Ascribing his dissertation had taken on an electrifying turn for the worse, Fournier took affirmative action.

"Can we have the next inquiry, please?"

A hand went up from a mustachioed, well-groomed man, exuding enough *joie de vive* to break into an impassioned rendition of the *La Marseillaise*. Receiving the green light from Fournier, he stood.

In acutely inflected French tinted English, he clucked, "Sir, we'd all be grateful, if you could kindly tell us about your impressions of London." Glancing into the throng and grinning, he qualified, "I mean as a foreigner to those parts."

Gawping at Alicia whilst shielding the microphone, Arron proclaimed, "Another sarky bastard. This guy must visualise I'm not English."

"You're *not*," Gilbert stipulated. "You're from Yorkshire!"

Raising her eyebrows at the stoic interlude participants, Alicia beseeched, "Doesn't matter. Just invent a wisecrack." Wafting at him disdainfully, she pressured, "Go on."

Refacing the circle, he indignantly clenched the lectern. "Well, speaking as a foreigner from York, my take amounts to London is mainly filled with Southern Jessie's, insipid beer and effete whoopsies." Defiantly, he curled his upper lip. "Do I satisfy your query?"

Demonstrably rattled by the retort, Frenchie responded, "Sir, your riposte has the sound of a very provincial attitude."

"Oh *contraire, mon frere*," Arron batted back, unable to resist lapsing into counterfeit French. "I'd uphold it is neither a provincial nor a metropolitan standpoint, but a deposition of fact."

More confounded whispers and hushed murmurs of consternation arose from the gallery. Increasingly distressed by the mind-blowing fracas, Fournier called for the subsequent enquiry. Aspiring to condense smooth waters from budding altercation, he gave the floor to a Dupree-shaped gentleman.

"Sir, we can all delight in your rather, shall we call them, jaundiced perspectives on democracy, but wouldn't you agree, it is the best system? After all, communism is dead." Holding a gold timepiece fastened by a chain to his waistcoat, doubtless he wanted to time the speaker's response.

Moulding a contrary dial, Arron considered his options. Should he go for peace-making, or persist his subversive viewpoint? He chose the latter.

"Where I come from, we don't mince our words, or change our minds because of fashionable opinions. We stick to what we know is right. Communism might be dead, but she will rise again, and be implemented the way

Marx saw it."

Leaving the Americans agape and unsure how to retaliate, Arron's response plunged the dagger deep into their central belief system, a salutary tryout few cared to salute, let alone challenge. Not bargaining for the nature of his voracious barrage, Fournier's turbulence worsened. Sensing the aggravated house mood, he skillfully brought the Yorkshireman's discourse to a finish, and directed the next ME7 speaker to the lectern.

Teeming with vim and vigour, Alicia sauntered frontwards to give the congregation an imparting from her *The Seventeenth Pilgrim* project, her articulate voice eclipsing Anglo-American language differences. With the delegates warming to her familiar transcending essay, Arron's nonconformism blast evanesced from recent memory. Witnessing their assenting body language, she went for broke, pulling out all her theatrical traits to make the allegory live. A near-to thunderous ovation transpired, Fournier smirking akin to a Louisiana swamp alligator feasting on a raccoon, Alicia's performance just what NOLS were expecting.

Materialising from behind the platform curtain Bernard joined Fournier, patting him on the shoulder in a veritable portent of approval, then ditching French in favour of domestic Louisiana American-English, he whispered a few complimentary remarks in Alicia's ear, though he did lapse into quasi-French superlatives with exultations of *magnifique* and *excellento*, whilst applause still rang in the foreground.

Extending a restraining hand aloft, Fournier called for quiet, then with an unmistakable connotation of pride, diligently told the multitude how NOLS unearthed ME7 Writers, before he threw speaker interrogation open to the equally enthusiastic emissaries.

Probing the assembly, an elderly but still noteworthy lady wearing a Scarlett O'Hara style dress, and endowed with splendid cheekbones and large penetrating eyes, drew his scrutiny, Fournier courting her address.

"Yes, can I ask Miss Alicia if she has any convictions on our acclaimed Southern writers, for example William Faulkner, Caroline Gordon, Thomas Wolfe, and Southern Agrarians like Allen Tate?"

Recapping from memory, Alicia appraised, "They are all fine writers, especially Faulkner and Wolfe. Inclusively, they do immeasurable credit to the Southern states' scholastic canon, I understand grew from the Pilgrim Fathers onwards." Lingering, she permitted auxiliary remembrances to come to mind. "My own personal darlings are Katherine Anne Porter and Nelle Harper Lee."

Apparently taken aback at the mention of Harper Lee, Scarlett grilled, "Do you mean, the author of *To Kill a Mockingbird*?"

"Yes, I do."

"Holy mother of God, an overrated fiction overly celebrated by opportunist politicians, and hardly emblematic of the width and breadth of the South's splendiferous literature."

Discerning an explosive argument mounting, Fournier intervened. "Excuse me, ladies, I wonder if we could possibly move on in the interests of time management."

Another hand went up.

"Yes, ma'am," Fournier authorised marking the quester.

"Maybe Miss Alicia could comment on the changing formulation and fettle of Southern literature in the wake of cultural and social changes since the end of World War II?" enquired a dainty lady undoubtedly in her twilight years, the antithesis of Scarlett, her semblance plain, her attire forgettable, but her examination insightful.

Encouraged by the querist's shrewdness, Alicia quizzed, "Do you have any particular writers in mind?"

"Yes indeed. I'd cite John Grisham and Tom Wolfe as being paradigms for the latest incarnation."

"Well, I do like Wolfe's sixties opus, such as *The Electric Kool Acid Test* and downstream labours like *Bonfire of the Vanities*."

"Don't you agree *The Electric Kool Acid Test* is corpulently unrepresentative of the South, with its psychedelic and drug fueled theme commendation of Ken Kesey and the Merry Pranksters?"

Glowering, like her confidants, Alicia realised she had misread the lady, mistaking her fascia and perceptiveness for the signs of a potential supporter. Laying a bear trap, she turned out to be as staunchly Southern in her mindset as Scarlett.

Trying to avert discord whilst still erring for the truth, Alicia cautiously accorded, "Yes, it is anomalous for the South, but I'd say perpetually representative of the United States as a whole, and the West in general, during the 1960s."

"Do you condone such a loaded premise, Miss Alicia?"

"A writer should be ethically neutral, neither being partisan nor overly critical of any doctrine, person or event. Taking primacy over naked involvement or criticism, the writer must remain an impartial bystander, if a faithful purification of creditable scribing is to be fulfilled. My view is, Wolfe honestly couched what he beheld."

"Good resolution," Natalia applauded to the rest of the team.

"Like many here, I'd acquiesce to the foundation of your sentiment," the dainty lady upheld. "Albeit, I'd categorize your reply as *à la mode,* substituting for the factual. Yes, a writer's grass root credential should be impartiality, but there is more of a hint in Wolfe's chronicle of pandering to the liberal-elitists of the northern metropolitan cities. Even, dare I say, writing to order, knowing a captive and receptive cortege existed, ready to buy the merchandise because it constituted their counterculture stocktaking of the world. I thus maintain *The Electric Kool Acid Test* is indubitably otherworldly of both the United States, and the world as a mass."

His controversy gauge on overload, Fournier motioned to another questioner. "Yes sir, can we please have your petition for Miss Alicia?" he virtually barked, practically curtailing the Wolfe quarrel.

Alicia's Q&A ended with more selections from the South's literati arsenal being batted to and fro, Fournier vigilant throughout, ready to metaphorically push the abort button should it chain-react into bitter rivalry.

Briefly returning to her brethren, Alicia then introduced Gilbert.

Making some introductory if not inflammatory allusions about civil rights and the plight of the indigenous American Indian, Gilbert then submerged into a yarn entitled *Strange Fruit —My role in the identification of the Klu Klux Klan Grand Wizard*. Employing his usual vehement and spicy enactment of the novella, he accentuated key aspects with thumps on the lectern, causing the microphone to vibrate and send ear-piercing feedback into the salon. Reciprocating sympathetically, the other ME7 Writers smiled with approbation at his dynamic performance.

"He's *definitely* on form today," Stanley euphorically extolled.

"Yes," Arron concurred. "All he needs is to be attired in a black suit, bow tie and hat, to approximate one of those Billy Graham-like evangelist preachers."

Continuing to be absorbed in Gilbert's dramatic execution, the English clan regarded him genially. Then Alicia made out some disquieting reactions from the floor, and the stage, the NOLS dignitaries colouring ruffled and disconcerted. Near to dribbling, his mug stationary in a contorted scowl, colloquium chairman Fournier's mouth inched into a wide yawn, as he slithered lower in his seat attempting to distance himself from the dissention, whilst Bernard visibly shrunk into himself, his routine sparkle and vivacity fully retracted. Out of the corner of her eye, she saw Dupree hurriedly moving along the hippodrome outside aisle making for the podium. Joining his bewildered NOLS compatriots, he whispered to them. Overhearing part of the message, Alicia differentiated, if need be, he aimed to pour oil over troubled waters.

Meanwhile, audience fizzle and hiss had magnified, Alicia surveying many delegates fixing Gilbert with an abhorrent glare. Others exchanged low volume innuendos and aspersions, the upheaval beginning to feel like a melting pot about to explode.

Oblivious to the furore he created, Gilbert strode on, his gesticulations emphasising principal elements, ever more thespian. Building the recreation to a crescendo, his intuitive sense of rhythm drove his crowning platitudes to a blistering climax, an implacable thump on the lectern echoing everywhere in the arena, signalling its finish.

Perspiring resultant from his sustained physical complement, he waited a few seconds to recover his breath before squinting at the NOLS hierarchy. Registering Fournier, Bernard and Dupree all appeared spellbound, though the last had the token of conciliatory reliance etched on his blood-vessel-bursting kisser, Gilbert stood bewitched awaiting Fournier's connecting reflections. Nothing happened, the gathering *en masse* rapt in silence and inertia. Reclaiming his own composure, Gilbert designated to Fournier for him to request queries from the floor, but the NOLS President resided transfixed, as if physically incapacitated by a black widow's sting.

Deciding to take the initiative, Gilbert refaced the gogglers. "Are there any questions?"

Peering into their midst, all at once aware of the fluster he had caused, tension ratcheted up a few more notches. A well-dressed gentleman with longish grey hair and pale blue eyes, balancing on an ornate silver-handled walking stick, caught the speaker's attention, Gilbert indicating for him to proceed.

"Sir, if I understood your footnotes accurately, you are hinting the South has a tainted history, and you personally intervened to identify what you call the Klu Klux Klan grand wizard. Am I correct?"

Perceiving the bait had been taken but knowing engaging in historical revisionism would be at cross purposes to the success of the English writers' visit, a wry visage propagated amidst Gilbert's contours. Instead of confrontation, he stuck with learned commentary.

Defending in generalist terms, he outlined, "Part of fiction's magic, conjecture allows the listener or the reader to decide *vis-à-vis* authenticity. Indisputably, proposition leaves loose ends, prompts speculation, loiters at least partially inconclusive, and thereby encourages detailed detective work." Desisting, he waited for the conflicting wrangle, but the catechist had reseated himself. "The author should be able to compose on any heading, without impunity or censorship," he continued without colouration. "There should be no sacred cows, everything up for debate, for analysis, the scour for answers even truth unsullied by rage impediments." He rested for effect. "Undisputedly, it is the paramount principle to be adhered to."

Envisaging a protest from the well-dressed gent, nothing came, the house reduced to out-and-out silence. Needing to layout exhaustive defiance, he specified, "A writer shouldn't avoid reality, even if it offends right or left-wing dogma. The narrative should be objective in the figure of digging for fact and nonaligned in its vitality for ferreting out prejudice of persuasion, but essentially, over-layered with mystique to accomplish the unique, meaning, an incitement creating startlement or curiosity, putting the hook in the reader. I leave it to you to decide the veracity of my function in naming the Grand Wizard."

Another hand shot up. By now Fournier had restored his cognition, ready to perform his role as session moderator again. Licensing airtime to a large lady with a bright complexion and bursting out of a too-tight dress coated in bows and bells, he sounded seamlessly *compos mentis* once more.

"*Yes*," she began in a vexed voice, "I'd like to ask the gentleman, if his drive for the equitable disclosure of fact and truth also encapsulates the scurrilous acts and contradictions of for example, the Clintons, O. J. Simpson, and those despicable Muslims responsible for nine-eleven?"

"To be sure," Gilbert clarified. "Those you mention are far from perfect, and unreservedly lay within the compass of my critique."

Incontestably wanting part justification for the scandalous exploits of the aforementioned, howbeit, the unheralded fairness of Gilbert's reply neutralised the lady's ardour.

"You *really* think so?" she entreated.

Falsely springing back pretending to be shocked, he challenged, "Do you have any basis to doubt me?"

"I suppose not," the lady admitted.

Behind the facade, Gilbert wanted to let fly with what he truly meditated, rationalising the duplicity of Bill and Hilary, the double standards of alleged murderer Simpson, and the Muslim terrorist atrocities stunning America, were symptoms of a divided society choreographed by pluralist factions pulling in opposite pathways, the twain never meeting.

After a few more malevolent explorations and equally candid replies, Fournier brought Gilbert's sermon to a conclusion, the meeting ringing with conjecture and speculation.

Rejoining at the lectern, Alicia made her prefatory remarks about Natalia's bookish background, then beckoned her to the stage centre. Ever modest, Natalia gave a meek bow to the listeners and positioned her topic in the most diffident and retiring terms, before setting out on a what-I-did-on-my-holidays account, in the vogue of Graham Greene's *Travels with my Aunt,* complete with acted voices and pantomime imbuing her tale with validity. Abounding with graphic description and striking dialogue, the odyssey recalled her expeditions to Cape Verde, Bali, Mauritius and Bahia.

Loving it, the Americans responded with oohs, sighs, and occasional gentle laughter when Natalia's travelogue tapped the comical, her classically English depiction just what the NOLS hierarchy had foreseen from ME7 Writers. Recording glows of thankfulness on countenances that only a few minutes previously had been wrought with perplexity at Gilbert's acerbic recital, her companions distinguished she had hit the sweet spot.

Feeding off the fruitful vibe, Natalia enriched her personality enactments with a variety of localised accents and foibles, the added theatre and bounce of her performance heightening impact, drawing supplementary warmth and esteem.

At her finish, Fournier conducted the applause, then held an arm up, ticketing for hush.

"My, my," he gushed. "What an elegant delineation of such an uplifting and pleasant array of recollections, mmmm, mmmm." Dwelling, as if temporarily drifting off into a sexual fantasy daydream, Natalia at its epicentre, he coughed to regain concentration before resuming.

"Miss Natalia, undeniably I speak for us all when I say you do have an auspicious way with words." Beaming convivially, he peeked at the huddle. "Ladies, gentlemen, please feel free to ask Miss Natalia any questions you may have."

Navigating the rally, he saw several hands go up, waving for advocacy. Gesturing to a gent dressed in ubiquitous white, his personae resembling the Orson Welles portrayed protagonist Charles Foster Kane in the movie *Citizen Kane*, he snapped, "Yes, sir."

Orson stood up. "Likely we all are curious to know more about your composition and performing method, Miss Natalia. Perhaps you can give us some insight?"

Pressing a forearm across her chest in an act of genuine humility, Natalia breathlessly enunciated, "I'm very flattered by your blessing, but there is nothing special about my anecdote, other than my limited ability to rouse it into life. I simply take an inkling, paint it into a backdrop with capacious concepts, then fill in the descriptive detail and overlay with barnstorming players, supporting extras and tenable keynotes." She beamed a self-effacing phiz, further seducing her newly acquired devotees.

"Unassailably, Miss Natalia is an unassuming wallflower," Fournier complimented. Refacing the summit, he crooned, "Which we do admire, mmmm, mmmm. Now, can we have the next query please?"

Gazing into the dimness of the lightly illuminated lecture theatre, he selected a small lady, barely tall enough to see above those seated in front of her when she stood.

"Miss Natalia," she began in a shrill wavering voice, "transparently, I speak for all when I say you have enthralled us with your vacationing escapades. Perchance you'd care to share with us, what you annex to be the best, the pinnacle of these sorties into the unknown?"

"Your ask is both excellent and challenging," Natalia acknowledged. "Let me see—" Lingering in search mode, she then glittered as if imbued with divine inspiration. "Because we are all lettering aficionados here, I will couch it in literary terms."

Recounting an occurrence from her early twenties, when she holidayed with her aunt in St Raphael, she instantly had patrons riveted. Regaled by a handsome aristocrat telling them about doomed love affairs making the area notorious for star-struck lovers, the incident reminded Natalia of Du Maurier's *Rebecca*, the handsome aristocrat approximating Maximilian de Winter, and she cast as the second Missus de Winter.

Just the kind of anecdotal memoir they foresaw, the delegates went wild for the tale. A flurry of ancillary inquests eventuated, Natalia adroitly explicating comebacks. Exhilarated on adrenalin rush, when she eventually withdrew from the lectern, the NOLS executive basked in her radiated adulation, confident their English posse were back on track forecast.

Finally, Alicia outlined Stanley's writer CV to the gathering before he wandered up to the microphone exuding a sinister ambience of menace.

"I'm going to carry on where Arron left off," Stanley gleefully announced, "with a piece entitled *The Gravy Train*. You might have concluded our Arron is a bit farther to the left of Karl Marx, steering for anarchy." Clutching the lectern he told them, "Having left all the political systems far behind, none of them delivering on promises made, I've also scurried down the disenchanted-with-polyarchy path. The only pure acts left are those of the indifferent anarchist. Ostensibly, this is the cornerstone of my dissertation today."

Preparing for another inflaming onslaught, both the NOLS executive and the conference goers settled back uneasily donning metaphorical tin hats, many ruminating, the outrageous views of Malcolm X were not so bad after all.

Stanley launched into his stanza about a rebel nonconformist uncovering the everyday excesses of the politicians' gravy train, and debunking all political systems as self-interested or self-righteous, narcissistic flimflam, geared to hoodwink or enforce by coercion, the assertion mixed in with a succession of spiky poems knitting the saga together. Appalled by what he said, the

CLIVE RADFORD

Americans sat motionless and aghast. Having estimated Arron's talk to be the acme by way of anti-establishment hyperbole, the NOLS executives were dumbstruck by Stanley's own stamp of disestablishmentarianism, certifiably not between the church and the State, but the people and the State.

Keenly enjoying the spectacle, Stanley revelled in the friction, peeping up occasionally in response to gasps and smirking. Taking a leaf from Natalia, he enacted the epic's characters. Voluble and intentionally histrionic, stagecraft took precedence over the written word, improvisation propelling the telling to its relentless finale.

Finishing with, "One ending plea, if I may? To quote the preeminent, contemporary American musician-poet, Robert Zimmerman, *don't follow leaders.*"

Polite but unenthusiastic applause ensued.

Near to apoplectic, Fournier's skin shade matched his pure white suit. Blinking at Stanley, his frontispiece enshrined in qualm, Dupree nudged his wrist, stirring him back to life.

Segueing into calmness, the NOLS President addressed the caucus. "Well, ladies and gentlemen, after such a searing discourse —" He rifled for the appropriate gratuitous verb. "I am certain we all cherished, I'd like to call for questions from the floor."

Oodles of hands sharply went up, Bernard and Dupree gulping in disbelief, their eyes widening, their body language fidgety. Regarding Fournier, they saw he had contracted back into his seat, cringing at the quickness of the audience clamour to mesh with the speaker. Superficially coughing, Dupree caught Fournier's absorption, the NOLS President sitting forward and singling out one of the questioners.

"Yes, sir."

A tall, well-groomed gent, with a pronounced sea captains' comportment and dressed in the inevitable white from head to foot took the floor.

"Sir, if I understand you correctly, you are implying political notorieties are all charlatans, out for themselves and uncaring for the people they symbolise. How can you justify this nihilistic sentiment?"

"Independent of party colours," Stanley maintained, "they ride the taxpayer-funded gravy train putting little in and taking a lot out. For example, in my country, we have public enquiries at the drop of a hat. Anything ranging from the momentous to the inconsequential is subordinated to years of taking evidence and drawing certitudes the unabbreviated nation has sussed out well before the damned enquiry ever started. They cost tens of millions but change nothing. They are merely deceptions, there to create the discernment change will transpire from deliberation and recommendation.

"In practice, public enquiries are just another assortment of jobs for the boys, the gravy train brigade. The same people demanding public enquiries intrinsically benefit financially from them. It's a self-perpetuating process enacted by the prevailing status quo, and no, I do not deem this to be a nihilistic view. On the contrary, it is a realistic portrayal with measurable parameters and documented evidence."

Not accepting the charge, Captain Gullible made a few contradictory evaluations, before relinquishing the floor, Fournier then firing up the next quester in the hope of evading incremental dissonance.

"Can we have the query from the bodacious lady in the fine, wide-brimmed hat?" he exalted. Suddenly identifying the investigator, he dissolved into a deferential register. "Oh, Mademoiselle de La Roux, you must forgive me. In the dimness I didn't recognise you." Amidst a frenzy of thrilled mutterings, a resplendent, caked in gusto Mademoiselle de La Roux rose to her feet, her magnificent head held high displaying quintessential, Greek goddess-like features, her blonde wavy curls floating gently about her shoulders, her vast, green-blue eyes sparking with fire and zest.

An exceedingly affluent local dignitary, her family lineage boasted a heritage going back to before the American Civil War. With links to the state governor, city hall, and a plethora of Louisiana landowners and industrialists, Madame de La Roux could claim to be potently well-connected with the state's major influencers. A life-long NOLS member, very well known within the city's artistic community, and respected universally in New Orleans for her charitable toils, she regularly grabbed the local press headlines.

Noting the sizzle she had caused, the English contingent exchanged a few hushed appraisals.

"Mademoiselle de La Roux unequivocally possesses all the regal attributes of the prototype Southern belle," Alicia accredited.

"With a touch of Cruella Deville mixed in with Mae West," Arron argued.

"Only dressed in the purest of white," Gilbert gibed.

"What else!"

"I'd like to ask the speaker," Mademoiselle de La Roux virtually breathed with feline cajolery, "if he has any sympathy for America's enemies, and whether he has ever, and I do mean ever, had a clandestine relationship with a Southern lady?"

Taken aback by the unpredictable left field poser, Stanley blanched. Heretofore, he had come up against some formidable English ladies whilst at the lectern, but the haunt of tantalising allure before him superseded all past experiences.

Cogitating on the tricky tease, he vindicated, "What the lady is so diplomatically trying to imply is, I am anti-American." Lingering to construct the right words, he appended, "I can say without reservation, I'm not anti-American, pro-Russian, anti-democratic, pro-communist, or any other system aimed at the subjugation of hearts and minds. For me, it's illogical to like or dislike unexpurgated nations or races or cultures. Only fools and the self-serving adjudge all brand x is good, and all brand y is bad. Judgment can only be made through personal participation. Accordingly, the liking or disliking of individuals is the only plausible demarcation.

"I have no singular beef with the United States. In fact, in principle, I'd go as far as to say, your country comes closest to nearing the utopian ideal. However, like in all systems, there are those bidding to slurp at the trough on the pretext of civic duty. The gravy train feeders as I call them, inhabit the epicenters of both the left and the right. It is this political class of pious, egocentric zealots who have destroyed the Pilgrim Fathers' enlightenment, just as the same type of virile opportunist has destroyed England, and every other Western country."

Noticing the convention's aura of vitriol had subsided, Stanley ceased. *Maybe they are buying it*, he contemplated. "As to the second part of your survey, Mademoiselle de La Roux, I confess I have not had the pleasure of any dangerous liaisons with Southern ladies. Mid-West, yes. My ex-wife is from Ohio."

"You don't say," she allowed. "Maybe we could discuss this failing offline?"

Good god, is she coming onto me, he pondered. "Erm…maybe."

With the exchange taking on an out-of-the-blue bearing, Fournier indicated to yet another well-heeled Southern gentleman, indubitably on the verge of eruption.

"Yes, sir, can we have your inquiry?" he solicited, much to Mademoiselle de La Roux's annoyance.

Holding a white straw boater, the natty gent stood. "Judging by the essence of his fable, I'd submit instead of playing possum with politics, the speaker would do well to join the fray and make an active contribution. What say you, Mister ME7 Writer?"

Sniggering at the suggestion, Stanley covered the lectern microphone with his left cuff, preventing any accusations of discourtesy whilst he prepared an offset.

"To quote Michael Dobbs famous political creation, Francis Urquhart, *you may think that I couldn't possibly comment*."

"It seems to me you are dodging the issue. I'd like a straight answer to a straight question."

"Whoa, you're trying to tempt me into indiscretions." Discontinuing, Stanley glanced at Alicia, as if petitioning for instruction. Like for Arron, she waved at him to make a reply, her annoyance at his antics plain. Conversely, Arron and Gilbert made goading cues to spur him on. "Well, further indiscretions," he joked, "but I can vouch, I have no ambitions in such a tendency. Politics is a very low occupation, even beneath the tiers of lawyers and investment bankers."

Another near-to-infuriated hand travelled skywards, Fournier granting airtime, Stanley clocking the irate examiner resembled General Stonewall Jackson in stature, with a huge moustache and beard, weather-beaten lineaments, and attired in the uniform of a Confederate army officer.

"Sir, I am beginning to assimilate your philosophy is not only politically agnostic, it is decadent as well. Can you give us some cheering words to dispel my postulation?"

Breaking into a glassy, baleful puss, Stanley stipulated, "On the contrary, in my view, decadence can be productive as well as appealing, dependent on the severity of moral turpitude. Maybe we should all be grateful to the Marquis de Sade for enriching our lives by providing the antidote to the sterility of conformist boredom."

Undoubtedly unconvinced, nevertheless General Jackson resumed his seat. Meanwhile, Alicia looked daggers at the male members of ME7 Writers, Arron and Gilbert exchanging superficial, mournful physiognomy in reply.

Supplemental enigmas were tabled and dealt with in rapier-like mode before Fournier informed attendees the ME7 Writers orations had overrun and needed to be curtailed to allow the succeeding round table by a group of traditional Cajun poets to begin.

That evening, he certified to Bernard and Dupree he had become more agitated by the possibility of a riot breaking out, if he didn't terminate the English delegation's enterprise, an unheard of rebuttal in the holistic chronicles of the New Orleans Literary Society, than about sustaining the popular protocol of permitting speakers' full reign.

* * *

Miffed when the afternoon confab broke up, Alicia had it in mind to castigate the ME7 Writers male members for going too far over the top to illustrate their points. About to commence her rebuke, they were joined by the NOLS hierarchy at a pre-dinner refreshments reception, necessitating her to put the censure on hold.

"Well, Miss Alicia," Fournier began, a hint of rebuke mixed with veneration in his voice, "your, shall we call it, colourful seminar content has affixed some extra dimensions to our annual event this year."

"Most definitely," Dupree assented. "The stark contrast between the er, let me call it, Miss Natalia's and your pastoral journals compared to what the gentlemen doled out, well, just let's say, unpredicted equates as an understatement."

Eyeing Arron, Gilbert and Stanley ruefully, Alicia made the standard official reply without much conviction. "At ME7 Writers, we make no constraints or mandates on what our members write about. We uphold an open-mic, deregulated inclination to the genre, creating some daring revelations. This is what sets the group apart."

"Yes, I er, I can kind of see your rationale," Fournier endorsed. "Since the founding fathers instigated the New Orleans Literary Society in 1875, we have had members, and guest speakers including Mark Twain, Walt Whitman, Tennessee Williams and Ernest Hemmingway, who have er…" Cracking a smile, Fournier lightened his tenor to continue the remembrance. "…often horrified the society with their recitals, but I must say, what the ME7 gentlemen writers rendered, fell into the stupefying category."

Not wishing to imply any censorship existed at NOLS, Dupree and Bernard made comprehensive affidavits designed to engender toleration of the gentlemen's subject matter. Notwithstanding the guarded subtlety, ME7 Writers sensed at the very least their hosts were seeking a smoothing out of the material.

Malcontented with his colleague's delicate call for restraint, before the gathering dispersed to freshen up prior to the evening buffet event, Fournier made a leave-taking solicitation. "Miss Alicia, Miss Natalia." He gaped at Arron, Gilbert and Stanley with a circumspect eye. "Er, gentlemen, let me be frank. You have probably spotted we have a potential powder keg moment here. You see, the New Orleans press will be joining us in the morning, and er—" He broke into a warm grin. "We don't want to give them fodder they could use to disparage either the society or your good selves, do we?" Adopting a congenial but authoritative countenance, he craved, "I wonder if I could call upon you to temper the more controversial sections of your readings for tomorrow's colloquium?"

"*Of course*," Alicia upheld. "I guarantee the ME7 gentlemen writers will accommodate you."

"Very generous of you, Miss Alicia," Fournier gushed.

"Mmmm, mmmm."

Gawking ahead, his engrossment cornered by increased delegate hum on the periphery of the crowded reception area, Dupree declared, "My oh my, I do believe we are about to receive a distinguished visitor."

New Orleans' high-society supremacy loomed into view in the form of Mademoiselle de La Roux. Sashaying her way over to the executive committee and ME7 Writers like Jessica Rabbit about to devour a feeble, unsuspecting male target, the crowd parted like respectful vassals, enabling the passage of a queen.

"Laurent, honey," she probed, "are you going to formally introduce me to your new compatriots?"

"Why I'd be delighted," Fournier concorded, as if he had obtained a request from a super deity. "Miss Alicia, Miss Natalia, gentlemen, it gives me enormous elation to introduce one of New Orleans finest ladies, Mademoiselle Madeleine Antoinette de La Roux."

"*Bonsoir*," greeted the seductive siren with enough passion to floor an inviolate regiment of hardened misogynists.

"*Bonsoir*," the ME7 Writers reciprocated in unison.

Suddenly, her effervescing glamour avalanched into a contemptuous smirk. "You know—" She hit Stanley with a derisory mug. "Stanley, is it?"

"Yes."

"We have a saying in Orleans going something like this. Don't knock the water carrier when you are dying of thirst."

"Meaning?"

"Isn't it *obvious*?" she lambasted. "Don't offend those who could save your life."

Feeling vulnerable, Stanley goggled at his comrades. Like him, they endured as perplexed by the local term.

"Incredible," she chirped. "You haven't comprehended what I

mean, have you?"

Persisting vacancy of expression, the ME7 Writers' confoundment continued.

Gyrating her head dismissively, their blazing inquisitor elucidated, "Many writers seduced by the NOLS annual writers' show kudos, go on to fashion lucrative careers for themselves. NOLS is revered worldwide as the South's premier literary society. An endorsement from the NOLS executive…." She waved an arching arm, encompassing Fournier, Bernard and Dupree. "….is the equivalent of being awarded a gold-plated access card to Fort Knox." Raking savagely at the English lobby, her eyes pierced deep into their psyches. "Are you beginning to understand what I am saying?"

Taking the initiative, Alicia affirmed, "Yes, Mademoiselle de La Roux, we are abundantly cognizant with what the NOLS seal of approval means to our authoring careers."

Moving nearer to Alicia, the antagonised southern belle grievously besought, "Then why have your colleagues insulted these gentlemen, the delegates, and the undivided city of New Orleans with their perverse expositions and flippant replies to fairly voiced questions?"

Flummoxed, Alicia stuttered out, "But, erm—"

"Miss Alicia," Mademoiselle de La Roux remonstrated, "are you aware of the consternation your gentlemen brethren caused at the afternoon rendezvous?"

"Well, we did notice—"

"Notice some irate delegates, perhaps?" she interrupted.

"Yes, some of them were perturbed."

"And what do you acclaim caused their agitation?"

"I'd prognosticate our gentlemen writer's theme content."

"Quite." She ambulated even closer, her eagle-like eyes aflame with condemnation. "What do you calculate the reaction could be in London, if a bunch of conceited, self-opinionated southern writers descended on one of your events, and proceeded to set forth the frailties of British society and your own chequered history?"

"It'd not be appreciated."

"Absolutely right." She threw her head back in disgust. "So why is it your colleagues suppose they can come here, and ride roughshod over the New Orleans Literary Society, sneer at every cultural and historical aspect of the great state of Louisiana, and denigrate the South in general?"

"Please be assured, Mademoiselle de La Roux," Alicia begged, "we never had any intention to offend."

"Look," Gilbert began, aroused by the scolding, "I don't see we have anything to apologise about. We merely recited what we genuinely feel, and—"

"Be *quiet*, Gilbert," Alicia admonished, glaring at him.

"*At last,* you get your veracious hounds under control," Mademoiselle de La Roux crustily applauded.

Crestfallen, the impact of the acidic imposition drove plumbless in Alicia's psyche, impeding her conversational competencies.

Sensing her inhibition, Stanley interposed, "May I mediate?" his inflexion sedate.

"*Huh*, the arch-anarchist craves an indulgence," Mademoiselle de La Roux taunted. "Go ahead, Mister Paris Commune. Let's see if you can keep a civil tongue in your head, and not resort to trendy, ultra-lefty nonsense with anti-society gibes and affections."

"Perchance, can I clarify where we are coming from?" he earnestly consulted.

"Go ahead, but please do not bring into play indifference to justify yourself."

"It's true to say Arron, Gilbert and myself are all capable of modelling the type of allegory fitting accustomed mentalities, but we've kind of left the mainstream barrier behind in pursuit of a touchstone more edgy and eye-catching." Extending his palms appealingly, he justified, "Like it or not, it invariably means challenging perceptions and nominating alternative viewpoints, many we know offend orthodox sensibilities. But it does kindle some astounding narrative, making people catechize their standpoints and faiths. To paraphrase Alicia, Mademoiselle de La Roux, a writer should be ethically neutral if a true distillation of creditable writing is to be achieved. No doubt you'd agree."

"And your point?" she briskly demanded.

"All I am saying is, in an attempt to present honest transcriptions from our archive, we broached the texts without colouration or prejudice of forethought. I admit we could have been more diplomatic with some of our replies, but we intended no offence."

"*Hah!*" She eyeballed him critically. "You are coherent, even passionate, Stanley, but you do not necessarily convince, let alone persuade."

Unsure of their eminence, sheepishness consumed the ME7 Writers.

Sensitive to their predicament, in his most compelling articulation, Fournier began, "Madeleine—"

"I trust you are not going to make excuses for these demagogues, Laurent?" she reproved.

Unflustered by the society icon's rage, he counseled, "I was about to suggest you reserve terminal judgment until after tomorrow's conclave."

"*Sacré bleu,*" she uttered, forging a glossy kisser before addressing the executive committee. "*C'est important de se souvenir de ses amis.*"

Fournier, Bernard and Dupree exchanged awkward glimmers before Fournier acted. "*Bien sûr*, Madeleine."

Stooping to Alicia's ear height, in a hushed intonation, Gilbert queried, "What did she say?"

Whispering, so the other ME7 Writers could hear, Alicia informed, "It's important to remember who your friends are."

"And Fournier's answer?" Gilbert persisted.

"Of course, Madeleine."

Coming across as suitably contrite, Stanley murmured, "I'm the chief culprit igniting Mademoiselle de La Roux's repudiation with my afternoon forum responses to her assertions."

"Howbeit, she's going to take it out on Laurent and his pals," Arron tendered.

"Yes," Gilbert okayed. "She's stunning, but I'd doubt she takes any prisoners."

Overhearing the ME7 Writers' whispers, Mademoiselle de La

Roux's veneer turned sour. Scintillating at Stanley, she advised in a venomous modulation, "I eat little boys like you for breakfast. You and your chums would do well not to incur my displeasure again."

Finalising her demolition job, she tossed her flaxen mane back and stormed off with an air of supercilious, feminine arrogance.

"One hell of a powerful piece of woman power," Bernard praised, his fondness for the flaming beauty palpable as she strode away, the crowd once again parting like Moses commanding the Red Sea to allow her passage.

"Indeed," Fournier supplemented. "The de La Roux family has been sponsoring the New Orleans Literary Society for...how many generations is it, Alexis?"

"Five generations comes to mind."

"My, my, five generations," Fournier reiterated. "Mmmm, mmmm." Offering the olive branch to the English, he beseeched, "Do forgive Madeline's flagrant rudeness. My, she can be a fiery vixen. I am optimistic you will value we have to permit some leeway for her indiscretions. I do hope you will not bear any malice against us."

"Oh no," Alicia snapped out. "It takes a lot to offend the group, bricks normally bounce off us. And on the contrary, some of us have misjudged just how far your tails can be tweaked. Let me safeguard, Laurent, we will be a whole lot more sensitive at tomorrow's summit."

"Ohh, that is so gracious of you and your collaborators, Miss Alicia," Fournier commended, deeming he had the situation under control.

"Erm...it's me Mademoiselle de La Roux wants to make an effigy off and stick pins in," Stanley volunteered. "I should have been more diplomatic and courteous responding to her at the afternoon clambake."

"Water under the bridge," Dupree proclaimed. "Water under the bridge. Why it's incongruous if some poor unsuspecting speaker didn't incur Madeleine's discontentment at these events. What say you, Pierre?"

"Yes, in recent times," Bernard recalled, "Madeleine has seen invitee speakers as fair sport for her prissy games. You mustn't chastise yourself too much, Stanley. If it hadn't been you, she'd have selected someone else to act as her plaything for the afternoon."

"All the same," Fournier requested, "please, let's have no repetition of today's controversies at tomorrow's event."

* * *

Vacating the reception to freshen up in their rooms before the main evening buffet, ME7 Writers piled into an elevator, contrition the prevailing mood.

"Clearly, I have allotted you too much freedom," Alicia chastised, glaring at Arron, Gilbert and Stanley. "It is one thing to be incisive and out on the rim of lettered contends, but you three went too far this afternoon, and now we are all paying the price for it. I can't begin to tell you how sorry I felt for Laurent, Pierre and Alexis when the paragon of Southern virtue tore into them." She adopted a conciliatory posture. "Fellas, these are really nice guys. They might not fit your archetypal mould for the door-kicking down, visionary writer, but they are in a position to help all our scribing efforts. And what do *you* do?" She flared her nostrils. "Abuse the privilege, and crap all over their society."

"Well," Arron wailed, "we can't all be goody two-shoes like Natalia."

"You're belittling me," Natalia scorned. "Just because I don't convey a bolshie bastard attitude like you three, it doesn't mean I haven't got the wherewithal to pursue disagreement. But there is a time and a place, and NOLS is not the venue for radical pronouncements and bogus highbrow bullshit." Delaying, she reminded them, "Revisit why we came here?"

None of the men reacted.

"Let me refresh your memories," she prompted. "We agreed to participate in NOLS as a means of gaining international exposure for our output, not to create a shit-storm and come on as lofty, pseudo-intellectual know-it-alls."

"She's entirely right," Alicia supported. "You three might consider yourselves to be cerebral big dicks, but today you just came on as smart-arsed pricks. You made no allies and might have jeopardised our exhaustive mission."

"*Ohh*," Gilbert rejoindered. "You *don't* have any room to claim immunity from controversy."

"What do you mean?"

"Well, you weren't exactly squeaky clean with your defence of Wolfe, were you?"

"My discourse played as a purely aesthetic argument, Gilbert," Alicia argued. "Contrast the intent with how you went out of your way to appear superior and arrogant."

"I adjudged I'd held back," he protested.

"Maybe, but as Natalia said, there is a time and a place to fly the 'everything we do is beyond anarchy' flag. It sits well with the loony left brigade back in England, but incontrovertibly, not here in the conservative boondocks of America." Ceasing, her critical phizog intensified. "You won't make any converts, Gilbert, not even amongst the adolescent set. They will all grade you as far too radical to tie their colours to your 'let's ignite society mast.'" She thrust an intransigent finger at the corpus of her scorn. "And it goes for you too, Arron, and you, Stanley. Let's have no more Leon Trotsky alter ego exhibitions."

"Yeah," Stanley corroborated. "You're completely right."

"*What!*" Arron and Gilbert shrieked in chorus.

"It's no good, chaps. We got it wrong. No profit in pretending otherwise. We lost sight of the attending NOLS objective."

"Aahh, the penny has irreparably dropped, has it?" Alicia ventured, making her male associates undertake an amenable carriage. "Now, when we go back, let's be civil, courteous, and above all respectful. Clear?"

* * *

Many society members and guests took advantage of the 'just too good an opportunity to resist' gratis bar at the sumptuous evening buffet reception, many migrating into a worse for wear alcoholic haze.

With a penchant for oysters and *Chateau Lafite Rothschild*,

Dupree informed the English troupe, "To quote your noteworthy English playwright Oscar Wilde, *I can resist anything but temptation.*"

Even Fournier slurred his habitually precise speech, his own particular predilection for rye and champagne, reducing his customary tag of delicate authority a notch or two. Settling into a lavish chair, he recounted the proud heritage of NOLS to ME7 Writers, other delegates and society members, his listeners attentive whilst simultaneously tickled by his merry deportment.

When Bernard sauntered up to the charmed group, it became patent, like for Dupree and Fournier, he had overdosed on his pet tipple. His knees buckling and on the verge of falling over, he leered at Natalia like a degenerate Mississippi tugboat master, baying, "*Bono estente*, pussycat."

Surprised by the impetuous change in the Southern gentleman's demeanour, Natalia reeled back.

"Ah, Pierre has gone into *Fast Show* mode," Dupree verified to Alicia. "He is a big fan of your English television humour." Smiling empathetically, he cooed, "You must forgive him, Miss Natalia, he still tunes into repeats of *The Fast Show*, and occasionally lapses into a mid-Mediterranean, eccentric spirit."

Also familiar with the series, Natalia mentally bawled, *bastardo.*

Close to passing out and leaning against her, Bernard garbled, "*Boutros Boutros-Ghali, scorchio, tha, tha…tha, tha, tha, Chris Waddle.*"

"Drunken old coot," Arron mumbled, seeing to it nobody heard him apart from Gilbert and Stanley. "Soon he'll be reprising, *small boys in the park, jumpers for goalposts* and, *I'm afraid, I was very, very drunk.*"

"How about, *does my bum look big in this?*" Gilbert jeered.

"No," Stanley corrected, "friend Dupree should narrate that alternative comedy catch phrase." Then a presage struck him. "Hey, if these guys are into *The Fast Show*, we should reprise the tailor's sketch."

"*Ohh, suits you, sir,*" Arron duplicated.

Sniggering, Stanley suggested, "With Pierre's obvious liking of

Natalia, we should voice, *Is sir, going to be rogering the young lady this evening?*"

Totally loosened up, they erupted into laughter, before Arron warned, "If we did, Alicia would excommunicate us from ME7 Writers."

Meanwhile, catching on to Fournier's sentimental playback, Dupree joined in, regaling about the society's deluxe heritage, his listeners fascinated by his over-elaborate, if not typical Louisianan speech code.

"Do you know, Orleans is an oasis of French Catholicism in a desert of Protestant bible-belt proselytes?" he posed, as if raising a never heard before remark.

Their earlier conversation about New Orleans religion resurfacing, Arron glanced at Stanley and raised his eyebrows.

"Many of us reckon our swish culture and much admired traditions can be traced back to our Catholic inheritance," Dupree acquainted the beguiled listeners.

"You mean, your religion has been a principal factor in the development of the Big Easy," Alicia suggested, "resulting in its world-renowned status today?"

"Well bless my soul, I do believe Tennessee Williams himself could not have put it any better," Dupree lauded. "Miss Alicia, you are beginning to understand the true personality of New Orleans." Loitering nearer, he whispered in her ear, "If ever you want to come back for a protracted stay, it'd be my joy to accommodate you, ma'am, mmmm, mmmm."

Widening out the conversation, Dupree and Fournier dived deeper into Louisiana's gilded French heritage, more of the society's guests flocking around the debonair gents, fascinated by both the proposers, and what they said.

In his element holding court, Dupree most notably milked their obvious adoration, resorting to adding florid symbols to emphasise his cardinal foci, his flamboyant act supplementing his worldly demeanour.

"The apex of sartorial elegance," Stanley feigned, pulling Arron's sleeve to attract him to the Dupree spectacle.

"An exemplary performer," Gilbert gushed. "I bet he's even

more entertaining behind a lectern, reciting extracts from Emily Dickinson, Longfellow or Emerson."

"But not Ferlinghetti or Ginsberg, mmmm, mmmm?" Stanley teased.

"Definitely not. There is diminutive convergence between the beat generation constitution and Dupree's phantasm of an American hinterland filled with classic 19th century poets and writers."

"Quite, but surely in broad terms, there is latitude for both in the mind of the enquiring ascetic?"

"Certainly, Stanley, but I have the distinct impression for NOLS, the American literature landscape ended with the deaths of Dorothy Parker and Ezra Pound."

"Yes, you are probably right. It begs the conjecture, why are Fournier and his fellow executives so taken with ME7 Writers?"

"Ah, I can enlighten you on the perceptible patronage. Alicia requisitioned me to take a call from Dupree before we came over. He wanted to give me a heads up on the future movement and superintendence of NOLS."

"Why you, and not Alicia?"

"He wanted to discuss language semantics, and Alicia told him about my article *The Guardian* published on the growth of the English language in the 21st century. You know, all those modern words and phrases largely emerging from internet social media organs and focus groups."

"Yes, I did read it."

"Well, it transpires Dupree had overseen research on behalf of NOLS, aimed at the younger generations' bookish habits. From what I could gather, finding out they use portable reading devices and read online, mainly new writers as opposed to the traditional giants, came as a shock." Breaking off, Gilbert scanned the participants. "Inspect about, Stanley." He did so. "Apart from us, can you see anyone under thirty-five?"

Taking in the foreground and squinting into the background, he replied, "No."

"Right. It occurred to NOLS, with an aging membership, and very few, if any, entrants in their late teens and twenties, the society might cease to exist if they cannot seduce new blood, meaning freshmen members. Dupree discovered ME7 Writers purely by off chance when he did a web search for writer groups. He scoped our 'About Us' page and liked what he read." Stopping momentarily, he then imparted, "Thereby, I submit the far-reaching component authenticating why we were invited to the shindig, is centred on enticing a teenage aegis."

"I did see one or two people managing to hobble in without Zimmer frames or crutches at the afternoon durbar. Maybe Dupree's strategy is working. Maybe the junior fraternity came to see us, rather than the more traditional orators?"

"Yes, but therein lies the dichotomy for NOLS. They need new recruits, but behind their Southern gentlemanly front, I suspect they recoil at the discernment of their society being overrun with modern poets and writers, extolling the virtues of minimalism, and let's call it, unorthodox words and ways of speaking contrary to Webster's dictionary."

"Unequivocally, you describe us…well, you, me and Arron. However, they must have been expecting all of us to recite in the same vein as Alicia and Natalia. Irrefutably, the girls acquired instant green lights from both the delegates and the NOLS executive." Extrapolating the notion, he articulated, "Traditional text coming through fledgling voices sustaining the genre is what they presumed."

Before Stanley and Gilbert could discuss the NOLS motivations further, Mayor of New Orleans Andre Girard, a statuesque gent with a regular politician's persona, and exhibiting a problems-to-solve posture, made an unscheduled entrance.

Giving the English cabal a somewhat irritated air, he quickly spirited the NOLS executives away into a Lafayette ante-room, Fournier, Bernard and Dupree rapidly recovering their pre-fleshpots imperative, and bearing bastions of sobriety replication under the mayor's gaze.

* * *

"Laurent," Girard began, his voice drenched in agitation. "I've been hearing some very disturbing reports about your invitees from England."

Fabricating calculating aspects of disquiet, the NOLS executives glided in on the mayor.

"Just what have you heard, Andre?" Fournier sought.

Assuming a flabbergasted disposition, he reviewed, "I am given to understand the drift of the prose they read today orbited in the spin of shall we call it, indiscretion, controversy, and bordered on sedition."

More anxious miens were traded before Fournier surmised, "You've been listening to Madeleine de La Roux, Andre."

"Yes, Madeleine, and others."

"Well, Mister Mayor, I'd not go so far as to describe what they presented in those specified terms." Shambling on his feet, he tried for a nimble physical stance. "I'd prefer to say the subjects were sagaciously stimulating."

"Possibly," Girard groaned, still not coaxed. "To be more specific, my sources tell me the ME7 gentlemen writers caused the donnybrook. Is the information correct?"

Breathing out heavily, Fournier grimaced then nodded at Dupree, indicating for him to remedy the mayor's query.

With his hands clasped behind his back in a scholarly manner, Dupree clarified the evolving situation. "It is true to say, the English gentlemen did exceed the norm in terms of social etiquette, but er, I do not moderate whether they advocated lawlessness or mayhem."

Skeptical about the viewpoint, Girard paced about the ante-room, brooding and insecure about his subsequent move. Not in their DNA nature to come forth with anything not reserved and confident, the NOLS executive lasted serene and relaxed, observing his travels.

Coming to a standstill, the mayor blinked at Dupree. Upholding his recalcitrant disposition, he cautioned, "You know, Alexis, the city press will be covering the event tomorrow?"

"They always do on day two," he substantiated. "It's a celebrated tradition."

Sitting, Girard rested his forehead on his right hand, his elbow propped up by a table, his comprehensible ambivalence increasing.

"What is it, Andre?" Bernard enquired. Strolling forward, he came to rest by the mayor. "What is *really* bothering you?"

Despite air-conditioning, palpably under pressure and digging for understanding, Girard perspired. Sitting up, he stared at Bernard imploringly.

"The State Governor is making a visit to the Big Easy tomorrow. It's a vital occasion not only for my career but also for the city. He's cogitating about granting more Katrina recovery funds, and with the city still largely devastated, we sure could do with it." Halting his news, he gauged the body language comeback from the executives, noting their receptiveness. "So, gentlemen, you will understand, we don't want him seeing any unsavoury press captions about a bunch of limey anarchists running amuck at the New Orleans Literary Society annual convention, do we?"

Glimpsing at each other, the well-read men said nothing.

Charged up with hyperactivity, Girard returned to pacing. Gawking at them, a thunderous outlook scarcely hid beneath his plaintive apprehension. "God, damn it," he declared. "This country had its revolution over 200 years ago. We don't want another one, do we?"

Turning formal, Fournier pleaded, "Mister Mayor, I can assure you we have the matter bottled up." Easing the lump in his throat, he then advised, "It'd be a grave mistake for the city authorities to intervene with, if I am interpreting you accurately, any measures along the lines of censorship." Lingering, he let Girard digest the message. "We already have a commitment from ME7 Writers they will mollify tomorrow's content."

Gathering around Girard, the society's father figures brought his wandering to a standstill, their aim to neutralise his fears, and build confidence in him to rely on their judgement.

"Andre, we honour it could be perceived that the ME7 gentlemen act like a cipher for disorder," Bernard approved, "but there will not be an iconoclasm tomorrow. On the contrary, I arbitrate their talks will steer more towards the submissive."

"*Submissive!*" Girard exclaimed, his eyes bulging. "You haven't organised a festivity at Madame Beauvais's house of ill repute for the ME7 gentlemen, have you?"

"No, no, no," Bernard validated, fanning out his digits as a stamp of guarantee. Smirking at Fournier and Dupree, the mayor's misinterpretation also had them on the verge of laughter. "You misunderstand. They will not be going anywhere near Danielle's illustrious pleasure palace. I am referring to their code of conduct."

"Thank God for small mercies," Girard blurted. "I'd hate to picture what the media would make of any liaison between these Englishmen and Danielle's voluptuous ladies." The timbre of his voice raced away. "And if the Governor ever found out..." Panicked by the prospect, he lost his thread.

"Calm yourself, Andre," Fournier begged. "The Governor is never going to know about any of this."

"Submissive," Girard repeated, grimacing and unsold on the passive term.

"Yes," Bernard settled. "As in being accommodating, deferential, even obedient, call it what you like." Procreating compelling physiognomy, he explained, "We are beginning to understand the temperament of the English faction. Oh, I can see through their premeditated bluster, they are capable of achieving substantial controversy, but you might mull over the commercial element."

"What do you mean, Pierre?"

"Well, er, let me see. Wordsmiths come here with ambitions of attaining advocacy, and thereby selling their creations. To present at NOLS, is a much-treasured endorsement. Publicity remains the gold panacea for marketing and selling literature. I, er, might be impugning our guests, but beneath their egalitarian exterior, I evaluate you'll find some commercial determinants."

Mayor Girard began to lighten up. "You mean it's an act, designed to be controversial, so as to create a bear pit?"

Nurturing insightful features, Fournier endorsed, "It could be, Andre, it sure could be." Bolstering his assertion, he shared, "They've already stirred up a hornets' nest. Word has gone far and wide. Now, if they are smart, they will have sussed out another combustible storm could be counterproductive to flattering publicity and thereby book sales. To prosecute such an altercation path equates with a negative effect, empathy, even sympathy turning to anger. You understand what I am saying?"

"Oh, yes," Girard confirmed, virtually purring. "Your syntax is without colour. Remember, you're talking to a politician. Empathy and sympathy are our stock in trade."

* * *

As part of the sequent day's symposium, ME7 Writers read more passages from their individual oeuvres, softening theoretical, controversial gists, and echoing to the audience with civility and due deference. Occupying the session moderator chair, Dupree regarded proceedings with a satisfied smile. Worse for wear from the foregoing night's fleshpot excesses after Mayor Girard departed, Fournier and Bernard took auxiliary posts at the moderator's station, holding their flagging chins with faltering hands.

At the culmination of the ME7 Writers seminar, Dupree called for final questions from the floor. Motioning to a trim gentleman dressed in the colonial style, replete with a pith helmet and monocle, an erstwhile dead ringer for Dr. Livingstone according to Arron, he pumped, "Yes, sir."

"Delegates from yesterday's confabulation led me to expect some fireworks from ME7 Writers." Browsing the association, the good doctor complained, "What we got today can be likened to a damp squib!"

Responding, Dupree petitioned, "Sir, just *what* were you expecting?"

Scanning about, the chic gent then swept an arm around the attendees. "We were expecting a more sizzling yardstick. What we got had all the hallmarks of a diluted or censored version."

"Sir, I can pledge, the New Orleans Literary Society has never and will never censor the contributions of writers taking part in our annual quorum."

"If so, how about giving us the real deal, then?" Amplifying the appeal, Livingstone thrust himself frontwards. "So, we can judge for ourselves."

Surging into hushed secondary valuations from the floor, the dispute ignited Fournier's and Bernard's sensory control. Alert again, they joined Dupree in debate with Doctor Pith Helmet, whilst still clustered at the speaker platform, ME7 Writers monitored the exchange with eagerness.

Ex post facto, Dupree canvassed the assembly for silence. "Ladies, gentlemen, if I could please have your attention. The executive has decided to request our erudite wayfarers from England to re-run their powwow again, only bringing out the feistier elements of the chronicles. Ergo, we will delay the Cajun poet's talks for one hour."

Unveiling a live one in the making, the New Orleans newsmen moved onward, taking up positions either side of the speaker's lectern, their flash cameras and camcorders ready to record the action.

After a short internal discussion, Alicia consoled the delegates. "We empathise with your yearnings, so what we are going to do is unique to this forum. Instead of re-running the content in the format we did yesterday, we're going to act out a parody vignette written by Stanley, entitled *Tribal Gatherings*."

Whilst a ripple of applause arose from the gallery, praying for providence, Fournier, Bernard and Dupree gawped to the heavens, hoping they had made the right call to Girard, and the press construed the limey's enactment favourably.

Reengaging, Alicia informed, "I will act as narrator, and the other members of the group will play the parts." As the lights lowered, and the lecture hall fell silent, electric anticipation tangibly streamed in the collective. "Think about this as a radio play, a skit for voices centralised on itinerant people rebelling against the status quo. Natalia plays a young woman once backing the political sect in government known as the Party, and favouring the State Broadcasting Corporation, the SBC, but she has seen too many contradictions to keep being a part of the machine and wants to go public with her depositions. Arron is her co-schemer.

He has also seen the light. Both are SBC employees. Gilbert plays the SBC human resources director, and Stanley, the director general of the SBC." Pausing, she enfranchised the attentive mass to grasp the plot summary.

Alicia

The opening scene takes place in the DG's executive suite at State Broadcasting House.

Stanley

You know, Gilbert, we can't tolerate non-conformists at the SBC. Their ranks could increase, moulding disenchantment and capping in our funding being reduced by the Party.

Gilbert

Yes, we don't want our gold-plated parachutes to be cut to shreds. I've already had to sack several dissenting rebels this quarter, for contradicting the edicts of the conformity tsar. She will not stand for anything challenging the SBC status quo line, on any issue.

Stanley

Good, in fact excellent. You've got to wheedle them out, Gilbert. Set traps, and get the watchers fired up to inform on them. Before the reactionary contagion infects the core, we get the perpetrators in front of their audio-video thought crime evidence, and dismiss them under the terms of the Emergency Anti-Dissident Enablement Act. The Party commands it. If people are allowed to contest, the Party might not get re-elected for a fourth consecutive term. And you know what that means, don't you?

Gilbert

The Opposition taking power and cleaning the stables at the SBC.

Stanley

Precisely, and in the process, the executive being replaced, and our inflation-proof pensions cancelled.

Gilbert

I know, I know. If it happened, we'd also lose our taxpayer-funded, five-bedroom houses in Islington and chauffeur-driven Bentleys.

Stanley

Track them down, Gilbert. Safeguard the conformity tsar's watchers with your undercover informers. Find the detractors, and let's have them out of the SBC.

Alicia

In another part of State Broadcasting House, two dissident technicians, Natalia and Arron, are leaving a conformity tsar information meeting.

Natalia

It's all rubbish, carefully conceived soundbites designed to mask off, contort or destroy the truth.

Arron

Yes, but we can't uncover our true sympathies yet. I'm adamant they suspect we're not committed to the Party. We must find more like-minded people, then approach the Opposition, and tell them what's going on at the SBC.

Natalia

As if they didn't know already! Arron, we have to take action soon. We can't go on day after day living this lie. We must equip the Opposition with evidence of the treachery happening at the SBC.

Arron

And the falseness of the Party. Ssshh, here comes the conformity tsar.

Alicia

The conformity tsar is suspicious of Natalia and Arron. Their body language and behaviour indicate they have turned away from the order. She quizzes them about their credos, tarrying dissatisfied the stock answers they give are not credible. On return to the executive suite, she marches into Gilbert's office. She tells him of her suspicions, and requests surveillance be kept on the pair, using the informer network. Gilbert tells her, the suspects have been under observation for some time, but he agrees to beef up the vigilance. Back in the studio technical support department, Natalia and Arron continue their conversation.

Natalia

That was close. I guarantee she suspected us of thought crime.

Arron

Yes, we're going to have to be more careful than I imagined, especially amongst Party stalwarts, many of whom are thought crime informers.

Natalia

Just to think, I used to believe all the junk they preach and broadcast to the nation. It makes me mad. I must have been a gullible fool to fall for their self-serving agenda. It's destroying England and all her cherished belief systems and traditions.

Arron

Don't reproach yourself, Natalia. Along with millions of English people, they duped me as well, but I have a hunch the Party and the SBC are running scared. They know the number of dissidents is on the increase. They're getting desperate to expunge them from the SBC, before the lead up to the next general election, just in case we influence voters, not that the vote means anything in this day and age.

Natalia

Yes, democracy is just an illusion. The will of the majority means nothing.

Arron

We are ruled by self-concerned, self-perpetuating minority groups, all acting under the banner of the Party. How on Earth did it ever come to this?

Natalia

Did you know Simmons in the *Yesterday* programme studio support team got the sack?

Arron

No, no I didn't. What happened?

Natalia

I overheard two watchers talking about it in the canteen. Apparently, Simmons refused to aim the studio camera at the Minister for Justice when his opposite number spoke. The *Yesterday* programme tried to portray a beneficial image of the minister and denigrate the Opposition to persuade viewers to back the official party line. Simmons kept the camera on the Opposition spokesman when he spoke. Afterwards, the HR director summoned him to his office, roasted him, then sacked him on the spot.

Arron

How do you know they were watchers?

Natalia

I've seen them before at the morning Party anthem chant. The watchers can't resist demonstrating their true colours by singing the Party anthem louder than others doing it through obligation, like us.

Arron

Natalia, we have to be careful what we say, and who we trust. The watchers could be anybody from canteen waitresses to top-floor executive staff.

Natalia

I agree. But I am more concerned about the informer network. Literally, *they* could be anybody. It's well known they occupy grades at every stratum in the SBC.

Arron

Come on, let's get out of here, before someone comes in and demands to know what we are doing.

Alicia

Over the last ten years, the Party had insured its own advocates occupied positions of dominion at the SBC, and those opposing their regime either sacked or neutralised by blackmail or subversion. The SBC has been assigned as the indoctrination machine for the Party, censoring news putting the Party in a bad light, endeavouring to ensure its programme schedule supports the Party's agenda, and making every effort to discredit all opposition. The Party deemed the measures necessary to preserve outright control over the nation. Back in the DG's executive suite, the SBC Director General and HR Director appraise their options.

Stanley

I want to see some more examples made, Gilbert. We must deter potential dissidents. If necessary, drum up some false charges contravening the Emergency Anti-Dissident Enablement Act.

Gilbert

Yes, Director General.

Stanley

The Party's chief whip called me this morning. He said the P.M is very concerned about the increasing count of dissidents, explicitly here at the SBC. He expects results.

Gilbert

What did you tell him?

Stanley

I told him, the conformity tsar's resources, and budget had been increased ten-fold over the past three years, and you spend most of your time catching dissidents.

Gilbert

How did he respond?

Stanley

He said, even more draconian laws are about to be instantiated to supplement the Emergency Anti-Dissident Act. These will license all public sector executives, incorporating the SBC, to deal with malcontents instantly.

Gilbert

Does it imply shooting them?

Stanley

Under the current purge, I'd not rule out anything.

Alicia

A few weeks thereafter, Natalia and Arron retire to the studio technicians support centre, presuming it is a safe place, not often monitored by the conformity tsar's watchers and roving informers. They have decided they cannot wait any longer to go public and have arranged to meet what they believe is a sympathetic supporter from the SBC news department having contacts with the Opposition.

Natalia

Where the hell is he? It's dangerous to stay here for too long. You never know who might stumble into the support centre and ask us why we are here.

Arron

Relax, it's normal for studio support technicians to be in here. All the same, we did say 5:30 and its 5:40 now.

Natalia

Oh, Arron, if he's not here in a few minutes, let's go. I don't want to get caught and be grilled by the conformity tsar and the DG. I've heard people assumed to be dissidents are subjugated to psychological interrogation.

Arron

It's just hearsay, Natalia. I remain unconvinced about the stories. Not even the Party and the SBC could get away with those inhuman methods.

Natalia

I'm not so sure. Do you recall Becky Daniels? She used to be in programme research and got the sack for suspicion of being a dissident.

Arron

Yes, I do.

Natalia

Six months after the SBC fired her, I saw her in Shepherds Bush. She just walked past me like a zombie, staring ahead like she'd had a frontal lobotomy. I tried to check her, but she didn't appear to recognise me. Her eyes were dead, like a doll's eyes. She looked dreadful. I tried to get her to speak, but she just kept on slowly walking along the Goldhawk Road. It was ghastly, Arron.

Arron

My God, why didn't you tell me sooner?

Natalia

I didn't want you to condemn me as being overly dramatic. Oh, where's that news department man?

Alicia

Suddenly, Natalia and Arron hear a booming voice coming from somewhere in the support centre. 'He is not coming. He is one of us. He is a watcher, like all news department members.' Natalia and Arron rush to the exit doors. 'Stop where you are,' said the voice. They run anyway, but the exit doors have been locked. A few moments pass, then the Director of Human Resources and the conformity tsar flanked by six security guards enter the support centre from a concealed entrance. Descending on the dissidents, the guards handcuff them while the conformity tsar reads out the charges against them contravening the Emergency Anti-Dissident Enablement Act. Natalia and Arron are hauled to the DG's executive suite, towering way above ground level in State Broadcasting House.

Stanley

You are dissidents and guilty of thought crime. What do you have to say for yourselves?

Arron

We haven't done anything. You have no right to treat us like this.

Gilbert

We have every right. You know thought crime has been outlawed under the terms of the Emergency Anti-Dissident Enablement Act. It is no use making any denials. We have evidence of your crimes.

Alicia

The DG plays a video tape of Natalia's and Arron's indiscreet conversations, not only in the support centre, but on multiple other occasions going back three months.

Stanley

Your crimes against the Party and the SBC are undeniable. Gilbert, do your duty.

Gilbert

You are both sacked without any appeal. All your benefits are forfeited, including your pension and this month's salary. These tapes will be sent to the Ministry of Justice, and no doubt you will both be brought to trial for thought crime.

Stanley

However, before you are surrendered to the Party's inquisitors for ancillary cross-examination, we need to know about your accomplices at the SBC. Conformity tsar, take them away. Get the truth out of them.

Alicia

Natalia and Arron are led away, still protesting about their civil rights. Scoffing at their remonstrations, the conformity tsar breaks into a nauseating laugh as the door slams shut to her interrogation centre. A few minutes later, a passing SBC employee hears screams as psychological torture is applied to Natalia and Arron.

Continuing to its bitter and revelatory conclusion, ME7 Writers feverish rendition of *Tribal Gatherings* had the entire congress moonstruck, it's theme resonating with reported incidents in the corridors of the mighty, worldwide.

With the auditorium still silent, Alicia tendered, "Our miniature passion play is a wakeup call to all people. Our message is, we must question those ruling us, ascertain if they are acting in our best interests, and most essentially, prevent them usurping absolute power and subjugating the people to tyranny."

An audience clapping ripple began ringing back and forth before turning into a raging ovation. Photographers let rip and journalists surged to the speaker rostrum in pursuit of exclusive interviews.

* * *

Bulging with pride, the subsequent day, an elated Dupree presented ME7 Writers with the *New Orleans Tribune*, its arts section headline proclaiming, 'English writers show America the light'.

Afternoon saw Mayor Girard accompanied by Mademoiselle de La Roux visit NOLS, both frothing with rejoicement at the *Tribune* review, Fournier inexpressibly bowled over by their tributes, Bernard stating the splendid tradition of allowing uncensored material had paid dividends, and Dupree effervescent with glee his invitation to ME7 Writers had been vindicated.

When the English contingent were eight miles high over Louisiana bound for Heathrow, they felt a distinct cognizance of achievement. Having pulled victory from the jaws of disaster, Arron, Gilbert and Stanley took an action from Alicia and Natalia to park their anarchic tendencies when reciting narrative to bedrock establishment institutions. Taking onboard the folly, they knew they had intentionally shocked the conservative New Orleans coterie for insular and infertile reasons. It had sensationally backfired, not resulting in converts to anarchy, but a hardening of traditional views until the delivery of *Tribal Gatherings* corrected the balance.

A salutary lesson, Alicia hoped her gentlemen writers sustained their commitment, and control of their cold-blooded alter egos.

THANK YOU FOR READING

* * *

Don't miss out on your next favorite book!

Join the Melange Books mailing list at
www.melange-books.com/mail.html

* * *

Did you enjoy this book?

We invite you to leave a review at the website of your choice, such
as Goodreads, Amazon, Barnes & Noble, etc.

* * *

DID YOU KNOW THAT LEAVING A REVIEW...

- Helps other readers find books they may enjoy.
- Gives you a chance to let your voice be heard.
- Gives authors recognition for their hard work.
- Doesn't have to be long. A sentence or two about why
  you liked the book will do.

ABOUT THE AUTHOR

Clive Radford began writing at school, then university but mainly through subsequent life experience.

A series of his short stories and poems have been published by Ether Books. The Arts Council has sponsored publication of his novels 'One Night in Tunisia' and 'The Sounds of Silence'. His contemporary satire 'Doghouse Blues' was number one in Harper Collins Authonomy chart and has been awarded gold medal status. It has been published by Black Rose. His spy thriller 'Zavrazin' has been published by Triplicity Publishing. It's companion sequel 'Nexus Bullet' is published by Ex-L-Ence Publishing. His three-book coming of age series 'Disclosures of a Femme Fatale Addict' has been published by both Wild Dreams Publishing and Miraclaire Publishing. His science fiction novel 'Maggie's Farm', suspense-thriller 'Incident at Lahore Basin' and his satires 'Doghouse Blues 2', 'Doghouse Blues 3' and 'Doghouse Blues Revised and Remastered' are published by Rogue Phoenix Press. Melange Books has published his mystery thriller, 'Monsoon in the Making'.

The 'Zavrazin' screenplay is under contract with Story Merchant/Atchity Productions for film production.

Rogue Phoenix Press will be publishing his contemporary thriller 'Alpha Centauri' February 2022.

Currently, he is crafting a number of works including 'Desolation Argonauts', a rite of passage sojourn along Route 66, 'Three Cheshire Boys' a comedic thriller, 'Colby Richmond: The

University Years', the coming of age sequel to 'Disclosures of a Femme Fatale Addict' and 'Mozart meets McCartney', a mystery.

His work has a distinctive voice setting it apart and appealing to those fascinated by intrigue, and who question status quo accepted views.

[f] facebook.com/clive.radford.9

[BB] bookbub.com/authors/clive-radford

ALSO BY CLIVE RADFORD

WITH MELANGE BOOKS

Monsoon in the Making